THE SILENT RESISTANCE

a&b

THE SILENT RESISTANCE

Anna Normann

Allison & Busby Limited
11 Wardour Mews
London W1F 8AN
allisonandbusby.com

First published in Great Britain by Allison & Busby in 2024.

A CIP catalogue record for this book is available from
the British Library.

First Edition

ISBN 978-0-7490-3216-6

Typeset in 11/16 pt Sabon LT Pro by
Allison & Busby Ltd.

The paper used for this Allison & Busby publication
has been produced from trees that have been legally sourced
from well-managed and credibly certified forests.

FSC
www.fsc.org
MIX
Paper | Supporting
responsible forestry
FSC® C171272

Printed and bound by
CPI Group (UK) Ltd, Croydon, CR0 4YY

To my Tante Berit who lived through the war in Haugesund as a little girl and remembers so much.
Natalie.

To my wife Maria for her support and inspiration.
Anan.

Chapter One

Ingrid, seven years old
Haugesund, Norway, September 1945

Ingrid kept her head down and ran through the schoolyard gates as fast as she could. She needed to get away quickly, before the other children noticed. She stopped abruptly on the kerb to check that it was safe to cross.

A convoy of military lorries passed by, filled with German soldiers sitting in the back, guarded by Norwegian soldiers. Last year, the German soldiers had been billeted at the school. Ingrid remembered how they used to give the children sweets.

It was peacetime now, yet many of the German soldiers remained. Her *besta* had said that Germany was so destroyed, their soldiers had to stay in Norway and wait until they could be sent back to their own homes.

She shivered despite the heat. She wished they would all go away. She wished she could go away. She wished she could find Mamma, and she wished she didn't need to feel scared anymore.

Ingrid held her breath, waiting for an opening in the traffic so she could run across. All the while, she kept looking over her shoulder.

From the schoolyard she heard children laughing and yelling, eager to get home after a long day. She had to be gone before any of them caught up with her.

She was almost in the clear, had one foot on the road, ready to run, when someone grabbed her by the neck and pulled her back.

'Oh no, you Nazi bastard. You don't get off that easy.'

Ingrid looked up at the older boy. Runar who only months earlier had been her friend, and now here was so much anger and hate in his eyes, and she knew what was coming. It had been the same ever since she started first grade at Gard Primary School in August, a few weeks earlier. From the first day, she had been singled out. Nobody wanted to play with her, be near her, and nobody talked to her. In the classroom, they'd pull their desks away from her and whisper behind her back. Even the children that had been in Mamma's crèche didn't want anything to do with her.

At some point Ingrid gave up trying to befriend anyone and accepted that this was how her school life would be. She kept her head down and tried her best to be invisible.

Runar was the worst. And it hurt so much more when Runar picked on her than when any of the other children did. He had been her *best* friend. Then the war ended, and everything changed.

'Nazi spawn like you shouldn't be allowed to go to school,' he continued. 'My father says you should all have

8

been drowned at birth, and then . . . and then hung like those Nazi fathers of yours. You're worse than that bastard Quisling, and he'll be executed any day now, Father says.'

He spoke so angrily, he was spitting in her face. Ingrid squirmed to get loose, but he only held her harder.

'My Pappa is in England, and he's not a Nazi!' she said.

'As if anyone believes that. Why isn't he here, then?' Runar was fuming. 'Your real pappa is one of those Nazi officers. Admit it!' He took a firmer grip on her collar.

The dress would tear, Ingrid knew that, and then she would have to lie to her grandmother about how it had happened. She didn't want Besta to know what they were calling her pappa.

Ingrid made fists with her hands and tried to hit him. That only made him laugh. He shook her so hard she could barely breathe.

While he was holding her with one hand, he put the other in his pocket and pulled out a piece of charcoal. He looked at her, then drew something on her forehead with hard, angry strokes. Then he threw the charcoal away. Ingrid could hear it shatter when it hit the ground.

'What did you do?' she yelled. She tried to pull away again.

The collar of her dress tore, and she fell to the ground again. From the corner of her eye, she spotted other children gathering against the fence, cheering him on. Laughing and screaming at them.

'Nazi bastard! Nazi bastard!'

Ingrid looked around for a way out, but there was another car coming, and she couldn't run into the road. She didn't know what to do. There was no place to run or hide.

Runar stood over her, feet apart, hands raised and a pained expression on his face. For a second she thought he was going to kick her. She tried to crawl backwards, away from him, but he followed her.

Ingrid swallowed. He wasn't going to let her go this time. He would keep on beating her. Something inside her shifted. It felt as if she was burning.

'I'm not a Nazi!' she yelled, and managed to get up on her feet. 'You're the bastard!'

'My father says your mamma is a Nazi slut, and that makes you a Nazi bastard! Everyone knows that!' he shouted at the top of his lungs.

Ingrid lost it when he berated her mamma. She hurled herself forward and hit him with both hands in the chest, so hard he lost his breath and almost fell over.

'My mamma is not a Nazi slut! Take that back, you . . . you ugly shit,' she said, remembering a bad word her grandmother used. 'And your father is a big, fat liar and a bastard!'

Her tiny fists hammered at him, but he was a year older, and heavier and taller. Runar tried to hit her back, but by now she was so furious her hands kept hammering at him. The best he could do was to protect his face.

'What's going on here?' One of the teachers came out from the schoolyard and pulled Runar away from Ingrid. 'Stop that!'

While the teacher was holding Runar by the ear, forcing the boy to stand on his toes, she turned to the gawping children on the other side of the fence. 'Anyone standing here in the next minute will have detention for the rest of the month.'

In a flurry, the children scampered off and disappeared.

Ingrid barely noticed. She held her fists high, ready to defend herself from Runar again.

'She started it,' Runar muttered, not looking at her.

'Liar!' Ingrid yelled, trying to get to him.

The teacher pulled Runar further back. Ignoring Ingrid, she looked at the boy. 'Did you do that to her face?'

Ingrid remembered the charcoal and touched her forehead. When she looked at her hand, her fingertips were smudged.

She scowled at Runar. 'What did you do?'

The teacher still ignored her. 'You know better, Runar. That's detention for you for a week for fighting.'

'But my father . . .' Runar said, his lower lip quivering.

'Yes, I know your father, but there's no excuse for fighting. Especially not with a girl younger than you. One week,' the teacher said, grim faced and clearly angry.

She finally looked at Ingrid.

'And you. This is the second time you're fighting. I don't understand why you're not like the other little girls. Run along home to your grandmother now,' she said.

Ingrid caught her breath. She looked at her, determined to have her say. She pointed a shaking finger at Runar. 'My mamma is not a Nazi slut, and my Pappa lives in England,' she said. 'You're a liar!'

The teacher looked at her, her eyes cold, and Ingrid knew. Her teacher believed the lies, same as Runar and everyone else.

'Run along, I said. Now, before I change my mind and give you detention too.'

Ingrid wished she could say more, wished she could make

them understand. Instead she scowled and turned away.

Safe on the other side of traffic, she suddenly couldn't take it anymore. She turned and looked at them. 'My Pappa is a hero. He sailed for Norway the whole war, fighting the Nazis, and you all know it. You're the bastards,' she yelled at the top of her lungs.

The teacher ignored her, and brought Runar back to the schoolyard.

Ingrid turned her back on the school. Her anger had given way to tears. She was crying so hard she could barely breathe. She rubbed her nose with the sleeve of her dress.

The dress was torn and dirty with coal dust. *Besta will be so mad*, Ingrid thought. This was her best dress, the last one Mamma made before she went away. She couldn't bear to show the state of it to Besta. Not again.

She ran as fast as she could to get away from that horrible school. *I hate them*, she thought. *I hate them all.*

She didn't stop until she came to her house. The house she had shared with her mother, not where she now lived with Besta. It was empty, of course, all the doors and windows locked. Her mother had left in June, when the war ended, and she hadn't come back yet. *Mamma will come*, Ingrid thought. She knew it was true, because her mamma always told her she would come back for her. Always.

Ingrid still had her mother's house key. It felt important. She slipped into the house, closing the door behind her.

It was hot and dusty inside, and when she climbed up the stairs, she spotted spiderwebs in the corners. In the bedroom, the bedding was still on the bed. The flowers in the vase on Mamma's nightstand had withered and died long ago.

Ingrid went over to the vanity table, and looked at herself in the mirror. On her forehead Runar had drawn a mark. She recognised it, of course. It was the ones the Germans had on their flags.

She rubbed at it with her hand until there was only a smudge left. Then she looked at herself. 'I hate Runar,' she said. Hating Runar was easier than missing Mamma.

She threw herself on the bed and tried to remember Mamma. Nothing smelt like her any more, but when she shut her eyes real hard, she could almost see her face.

Every day she tried with all her might to keep the memories alive, but all their pictures had vanished, Mamma's clothes were gone, and it was like Ingrid had never slept in this bed, next to Mamma.

Ingrid couldn't stand staying in the empty bedroom any longer. She grabbed Mamma's bedspread and dragged it behind her down to the cupboard under the stairs. Their secret place.

She crawled inside and wrapped the bedspread around her.

Inside the little room, she finally felt safe. This was where Mamma had told her to hide if the bad men came.

Ingrid cried until she fell asleep, curled up under the dusty blanket.

She woke up to a door slamming shut. It took her a minute to realise she was in the old, secret cupboard.

Oh no, she thought. Had Besta or someone else seen her come here? Besta didn't like it when she had to come and pick Ingrid up from here. Last time it happened, she had said she would change the locks.

Ingrid pulled away the blanket and sat up on the floor. The only light in the cupboard came through the crack in the door.

Steps approached and she held her breath, remembering Mamma's word: *Don't come out until it's safe.* She knew no soldiers would come now; they were all gone, but still, she was terrified. Maybe Runar or some of the other children had followed her.

Unsure what to do, she remained completely still.

'Ingrid? Are you in here?'

Ingrid recognised Besta's voice at once and her whole body flooded with relief. She pushed up the little door and peeked out. She couldn't see her.

'I'm here, Besta,' she called back.

'Ingrid, what are you doing?' Besta came into the hallway and looked at her with a frown. 'When you didn't come home from school, I didn't know where you were, or what had happened to you.'

'I'm sorry,' Ingrid muttered, scooting outside.

Besta sat down on the floor next to her. 'That's good, but not good enough. You know that, don't you?'

'Yes, Besta,' Ingrid said, struggling to hold back tears.

'What happened this time? And don't lie to me, little one. I can tell when you're lying.' She took her hand and held it between her big ones.

Ingrid slumped. It was true. Besta always did. 'It was one of the boys,' she muttered. 'He said bad things.'

'He did? Did you fight him?' Besta touched the rip on her dress.

'Yes, he pushed me and I hit him.' Ingrid pulled her other hand under her nose. 'He was mean.'

'Was it Runar?' Besta's voice was so soft, so kind, Ingrid started crying again.

'Yes, but it's not only him. They all think it, even the teacher.'

'What does the teacher think?' Besta patted her hand. 'You can tell me.'

Ingrid sniffled, then pulled the sleeve of her jacket under her nose. 'I'm not a Nazi bastard, am I?'

Besta pulled her close and kissed the top of her head. 'Good heavens, of course not. You were born two whole years before the Germans came. Anyone saying that is an idiot who doesn't understand basic maths or biology – you can tell them I said so. Now tell me everything that happened. You're not in trouble, I promise.'

Ingrid sighed. When Besta talked like that, she knew she would have to be truthful. She told her everything, sniffling as she talked.

'I'm sorry about my dress,' she muttered, rubbing her eyes.

'Don't worry about the dress. It's nothing that can't be mended. You don't have to apologise for defending yourself, Ingrid.'

Ingrid looked at her. 'Why do they hate me? They never used to. Why do they call Mamma bad things?'

Besta didn't answer those questions; she never did. Instead, she patted Ingrid's hand and smiled at her.

'Before you started school I was so worried about you. I know what they're gossiping about, bunch of wet hens, they are. Then my worst fears came true the first time you came home like this. That's why I have written a letter to your father.'

Ingrid's mouth fell open, but Besta didn't seem to notice.

'I told Lars that if he insists on living over there in London, at least he has to do right by you. And I got word from Lars yesterday. He's coming to bring you to London to live with him.'

Her father hadn't been home once since the war ended. He had been sick, Besta had said. But she never said what was wrong with him.

Ingrid looked at her. 'Leave here?'

'Yes. You're unhappy and you need a change. That lot at the school will never let you be. I can't . . . I won't have you paying the price for . . . for someone else's sins.'

Ingrid didn't understand what she meant by that, but she shook her head. 'I have to stay here, Besta.'

'Ingrid, I will not have you come home with bruises and torn clothes every other day,' Besta said, frowning. 'No, this is how it will be. Even if it means sending you away . . . You're not going back to school before you leave. We have a lot to do to get you ready. I don't think Lars will stay for long.'

Even the surprise that her father would finally come back didn't stop Ingrid from protesting. Did Besta not understand?

'But what if Mamma comes home and I'm not here? How will she find me?' Ingrid shook her head several times. 'No, I can't go away.'

Besta patted her hand. 'You don't have to worry about that.'

'Mamma will come back for me,' Ingrid said, trying desperately to make Besta understand. 'She promised she would, and she always does. She will come.'

Besta got a strange expression on her face. 'I promised Anni that I would do everything in my power to take care of you, and that's what I intend to do. If Anni comes home, I will tell her where you are. But it's not easy for her to return, you know that.'

Besta hadn't told her where Mamma was, only that she had to go on a trip and that she didn't know when she would return. Ingrid wanted so badly to know where she was. She dreamt about her at night and she thought about her every day. When she asked Besta, she wouldn't say, not properly.

Besta put her hand on her chin. 'I know it's difficult. The world is still in so much chaos from the war. But I know your mamma wants you to be safe and happy, and in London nobody will know what happened here. Do you understand?'

Ingrid folded her hands so hard her fingers hurt. 'Yes, Besta.'

'Now, come with me back to the farm for your supper and we'll talk no more about this.'

Ingrid knew what that meant. She was not to mention Mamma again. It was so frustrating that no one would tell her what her mother had done to make everyone so angry.

But Besta is wrong, she thought. *Mamma will come and find me. She always finds me.*

Perhaps Mamma would come before she had to go to London. She hoped so.

Chapter Two

Anni, twenty-four years old
Haugesund, Norway, November 1944

The autumn storm bit down hard. The little house by the sea creaked and moaned as the wind shook it.

Anni could only hope the roof and the windows would last them another winter.

With Lars gone, she had to manage everything herself, but she had a strong suspicion that fixing the roof might be beyond her abilities.

'Look, Mamma. There's fog on the window when I blow air on it,' Ingrid said.

'That's because the windowpane is cold and your breath is warm,' Anni said, smiling at her six-year-old daughter. 'Where's your *kofte*?'

'I don't know.' Ingrid was busy breathing on the glass, delighted when the fog appeared. She still had a bit of a cold. Taking her outside in this weather was probably not the best idea. The other mums would also not be thrilled if their kids picked up Ingrid's sniffle. But they needed all the money they could get, and the impromptu crèche she ran at the little prayer house was not something she could afford to lose. Normally Guri, her mother-in-law, would look after Ingrid if necessary, but she was out in the hinterland, and Anni didn't have anyone else. A quick look at her watch told her they would soon be late. She didn't like having the children wait outside the prayer house in the rain.

'Your *kofte*?' she repeated while trying to find the item in question.

Ingrid grinned from ear to ear, pointing at the knitted jacket she had on. 'I'm wearing it, Mamma,' she said.

Anni laughed. 'Yes, you are. How clever of you to hide it by wearing it!'

Ingrid giggled. 'I can put my coat on myself.'

'Good girl. I'll help you with your boots. The other children will arrive soon, and we want to heat up the room first, don't we?'

Ingrid's boots were worn down almost to the sole and they were getting too small for her feet. Anni sighed. Ingrid had only had those boots for six months. How she could grow so fast on the rations they were getting, was a mystery.

'We're taking a trip to town tomorrow, and then we can see if we can't get you something better for your feet.'

She had to try to hand over the new illegal newspapers Martin had brought, and looking for boots was a valid excuse to make the trip into town.

'I still have some old jumpers of your pappa's we can barter with,' she said.

'But won't Pappa need them when he comes home?' Ingrid said.

'I'm sure he has new jumpers by now.' *Hopefully*, Anni thought. She hadn't seen Lars since 1940, shortly before Ingrid's second birthday. Somehow a Red Cross letter had found its way to her in 1941, telling her he was on a cargo ship heading for Canada, and that was the last she had heard from him.

Anni tried not to dwell on it too much. Not knowing where he was, or even if he was alive, was too hard.

He could be anywhere in the world by now. When the Germans attacked, most of the Norwegian merchant marine, hundreds of ships and thousands of sailors, refused to return to Norway, and instead joined up with the Allies to help defeat the Nazis.

Anni sighed. She was so proud of Lars for doing his part. But now, after all this time, she didn't know if he was still on the same ship, if he had been transferred, or, God forbid, torpedoed. Tossing and turning at night, her mind cruelly kept picturing him in the sea, waves pulling him down, with a sleek, ugly, Nazi U-boat circling the waters like a giant shark.

She shook her head. *Don't think like that*, she reminded herself. Letting her mind play out her darkest fears and sleeplessness didn't help anyone. She needed to believe things would work out, needed to stay strong for Ingrid. *He'll come home*, she thought.

Every month she went down to the shipping company Lars sailed for to collect money from his paycheck, like she used to do before the war. It wasn't much, even they were struggling now that most of their ships were abroad. But it was enough to keep them afloat. She clung to the hope that as long as the payments arrived, Lars was still alive. He had to be.

'Does Pappa miss us?' Ingrid leant against her.

Anni smiled, happy to be interrupted. 'Of course he does. He loves you so much, and he thinks of you all the time. When he left, he said he would come home to you as soon as possible.'

'But then the soldiers came,' Ingrid said.

'Yes, they did, and nobody knew that would happen. And your pappa can't come home to us yet. But he will,' Anni assured her daughter.

'Do you promise? Do you cross your throat promise?' Ingrid frowned.

'Cross my throat promise,' Anni said, planting a kiss on the top of her head. 'And when your pappa's ship arrives in Haugesund, we'll be right here waiting for him.'

'But can he come for Christmas?' Ingrid didn't give up that easily.

Anni thought about how the war was progressing. France had been liberated in August, the Russians crept ever closer to Germany in the north, and the Germans were getting more and more antsy by the minute. Dreaming of the war to end wasn't a pipe dream any more. It was a possibility.

'I can't promise he'll come home by Christmas, but I hope so, sweet pea, I really do.' Anni wouldn't allow herself to think anything else. Lars would come home, and that was what she wanted Ingrid to believe too.

Ingrid seemed happy with her vague reassurances, and Anni breathed a sigh of relief. It was becoming such a challenge coming up with stories about Lars. Ingrid had been so little when he left, still a baby. She only knew him from their wedding photograph. But it helped Anni too; it helped keep Lars a part of their lives and make Ingrid excited to meet him.

Please come home safe, my darling, Anni thought. *Just come home.*

Ingrid put her hands on either side of her face. 'Mamma, we have to go now. The prayer house is cold for the children.'

She looked so much like Lars, Anni had to blink to stop her eyes from getting teary. 'Yes, we must go now.'

Anni put on her own coat, an old seaman's coat Lars had left behind, and frowned when one of the buttons came off and broke in half when it hit the floor. She picked up the two pieces and sighed. Finding new buttons was a nightmare, and involved bartering on a whole new level. She would have to be extra creative this time.

There was no time to worry; she would have to manage. Either make a new button with some yarn, or see if she could locate a safety pin. Although that was probably as impossible as finding a new button.

She was too engulfed in the drama of the broken button to hear the rumbling engine outside their house.

'Mamma! Look! Look! Soldiers are coming,' Ingrid shouted, pressing her face against the window.

Anni took a quick look out the window, and saw a big, black car pulling up outside their drive.

Familiar fear started to creep up along her body. She closed her eyes for a second. She couldn't show Ingrid how terrified this made her.

They were here. After all this time, they had finally caught up with her. *Thank God Guri isn't here*, she thought. *Now all I have to do is to keep my mouth shut until the others can escape.*

She took a deep breath and pulled herself together. This was it. *They're coming for me. I have to keep calm*, she thought. All she wanted to do was grab Ingrid and run.

'Come away from the window, sweet pea.' She didn't want them to see Ingrid.

Her mind was racing. She tried desperately to remember what she was supposed to do. *I know this*, she thought. *I have a plan. We have a plan. All I have to do is remember the plan and stick to it.*

Every morning she woke up, expecting Gestapo to kick down the door and take her away. She had made preparations and drilled into Ingrid what to do if the worst happened. It was a delicate balance between not scaring her too much and still making her remember what to do, but she couldn't pretend that the war wasn't everywhere.

Even a six-year-old knew it was dangerous. Ingrid knew to hide when the RAF bombers flew over the house, when the soldiers in the schoolyard started yelling, and to stay behind Anni when there were patrols in town. But then, Ingrid also chatted with the soldiers over at the school, hoping they would give her sweets, so it wasn't a perfect system.

Anni listened to the slamming of car doors and knew there wasn't much time. She turned to Ingrid. 'This is it, sweet pea. You know what to do?'

'Yes, Mamma. Hide in the tiny room under the stairs until they go away, then run to Besta when everything is quiet,' Ingrid said, rattling off the words like a nursery rhyme.

'And when Besta isn't home, like today, then what do you do?'

Ingrid frowned. 'I . . . run to Mrs Olsen, even if I don't like her, and she doesn't like us, and Besta thinks she's an old bat.'

Normally, that would make her smile, but today *they* were outside her door. The Olsens were Guri's closest neighbours, and despite their fondness for all things Nazi, they would not dare to turn away Guri Odland's granddaughter.

'Good girl. Your grandmother will be back tomorrow and she'll look after you. Go on, hide now,' Anni said. 'And don't come out whatever you hear, even if you hear yelling.'

Especially if you hear yelling, she thought.

Anni waited until Ingrid had crawled into the closet under the stairs. The little girl scooted underneath all the rubble Anni had carefully put in there, to make it look unused. Inside the walls, behind the old wallpaper, the illegal newspapers were hidden. She could only hope they didn't ransack the house too thoroughly. *Thank God the basement is empty*, she thought.

If they didn't do a thorough search she might wriggle her way out of whatever they were coming to arrest her for.

She put some old clothes on top of Ingrid, making sure she could breathe under there.

'Mamma? Can I ask something?' Ingrid whispered.

'Say it quickly,' Anni said.

'Can I run to Runar instead of the Olsens? He'll be at the prayer house by now.'

Why didn't I think of that? Anni thought. 'Yes, you can run to Runar and stay with him and his mum until Besta comes home. But now you must stay absolutely still. Like a tiny mouse hiding from the naughty cat,' Anni whispered.

Ingrid giggled but stayed hidden. Anni stood up and closed the door. It was almost invisible. Almost would have to be enough.

Goodbye, my sweet girl, Anni thought.

She closed her eyes for a second, saying a small prayer that she would be able to stay strong. Too many people depended on her.

When the knock came, she braced herself, took a deep breath and opened the door before the soldiers could knock it down and drag her away.

The wind wasn't as strong as it had been earlier. The rain had calmed down some. Anni suppressed the urge to run. The moment of truth had arrived, and she had to stay calm.

The car was parked in her yard, and she could see the driver sitting quietly.

A man in a heavy coat stood with his back to her, looking at the scenery. She knew what he was watching. The tip of the monument's mid-pillar, and the ramshackle sheds lining her property.

She noticed he was holding an umbrella in one hand, and that he wasn't wearing a uniform. For a second, it threw her. He was a civilian. Her mind couldn't wrap itself around it. What was a civilian doing here? He had to be Norwegian, she was sure of it, but the car confused her. Was he a quisling? One of the people who happily joined the Nazis?

Anni stood absolutely still, with her hands folded in

front of her. He was alone, except for the chauffeur. There was no sign of the company of soldiers she had anticipated.

She had seen people getting arrested in town. There were usually a lot of soldiers present, a lot of screaming and shouting. And now, for her, there was only this one man, standing in her doorway as if he was a friendly visitor.

Anni waited, afraid to say something, until he turned to look at her. 'Frau Odland?' he said, smiling slightly.

She nodded. '*Ja*,' she said. So, not Norwegian, then. Not when he called her 'Frau'.

'I know you speak German, so I think we can talk, yes?' He frowned slightly as if he expected her to lie.

Anni nodded again. Although her German was far from perfect, it was good enough to get by.

'My name is Hugo Kerber. I'm in charge of the administrative office at Hagland Fortress,' he said. 'Including this whole area and the soldiers' camp at Gard's primary school.'

'I see,' Anni said, puzzled by why he was telling her this, and confused about why he hadn't arrested her yet.

He didn't talk like any of the few German officers she had met, and while she knew that the Germans had German civilians working for them, she had never met one.

Then her scrambled brain realised he wasn't from the dreaded Gestapo, and she thought – she hoped – there was a slim chance he wasn't there to arrest her.

'I arrived at Hagland Fortress a few days ago,' he said. 'You know the place, yes?'

Anni nodded. 'Of course.'

The Hagland Fortress was further north from her house.

The Nazis had been building coastal batteries out there, ever since they arrived, preparing for the British invasion that so far had failed to materialise.

Anni was trying to muster the courage to ask him what the bloody hell he was doing at her house, but she was too scared. She hated that feeling, especially when all she could do was wait, and try not to panic in the meantime.

'I was told you and your child live alone in this house? I hope it's not an inconvenience if I take lodgings here,' he said, with a surprisingly friendly smile. 'To billet, you understand?'

Anni blinked. She wasn't sure if she did understand what he said. This was the last thing she had expected. She hoped her face didn't reveal the shock and the fear she was struggling to hide from him.

'We . . . we only have one bedroom,' she finally said. It wasn't strictly true, but since Lars left, Ingrid slept in her bed. 'The . . . there is a second bedroom, but it's small, barely more than a closet, where my daughter used to sleep. It's not suitable for an . . . an adult,' she said, in case he would think her lying.

'What about downstairs?' He looked around as if he was expecting a bedroom to materialise out of thin air.

Anni didn't dare to lie. 'There's a lounge where we spend most of our time, and then there's the dining room. But we don't use that.'

'May I come inside and see for myself?'

His friendly politeness scared her more than anything. Silently, she opened the door all the way, stepped aside and let him in. She was sure he could hear her heart pounding. She was convinced she could hear it herself.

He left his umbrella in the corner by the door, took off his hat, revealing short, dark hair, and placed the hat under his arm while he looked around as if he was appraising the house for a possible sale.

The whole situation was extremely absurd.

Anni wasn't sure what to do. Should she follow him into the lounge or stay in the hallway, hoping he would bugger off soon?

He solved the mystery for her by looking over his shoulder.

'This is the lounge, yes?'

Anni nodded. 'It's difficult to heat the whole house during winter,' she said, her voice shaking slightly. 'The . . . the dining room is larger and also has its own fireplace.'

Why the hell did I tell him that? Now I sound like a landlady talking to a prospective lodger, she thought. *This is becoming more absurd by the minute.*

'May I see it?' he asked, in the same calm tone.

Anni pointed towards the kitchen. 'It's through that door. There's a narrow hallway between that room and the kitchen. You might be disturbed when we eat, I'm afraid.'

Why am I telling him all this? Anni followed when he walked in front of her into the lounge.

He's a bloody Nazi, he can do what the hell he wants to, he can throw us out of our house if he gets a fancy, and then we have to go and live with Guri and her damn goats.

She shuddered at the thought. As much love and respect she had for her mother-in-law, she had no desire to live with her.

I should tell him the ceiling is leaking or that the

*windows are draughty, or that we have rats in the basement.
Something to make him change his mind*, Anni thought, swallowing her anger. His politeness was getting on her last nerve. His behaviour, all gentle and nice, was unnerving.

'The fireplace hasn't been used for a long time, so I don't know what condition it's in,' she said instead. 'We are unable to warm up more than one room.'

All he did was smile, and Anni felt as if she would faint if he didn't stop being there, in her house, soon.

'Because of the shortage of firewood,' she added, but realised that he most likely already knew that. Not that any of his people would suffer from shortages of any kind. *God knows they've been robbing us dry*, she thought, looking down so he wouldn't see the flare of hatred in her eyes.

He didn't seem to hear what she said, or perhaps he didn't care.

She watched him from the doorway, seeing her house through his eyes. It was worn down. The curtains were made from cheap materials. She had used the good pre-war drapes to make clothes for Ingrid. The furniture had all seen better days, and what little they had once owned of good and useful things she had sold or bartered to keep them warm and fed. She had tried her best to make it a home for Ingrid and herself, and this man was an intruder.

I don't care what he thinks, she reminded herself. *He's a bad person, one of* them.

He walked into the dining room and stood still. *Perhaps he doesn't like it*, she thought. *Perhaps he'll go and live with the neighbours instead.* Perhaps she should suggest that.

'There's no furniture in here,' he said, looking at her.

'No, there isn't,' she said, unwilling to tell him that she had used the table and a few of the chairs as firewood last winter.

'My . . . my neighbours up the road have a bigger house. You passed it when you came here,' she said, her voice slightly shaking again. They were also strong supporters of the new regime, but she didn't say that.

'Yes, I am aware,' he said, ignoring her statement.

Anni frowned. He seemed to know an awful lot.

He stood in the middle of the room and looked very comfortable. 'I understand that you have lived here for some years?' he said.

'Yes, I have. We moved in here in 1937.'

'And you are taking care of the little prayer house down the road?'

'Yes, I do. I look after children when their mothers have to work, and . . . and sometimes they have to come here,' she said, desperately hoping that would scare him off.

She had done everything possible to stay out of sight from the occupants, keeping her head down at all times, not engaging with any of them. And yet, here was this Nazi officer, no, Nazi civilian, indicating that he knew things about her.

Anni put her hands behind her, and knitted her fingers as tightly as possible to keep herself from revealing her emotions.

'Good, good. It's important that children receive proper care.' He smiled at her, like a person who wasn't representing the enemy.

Anni couldn't make herself smile back. She watched him warily, as if he was a wolf loose in her lounge.

He went over to the window. 'Lovely view. What are those pillars?'

She knew what he was looking at. 'That's Haraldshaugen. It's a memorial for a battle that happened in Hafrsfjord about a thousand years ago, and it's also the presumed burial site of King Harald Fairhair. What you see is the middle pillar. There are smaller ones, surrounding that one. The smaller pillars represent the counties that surrendered to him.' Anni stopped.

'He was the Viking king who unified Norway under his rule, yes?' Herr Kerber looked at her for confirmation.

'According to legend and tradition, yes, that's what he did,' Anni said.

'And why was he called Fairhair?' Herr Kerber didn't look at her when he asked.

'Supposedly he refused to cut his hair until Norway was one kingdom, and it became very long and very pretty,' she said.

She knew she was babbling, and she almost screamed at him to leave, but she forced herself to keep still. Even when he picked up her wedding photograph standing on the shelf.

'Are you a widow, Frau Odland?'

For a second she hesitated, but decided not to lie. He probably already knew. 'No, I'm not.'

He put the photograph down. 'Of course not. Your husband is a sailor, yes?'

'Like most men in this town have been for centuries,' Anni said, defiance creeping into her voice.

She almost told him that Lars was a third officer. She held her tongue and refused to give him more information.

For all she knew, Lars might have made captain by now.

He waved his hat around, before putting it on his head again. 'This will do fine. You will of course be paid for the inconvenience.'

Damn, Anni thought, hoping against hope her reaction didn't show on her face.

'I . . . see. You should know that there's only cold water in the sink, there's no bath and the . . . the facilities are outside. In the outhouse,' Anni said, in a last desperate attempt to make him change his mind.

'I am aware of that.' His smile widened.

Anni almost took a step backwards, to get away from him.

He seemed unfazed. 'You will hardly notice that I'm here, Frau Odland. I'll leave early in the morning and likely come back late in the evening. I'll also be travelling in periods. I'll take most of my meals at Hagland. All I need is a peaceful place to sleep.'

It was such a strange thing to say.

Anni didn't know what to think about that. 'I see,' she said again, not knowing the right response.

Soldiers were billeted all over town. Hers was by no means the only house commandeered by the Nazis. And there was absolutely nothing she could do about it.

'Good,' he said again, heading for the door.

A thought occurred to her. 'There's not even a bed in there,' she said, half expecting him to say he'd take hers.

'I will send a car with everything I need.' He turned and held out his hand. 'One more thing. Do you have a house key for me, or do you leave the door open?'

Anni opened the key box by the door, took out the

keychain Lars had left behind and forced herself to hand it over. 'This is the only spare I have,' she lied.

'*Danke*,' he said. 'I will be quiet when I return.'

He suddenly smiled again, his features softening. 'You have a lovely daughter,' he said.

Anni turned around quickly and discovered Ingrid sitting on the floor, with the secret door wide open behind her, staring wide-eyed at Kerber. Her heart sank. All he needed to do was give the closet a search and she would be done for.

'*Danke*,' she said, turning back.

'May I ask her name?' His eyes softened when he looked at the little girl. Anni thought she could see longing and perhaps sorrow. It was disturbing. She wanted to think of the enemy as the monsters they were, not as actual humans with feelings.

'Ingrid,' Anni said, almost whispering.

He smiled then, and Anni almost lost her breath. She hated his smiling. It was unnerving, and she didn't like it.

'That's a good, strong name for a lovely girl.'

Herr Kerber put on his hat.

'*Auf Wiedersehen*, Frau Odland,' he said, then bowed and left the house.

Anni closed the door after him, hardly able to breathe.

She wanted to scream at the top of her lungs. But that would scare Ingrid and alert the German.

Instead, she swallowed her scream and leant against the door frame, sliding down onto the floor, willing her heart to calm down. Most of all, she wanted to cry, but she fought it with everything she had.

'Mamma? Was that a bad man?' Ingrid slid over to her,

and put her hand on her knee.

'No, no, sweet pea, he's not.' Anni leant forward. 'Why did you come out? I told you to say in there.'

Ingrid's eyes filled with tears. 'I'm sorry, Mamma. I thought he had left. It was so quiet.'

'Don't cry, sweet pea. I'm not angry.' Anni pulled her close and hugged her tightly.

Her thoughts raced, and she managed to stop herself from crying in front of Ingrid. Instead, relief filled her whole body.

Oh my God, she thought. *I'm not on my way to the Gestapo house. I'm not being tortured. Guri, Martin and Nina are safe. I'm still here and I still have my girl.*

The reminders kept her calm.

After a while, Ingrid wriggled loose, and looked up at her.

'The children,' she said.

Anni had forgotten the children. They would be waiting outside the prayer house by now, standing in the cold.

Chapter Three

Anni cracked open the door and peeked out, to see if the car was still there, but they were gone. *Thank God*, she thought.

'Let's go. The poor children must be freezing. We have to run,' she said.

'Can we run faster than the wind?' Ingrid seemed to have forgotten the visitor already.

'We can try,' Anni said, looking around the room to see if she had forgotten anything.

Ingrid waited by the door, humming to herself, looking like a tiny, adorable fisherman in her rain clothes.

Anni locked the door behind them. When she turned around to take Ingrid's hand, her eyes fell on the outhouse.

'Oh, that's not good,' she muttered. She looked at Ingrid. 'Wait here. Don't leave this spot.'

'Why?' Ingrid looked up from under the sou'wester.

'So I know where to find you when I come back in.'

Anni ran over to the little shed and opened the door.

As quickly as she could, she pulled down the magazine pictures of the royal family, making apologies to His Majesty and the rest of them.

'Apologies, Your Majesties, but I can't risk getting arrested if this idiot sees you,' she muttered.

There was a pile of newspapers and a few pre-war magazines on the bench next to the sitting holes.

'Filled with more royal pictures,' she muttered to herself.

She grabbed the magazines but left the newspapers. They were softer than the toilet paper they sold in the store. They were also filled with propaganda and lies. *Let him wipe his bum with that*, she thought.

She would bring the magazines to the prayer house and burn them. She stuffed them inside her rucksack, and headed over to Ingrid, who was entertaining herself by jumping up and down on the bottom step of their front steps.

Anni grabbed Ingrid's hand. They ran and skipped down the gravel road.

A few minutes later, they stood outside the gate to the tiny, white prayer house. A burly boy, a year older than Ingrid, jumped up from the front steps.

'Mrs Odland is here!' he yelled.

From behind the fence, five more heads popped up. All dressed in more or less the same hand-me-down fashion as Ingrid.

'Good morning, children,' she said.

'Good morning, Mrs Odland,' they echoed.

Anni opened the gate and let Ingrid inside the small garden. 'Have you been waiting here long?'

The boy took charge. 'Not for long. We hid when the big car drove past us. Why did they drive up the road?'

Anni smiled at him. 'They came to tell us something, Runar,' she said.

'What did they say?' Runar was the responsible one of her kids, the one who always took care of the others. That made him bossier and certainly more curious.

Anni was not about to tell any of the children that a Nazi officer was moving into her house. She knew they'd find out soon enough. She had to inform the reverend first, then the parents. No need to scare them before she had to.

She smiled at him. 'Nothing that would interest children.'

Runar narrowed his eyes, obviously not believing her. Anni turned to the others before he managed to ask again.

'Inside, children. It's too cold and wet to stay out here,' Anni said, shepherding them all inside.

Still four children short, but that wasn't unusual. She wasn't a teacher or childminder in any formal capacity. But some of the other mothers needed to work, and then they would send their youngest children to her. And since she already worked as the caretaker of the little prayer house, she had talked to the reverend and persuaded him to give her permission to open a small informal crèche.

Sometimes the children didn't come. Like today: either because they lived too far away and couldn't get a ride, there was no food at home, they didn't have warm shoes, a sibling needed the wellingtons, or one of the million other things that made everyday tasks hard under the Occupation.

'Mrs Odland?' One of the girls pulled her hand. 'It's cold in here. Can we keep our coats and hats on?'

'Of course you can. I'll get the room warmed up soon enough,' Anni said.

'Who wants to tell us how their weekend was?' she asked, to keep the children busy while she struggled to fire up the ancient oven.

One of the girls put up her hand. 'Me, Mrs Odland, me!'

'All right, tell us, Liv,' Anni said.

The old wood burner in the prayer house wasn't always cooperative, especially when it was raining. She tore out pages of the magazines, twisted them and put them under the firewood before lighting it.

'We had to slaughter one of our hens. It wasn't laying any more eggs and Mamma cooked it for Sunday supper,' Liv announced proudly. 'And do you know, she had to boil it for hours and hours and hours, she did, but it was sooo delicious.'

The other children looked both impressed and jealous at the same time, and Anni hid a smile. None of them were starving, but a constant diet of potatoes, turnips and salted herring took its toll. They were too skinny, too pale all of them. Every sort of food was rationed, but a ration card didn't make much difference when there was nothing to buy. Meat was a luxury so rare, it was hard to remember what it tasted like. The same with the milk. The fatless milk that was available was called 'blue milk'.

She sighed. Sometimes all she could think of was the food she missed. It made her feel embarrassed. She looked at the children. It was different for them.

These little ones couldn't remember sweets or sugar.

They were too young to have tasted the real thing, they had no idea what marzipan or raisin buns tasted like and couldn't remember a time when they could slather a freshly baked slice of bread with real butter and proper sugary jam.

The memory made her swallow. She could almost taste the bread and the melting butter. *Oh, butter*, she thought, trying to ignore her growling belly.

While the heat slowly spread through the room, she went over to the window facing the primary school across the road. The children talked eagerly behind her, exchanging stories about their weekend. The bragging became more and more exaggerated, and made Anni smile despite the sadness the sight of the school brought her.

Gard school had been used as barracks for Wehrmacht soldiers since they came in 1940. She remembered when the schoolyard was filled with happy, playing children. Now they had to walk to the old restaurant in the park about two kilometres away for their schooling.

'Mrs Odland, can we take off our coats now?' Runar said.

'You can all do that, but keep your wellies on,' Anni said, glad to be taken out of her own thoughts.

She had to help a few of them. The mothers would layer them up to keep them warm, and it took a good deal of time to unwrap them all.

'You're like a Christmas gift, aren't you?' she said, pulling a second jumper off one of the boys.

He giggled. 'I can't be a present, Mrs Odland.'

Finally, they were all ready. They stood straight and said their morning prayers in shaky unison.

'Well done. Now, let's do some jumping and running around, to get warm.'

'Can we sing?' Liv asked.

'As loud as you can, please,' Anni said.

They jumped and skipped, and she was happy to see them enjoy themselves. *I wish I could*, she thought, thinking about Herr Kerber.

She knew she had to get a message to Martin, the leader of their little resistance group, and she had to tell Guri as soon as she was back at the farm. As long as this man stayed with her and Ingrid, there could be no refugees, no illegal newspapers or anything that could hint at what she was involved with in her house.

Martin wasn't going to be pleased.

Oh, bother him, she thought. *I'm the one who has to have that man in my house, not him. And if he gives me any grief over it, I'll give him a piece of my mind.*

Behind her the children had calmed down, and she shook her head. Time to start the day.

'Have you had breakfast today?'

They all nodded in unison.

'We had the last of the bread, but Mamma says the milk store will have bread today,' one of the girls said.

'We had fried potatoes for breakfast,' one of the boys announced, looking smug. 'And half an egg each.'

'That sounds lovely,' Anni said. 'Also, good. Because Christmas is coming, and we have some serious drawing to do today, and your heads had better be working.'

The children giggled and started getting their paper and colour pencils. It wasn't difficult to keep them occupied. Sometimes they did little projects, or they sang and danced, and when the weather allowed, they would spend most of the days by the monument or on the beach.

Anni forced herself not to think about Herr Kerber. Something about him unsettled her. Something beyond the fact that she couldn't do anything to stop him from moving into her house.

When Anni opened the door to her house, she could see the Nazis had already been there. The thought infuriated her. Wasn't it enough that they had invaded her country, now they wanted her home too? She ground her teeth in frustration.

Ingrid looked at her. 'Mamma? Are you mad?'

'I'm not, sweet pea. I'm hungry.' She smiled at her. 'Wait here in the hallway.'

After a quick search, Anni relaxed. No one was there now, and nothing of hers had been disturbed, not even Ingrid's hiding place under the stairs. She allowed herself a sigh of relief.

'Mamma, is the man here?' Ingrid took her hand.

'No, nobody is here. I'm being silly.' She started taking Ingrid's outer clothes off, tickling her in the process.

Ingrid giggled. 'You're silly, Mamma.'

Anni put away their coats and boots. 'Yes, I am. Now go and play in the lounge, while I make us something to eat,' she said.

On the way to the kitchen, she passed the dining room. The door was closed. She hovered with her hand over the door handle, then pulled away.

He might be in there, she thought, and hesitated. Then changed her mind.

To hell with him, it's my house, was her next thought.

Determined, she opened the door and looked inside.

'Oh,' she said.

The room was furnished. Sort of. By the window, there was now a bed that looked like a military bunk, with a pillow and a couple of thick blankets placed on top.

The bunk didn't seem the least bit comfortable, but perhaps that was what he was used to.

They had also put in a big metal chest. For his belongings, she assumed. And there was a bedside table, a narrow bookshelf and a lamp. All of it very military looking. Not even a rug on the cold floor.

She blinked. The room had been empty and unused for such a long time, but she remembered the Sunday dinners they used to have in there: Lars cutting the steak, Guri telling him he was doing it wrong, and Ingrid slamming her spoon on the table, sitting in her highchair. It seemed so . . . so horrible that this room where she had such fond memories should now house a Nazi.

'Mamma, what's in there?' Ingrid came over, dragging her doll behind her.

'Nothing for us, darling. But from now on, we are not to go in there. Not you and not me.' Anni stopped her before she could enter the room.

Ingrid looked wide-eyed at her. 'Why?'

Anni sat down in front of her. 'The man that was here this morning, you remember him?'

Ingrid hung her head. 'Is he a bad man?'

Oh dear, Anni thought. 'No, sweet pea. You don't have to be afraid of him. He won't harm us. We'll barely see him. But he'll sleep in that room, and we are not to disturb him. He's a lodger. Do you understand?'

Ingrid nodded with her finger in her mouth.

'Good. That's my girl. Now let's eat. You can bring your doll.'

Ingrid climbed up on one of the kitchen chairs.

'What's going on, sweet pea? You look very serious,' Anni said.

Ingrid sighed. 'Is Besta coming home tomorrow?'

'It might take another day or two.' Anni wasn't looking forward to it anymore. Her mother-in-law was sharp as a hawk, and just as tough. She would not be happy about the new development.

'Do you think she'll bring me something yummy to eat?'

Anni laughed. 'It's that all you're thinking about? Filling your tummy with yummies?'

'Yes!' Ingrid giggled.

'I'm sure she'll bring you something. She never forgets.'

Guri somehow managed to find special treats whenever she travelled to the hinterland. Since the war came to Norway, she had become quite the smuggler.

Anni turned away from Ingrid, so she wouldn't see her concern. With Kerber in the house, they would have to be a lot more careful. Her home had been a sanctuary, a place to feel safe, but now the danger was inside her house. She had no idea how to deal with it, and that scared her more than anything.

Chapter Four

The next morning, they took the bus into town. The old bus creaked and moaned up the hill, leaving behind small clouds of black smoke from the woodchip engine.

Ingrid sat by the window, excited to be on a trip. She pointed at all the things she loved. Mostly at the fairground that was closed for the winter.

'When will they open again, Mamma?' She was pressing her nose against the cold window.

'Not until next spring,' Anni said. She missed it too. The music and laughter that carried down to their house in the evenings reminded her of better times, pre-war times.

'Maybe Pappa can go with us then,' Ingrid said, turning away from the fairground.

'I'm sure he misses it too.' Anni put her arm around Ingrid and pulled her closer.

Mostly she would leave Ingrid with Guri when she went into town, especially when she was delivering newspapers to Martin. Anni felt uncomfortable and exposed among the German soldiers that walked around, looking as if they had every right in the world. Every minute she spent in town, she expected a heavy hand on her shoulder. Now that same feeling gave her a sharp pain in the pit of her stomach.

Anni carried an old rucksack with a couple of jumpers she hoped she could exchange for a pair of wellingtons for Ingrid. The wad of illegal newspapers was hidden in a secret pocket in the back of the bag. She had also brought their ration cards, both for clothes and food, even the useless ones, like tobacco cards.

Finding a shop that had tobacco was a pipe dream, but she brought the cards along anyway. There was always hope. The bartering you'd be able to do if you had some tobacco!

'Can we have oranges, Mamma?' Ingrid looked hopeful.

Guri had given her a couple of oranges last Christmas and Ingrid still remembered. She had eaten a wedge every day, then Anni had helped her dry the peel so it would smell pretty in her secret room under the stairs.

'I doubt there are any now, sweetie.'

'But can we look?' Ingrid wasn't about to give up.

Anni laughed and put her hand on her head. 'We can look.'

The bus passed Flotmyr, once the town's rubbish dump, now the largest military camp in the area, before turning right and down the road leading to the town centre.

The bus stopped at the pyramid-shaped concrete blocks the Nazis used for roadblocks, hindering anyone from entering town unnoticed.

'Damn Hitler teeth,' someone behind Anni muttered. She hid a smile.

Silence settled among the passengers when a soldier entered. He had his weapon over his shoulder, and started asking people for their travel passes.

Anni kept calm and had their *Grenzzonen-Bescheinigung* ready to show the soldier.

With a bored look on his face, he walked slowly from person to person, glancing at their passes, sometimes asking to have a look in their belongings, before continuing to the next one.

Like everyone else, Anni kept her eyes cast down, clutching Ingrid close to her. Her rucksack was on the floor between her feet, and she carefully pushed it under the seat. Ingrid leant against her arm, watching the soldier.

Anni handed him their passes. He looked at them and handed them back. 'Rucksack, *bitte*,' he said, pointing at her feet.

Damn, she thought. She leant down and started slowly pulling at the rucksack. Hoping against hope that he wouldn't bother, she was about to lift it up when Ingrid squealed.

'Bon-bon!' she said, holding out her hand.

The soldier looked at her, frowning slightly.

Ingrid gave him a toothy smile. 'Bon-bon, *bitte*,' she insisted, waving her open hand at him.

Anni turned to her. 'Ingrid, what are you doing?'

'He's one of the bon-bon soldiers at Gard, Mamma. I know him,' Ingrid said.

The soldier relaxed his shoulders and smiled at the little girl. For a minute he looked young and harmless. He put his hand in his pocket and fished out two boiled sweets. Ingrid grabbed them and smiled even wider.

'What do you say, Ingrid?' Anni played along, gently pushing the rucksack back under the seat.

'*Danke*,' Ingrid said. 'Thank you.'

The soldier nodded to her, then checked the passes of the rest of the passengers and left the bus.

As soon as he was gone, every passenger relaxed, then stood up to leave the bus. They exchanged smiles, even laughing a little.

Anni looked at her daughter, happily busy opening the wrapping paper and popping the sweet in her mouth. 'You are something else,' she said.

'For you, Mamma.' Ingrid held up the other sweet for her.

Anni shook her head. 'Thank you, but you keep that for later,' she said.

'Can I give it to Runar?'

Anni smiled. 'If you want to.'

Ingrid got even more excited the moment they entered Haraldsgaten, the main shopping street in town. There were lots of people milling about, enjoying a day of rare sunshine while standing in queues.

From the top of the street, they stopped to look down to the harbour where a few fishing boats intermingled with German warships. Anni closed her eyes for a second, imagining it was Lars's ship down there. That some kind of normal life existed where they could walk the streets in their town without fear.

Ingrid pulled at her hand. 'Mamma? Why are you staring at the fishermen?'

Anni smiled. 'I like them.'

The statue of the two fishermen stood in the middle of the hill. They had their oilskins and their sou'westers on, leaning forward and pointing out at sea, reminding everyone that Haugesund was built on the herring fisheries.

'Stay close to me and don't let go of my hand,' Anni said, smiling at Ingrid.

Ingrid held her hand tight, but Anni could see it was hard for her to focus. There were too many people, too many shops. Ingrid found everything equally fascinating.

'Let's go to the barter shop first, and then we'll see what else we can do. Maybe we'll find a place and treat ourselves to some hot soup. Would you like that?'

Ingrid nodded. 'Do you think they'll have cauliflower soup?'

'We'll have them surprise us, I think.' *Doubtful*, Anni thought. The only thing they had to look forward to was likely some kind of turnip soup. She frowned at the thought.

Outside the barter shop, there was a queue of women and children waiting patiently to be let in. Anni was relieved to see the queue wasn't too long. She smiled at the women as she found her place at the end.

Some of them she knew from other queues. Everyone scoured the daily newspapers, looking for announcements of anything else to eat other than turnips and potatoes. It seemed like life mostly was standing for hours outside a shop, in the faint hope there would be something to buy.

She could see that some of the women had parcels in their hands, clearly bringing things to barter, like she did. All part of the daily struggle to somehow keep their children warm, fed and safe. The shop would also take money, if you had any to spare. Anni tried to barter as much as possible, needing her coins for more important things, like food.

'Can I play?' Ingrid pointed at another little girl in the queue.

'Yes, but stay close, and don't run into the street,' Anni said.

She put her rucksack on the pavement and rubbed her hands together. She smiled at another mother. 'Have you been waiting long?'

'I came here twenty minutes ago,' she said.

Anni frowned. 'And there are so few people?'

The other woman nodded. 'There are rumours of fresh cod, so most people have gone to the fish market, I think. I'm here to see if I can get a winter coat for my boy.'

Anni nodded at Ingrid, who was showing her new friend her doll. 'She needs new boots. I swear, I can see her feet growing from day to day,' she said, laughing a little.

The other mother chuckled. 'But they do! I found my son a winter coat before Easter and already the sleeves are too short.'

There was a hush in the queue, and Anni turned her head. A young woman was coming towards them, arm in arm with a soldier. Anni could see he was an officer. Instinctively, she pressed her back against the building.

'Look at her,' one of the other women whispered. 'Flaunting her shame like that. If I was her mother, I'd never allow something like that.'

Anni noticed the woman was pregnant. When they passed the queue, the woman lifted her chin, and held on to her lover's arm, so hard Anni could see her hands pale.

49

How scared she must be, Anni thought.

Another woman spat on the ground, and the others whispered between them. 'German slut,' one of them muttered.

Anni didn't participate. She couldn't understand why those women would openly choose to be with an enemy soldier. How could they love a man who represented all the horror of Nazi Germany? *It beggars belief*, she thought. But that didn't mean she hated them or would spit at them on the street.

Their choice would haunt them later. She knew that. The illegal newspapers from the exile government in London had made it clear that women like them were to be regarded as collaborators and traitors. The shame they carried, Anni thought. *I hope it's worth it for her.*

The queue gradually moved forward and soon Anni could go in with Ingrid in tow. Inside, there were several tables and shelves, with clothes, shoes and anything else people had brought in hope of finding something they needed more. Everything was organised by size, and she could see at once that the selection of shoes and boots were slim.

At least that's not the only thing I'm here for, she thought with a sigh.

The shop was run by volunteers, and at first, she couldn't see the person she needed to talk to, then she spotted her behind the counter.

'Anni! I didn't know you would come today.' Nina was Martin's daughter, and the main reason for coming to the shop. She was in on most of what they were doing, apart from the more dangerous operations. Martin didn't want to put his nineteen-year-old daughter in danger. On those occasions she was a trusted babysitter for Ingrid instead.

Anni smiled back. 'Hello, Nina. I've brought these today.'

She opened the rucksack and pulled out one of the jumpers she had found. With a quick movement, she also pulled out the newspapers, and wrapped them in the bottom jumper. It was the last bundle she had, and she wouldn't be able to smuggle any more for the foreseeable.

Nina very efficiently put the jumper under the shelf, out of sight of curious eyes. She smiled at Anni, giving her a quick wink.

Anni hid a smile. 'You have to be careful, Nina.'

The young girl pulled a face. 'I am. I really am, Anni.'

'Thank you. I'm also here to see if you have any boots for Ingrid. The ones she's wearing are too worn down.'

'Do you have anything to barter with in addition to the jumper?' Nina leant over. 'I can't be seen to show you any favours, you know.'

Anni pulled out a second jumper and put it on the counter. She left her hand on it.

When Nina reached out to take it, Anni hesitated.

The oldest, and most worn-out, garment was Lars's fishing jumper. She knew it was only useful for the wool now, perhaps to knit something for Ingrid. But it belonged to Lars, and she didn't have much left of his.

She couldn't seem to move her hand away from it.

Nina lowered her voice even more. 'This is the third time you've brought me this jumper, Anni. I think you're meant to keep it.'

'No, I don't think I can.' Anni sighed. 'Ingrid will freeze without a better pair of boots.'

Nina shook her head. 'Don't worry about that. I have what you need in the back. The other jumper and Ingrid's old wellies will do fine.'

Anni knew she was acting silly. It was sentimental and foolish, and still she couldn't let go of the jumper. 'Thank you,' she said.

Nina looked at Ingrid. 'You have to stop growing, little one. Especially those toesies of yours.'

Ingrid giggled. 'I can't help that,' she said.

Anni looked around. Nobody seemed interested in what they were doing.

'I need to see Martin tonight,' Anni whispered.

Nina looked around too, before answering. 'I might not be able to get a message to him that quickly.'

'It's an emergency,' Anni said. 'I need to talk to him.'

One of the other volunteers came over to them, and Nina straightened up.

'I'll take these in the back and see if we have something that might fit you. You two can wait over there,' Nina said, pointing at the corner by the shoe racks.

Anni took Ingrid's hand and went over to one of the side tables.

There was a scant collection of children's shoes and Wellingtons, most with worn-down soles like the ones Ingrid already had on. Anni couldn't see any that would fit Ingrid. She didn't mind if they were too big; that only meant her feet would have room to grow and for an extra pair of warm socks when winter arrived proper.

A few minutes later Nina returned with a pair of laced boots in her hands.

'Here, I think these will do,' Nina said with a huge smile

and handed them to Anni. 'They came in yesterday, and I've been keeping them for you.'

Anni looked at the boots and could have cried. They were brown, scuffed on the tip, but they had proper soles that looked thick and almost brand new.

'This is real leather,' she said in awe, looking at Nina.

Nina frowned. 'I know they're not wellingtons, but they will do fine even when it rains, I promise.'

Anni held the boots out to Ingrid. 'Let's see if these will fit you,' she said.

'Are they for me?' Ingrid looked at the boots in awe. 'Truly?'

'If they fit,' Anni said. 'Let me help you with the laces.'

Ingrid shook her head. 'I can do it myself, Mamma.'

'Good girl.' Anni looked around. Nobody had taken notice of Ingrid's boots. She looked at Nina. 'I'll be at the monument at eight. Tell him that under no circumstances can he come to the house. It's dangerous.'

Nina paled, understanding the situation. 'I will find him.'

A woman grabbed Nina's arm. 'Please, do you have any jumpers for a ten-year-old boy? I swear, he'll be taller than me soon.'

Nina nodded. 'Let's see what we can find, shall we?'

She left and Anni turned to Ingrid.

Ingrid had managed to take off her old Wellingtons, put them nicely to the side for Nina, and held out her hands for the new boots.

Anni waited patiently while she pulled them on, and then tried to tie them without much success.

'You want me to help?' Anni sat down to look at her.

Ingrid shook her head. 'I can do it, Mamma,' she said.

Finally, there were loopy bows on both boots, and Ingrid stood up. She took a few tentative steps, then looked up at Anni with a huge grin.

'They're so good, Mamma.' Ingrid jumped up and down.

Anni pressed her thumb gently on the tip of the boot. 'Plenty of space for toes to grow,' she said.

'I can have them?' Ingrid beamed.

'Yes, you can. Now we'll go and have soup, and then see if there is anything good in the shops before we go home. Does that sound like fun?'

Ingrid nodded. 'Can I keep them on?'

'Yes, that's the idea, and if your feet get wet, you have to tell me,' Anni said.

Ingrid nodded. 'I will, Mamma.'

Anni took her hand and waved to Nina on the way out.

Hopefully Nina could find her father and give him the message. Anni needed help. The situation was too dangerous for her to handle on her own. So many things would be jeopardised if this man was allowed to stay in her house.

She tried not to think too much about it as they strolled up Haraldsgaten again, looking for a café where they could get a sandwich or some soup. Anni remembered when the bakeries would offer cream-filled pastries, covered in chocolate and marzipan, huge soft buns with raisins, and waffles with melted butter and proper strawberry jam. The thought made her stomach rumble.

Ingrid was skipping next to her, singing about cauliflower soup. Anni straightened her coat and smiled at her. She didn't know what she was missing, and fully enjoyed the treats that were available.

When this bloody war is over, I swear I will take my

54

girl to the best bakery in town and let her stuff herself sick on anything she wants, she thought. Plenty of fresh cream, strawberries and whatever else she fancied.

The café was half full when they entered. Anni closed her eyes for a second. With a little help from her imagination, she could almost smell a faint coffee smell, though the only thing they served now was a roasted acorn and rye mix, and probably something better left unknown, but that tasted nothing like coffee.

Ingrid looked up at the blackboard and carefully spelt out the few dishes they had on offer.

Then she looked up at Anni. 'No cauliflower, Mamma,' she said, not able to hide the disappointment.

'No, but they have fish soup. You like that, don't you?'

Ingrid nodded. 'Yes, I do.'

Anni ordered two bowls of soup and found them a table by the window. Ingrid loved looking out on the street. She had a running commentary on everyone and everything she saw.

'Look, Mamma. They're playing music,' she said.

Anni watched the marching band of uniformed Wehrmacht soldiers playing their marching songs. At least they weren't singing, she thought. Their military songs grated her nerves.

Ingrid frowned as the fish soup was brought out. 'Where's the fish?'

Anni pointed with her spoon. 'Look, there's the little dumplings, and there's some smoked porbeagle,' she said, pointing at some small, greyish balls, and darker pieces of smoked fish. 'And those are peas. You like peas.'

Ingrid nodded. 'I love peas.'

Before the war, the soup would have been made with real cream and filled with big chunks of fresh fish and pink, salty shrimps. Now it was made from 'blue milk', potato starch and salty broth. They had put a generous amount of dried chives in it, though. That helped.

Ingrid tested the soup and nodded her approval. 'Good, Mamma.'

'I'd better trust you, then,' Anni said, smiling at the eagerness with which Ingrid attacked the soup.

Anni made a decision not to worry about the German in her house and enjoy the day with Ingrid. There would be trouble soon enough anyway. But she couldn't help worry about Nina getting the message to her father. She was sure it would help appease Guri if she could tell her what Martin thought about the new situation.

By eight o'clock, there was still no sign of her new lodger. As soon as Ingrid was sound asleep, Anni pulled on her coat and wrapped a scarf around her neck.

It wasn't something she wanted to do, leaving Ingrid alone in the house, especially while expecting a stranger. But she had no choice. Martin needed to know as soon as possible.

Before leaving the house, she found an old shopping bag she used for carrying firewood from the woodshed. She needed an excuse if the German suddenly appeared.

She put the basket inside the woodshed, then carefully walked towards the monument. There were no lights anywhere, thanks to the mandatory blackout; everyone had to cover their windows with black paper so the RAF didn't have anything to aim for. And now it was so dark, she could barely see where she was going. But she knew the area well and trusted her feet.

When she arrived at Haraldshaugen, the dark pillars somehow made her feel safer. In the middle was the tall obelisk marking what was believed to be King Harald's grave. The smaller ones, forming a square, represented the counties that existed back then. They were like old friends.

Memories of how she and her friends had dug around for the treasure that the king was supposed to have with him in his grave made her smile. They never found anything, but that didn't stop them from imagining the Viking riches hidden in the dirt. And now Ingrid and the other children played the same game.

From a distance she could hear waves breaking against the shore. The sound always calmed her. She had lived near the sea all her life, the one constant that was always there.

Anni hid behind the pillar furthest away from the house, burrowed her hands in her pockets and waited. Why the hell wasn't Martin there already? She couldn't stay long in case Ingrid woke up, or that . . . that *man* showed up, whichever came first.

Finally, she could hear footsteps on the gravel road and turned to face Martin. He was the liaison officer between their little group and the Norwegian base on Shetland. He was also Lars's oldest friend, from the first time they were deckhands together, and the one who had recruited Guri and herself into the resistance.

Martin was dressed in a thick, patterned jumper, a long coat, a hat pulled down over his forehead and heavy fisherman boots. He didn't stand out from any other man in the area.

Normally he was cordial and friendly; tonight, however, he looked cross.

'We're not supposed to have any contact until next week,' he hissed. 'Nina had to travel out to Karmøy to find me.'

Karmøy was the large island off the mainland. It was quite the journey these days, with constant German controls on the ferries. 'I'm sorry, but it couldn't be helped, Martin.'

'Is it Guri? Has something happened to her?' Martin looked concerned.

'No, she's still in the hinterland.'

'Then what is it?'

Anni wrapped the coat tighter around herself. 'A German civilian showed up at my house yesterday. His name is Hugo Kerber, and he told me that he's in charge of the administration at Hagland,' she said.

Martin looked confused. 'What did he want with you?'

'Nothing with me, but he has decided to take lodgings in my house.'

Martin swore under his breath. 'That's bloody inconvenient, you know. Couldn't you say no? Or suggest another place, or something like that?'

'As if I had any choice.' Anni scowled at him. 'How the hell could I refuse? I don't want him in my house, and I damn well don't want him anywhere near Ingrid. But you know there's no bloody chance he's going to give a sod about that, is there? Now, you tell me how I could have dealt with the situation.'

'I need to think.' Martin went silent for a moment, staring ahead as if King Harald himself would tell him what to do.

Anni looked at him with growing impatience. After a few minutes she'd had enough.

'Martin, I can't stay for much longer. Ingrid could wake up, or he might return,' she said. 'He might find it odd that I'm on an evening stroll while my child is sleeping in an empty house.'

'I understand. Of course I do.' Martin nodded. 'The problem is that we're expecting a shipment any day now, and we don't have anywhere to put the cargo. We were counting on you and Guri.'

They would store contraband and equipment to help the resistance in one of the sheds until someone could come and collect it, and so far, there had been no problems. Her house and Guri's farm were well suited for clandestine operations, both being fairly isolated and located so close to the sea.

Anni frowned. 'You have to find other arrangements. I can't bring anything or anyone in the house now. I can't risk Ingrid, or you and Guri.'

Martin nodded. 'I agree, we can't risk either of you. That might have serious consequences. I'll find another way. You don't have to worry about that. You and Ingrid are safe. Have you told Guri?'

He interrupted her before she could protest. 'Sorry, you just told me about her.'

Anni put her hand on his arm. 'One more thing before you go. Can you find out about him? I need to know what kind of man he is.'

Martin looked confused. 'Why? They're all the same sort of bastards, aren't they?'

Anni sighed. 'I should think that's obvious. I want to know if he's likely to attack us, or invite his Gestapo buddies for breakfast and beat us to death because it amuses him.'

She could hear the shrill note in her voice and knew Martin could hear it too. 'Can you do it?'

'Yes, yes, I know. I'm sorry, Anni.' He nodded again. 'You're absolutely right. We need to know everything about him. I'll let you know what I find out, as soon as I can. Nothing could be more important right now.'

'Thank you. Guri isn't here, so I can't send Ingrid to stay with her. Until I know more about him, we won't be safe. Or as safe as we can be these days.'

Martin looked at her, every sign of annoyance gone. 'Do you want us to take you both to England? I mean all three of you? I know you'd never leave without Guri. All you have to do is say yes, and it's done. God knows you've both deserved it.'

Anni knew that would create an even bigger problem for the resistance, and she didn't want to stop helping them. It was too important. Besides, there was absolutely no chance Guri would ever go with them. No, they would have to stay on, doing their best to get through the damn war.

She had an idea.

'No, not yet, anyway. Listen, depending on what you find out about him, we could possibly use this. He might bring papers back to the house, or, I don't know, other things. Maybe he talks in his sleep.'

Martin's jaw dropped, and it was obvious what he was thinking.

'No, not *that*.' She glared at him. 'For God's sake, Martin. I'm talking about gathering information. Maybe he'll bring other people, his people, over for a party and I can eavesdrop. He's at Hagland, and that means he'll know things that can be useful for us, don't you think?'

Martin looked relieved. 'Don't worry, I'll find out as soon as I can.'

'Make it sooner. If he's dangerous, I don't want to keep Ingrid in the house.' Anni's mind was racing now that she had thought about using the situation to their advantage.

'Right,' he said. 'I'll get on it at once.'

Anni put a hand on his arm. 'Martin, he knows things about me.' She shuddered at the thought.

'Like what?' Martin looked concerned.

'That I speak German, that I take care of the prayer house, that I have a daughter, and that Lars is a sailor. I'm worried he's in my house to keep an eye on me, maybe even on Guri. We have to be extra careful from now on. You and Nina can't be seen with either of us.'

Martin looked even more concerned. 'I understand. Keep your head down and stay calm as much as you can. Maybe try to be friendly, so he has no reason to suspect anything.'

Easy for him to say, she thought.

Anni waited until he disappeared into the shadows, before running back to the house.

She remembered to stop at the woodshed for the shopping bag. While she was in there, she heard a car roll in and stop in front of the house.

Anni froze, too scared to move. *They must have seen me coming from the monument*, she thought. The timing seemed too convenient. Had they been somewhere out there since she left the house, with the engine turned off? Without the faint light coming from the headlights, she would have been none the wiser of what hid in the dark.

She peeked out the door of the shed, trying to see if it was only him and his chauffeur. She couldn't see either of them. Only the dark outline of the car.

I can't stay in here all night, she thought, knowing full well that if it hadn't been for Ingrid sleeping in her bed, she might have.

Be calm, she told herself. *Be calm, and don't show them how scared you are. They like that, for sure.* She had seen it often enough in the last four years.

Anni took a tight grip on the handles of the bag, stepped outside and headed towards the house, making sure to keep her eyes down.

The car backed out and drove away.

Kerber stood on the porch, looking through his pockets. *Or pretending to*, Anni thought. He didn't seem surprised to see her, which increased her unease. She had to force herself not to look back at the monument.

'Good evening, Frau Odland,' he said, and bowed slightly.

'Good evening, Herr Kerber,' she said, surprised she managed to speak at all.

'May I?' He didn't wait for her answer, and gently took the bag from her, before letting her go inside first.

Anni tried to hide her surprise, and was pretty sure she had made a right mess of it. He didn't seem to have noticed.

'Is this what you use for heating?' He looked at the dried peat in the bag.

'That's the only thing there is at the moment,' Anni replied.

'If you allow me, I will bring some proper firewood from Hagland,' he said, and sat the bag next to the wood burner in the lounge.

Anni nodded. 'That's good. For you, I mean. Like I said

yesterday, we don't have enough to keep a fire going in the dining room.'

She could feel his eyes in the back of her neck as she moved through the room. *Calm down, Anni*, she told herself. *There are no troops with him, no Gestapo lurking in the darkness outside. I'm safe for now.* She made sure to keep her face normal when she turned to him.

'It's probably cold in your room. Help yourself from here tonight. I have more in the shed,' she said, pointing at the peat.

He didn't say anything but simply looked at her, making Anni uncomfortable. She didn't like the way it made her feel, as if he could see right through her attempts to keep a brave face.

Anni cleared her throat. 'I'd best go to bed,' she said.

'Thank you, Frau Odland,' he said in his quiet voice.

She turned towards the hallway and the stairs and managed to resist the urge to run up the steps, away from him. She didn't want him to know how terrified she was. Something about him wasn't right, and it bothered her more and more.

On top of the stairs, she couldn't help herself. She stopped and looked down.

He was still standing in the doorway, still with his coat on.

'*Gute Nacht*,' he said, with a slight nod.

'Good night,' Anni said.

She found it infuriating that she had looked back, and that nod annoyed her even more, but she forced herself to walk at a normal pace, before almost diving into the bedroom and closing the door behind her, making sure it was properly closed.

After checking that Ingrid was fast asleep, she went over to the water bowl, and rubbed her hands in the cold water. She took a few deep breaths, before getting undressed and slipping under the covers.

Ingrid stirred but didn't wake up. She had slept through some of the worst RAF bombings, so Anni wasn't surprised.

Anni rested her head on the pillow, and watched the little girl.

Her blonde fringe was hiding her eyes and she had bed hair in the back. *Angel hair*, Anni thought.

She touched her soft cheek gently.

'I wish Lars could see you. He's missing out on everything,' she whispered.

She sighed. Lars wouldn't be back before the war ended. When the Germans came, the Occupation forces had ordered all Norwegian ships to return to home base immediately. None did. Apart from the ships already in Norwegian waters, the rest of the merchant fleet never came home. The new authorities were furious at losing one of the largest fleets of merchant ships in the world. It was a huge blow to their plans.

Anni smiled at the thought. It had taken some time before they realised what had happened.

The King and the government had managed to escape German captivity in 1940. They relocated to London, and the 'London-government' became the name Norwegians called their proper government. Which was to the great chagrin of the 'minister president' Quisling, who had fancied himself the role as Führer of Norway, and instead became the puppet for Hitler's appointed *Reichskommissar*, Josef Terboven.

One of the first things the London-government did had been to reorganise the merchant fleet into one shipping company, Nortraship, with the blessing of the various shipping companies. She knew that was a good thing, even if it kept Lars out of the country.

Anni looked at Ingrid again, and swallowed a lump in her throat.

He didn't even know how much Ingrid had changed since he saw her last. She had been a month shy of two years old when he left, walking and talking, but still a chubby baby. He had missed so much. Anni knew that must be hard for him.

All she could do was wait and hope that the war would end soon. And in the meantime, remember him in her heart.

They had met at a dance when she was in the last year of school. Anni smiled to herself. She had wanted to study to become a teacher, and she had good grades in middle school, so it would have been possible.

Lars had been soft-spoken and charming, and they met every day until he had to leave again. After that, he made sure to find her if the ship he was on had a stopover in Haugesund.

They had been in love, she was sure of that, and when they married in the little white church up the road, she had been happy. It had been a good marriage, she was sure of that too. But right now, in the darkness, in the bed they had shared, she couldn't remember the touch of his hand, the smell of his skin. Even if she closed her eyes, it wasn't there.

Sounds from downstairs interrupted her memories. Anni could hear Kerber moving around. She had forgotten that the dining room was right below her room.

Anni thought about him, trying to make up her mind how dangerous he could be. He was polite and quiet, but she wasn't fooled. Some of the Nazis behaved so nicely and politely when you talked to them, butter wouldn't melt. But they could not be trusted. And then there was the Gestapo. They all knew what was going on in the Gestapo houses across the country . . .

She'd been spared that when Kerber arrived. She was still here.

Anni closed her eyes and snuggled into Ingrid. The tiny, warm body was her anchor. Without her, she would be lost. Ingrid was the only thing that mattered.

Hopefully the German would be fed up driving back and forth and decide to stay at Hagland Fortress, and they would be safe again, or as safe as they could be in the middle of the war.

Chapter Five

Anni watched Ingrid skip down the narrow pathway running along the monument. Her new boots clearly stood the test of wet and cold weather. *Thankfully*, Anni thought.

'Don't run too fast,' she called. 'It's slippery.'

Ingrid turned around and grinned at her. 'My feet are toasty!'

I wish mine were, Anni thought and waved at her. She shivered from the gust of wind coming in from the sea.

Martin had said there would be a shipment coming from Shetland next week. Cargo, he had said, and Anni knew that could mean anything from passengers, black market food and medicines, or weapons. She knew the boat would be in for a rough crossing.

The weather was unpredictable this time of year. Still, the boats didn't have much choice. They needed the darkness to hide. She knew the skippers knew the coastline well, even in the dark, but after four years of Occupation, the German patrol boats weren't that ignorant anymore.

Anni pulled the scarf tighter around her neck. *The new lodger might know about patrol boats and patrols, maybe even planned raids. If he does, and I can gain access to that kind of information, perhaps the risk will be worth it. That's a lot of ifs and maybes*, she thought.

Now it was a question of how much she should tell Guri.

'She's going to hate this,' Anni muttered.

Her mother-in-law's farm was on the other side of the monument, and they always took the pathway by the monument, away from the road. Walking along the main road, there would be military lorries and cars constantly passing by. She didn't feel safe, and Ingrid would not be able to skip.

Ingrid stopped and pointed ahead. 'Look, Mamma,' she yelled. 'Besta!'

'Then run along.' Anni waved at her mother-in-law, who waved back.

Guri was busy cutting down brushes by the fence. *Never one for sitting still*, Anni thought.

When Ingrid came running towards her, Guri pulled off her gloves and greeted her granddaughter with a big hug.

Anni smiled at the sight of them. She had no idea how she would have managed without Guri. *That was the one good thing about the war*, she thought. It had brought them closer together.

Most of the family land had been sold off by earlier generations, but Guri still owned her house, the farm and enough land to sustain a few goats and herself. Before the war she had kept cows, but they were taken by the Nazis. Later she tried to raise pigs, but those proved popular with both soldiers and locals, who didn't have any reservations about stealing the piglets.

Anni remembered how difficult it had been at the beginning, when Lars first introduced her to his mother. There was no immediate love from her, no hugs and welcome to the family. Guri didn't think much of the town girl, marrying her only son. It had taken a war and an occupation by a foreign power to make Guri warm up to her.

The bond between Guri and Lars was one she recognised with Ingrid. She could understand that. For the longest time it had only been Guri and Lars. Guri's husband had died on a fishing boat, during a winter storm in the herring fisheries when Lars was a few years older than Ingrid.

Guri didn't talk much about it, but it was clear that she worried about him.

Anni wondered again how Lars was doing, where he was, if he even was alive. She had been so sure she would be fine alone, when he sailed out that last time.

She had followed Lars down to the harbour, one crisp morning in March 1940. There had been a touch of spring in the air, but she had felt the winter chill. Ingrid had been in her pram, happy as ever.

Lars had held his arms around her and promised he would return before Christmas, with presents from America.

He knew she worried about him, more and more as the war in Europe developed. 'I wish you wouldn't go,' she said. 'There's a war, Lars.'

He had shrugged at that. It still infuriated her when she remembered that. 'That's not going to affect us. Norway is neutral, remember? I promise you, it will be like the last war. Shipping in Norway, and especially Haugesund, will thrive, and everyone will make tons of money. Even us.'

Anni remembered how angry that had made her, and that she had almost yelled her reply. 'Don't you dare say that to me. I read the papers too. Since the British declared war in 1939, how many dozens of our ships have been torpedoed? Nine from Haugesund. The Germans couldn't care less about our neutrality. What if they come here?'

'That's ridiculous. The Germans have more use of us when we're neutral. We're trading plenty with them,' Lars had said.

She had known he was trying to make her feel better, but it had only made it worse. 'You don't know that,' she had said, tired of the whole argument.

Lars had only laughed and then kissed her. 'Trust me, I'm not going to be torpedoed. I love you, and I'll see you both soon.'

He had bent down and made a fuss about Ingrid, making her laugh in the shrill, birdy kind of way she did.

Anni had a bad feeling watching him walk up the gangway. Ingrid sat on her arm by then, waving back at him. Anni had forced herself to smile and wave when he dropped his bag on the deck and stood there until she couldn't see him anymore.

Afterwards she had taken Ingrid for a stroll in town, bought herself a cup of coffee and a waffle for Ingrid, and an hour later the feeling was mostly gone. She walked home to take care of the house and the baby, and to wait for Lars to return.

After all, she would only be doing the same as every

woman on the coast had done, what Guri had done, and like countless other women whose husbands, fathers and brothers had sailed on a Norwegian ship in foreign waters since before the Vikings.

And then the Occupation forces came and everything changed.

Anni shuddered. *I should have stopped him*, she thought now. *I should have acted on my bad feeling. Then Lars would have been home, and no damned Nazi would have dared to move into our home as if he owned the place.*

She caught up with the others just as Ingrid was showing Guri her new boots. 'Mamma said they are real leather,' she said.

'They are pre-war quality,' Guri said, clearly impressed.

'We went into town,' Ingrid declared. 'I had fish soup with dumplings in the café.'

Guri smiled at Anni. 'Was it as good as my soup?'

Ingrid hesitated, then shook her head, grinning. 'Your soup is the best in the world, Besta.'

Guri laughed. 'You are a terrible child. Did you miss me?'

Ingrid nodded. 'All the time. Because now we have a bad man at home,' she said. 'Can you make him go away, Besta? He'll be scared of you, I'm sure.'

So much for trying to make her forget about Herr Kerber, Anni thought.

Guri looked at Anni again, narrowing her eyes. 'What is she saying? A bad man?'

'Ingrid, go inside the house, please,' Anni said. 'Now.'

Ingrid sent her a worried look. 'But Mamma,' she whined.

Guri patted her on the head. 'Run inside and see what I brought you. It's in the kitchen.'

Ingrid lit up. 'For me?' All thoughts of the bad man forgotten. *I wish it was that easy*, Anni thought.

'Yes, run along,' Guri said. 'And don't touch the food! You can look, but not touch.'

The moment Ingrid disappeared into the house, Guri turned to Anni with a furious look on her face.

'Not in my wildest imaginations would I've thought you would be unfaithful to Lars,' she said.

Anni tried to interrupt her, but Guri wasn't having it.

'What do you think Lars will feel when he comes home after all these years and . . .' Guri stared aghast at her. 'Ingrid only calls *them* bad men. I can't believe it. What do you think Lars will say when he finds out you've been with . . . with one of those bastards? You'll disgrace us all, not only yourself. And don't think for a second I won't tell Lars when he comes home!'

Anni rolled her eyes. 'For goodness' sake, Guri. Of course I'm not unfaithful to Lars. I would never do that. Not with a German, not with anyone. How can you even think that?'

'Then who is this bad man?' Guri didn't seem convinced.

So much for telling her gently, Anni thought. She threw herself into it.

'A German civilian came to the house two days ago, said he runs the administrative office at Hagland from now on, and that he had decided to pick my house for lodgings. You know I wouldn't have let him across the threshold if I had any choice.'

She looked relieved, almost happy for a second. 'I'm glad. I mean, I'm not glad he's in the house, but I'm glad about you.'

'Maybe next time you're not so quick to doubt me,' Anni said, still frowning. 'How could you even think I would do something like that? I'm Lars's wife, and that means everything to me.'

'I'm sorry,' Guri said, looking dejected. 'I shouldn't have doubted you.'

'No, you bloody well shouldn't have.' Anni sighed.

Guri looked at her. 'I would be lying if it hasn't crossed my mind that you, you know, might find . . . comfort.'

Anni looked at her, gaping. 'Oh my God, you didn't say that. That's horrendous, Guri.'

Guri seemed unfazed. 'You have been apart for over four years. That's a long time to be alone for a young woman.'

'True, but that's no reason to jump into bed with someone else. And how could you for a second believe that I would go with a German, when they are the reason Lars isn't home with us, like he should be?' Anni said, furious now. 'And just so you know, when Lars comes home, I want to be able to look him in the eyes and know that I've been faithful to him.'

Guri smiled, clearly touched by her words. 'I know that. Of course I do. I'm sorry for doubting you, Anni. I didn't mean any of it. I was surprised.'

The idea that Guri would think she had an affair going on with . . . with that man was unbearable. Anni took a deep breath. 'It was quite the surprise to me too,' she said.

Guri looked at her and chuckled. 'Now what do we do?' Guri looked towards her house. 'How do you feel about this situation?'

They couldn't see it from here. The only thing visible was the top of the monument.

'How do I feel about having one of them in my house? This is a gigantic problem.'

'I knew something bad had happened.' Guri looked annoyed.

Anni doubted that. 'How? It happened two days ago while you weren't here.'

Guri's expression softened. 'I knew something bad had happened the moment I saw you. God, I hate those bastards.'

'We're in a war, Guri. Bad things happen all the time,' Anni said. 'Soldiers are billeted all over the country, in all sorts of houses, and the people who live there don't have a say.'

'Of course.' Guri frowned. 'But why did this man choose your house? He could have found a house closer to Hagland, or he could have slept at the school, like the rest of them.'

'His explanation was that he wants a peaceful place to sleep,' Anni said.

'That's an odd thing to say, especially for a German.' Guri gave it some thought. 'Or maybe not. It must be exhausting with all that shouting, marching and torturing people they do all day.'

Anni tried to hide a smile, but when Guri grinned, she couldn't help herself. 'I suspect you're right.'

Guri wasn't done yet. 'What did you say to him?'

Anni folded her arms over her chest. 'I told him we didn't have a spare bedroom, so now he's sleeping in the dining room. They do what they bloody well want to. You know that.'

'Yes, yes.' Guri shook her head. 'What kind of officer is he?'

'I told you. He's not an officer. He's a civilian, working for the Wehrmacht. Not that it makes much of a difference, I suspect.'

'Still, it's better than if he was Gestapo or SS,' Guri said.

'I suppose.' Anni rubbed her temple. 'I've no idea what to do about it, to be honest.'

'This will probably not help, but have you told the reverend yet?' Guri said.

'I don't expect there to be a problem. We all understand the situation we're in.'

'It's a nightmare that won't stop, isn't it?' Guri frowned.

'Yes, but there's only so much we can do.' Anni took a deep breath. 'I met Martin last night. I couldn't risk him coming to the house. Not now.'

'I expect he wasn't happy about the situation?' Guri said.

'Not even a little bit. There's a shipment expected next week, so he'll have to find other arrangements.'

'More weapons? You'd think this coastline is riddled with guns by now.' Guri had a grim expression on her face.

Anni shrugged. 'They're preparing for the end of the war. But I can't have people or goods on my property as long as that man is with us.'

She wondered if she should tell Guri she planned to spy on the German. What if she never found anything? *No need to scare her*, she decided.

'Guri, we're so lucky there wasn't anyone hiding in the basement. We can't take risks like that anymore.' Anni put her hand on her arm. 'Please don't hide anyone in your house until we know more.'

Guri looked annoyed. 'I'm not reckless. You know that.'

'I know you're not. But I need you to promise me this,

because if they arrest me you're the only one to take care of Ingrid. She doesn't have anyone else. Not with Lars gone.'

'Don't even say that.' Guri shuddered. 'That can't happen. It won't.'

'I don't want it to.' Anni knew they had to be practical. 'But we've known the risk ever since we started this. And we don't know if this man is here to keep an eye on me or if he's what he says he is.'

Guri's face darkened. 'Did he say or do anything to make you think that?'

Anni took a deep breath. 'He knew a lot about me. That scared me.'

Guri looked horrified. 'You have to let Ingrid stay here with me. What if something happens?'

Anni shook her head. 'He's already seen her. Otherwise, I would've told him she lived with you. Now, if she's not at home, he'll know I'm afraid. It will make me look even more suspicious. We have to appear as if nothing is amiss.'

'Are you sure?' Guri wasn't about to give up that easily. 'You know Ingrid loves to stay with me.'

'Yes, of course she does, you spoil her rotten. I appreciate everything you do for us, Guri, but she has to stay with me, at least for now,' Anni said firmly.

Guri nodded. 'For now,' she said.

Anni didn't comment on that. Guri wouldn't understand. Staying in the house, alone with that man, scared her more than having Ingrid there with her. And she refused to talk to Guri about it, or even acknowledge it to herself.

'Do you have anything illegal in the house now?' Guri had a concerned look on her face.

Anni shook her head. 'Nothing. I got rid of the last of

the newspapers yesterday when I went to the barter shop.'

'There's half a blessing,' Guri said.

'And you, did you hand over the radio parts?' Anni knew that was the real reason for her trip.

Guri looked pleased with herself. 'Of course I did. I know you're worried, but they pay no attention to little old ladies like me. I play the dimwit and they let me through.'

'That doesn't mean you have to take all the risks,' Anni said, knowing full well it was a waste of breath.

Guri put her hand on Anni's arm and gave it a gentle squeeze. 'We will get through this. We have managed so far, haven't we?'

Anni smiled. 'Yes, we have. But we must be even more vigilant now.'

Guri shook her head. 'I hate this,' she said, lowering her voice.

'There's not much we can do about it.' Anni straightened her shoulders.

'We know they're losing now, France is liberated, the Brits are in Greece, and the Allies are making headway in Germany. That makes the bastards nervous and scared,' Guri said. 'When snakes know they're trapped, that's when they are the most dangerous.'

'So, we keep our heads down,' Anni said, smiling at the older woman. 'There is an upside, though.'

'I'm scared to ask,' Guri said.

'He'll pay rent.' Anni laughed when Guri looked shocked before bursting into laughter herself.

They were interrupted by Ingrid, who came barrelling out of the house. 'You have to come inside, Mamma. Come see!'

Anni put a hand on her head. 'Why?'

'You must come and see!' Ingrid said, tugging at her hand.

Ingrid danced ahead of them into the farmhouse. Inside the smell of goat permeated the house.

'Did you leave the goats inside again?' Anni tried to breathe through her mouth.

Guri nodded. 'I wasn't going to leave them outside for someone to pinch them, was I?'

'I could have looked in on them and let them out in the pen, during the days.' Anni felt bad she hadn't even offered.

'No need – I was only gone for two nights. They had water and food.' Guri showed no signs of being bothered by the smell.

In the kitchen, Ingrid was standing by the table, jumping up and down. 'Look, Mamma.'

The table was full of packages, wrapped in brown paper and string.

'You can keep the food, but hand over the paper and strings,' Anni said, making Guri laugh.

'You can take home some of the strings. Can you believe they wrapped it up like that? It's more valuable than gold right now.' Guri smiled at Ingrid. 'You can unwrap the big package, Ingrid. That one is for you.'

Ingrid started on the knots.

'Now, what kind of edible treasures did you barter on your trip?' Anni looked at her mother-in-law.

'A few eggs, a side of pork belly, and the one thing we all crave: real butter,' Guri said, smiling at her. 'You see, keeping goats isn't so dumb, after all. My goat cheese is popular.'

'My stomach is growling,' Anni said, and she wasn't lying.

'I've put some away for you,' Guri said, before her face fell. 'I didn't think of that. You can't take food home, can you? That man would know it's not from the shops, wouldn't he?'

Anni could have cried. 'Yes, he probably would. I can't hide anything in the house now.'

'I'll cook the pork for Lars's birthday dinner. We'll have a proper meal on the day for once.'

Anni nodded. 'I'd like that,' she said softly.

It had been their own little tradition since the Occupation started. Partly to remember him by and to make Ingrid feel that he was a part of the family, and partly to remind themselves that life would be normal again one day.

Guri sighed. 'Can I give you two eggs at least? If he asks, you can say one of your kids from the prayer house gave them to you, can't you?'

'I think that will be fine,' Anni said, unable to resist the temptation.

'Good. You can have boiled eggs for breakfast. I'll give you butter too. Enough to enjoy with the egg. You can hide the food in your bedroom until he's gone.'

Anni smiled. 'How can I refuse?'

'You can't. The eggs and the pork alone cost me my last two thread spools,' Guri said. 'But with the sugar and flour I have saved up, we'll have a proper cake too.'

'She's going to love that. Perhaps you should save the eggs for the cake,' Anni said.

'I've already put the rest of the eggs in sand, so they'll keep.' Guri grinned. 'I've kept one egg for my breakfast too. I'm not some kind of ascetic, for God's sake.'

'I'm done,' Ingrid said with pride.

'What did Besta bring you?' Anni walked over to the table and looked at the gift. 'Aren't you the lucky one?'

Ingrid held up a blue dress, almost dropping it on the floor that was in dire need of a good sweep and scrub.

'Isn't it lovely, Mamma?' Ingrid pressed the dress to her chest.

'It's too big,' Guri said. 'But you can fix that, can't you, Anni?'

Anni smiled at Ingrid. 'I'm sure we can. It's lovely, Guri.'

'It's for Pappa's birthday, isn't it?' Ingrid couldn't stop admiring the dress.

'I'll have it ready by then, I promise,' Anni said.

'You're lucky to have a mamma who can sew, Ingrid. Me, I only had one boy and he didn't like dresses,' she said.

Ingrid giggled. 'Boys don't wear dresses.'

'That's exactly what Lars said.' Guri started putting away the food, and making a parcel she put in Anni's rucksack, ensuring the dress was on top. 'Don't forget the milk pail for Ingrid. Don't let *him* take it,' she said.

'I'm sure he won't take milk from a little girl,' Anni said, remembering how he had looked at Ingrid, but she didn't want to tell that to Guri.

'Don't be naive. They've stolen half the world. I doubt one little girl's milk matters much to them,' Guri said.

'He can have my milk,' Ingrid said, frowning when they laughed. 'Who is he?'

'Nobody, darling, that milk is for you. Because you need your milk to grow big and strong.' Guri filled the pail with milk and handed it to her. 'Be careful and don't spill any.'

Ingrid nodded. 'I won't, Besta.'

Guri and Anni smiled at each other, before Anni put the rucksack on and they headed out again.

Guri held Anni back. 'Let me know as often as possible how you're both doing. I'm worried with that man in your house.'

'If anything should happen, Ingrid knows to come to you.' Anni smiled thinly. 'We'll practise more on how she should hide in the closet, and not come out at all. A lot more.'

'Then I'll stay here on the farm. I won't leave town again in case you need me,' Guri said.

Anni wanted to protest but held her tongue. Guri was right. If she stayed at the farm, it would be easier to keep Ingrid safe. There was no ignoring how dangerous the work they did was.

'Thank you,' she said instead. 'I'd feel a lot safer with you here.'

Guri nodded. 'So will I.'

Guri walked with them to the path, then waited there. Anni took Ingrid's hand. She wasn't skipping now that she was holding the milk pail.

'Can I have the dress for Pappa's birthday, Mamma?' Ingrid looked up at her.

'That's why Besta got it for you. And then after that, you can wear it on Christmas, and maybe next year when you start school.' Anni could barely think that far ahead.

'Yes.' Ingrid nodded, then looked at her again. 'Are you leaving, Mamma?'

Anni stopped and looked at her. 'Why would you say that?'

Now she had such a worried expression on her little face. 'I heard what you said to Besta. That if . . . if anything happens, she will look after me.'

Anni sat down in front of her. 'Nothing will happen to me. I promise.'

'You're not leaving?' Ingrid looked so small.

Anni forced herself to smile. 'Now you listen to me, sweet pea. I will never leave you.'

Ingrid narrowed her eyes. 'But sometimes you leave, and I stay with Besta.'

'Yes, sometimes I do, but I always come back, don't I?'

Ingrid nodded. 'Yes, and then you bring me something, like Besta does.'

'That's right, clever girl.' Anni kissed her on the nose. 'I will always come back for you. Never, ever forget that.'

Chapter Six

Ingrid, fourteen years old
London, 1952

Ingrid burst into the little sweet shop, inhaling the smell of all the scrumptious treats. She never got tired of it.

'Hello, Mum.'

Esme put away the duster she was using. 'Hello, pet. How was school?'

Ingrid smiled at the woman behind the counter, and dropped her schoolbag on the floor. 'So boring.' She rolled her eyes.

'You mean, you didn't learn a single thing today? Not even a little long division or how to spell "mischievous"?' Esme raised her eyebrows.

'No. Not a thing.' Ingrid put a thick envelope on the counter. 'This is all the postman brought for us. I ran into him on the way.'

Esme looked at it. 'Hmm,' she said.

'It has Pappa's name on it. See? Lars Odland.' Ingrid pointed. 'What do you think it is?'

'It looks official, that's for certain,' Esme said, then looked closer. 'Why is there a hole in the paper?'

'The postman's lad is collecting stamps, and he doesn't have any from Norway. I had to promise to give him every stamp I get from now on,' Ingrid said.

Esme didn't look as if she was listening.

'It's from Besta, isn't it?' Ingrid said, worried now.

'I don't think so, it looks far too official,' Esme said, turning the envelope in her hands.

'Where is Pappa?' He was usually in the shop with Esme, and she was surprised not to see him.

'Upstairs in the lounge, taking a nap. He's been looking forward to you coming home,' Esme said.

Ingrid frowned. 'Is he OK? He doesn't usually nap in the middle of the day, does he?'

Esme put her hand against her cheek. 'Don't look so worried. You know how he is. You can go up in a minute.'

Ingrid nodded. Her father had his spells. She knew he had been torpedoed during the war, but he never spoke about anything from the war. Nor did she, apart from the times she had asked him about Mamma. He didn't like that, and she had stopped asking now.

She threw a stolen glance at the envelope. What if whatever was in there was about Mamma? What if Besta had finally found her? She had promised to make enquiries, but that was a long time ago, before she even came to London.

Ingrid knew Esme was worried and felt bad. She smiled at her stepmother and looked around the shop. 'How can I help?'

Esme cheered up at once. 'We need to fill those two jars with lemon sherbets and toffees.'

'May I have one?' Ingrid loved toffee.

'Only one. I don't want you to rot your teeth and spoil your tea,' Esme said.

Ingrid giggled and stuffed a piece of toffee in her mouth. Esme always said that, and she would always let her have more than one.

'I have to tend to the till before we go upstairs,' Esme said.

Ingrid walked over to the huge glass jars filled with different coloured sweets. Some wrapped, some showing off their glorious colours. Esme had grown up in the shop, and they lived upstairs. She thought it was the most magical place in the world.

A glass jar filled with sweets, wrapped in transparent cellophane, caught Ingrid's attention. 'These are new, Mum,' she said.

Esme looked over her shoulder. 'Yes, they came in today. Some kind of liquorice flavour, I think.'

'I like liquorice,' Ingrid said, smiling when Esme gave her a quick glance.

Ingrid opened the lid and took out one. She put it up to her nose and frowned. A memory from the back of her mind popped up. She was outside the white school building with Runar and they were talking to one of the soldiers. He gave them sweets like these.

She unwrapped the sweet and sniffed it again. Not quite the same, but close. 'Bon-bon,' she said quietly.

Esme looked up. 'What, pet?'

Ingrid turned towards her. 'I think the soldiers used to

give us sweets like these. We called them bon-bons.'

Esme smiled. 'That was nice of them. Although not something I would expect from German soldiers.'

'Maybe they were not all bad.' Ingrid tried to remember more. There was a man in the house. He was nice. She could see him smiling to her mamma in her mind. But she couldn't remember his name or who he was. But she remembered Mamma smiling back at him.

She turned away from Esme to hide the sudden tears, cursing the confusing memories.

'Are you all right?' Esme's voice seemed to come from far away.

'I'm fine.' Ingrid breathed through her nose and quickly regained control over herself. 'It's nothing. We're low on Bassetts Allsorts too.'

Esme didn't ask again.

Ingrid knew she worried about her. She turned around and smiled. 'I think I'm done here. I'll go and wash up for tea.'

'I'll come and get you when Lars is up and ready,' Esme said with a smile.

Ingrid gave her a hug, then picked up the schoolbag and ran upstairs.

Ingrid sank down on the bed and folded her hands in her lap. It was hard to remember details from home. She had lived in London just over seven years now, and if it hadn't been for the picture of Mamma and herself hanging on the wall, she might have forgotten her face.

The little box room had yellow curtains with daisies and a small wardrobe. There wasn't much room for anything else.

Her books were on top of the wardrobe, mostly English, but also Norwegian books Besta had sent her over the years.

She had felt safe in this room from the moment she arrived. It had been terrifying at first. The only one she could talk to was her father, and he didn't say much. Esme had decided that she would teach her English, and within a month she had known the name of every sweet in the shop.

And when she started school and had to wear a uniform, nobody picked on her, called her Nazi bastard or said mean things about her mamma. Instead, the other children included her and played with her, and her English quickly improved.

Ingrid rubbed her neck. Sometimes she had nightmares that felt like memories. More frequent when she was little, rarely now. *I have forgotten so much*, she thought.

Maybe that letter was about Mamma. Maybe Besta had found her, but why hadn't Besta written herself?

Every time she wrote Besta a letter, she would beg her for information about Mamma. And every time Besta replied with the same answer. She hadn't returned, there was no letter from her, nothing to tell Ingrid what had happened.

Ingrid wanted to run downstairs and ask Pappa about the envelope. But she knew she had to wait until Pappa woke up from his nap. After a while, she went into the bathroom and washed her face and hands. *There was cake*, she thought. And tea. And then she could ask about the envelope.

She could hear them talk when she came down the stairs. Esme first, then Pappa. He sounded cross.

Ingrid sat down on the step. She smoothed her skirt under her knees and waited for the right moment to pretend she had only just come down the stairs. She knew they were talking about whatever had come in the mail, and it didn't take long before she knew it was about her. She also knew if she came in now, they wouldn't say anything, and she needed to know.

Esme was pleading with him. 'You cannot hide this from her, Lars. If you don't tell her, I will.'

'I disagree. She's too young, and she's been through too much for someone her age. I don't want her to suffer more loss,' Pappa said.

'It doesn't matter. You have to. I can promise you she'll never forgive you if you hide something like this,' Esme said, in the voice Ingrid knew allowed no arguments.

'I'll think about it,' Pappa said.

Ingrid heard Esme leaving for the kitchen. She stood up, then trampled down the rest of the stairs, making sure she made noise.

In the lounge her father sat in his chair, chewing on his pipe. In his lap, Ingrid spotted the mysterious envelope. He looked up when she came in and smiled at her.

'There you are. How was school?'

'Fine.' Ingrid sat down on the footstool and folded her hands in her lap.

Lars took out his pipe and started to clean it. The smell was one of Ingrid's favourites. It was the first thing she remembered from the first time she met him.

He had come into Besta's kitchen with a soft toy, a Peter Rabbit in his hand. It was sitting on her bed now, and she had known immediately he was her pappa. For the first time since Mamma left and the war ended, she had felt safe.

From the kitchen, Ingrid heard the sounds of Esme preparing tea. There wasn't much time.

'Is the envelope about Besta?' she asked quickly. 'Did it say anything about Mamma too?'

He sighed. 'Did you expect there to be?'

Ingrid was knitting her fingers so hard together they hurt. 'No,' she whispered.

He put down his pipe. 'I'm sorry, Ingrid. This is not going to be easy for you. These are papers concerning the farm and the house. And Mother's will is in there too.'

Ingrid frowned. 'Why would Besta send those to you?'

He looked at her, and his eyes told her how serious it was. 'Oh,' she said.

'Your grandmother passed away,' he said.

Her heart felt as though it were falling apart, and she bit her lower lip to stop her from crying. 'Besta is dead?'

She couldn't bear it. Besta was the only bond she had to the past, to Mamma, to Norway. The thought that she was gone was unbearable. How could she live not knowing Besta was there? She had always been there for her.

She stood up. 'I don't want any tea,' she said, then ran upstairs and into her room.

Ingrid managed to close the door behind her before she burst into tears.

She was crying so hard, her chest hurt. Her whole body hurt. Ingrid burrowed her face into her pillow, trying to stop the crying. She didn't notice the door opening, until Pappa sat down on the bed. He put his hand on her back.

'I'm so sorry,' he said.

Ingrid turned around and threw her arms around him. 'I'm sorry too, Pappa.'

He handed her a handkerchief. 'I should have told you at once, but I didn't know how.'

'When . . . when did it happen?' Ingrid blew her nose and tried to stop crying. She didn't manage.

'About a week ago. You were at school when they rang me. Mother had suffered a heart attack, and the farmhand discovered her when he came to work and didn't find her outside. The doctor said she passed away peacefully. There was nothing they could have done,' Lars said.

Ingrid could hear his voice strain. 'You should have told me then,' she said.

'Yes, I should. I felt so bad about leaving her alone over there. But you know how she was. We tried to talk to her about it when she was here last Christmas, remember?'

Ingrid nodded. 'Yes, she didn't want to leave the farm.'

They fell silent for a moment, and Ingrid tried to breathe slowly. There was still one thing she needed to know, and he probably wouldn't like it. She looked up at him. 'What will happen to the farm now?'

'What we want to happen, I suppose. Mother left it to you and me in her will, including all the land and the house where you lived with your mother.'

'I don't want to sell any of it,' Ingrid said quickly. 'Not ever.'

'Are you sure? If we do, I'm sure we'll get enough to pay for your education and maybe some savings,' he said.

Ingrid shook her head. 'No. I don't want to sell.' She looked at him again. 'Can you sell it? Without me, I mean?'

Lars smiled. 'No, I couldn't even if I wanted to. Mother made sure there's a stipulation, that even if you're still a minor, I can't do anything without your consent. You and I have to make all decisions together.'

'Good.' Ingrid felt a huge relief rush through her body.

Besta had known how important it was for her. In her heart she knew that the house and farm would be the first place Mamma would go when she returned. And if other people lived there, how could she find her?

Lars put his hand around her shoulder. 'I understand this is a shock for you. You loved her, and she loved you.'

Ingrid leant in on his shoulder. 'What happens to Besta now?'

'There will be a funeral, of course.'

'Will you go?' She didn't look at him when she asked.

'Yes, I have to. I'll arrange the travel tomorrow,' Lars said.

'Can I come with you?' Ingrid already knew what he would say, but asked anyway.

'I'm sorry, Ingrid, but I think it's better you stay here with Esme. The trip is expensive and you have school. I'll be back in a week or so,' he said.

'And you promise you won't sell the farm?' This time she looked him right in the eyes.

'Yes, I told you I can't do that.' Lars frowned. 'Why don't you want to sell it?'

Ingrid felt tears burning again. 'When Mamma comes home, she needs to find me. If the farm is sold, she won't know what to do,' she said.

Lars sighed. 'I know you want to find out where Anni is, but the truth is that I have enquired, so did Mother, and the authorities in Norway have no record of your mother anywhere. I don't know what else to tell you.'

Ingrid looked at him. 'Then Mamma must be alive somewhere. Because if she was dead, you would have found a record of it, wouldn't you? I mean, they register deaths in Norway, don't they?'

He got a pained expression on his face. 'Yes, of course they do. But that doesn't mean that she's alive. It doesn't mean anything. The war . . . it made things messy and chaotic, and not everything was done the way it should have been. You understand, don't you?'

It was a circular discussion, always starting and ending in the same manner.

'I understand, Pappa,' Ingrid muttered.

'Good girl.' He hugged her before standing up. 'Will you come down for tea?'

Ingrid couldn't bear the thought of food. 'Can I stay here?' she said.

He nodded. 'Of course. You come when you're ready.'

As soon as he closed the door behind him, Ingrid lay down on the bed and pulled the cover over her head.

She found it hard to understand she would never see Besta again. She had so many memories of her, standing in her garden, picking vegetables. The smell of the earth and all the summer roses climbing the wall of Besta's house.

Ingrid smiled when she also remembered how the goats used to chase her and headbutt her when they caught up.

Mamma was in the memories too, laughing and chasing the goats, making Besta scold them for scaring the milk sour.

As if that was possible, Ingrid thought. She pressed her eyes shut, trying to stop the tears, trying to avoid the pain in her chest again.

But she couldn't. Every memory of Besta was also a memory of Mamma. And now, without Besta trying to find Mamma, there was nobody to look for her.

I will, Ingrid thought. *I will never give up.*

Chapter Seven

Anni

Haugesund, November 1944

Fortunately, Kerber left at six every morning, leaving them to their normal routine. Every day she hoped he would not back.

She could hear the rain hammer on the roof. It was a comfortable sound, cosy even, as long as they didn't have to go outside. There was no crèche today, and that meant they would stay inside all day.

The door to Kerber's room was closed, and she kept looking at it. *He lives in my house*, she thought. *There's probably nothing useful for Martin in there, but I have a right to know more about the man, don't I?*

Her thoughts were interrupted by Ingrid rambling down the stairs. She wasn't a morning person and needed some time to ease into the new day.

'Good morning, little troll.' Anni lifted her up on the

counter. 'Did you sleep well?'

'I dreamt something bad,' Ingrid said.

'What did you dream?' Anni put a plate with two pieces of bread next to her.

Ingrid frowned. 'I don't remember.'

Anni kissed her on top of her head. 'Then it's nothing to worry about. Eat your breakfast.'

Ingrid looked at the bread. 'Is there more blueberry jam?' she said hopefully.

'We used it all for pancakes the other night, remember? There's carrot and rhubarb jam. You like that.' Not that she had any choice. These days, they managed on what there was.

Ingrid munched on the sandwich and seemed to perk up. 'Here, drink your milk,' Anni said and put a glass of goat milk next to her plate.

'What will we do today, Mamma?' Ingrid said.

Anni pointed at the window. 'It's miserable weather outside, so we'll stay home. How does that sound?'

'Good. I like it when it's warm inside.' Ingrid had noticed the improvement of firewood since Kerber arrived. The house was infinitely warmer. Especially since he lit the oven every morning before he left. She wasn't used to coming downstairs to a warm house. Perhaps he wouldn't notice if she took some firewood to the prayer house.

'We need to start on your dress. It's time to make it fit you,' Anni said.

'My dress!' Ingrid jumped from the counter and Anni caught her mid-air.

Anni held her tight, savouring the hug for a second before going into the lounge.

The dining room door was still closed. She knew he had left. Still, after putting Ingrid down on the floor and telling her to find her toys, she took a quick look in the hallway. His boots and coat were gone.

The house was theirs. She decided to focus on Ingrid. Her dress was on a hanger in the lounge, next to Anni's old sewing machine.

'Can I try it on?' Ingrid touched the dress.

'Yes, otherwise I can't see how to make it fit, now can I?' She helped Ingrid out of the pyjamas and pulled the dress over her head. The shoulders drooped and the arms were far too long, with the hem hitting the floor.

'It's too big, Mamma.' Ingrid lifted her hands and looked like an overdressed angel.

'No, it's not. I thought that I would make it longer and maybe have another arm in the back or a fluffy, pink tail. What do you think about that?'

Ingrid giggled. 'You're silly.'

'Yes, and now I'll make you look silly, too.' Anni blew a raspberry kiss on Ingrid's cheek, making her squirm and squeal.

Later, when the pins were in place and Anni was all set to split up the seams, Ingrid was running in circles on the floor next to her, making growling noises.

'What are you playing, sweetie?'

Ingrid stopped. 'I'm the good men,' she said. 'When the planes come, that's the good men.'

Good men, yes, but that didn't mean the RAF planes didn't do proper damage when they came, Anni thought. It wasn't that long ago they had bombed the harbour in town.

'What do you want to do on Pappa's birthday?' she said, to distract her, and herself if she had to be honest.

Ingrid sat down on the floor. 'I don't know. What do you think?'

'We're going to Besta's for dinner, and you'll be wearing your new dress.'

'With cake?' Ingrid had stars in her eyes at the thought of yummy food.

'And she'll make us a proper roast. What do you think about that?'

Ingrid pulled her feet up and rested her chin on her knees. 'Can Runar come?'

'Do you want him to?' Anni smiled at her.

Ingrid nodded. 'I want Runar to be there. He's my best friend in the whole world.'

Anni ruffled her hair. 'I'll ask his mother if he can come.'

'We can play and I can show him Besta's barn and the goats. Do you think Runar likes goats?'

Anni nodded. 'I'm sure he does. Is there anyone else you want to ask? Some of the girls from the crèche, maybe?'

Ingrid shook her head. 'No, only Runar.'

Then Runar it is, Anni thought. She looked at the dress and decided to hem it. In a year or so, Ingrid would fit into it the way it was now.

She concentrated on the work, keeping an eye on Ingrid, who busied herself with throwing a party for the doll and the battered old teddy bear Lars had brought to the hospital when she was born.

Her thoughts wandered. The house had been a haven for her, from the first time Lars had brought her to see it. And now she kept looking towards the door, expecting *him* to come in. He had stolen her peace and thought nothing of it.

When she heard knocking on the door, with full force, Anni jumped up out of the chair.

'Stay here,' she said to Ingrid.

The little girl stared wide-eyed at her, then scooted under the table, clutching her bear.

Anni went out into the hall, opened the door and took a step backwards. 'What are you doing here?' she hissed.

Martin looked slightly taken aback. 'You wanted to know about the German,' he said.

'Yes, but you can't come here! He might come back.'

Martin shook his head. 'Not bloody likely. I was at Hagland when he arrived. Can I come in? It's bloody freezing out here.'

Anni hadn't noticed that he was drenched.

'I'm sorry, Martin. Come inside. You look like a drowned rat.'

Martin closed the door behind him. He carefully shook his coat, and the water pooled around his feet.

'I'm sorry too for barging in like this, but it couldn't wait,' he said.

'What did you find out?' Anni felt bad for him now. 'Can I get you a towel? I have some tea, if you want.'

That made Martin smile again. 'It's better if Ingrid doesn't know I'm here. She might mention my name.'

'Yes, you're right. Tell me,' Anni said, smiling back at him.

Martin frowned. 'He's a civilian, like he said. But he might be of some importance. The Wehrmacht officers seem to treat him as such.'

Anni leant her shoulder against the door frame. 'This is odd,' she said. 'I don't understand.'

Martin looked concerned. 'I've been thinking about what you said. He might be here to keep an eye on you and Guri. You need to be careful.'

'I am, and so is Guri now,' she said.

'I don't like this at all. Perhaps we should get you to Shetland.' Martin was sincere, she could see that.

Anni drew a sharp breath. 'It's too late for that. Guri won't leave the farm, you know that. And if I go, they'll come after her. I need to stay here.' She hugged herself. 'You said he's not an officer. He doesn't have the authority of the Wehrmacht, then, does he?'

'You can't think like that. He's as much Wehrmacht as the rest of them. People like him, they sit in an office and fill out forms, register deaths and slaves, and how little food they can get away with letting people have, and . . . and calculating how many of those miserable Russian POWs will fit in one grave.' Martin stopped when he realised she was staring at him. 'He might not wear a uniform, but he's still the enemy,' he muttered.

'I'm not going to underestimate the man. But, whether or not he's here to spy on me, I think we have an opportunity to turn the tables on him.'

Martin frowned. 'You can't get into the offices at Hagland. Trust me, we have tried.'

'No, of course not, but I can go through his room when he's not here, and I can be nice to him, treat him as if he's a proper lodger. He would be privy to all sorts of useful information, wouldn't he?'

'About the fortress, for sure. Maybe even other things.

Loads of information comes through his office. But, Anni, that's dangerous.' Martin didn't look convinced.

Anni smiled. 'I've been in danger since the beginning of the war, Martin. And we have successfully managed to stay under their radar, haven't we? I think we need to take advantage of the situation.'

'He's living in your house. You can't avoid him. He can snoop too, as much as you can.' Martin shook his head. 'It's too risky.'

'Obviously, I can't keep illegal papers or anything else here anymore. I've already talked to Guri about that. But I can go through his things. Be . . . friendly to him, like you said.'

'I'm not sure I should have said that,' Martin said.

'I'm simply going to be nice, so that he thinks I'm a boring *hausfrau* who knows nothing about anything. Perhaps he'll bring back papers or he'll talk too much.'

'Please be careful, Anni. I don't want Lars to think I've thrown his family to the wolves.'

Anni smiled at him, touched by his concern. 'I can take care of myself, you know that.'

'You'd better.' He opened the door, but she stopped him.

'You be careful too.'

Martin smiled, before disappearing into the storm. Anni had to use force to close the door behind him.

When she came back inside, Ingrid was still hiding under the table.

'You can come out, sweet pea. It's safe,' Anni said.

Ingrid popped her head out under the tablecloth. 'Are you sure?'

'Yes, I'm absolutely sure. Is your teddy scared, maybe?'

Ingrid nodded. 'Yes. She doesn't like it when people knock on the door.'

'Nobody is knocking now. It was a messenger, nothing to worry about,' Anni said. 'I'll read you a story.'

Ingrid jumped up. 'Can I choose the book?'

'Yes, run up and find the one you like,' Anni said.

'I will.' Ingrid ran upstairs, singing to herself.

Anni turned to clear away the toys and kept looking at the door to Kerber's room. If she was to befriend the man, she needed to know as much about him as possible.

She ran her hands against her skirt, walked quickly over to the door and opened it before she could change her mind.

This time the room looked more personal. The first thing she noticed was a framed photograph next to the bed.

Anni looked over her shoulder, scared to see him there, but she walked into the room, nonetheless. She picked up the photo.

Kerber and a young, blonde woman. Between them an adorable little boy grinning at the photographer. His son. She could see the resemblance.

He must be missing his family, Anni thought. That explained the soft expression on his face when he saw Ingrid. She wondered how long it had been since he had seen them. The photograph looked worn and creased, as if he kept it in his wallet or his pocket.

Her lips trembled. *At least he has a picture of his family*, she thought. Lars didn't even have that of Ingrid. They had planned a family photo when he came home, and he never did.

Anni rubbed her hand across her eyes. *What am I doing?* Suddenly she couldn't bear staying in his room.

She hurried out and closed the door behind her.

Better not be caught crying in his room, she thought, and rubbed her eyes again.

Then she put on a brave face and went into the kitchen to make Ingrid a snack.

Chapter Eight

It took Anni a week to muster enough courage to enter Herr Kerber's room again, but she couldn't postpone it any longer. She could feel her muscles stiffen in her neck by the hour.

She could hear Ingrid scolding her doll in the lounge, and knew she only had a few minutes.

Taking a deep breath, she opened the door and walked inside.

Anni scanned the room. There had to be something useful somewhere. A small stack of books on the table caught her interest.

The book on the top was no surprise; she supposed *Mein Kampf* would be obligatory reading for any German. Never having read it, she picked it up and opened it to see what it was like.

It took her few seconds to recognise the first lines of *All Quiet on the Western Front*. The pages were worn, as if the book had been read over and over again.

'I'll be damned,' she muttered.

A quick look through the rest of the book stack revealed that the jackets were all hiding other books inside. *Der Steppenwolf*, *The Great Gatsby* and *A Farewell to Arms*. Apart from being wonderful books, they were also banned by the Nazis.

She knew the books; some of them were in her own bookshelf. It was a surprise, and an unnerving one. Anni didn't know if that changed anything. He might have put the books out for her to find, as a ruse to make her think he wasn't a fanatic Nazi.

Anni pulled a face. *I'm getting paranoid*, she thought.

It didn't prove anything about him, except that he had good taste in literature. Perhaps that was why he wanted to live away from the fortress and the school.

If it wasn't an attempt to entrap her, then he was terrible at hiding stuff. What would happen to him if somebody found out?

Could he be hiding anything else?

Anni quickly and systematically went through his room, checking everywhere. It took all of five minutes; there weren't that many hiding places.

Nothing. Apparently, he didn't bring his work home.

Anni sighed. It was a long shot, so she shouldn't be disappointed. If she had to have the man in the house, the least he could do was be useful.

She looked at the books again. On impulse she opened each book and shook it. Nothing remotely interesting fell out, except for a bookmark fluttering down to the floor, sliding under the bed.

'Ah, bugger this,' she muttered.

When she bent down to pick up the bookmark, her eyes fell on a small envelope sticking out from under the bedsprings.

Anni pulled it out as gently as possible and opened it. It contained a single piece of paper with a list of names.

She had no way of knowing who the people on the list were, or why he was hiding it under his bed. Perhaps Martin could make sense of it. She copied the names in her notebook, then put the paper back in the envelope and left it where she had found it.

Afterwards she took one final look at the room, and hoped he didn't have a photographic memory.

'That would be bad,' she muttered.

'Mamma?' Ingrid's voice made her jump.

Anni spun around. 'You startled me.'

Ingrid held one hand on the door. 'Why?'

'Because you're as quiet as a little mouse,' Anni said and lifted her up after shutting the door behind her.

Ingrid squealed and kicked her legs. 'No tickles, Mamma!'

Anni carried her into the lounge and dropped her on the sofa. 'Yes, tickles.'

She pretended to attack her, and Ingrid tried to fight back. Anni couldn't stop wondering what the list meant. She had noticed one thing that was odd. The names were all German. Why would he keep a list of German names hidden like that? It made no sense. At least it proved he didn't have a photographic memory. He wouldn't need to hide a list if that was the case.

* * *

Every night Anni made sure she was in bed before Kerber came back. Lying awake, she could hear the military car arriving outside, and then again in the morning when he left. She knew his routine. He had stayed true to his word. She never saw him.

But tonight, that would change. She made sure the kettle was on the hob, and had a cup on the counter, filled with Guri's special tea for calming the nerves. If that was true, she might need to drink a gallon. Her hands were sweaty. *A glass of brandy would have been nice*, she thought.

She took a few deep breaths to steady herself. *I have to act – pretend to be Greta Garbo*, she thought. *How hard could it be?*

She glanced at the kitchen clock on the wall. He would arrive any minute now. If there was one thing they had learnt about the Germans the last four years, they loved punctuality. This one was no exception.

Anni took a sip of the tea. It didn't taste of anything except brackish water. But it was the only thing she had.

She might have expected him, but when she heard the door opening, it still made her jump. She folded her hands around the cup and held her breath.

He came inside the hallway, and stopped when he caught sight of her. 'Oh,' he said.

'*Guten Abend*, Herr Kerber,' she said, and had to clear her throat. It felt as if it had tightened with every syllable.

He had a look of confusion on his face.

'*Guten Abend*, Frau Odland,' he answered, a tad hesitant.

'I hope I won't disturb you. I couldn't sleep and when that happens, I sit here in the kitchen and make plans for the crèche. Sometimes it's difficult to find new things to keep the children entertained,' she said, smiling. Not too much, not too forced. At least she hoped so.

'Yes. Preparing lessons always made me sleepy,' he said.

Anni blinked. Had he made a joke? 'Have you been a teacher, perhaps?'

Is my voice shaking? She didn't think so, but that made her even more nervous. *Don't let him know*, she thought. *Don't dry your hands on your skirt. Don't look at him as if he's a man.*

'Before all . . . this, yes, I was a teacher of mathematics in a gymnasium in Berlin,' he said.

That surprised her. 'I . . . you were not a soldier?'

He smiled properly this time, and she didn't like that. She felt a stab in her stomach, and she didn't think it was fear. Not all of it, anyway.

'My flat feet kept me out of the army. I thought that's how I would spend the war. And then, out of the blue, I was ordered to join the Wehrmacht,' he said.

Should I say sorry? Anni thought. *That would be strange, wouldn't it?* She tried to sort her thoughts and find some sensible questions. Greta Garbo had a script to work from. All she had was her own wit, and it was clearly failing.

'Why . . . why would they do that?' Anni bit her lip. Was that stupid to say?

'As the war progressed, the army didn't care about my flat feet anymore, and I was sent to the Eastern Front,' he said.

Anni was lost for words. This was more information than she had expected. 'How . . . how long have you been in the army?'

It was the only thing that fell into her head.

'Since 1942. It feels like a lifetime,' he added.

1942, Anni thought, wondering if he had been at Stalingrad. She didn't dare ask him about that.

'Norway must be very different for you, I think?' She smiled a little when she said it, hoping to keep him talking.

'Yes, it is. And hopefully I can stay the rest of the war here,' he said. He smiled, then seemed to pull back. 'I'd better turn in,' he said. 'Good night, Frau Odland.'

'Good night,' Anni said.

As soon as the door closed behind him, she breathed out. Her hands shook when she picked up the cup, and she spilt some tea on the table.

'Oh dear,' she muttered, before reaching for a tea towel.

She listened after sounds from his room. He was quiet. Somehow that seemed more unnerving than anything. Was he trying to see if she had been in his room? Had she managed to put everything in the right order?

Anni cleaned up the mess, then almost ran upstairs. For a long time she lay awake, going through their conversation over and over again. Did he think he had said too much? He'd left so abruptly. Or perhaps that was part of a plan to make himself sound interesting and harmless.

At least I didn't say too much, she thought, right before falling asleep.

The next morning, Anni came downstairs early, so early she bumped into him in the kitchen. She knew that the car wouldn't come for another half an hour.

'I'm sorry,' Kerber said at once. 'I hope you don't mind.'

He pointed at the kettle coming to a boil. There was a metal cup next to it. 'I was making coffee. We haven't had real coffee in a long time, and yesterday they gave us a tin each.'

He didn't explain who 'they' or 'us' were, and she didn't ask.

Anni was temporarily shocked by the aroma of actual, real coffee. It was intoxicating. She drew a sharp breath, then shook her head. 'Of course not. Use anything you want.'

She could hear Ingrid jumping upstairs. 'It's only . . . my girl comes down soon, and she . . . well, she . . .' Anni bit her lip.

He pulled a hand through his hair. 'I see. She fears us.'

'Not all of you. She doesn't mind the soldiers at the school. She calls them bon-bon soldiers because they give her sweets,' Anni said.

The expression made him smile. 'I understand.' He was about to say something else, but the water boiled.

Anni looked at the coffee, then looked away when he caught her.

'May I leave the box here in the kitchen?' he asked.

'Yes.' Anni searched for the right words, for any words.

He nodded, now with a serious look on his face. 'Thank you. And help yourself if you want to. I mean, if you like coffee.'

Anni hesitated. Wouldn't it be collaboration if she drank his coffee? But the temptation won out. 'I . . . thank you. I might,' she added.

He filled up his cup and pushed the coffee box towards the wall. 'I wish you a good day,' he said.

Anni almost smiled. 'You too.'

Why did I say that? I shouldn't say things like that, she thought.

When he'd left, Anni turned and stared at the coffee box, then opened it.

She closed her eyes, and her head filled with all the memories of times before, when the world made sense and coffee was on the breakfast table every day.

The thought that everything could change in one day, in a matter of hours, never occurred to her before the Occupation. The war had been far away, in Europe, fought between bigger nations than their little country up in the north. It had nothing to do with them. Until it did.

Nothing would ever be the same. The war had changed her, and she knew in her heart that it would have changed Lars too.

Life will be different once the war is over, she thought.

When she opened her eyes, she had to blink away tears. She put the lid back on and pushed the coffee tin away. *Better leave it*, she thought. *At least for now.* Maybe she could bring a little for Guri.

'That would shock her,' she said, almost laughing.

A few hours later, they headed for the farm. As soon as they got closer to the farm, Anni spotted Runar. He was crouched down outside the fence, staring at the house.

Ingrid yelped and started running. 'Runar!'

She threw herself around his neck, and the boy nearly fell backwards before finding his balance.

Anni smiled when they caught up with him. 'Why are you standing outside, Runar?'

'I . . . I was waiting, Mrs Odland,' he said.

He looks cold, Anni noticed. 'Let's go inside and see what kind of trouble we can get ourselves into.'

Runar stared at her. 'There's trouble?'

'No, it was a little joke. I'm looking forward to the delicious food,' Anni said.

He brightened up when she said that.

'What's in the bag?' he asked when they entered the yard.

'There's Ingrid's birthday present for her father, and something for Guri,' she said, winking at him.

Runar frowned. 'Is it her birthday too?'

'It doesn't have to be a special occasion for a gift, you know.'

Runar looked as if he had something to ponder.

Guri had seen them and flung open the door.

'Welcome to the party, my girl,' she said, and scooped Ingrid up in a big hug. 'Oh my God, you're getting too big to lift. Must be all that goat milk.'

Ingrid wriggled to get down. 'I'm not too big. I'm only six,' she declared.

Runar was almost hiding behind Anni, and she pulled him forward. 'This is Runar, Guri. He's Ingrid's good friend from our crèche.'

Runar blushed, but then held out his hand, and bowed his head. 'Thank you for having me,' he said slowly, clearly instructed by his mother.

Guri shook his hand and smiled at him. 'You are most welcome, Runar. We haven't had a man visit us for ages.'

That made Runar blush even more, and Ingrid stepped in to save him. 'Runar isn't a man. He's a boy,' she said.

'I'm sure he'll be a good man in a few years.'

Runar looked pleased with that.

The smell of roasted meat made Anni's stomach growl.

'It smells divine in here, Guri,' she said.

'It should. I've been working on it all day. Are you hungry, Runar?'

He swallowed. 'Mamma made a sandwich for me before I left. She said it wasn't polite to come hungry,' he added quickly.

Guri laughed. 'I used to have a little boy myself, Ingrid's father, and I can tell you that he was hungry all the time. He was like a bottomless pit, he was.'

Runar's eyes widened. 'Mamma says that about me!'

'There you go, then. We have plenty of food and there will be cake afterwards,' Guri said.

Runar took a small package out of his coat pocket and handed it to Ingrid.

'I made it myself,' he said, looking even more embarrassed when she took it from him.

Anni bit her lower lip. He was so serious and so sweet.

'For me? But it's my Pappa's birthday, not mine,' Ingrid said.

Runar blushed. 'I didn't know that.' He had whittled the cutest little boat, with a simple mast and sail. 'It's a sailing boat,' he said. 'You can sail it in the water.'

Ingrid looked at the boat with eyes filled with wonder. 'I can?'

'Yes, and . . . and it will float. Mamma helped with the sail, but I did the rest,' he said, brimming with pride now.

Ingrid held the boat with both hands, admiring it properly. 'Will you show me how to sail it?'

'Yes, but it's not hard,' Runar said.

Ingrid turned around, holding the boat out for Anni. 'Look, Mamma. Isn't it lovely?'

'Yes, it is. You are very clever, Runar,' Anni said.

She knew his father was a war sailor, like Lars, and they had no idea where he was. Runar's mother struggled, but she had a job in one of the occupied schools, cooking for the soldiers. They managed, like everybody else.

She ruffled his hair. 'I love your boat. It's the perfect gift for Ingrid.'

He blushed again and looked down.

Guri interfered. 'Boats are all well and good, but food is better. Not that I don't think your boat is fabulous, Runar. I do. But are you hungry?'

Runar nodded. 'Yes.'

'It's not quite ready, so you two go and play.'

Ingrid handed the boat to Anni, then took Runar's hand. 'Come, I'll show you the goats,' she said.

He looked confused. 'But I took off my boots,' he said.

'No, silly, they're inside. They are, aren't they, Besta?'

Guri nodded. 'Yes, they're in the backroom. You can say hi, but don't take them out of the room, please. They'll eat the cake if you do.'

The two children giggled and headed off to the back of the house.

Anni followed Guri into the kitchen. The smell of roast meat was even more intense here, and her stomach responded. 'God, I can't remember the last time a kitchen smelt this good,' she said.

'I've used rosemary and pepper, and we have potatoes. No turnips today,' Guri said.

'What will we eat for Christmas after this feast?' Anni said.

'We'll manage,' Guri said, with a wicked smile.

112

'Something always shows up, you know.'

Anni nodded. 'Yes, I do. Remember the reindeer steak you found us in 1941? That was to die for.'

Guri smiled at her, a little sad. 'I hope we'll get proper food again soon. I'm so tired of this bollocks.'

'Guri!' Anni couldn't help but laugh.

Guri shrugged. 'Oh, never you mind.'

'I have something to cheer you up,' Anni said, holding out the brown paper bag. 'It's not much, but if all goes well, I can get more.'

'No, no, you shouldn't bring me a gift,' Guri said, when she took the bag.

Then she opened it, and her eyes lit up in shock. 'Coffee?' she whispered.

'Yes, real coffee. It's probably barely enough for a pot, but I hope you'll enjoy it.'

Guri buried her nose in the bag and inhaled the smell. 'I can't remember when last I had a cup of coffee, made from real beans.'

'Me neither,' Anni said.

Guri frowned. 'Where did you get it?'

Anni looked over her shoulder and couldn't see the children. Even so, she lowered her voice. 'Where do you think? That doesn't mean you won't take it, will you?'

Guri scoffed. 'Not even a little bit. I bet they confiscated it from some crooked shopkeeper, and that means I'm only redistributing it back to us.'

'I love the way your logic works,' Anni said, making her mother-in-law smile impishly. 'But it's best not to use it while Runar is here.'

'I'll save it for Sunday morning breakfast and that

113

horrible Sunday paper,' Guri said, looking dreamily at her gift.

I may have to ask Kerber for a bigger tin, Anni thought.

While Guri hid her precious coffee, Anni called the children. Today Guri's big table was covered with her finest tablecloth and the good china.

Runar was fascinated by the plate. 'Why are there flowers and elephants on it?'

'That's because my husband, Ingrid's grandfather, bought it in India when his ship docked there. It was my wedding present,' Guri said.

'I've never seen plates with elephants,' Runar said, stroking his finger across the pattern.

Guri took it away from him, over to the stove, and filled it up with pork and potatoes, a thick, brown sauce and winter carrots from her garden.

Runar stared at the full plate. 'Thank you,' he whispered, remembering his manners.

'There's more where that came from.' Guri took the plates from Ingrid and Anni, and filled them up.

Anni looked at the plate. 'I can't possibly eat all this,' she said.

'I think you can. Today is a celebration and we haven't had many of those. Tuck in. And remember to save room for cake.' Guri looked pleased with herself.

Runar was holding his fork to his mouth. 'There really is cake too?'

'This is a birthday party. Even if the birthday boy isn't here,' Guri said, winking at Anni.

Anni looked at the plate again and felt like crying. This

dinner was like a pre-war dinner, a proper Sunday roast with all the trimmings. She was sure it had cost Guri a lot more than a few spools of thread.

The first bite almost had her moaning. The meat was soft and rich, and she could taste the herbs from Guri's garden.

She kept an eye on the children. They had quietened down now, not used to food like this at all. Runar stuffed another large piece in his mouth, chewing so much, it made him look like a squirrel storing nuts in its cheeks.

'Slowly, Runar. Or you'll make yourself sick. Smaller bites are better,' Anni said.

Runar swallowed a lump of meat that almost brought tears to his eyes.

'See, slower is better,' Anni said, smiling at him.

Ingrid was happily chomping down on her food, telling Guri in excruciating detail how they had finished the dress.

Anni looked at them and hid a smile. When they sat like that, with their heads together, she could see how alike they were. Sometimes she struggled to remember Lars's face, but he was still there, in Guri and Ingrid.

Anni blinked hard to stop the tears threatening to overwhelm her. Lars had missed four birthdays already. How many more would there be?

Later, when Ingrid climbed into bed, all she talked about was Runar's boat. 'He said he'll show me how to sail it soon,' she said.

Anni tucked her in. 'Did you have a good Pappa's birthday, sweetie?'

'Can we have another one tomorrow?' Ingrid put Runar's boat next to her in bed.

'No, we only get one each year, even your pappa. It wouldn't be very fun if we had them every day, now, would it? Think how old we will be in a year!' Anni kissed her cheek.

Ingrid giggled. 'Runar liked the cake, didn't he, Mamma?'

'I'm sure he did.' He had practically inhaled it, the poor boy. Hopefully he wouldn't go off cakes altogether.

Ingrid yawned. 'I'm sure I can't sleep now.'

Anni pulled the duvet up to her chin and tucked her in properly. 'See, now you're exactly like the tiny mice in the basement, all warm and snuggly. You'll be asleep before you know it.'

By the last word, Ingrid was fast asleep. Anni gently pressed a kiss on her soft cheek. 'Sweet dreams, sweet pea.'

She walked downstairs and into the kitchen, to get the leftover cake out of the cupboard. It had been a proper pound cake, considering how difficult it must have been to gather all the ingredients.

Anni smiled. Guri never did anything half-heartedly. All or nothing. There had been enough left over for Runar to take some home to his mum, for Guri's Sunday coffee, and for them to save as dessert.

She took the lid off the cake tin and looked at the cake. It was too late for coffee, but it was never too late for cake. Anni cut a small piece and put it on a plate, before sitting down at the kitchen table.

She didn't notice him until he stood in the doorway. '*Guten Abend*, Frau Odland,' he said.

Anni looked up, surprised she hadn't heard him come in. 'Good evening.'

'Did Ingrid have a good birthday celebration?'

Anni cleared her throat. 'She wants to have another tomorrow.'

That made him smile, a little sadly, she thought. 'My son loved birthdays. All he wanted was cake.'

'You have a son?' Anni knew it from the picture, but he didn't know she had seen that.

'Yes, I do,' he said again, avoiding looking at her.

Why was he so sad? Perhaps he hadn't seen his family in a very long time. She didn't know what she would do if she was unable to see Ingrid every day.

Anni fought a sudden impulse to reach over and touch his hand. *What the hell is wrong with me?* she thought.

'It's a whole day only for them. It's important,' Anni said, trying not stare at him.

He nodded. 'Yes, it is.'

Anni took a deep breath. 'Would you like some cake, Herr Kerber? My mother-in-law made it and she does miracles, even with what's available for us now.'

He hesitated only for a fraction, then nodded. 'I would love to. There aren't many miracles in army kitchens.'

Was he making a joke? Anni wasn't sure, and to hide her confusion, she stood up to bring him a plate. 'I haven't made coffee, I'm afraid. Too late.'

'Coffee keeps me awake,' he said, pulling out a chair.

'But cake won't,' Anni said, handing him the plate and a small fork to go with it.

She watched his face when he took the first bite. He half closed his eyes. 'I haven't tasted anything like this in years. Your mother-in-law is skilled.'

'We save our coupons to give Ingrid a memorable Christmas and birthdays. We do our best to create good memories for her.'

'Yes,' he said softly. 'She'll remember this.'

'I hope so.' Anni polished off the last crumb, and reminded herself what the mission was. She said the first thing that fell into her head. 'Where are you from?'

To her surprise, he started talking. 'I grew up in a small village outside of Berlin. My family has lived there for generations, farming the land,' he said slowly, as if it pained him to do so.

'I thought you were a teacher?' Anni wanted to keep him talking.

'My father realised I was more of a bookworm than a farmer. He was convinced I would be a great man if I went to the university.' He smiled ruefully. 'I'm grateful he never saw me go into the army.'

What an odd thing to say, Anni thought. 'But you're not a soldier,' she said, testing the water.

'Suits or uniforms make no difference. We are all soldiers in this Germany, Frau Odland,' he said. 'And what about your father?'

'He passed away when I was fifteen. He was so proud that I was born in our own country,' Anni said before she could stop herself.

He looked surprised. 'Your own country?'

'Yes, Norway became a sovereign nation in 1905, after ninety-one years in union with Sweden, and before over four hundred years with Denmark. He told me it felt as if the whole country could breathe.' Anni laughed a little. 'I always thought that was such a strange thing to say.'

'He wouldn't have liked us then,' he said quietly.

Anni met his gaze. 'No, probably not.'

'Nor would my father. He was a man of peace.' Herr Kerber stood up abruptly, as if he couldn't stand talking any more. 'Thank you for sharing your cake and your story, Frau Odland.'

'You're welcome,' she said.

He was so correct it was unnerving.

'Sleep well,' she added quickly.

Before he left the kitchen, he turned and looked back at her.

'Thank you,' he said again.

Anni sat for a minute after he was gone. It felt odd that he'd said that. He had already thanked her for the cake.

Still, his face kept her awake for a lot longer than she liked. Talking with him had been different from what she had expected. There was a gentleness in the way he spoke, which she hadn't thought possible in someone like him.

He's a Nazi, she scolded herself. *I can never allow myself to forget that.*

Chapter Nine

Anni

Haugesund, December 1944

What Anni hoped was the last of the winter storms came down with a vengeance. Gales tore into the roof, as if trying to tear it off.

Anni sighed. She had dragged Ingrid out of the house to the prayer house, in case some of the mothers had been silly enough to send their children outside.

'I'm the silly one,' she muttered.

Ingrid was jumping around on the floor, dressed in all the winter clothes she owned. *Poor baby*, Anni thought. *I should never have dragged her out of the warm house.*

'Let's go home, sweet pea. I'm sure everyone is in their houses, safe and warm, today.'

A few minutes later, they were outside by the gate. Anni struggled to open it. Already snowdrifts were building up against it. With a final push, she managed to get the gate open enough for both of them to squeeze out into the narrow road.

Anni looked towards the main road and the big school. It was eerily quiet, despite the wind. She couldn't see a single soul outside. She couldn't even see smoke from the chimneys.

She turned away and took Ingrid's hand. 'We can walk back in my footprints,' she said. 'Can you see them?'

The imprints were barely visible, more like faded dimples in the thick snow.

'Mamma, look!' Ingrid waved her hand.

Anni turned around and discovered a car was pulling into their road.

She pulled Ingrid back towards the gate. She recognised the car at once. What was Kerber doing coming back to the house? Had he forgotten something?

Maybe they should stay with Guri instead, at least until the weather settled. That way, she didn't have to deal with him for a few days.

She was so engulfed in her thoughts, she didn't notice the car stopping right next to them.

'Mamma? Why is it stopping?' Ingrid hid behind her.

Anni didn't move or acknowledge that the car was even there. Instead she looked straight ahead, hoping they would keep driving.

The rear door opened and Kerber looked out with a smile on his face. 'Frau Odland, please let us take you both up to the house,' he said.

Anni tried to form the German words in her head. 'It's not necessary,' she said.

'Your daughter looks half frozen and with all this snow, it's a long walk for short legs,' he said.

She looked at Ingrid, who had snow in her eyelashes again. The warm boots didn't help much when her coat was worn thin. Suddenly it felt too stupid to say no.

And maybe wise not to antagonise him.

'Yes, thank you.' Anni looked at Ingrid. 'We can go in the car, sweet pea. It's warmer.'

Ingrid didn't look convinced, but she didn't protest when Anni half lifted her into the car. She stayed close to Anni on the seat and stared at Kerber the whole time.

Anni put her arm around her. 'Thank you,' she said again.

He sat in the corner of the car seat, with sufficient room between them.

'Why are you out in this weather?' He smiled, and Anni tried to smile back. *It probably looked more like a cramp*, she thought.

'I had to be sure none of the children had showed up,' Anni said.

'You thought children would come?' He waved at the window.

'No, but I had to make sure. It's my responsibility,' she said.

'Is there no way of letting people know that schools are closed for the day?'

Anni looked at him. How could he not know? He looked at her as if he expected her to answer.

'It's not a school, it's more of a crèche. Very few families have telephones, and we're not allowed radios. We had to give them up in 1941,' she added.

'Of course,' he said. 'I'm sorry.'

Anni tried to see out the window, but it was all white.

She was sure she saw the path to the neighbour's house, but perhaps it was just another snowdrift.

He didn't speak again until the car stopped in front of her house. Anni opened the door and let Ingrid out first.

'Thank you,' she said to Kerber.

'*Bitte*,' he said.

Anni felt awkward and, to cover it, she hastened up the steps sending Ingrid ahead of her. She didn't see where she was stepping until it was too late and she slipped on one of the steps. She had a vision of herself falling through the air and landing on her back. With a broken leg.

A strong arm grabbed her elbow. 'Careful, please,' he said.

Anni had no choice but to let him pull her up. *How was it possible that this was even more awkward*, she thought.

'I'm sorry,' she said.

He smiled. 'Don't be,' he said, then proceeded to pull out Lars's keys and open the door for them.

Ingrid ducked under his arm and ran inside. Anni had no intention of ducking under anything. She walked inside with what she hoped was left of her dignity.

She was fairly sure he hid a smile, but she chose not to acknowledge it.

Inside Ingrid was standing in the hallway, staring wide-eyed at them.

Anni smiled at her. 'Let's get you sorted,' she said in the calmest, most mummy voice she could muster.

She focused on getting the winter clothes off Ingrid, trying not to look at him while doing so.

The entire time he'd been standing by the now-closed door, waiting patiently. A small pool of melting snow grew under his shiny boots.

'We're done,' she said, gently pushing Ingrid into the lounge, and then nodding to the kitchen.

'Wait for me in the kitchen, sweet pea,' she said.

The little girl ran clumsily across the hall and disappeared.

Anni turned to Kerber, who was about to unbutton his coat. 'I . . . thank you for saving us out there,' she said.

'You don't have to thank me,' he said, starting to hang up his long coat.

He looked at her before taking off his boots and putting them next to hers. 'I hope this is fine?'

'Yes, of course. Better there than dragging them through the house,' Anni said.

She briefly closed her eyes. *Get yourself together*, she thought. 'I have to look after Ingrid.'

She wanted so badly to ask him why he was there, why he was in her house in the middle of the day. He had said he would only stay there at night, but this was not the night.

He cleared his throat, and she almost jumped. 'Sorry. I will go now,' she said, then thought better of it. 'Your chauffeur, is he going to sit in the car? It might be cold. Unless he's a polar bear in a uniform,' she added, almost shaking her head.

'He's already returned to Gard,' he said.

'Oh.' Anni didn't know what else to say and the silence was more than awkward.

'Frau Odland, I can see you are uncomfortable with me being here,' he said in a gentle voice. 'Unfortunately it's my day off and I couldn't go to town because of the weather. I'd rather not stay the night at Hagland.'

It was so unexpected Anni just stared at him. 'Oh,' she said again.

'I have paperwork to do and will stay in my room. You will hardly notice I am here,' he said.

Anni could feel her face making an expression she was sure wasn't flattering to him. 'Of course,' she said, hoping that wasn't too . . . too much.

He raised his eyebrows and looked at her. Anni frowned. He looked like he was waiting for something from her.

'May I?' he finally said.

Anni realised she was standing in his way. She stepped back. 'Uhm, sorry.'

He started walking past her, and Anni felt bad. 'Herr Kerber, please feel free to use the kitchen whenever you want to,' she said in her most polite voice.

'Thank you,' he said. 'I appreciate that.'

'There's not much food, but there's coffee,' she said.

When he smiled at the little joke, she smiled back.

He nodded, then disappeared into his room.

Anni hurried into the kitchen and didn't stop until she stood by the counter. She got her breathing under control and tried not to think about him in his room.

'Mamma?' Ingrid crawled out from under the table. 'I'm hungry.'

'I'll make you a sandwich.' Anni picked her up and sat her down on the counter. 'What do you want? Bread and cheese, or bread and potato, or bread and jam?'

Ingrid giggled. 'Jam!'

'We only have the tart rhubarb and carrot jam, you know that, right?' Anni opened the breadbox and found the knife from the drawer.

'I know.' Ingrid nodded. 'I like jam.'

Anni cut a slice of the bread. Because Ingrid was six and

underweight for her age, she had coupons for whiter bread. It was by no means a pre-war loaf, but it was better than the grey, sticky bread she would have on her own coupons.

She slathered a generous amount of jam on the bread. 'Here, enjoy, and don't drop the jam all over your dress.'

Ingrid looked at her. 'It's too big. Can you cut it?'

'Yes.' Anni cut the sandwich in four equal pieces. 'I'm very sorry I didn't do that at once, madam.'

Ingrid giggled. 'You're silly, Mamma.'

'I absolutely am.' Anni tried to listen for sounds from his room, suddenly having a vision of him standing right outside with his ear pressed against the door.

The idea made her look at the door with a frown. That wasn't something she wanted to think about. She filled up the kettle and decided to use his coffee. Perhaps she could offer him a cup. She had managed to get the list of names to Martin, but had no idea if he could find out what it meant. *And I have to be friendly, right?* she thought.

'Do you want bread, Mamma?' Ingrid held the last piece out to her. Her hands and face were sticky with the jam.

'No, sweet pea. That's your special bread. I have my own, remember?'

'You have farty bread,' Ingrid said and burst into laughter.

'What? Where did you learn that?' Anni couldn't help laughing too. 'Did Runar teach you that?'

Ingrid giggled again. 'Yes,' she said.

He's not wrong, Anni thought. *Have you heard the new bread?* was a common joke.

'I don't want you to learn bad things from Runar. He's a naughty boy and I will tell him so next time I see him.'

'I'll tell Besta,' Ingrid said, her eyes shiny with mischief.

'Don't do that. She'll think I'm the one who taught you!' Anni pretended to be horrified, and Ingrid laughed so hard she almost fell off the countertop.

'So, little troll, what should we do today since we're snowed in?'

'Play?' Ingrid looked hopeful.

'Yes, you can play. Bring your toys downstairs, and you can play in front of the fire,' Anni said.

She waited until Ingrid had scrambled upstairs, before returning to the kitchen. She stopped the kettle from boiling over, and closed her eyes for a second, inhaling the smell of freshly brewed coffee.

Then with a determination that surprised herself, she filled a cup with the hot beverage, put the cup on a saucer and carried it over to his door.

She lifted her hand, and only hesitated for a second before knocking. Her heart was in her throat while she waited for his response.

'*Bitte*,' he said.

Anni imagined he was surprised, but when she opened the door, he was sitting on his bed reading. His jacket and tie covered the back of the chair, as if he had thrown them there.

'I thought perhaps you wanted some of your coffee,' she said, offering him her most social smile.

He stood up from the bed and came over to her. 'Thank you,' he said.

'I'm afraid I don't have a biscuit,' Anni said, handing him the coffee.

He took it and had a look of amusement on his face. Anni

127

tried not to stare at him. He seemed different somehow. Not so grave. It made her wonder what he was reading.

'The coffee is more than fine, Frau Odland,' he said politely.

Anni smiled again. 'Good. We'll be staying in the lounge today. I'm sorry in advance.'

'For what?' He frowned.

'We might play a bit loudly; it all depends on what we do,' Anni said. 'So, I thought I'd better warn you.'

He surprised her by laughing. For a split second she forgot herself, and saw him as a regular man, instead of what he was. She couldn't look away from him.

'Let Ingrid play as much as she wants to,' he said. 'I miss the sound of playing children.'

It was an odd thing to say, but perhaps where he had been, there hadn't been many children. 'Yes, of course, I'll leave you with your book, then. I'm sorry I can't offer you any food. There's barely enough for Ingrid today.'

'Don't worry about it, Frau Odland. I am expecting a delivery later. There will be plenty to eat, and I hope you don't mind sharing it with me,' he said.

Anni frowned and said the first thing that fell into her head. 'How can anyone drive in this weather?'

'My chauffeur is from Tyrol in Austria. They have worse weather than this. You'd be surprised. He'll manage,' Kerber said.

'Thank you,' Anni said, trying to hide her surprise.

Kerber looked at her. 'I know it must be difficult for you having me here, and I hope the extra food will make up for some of the inconvenience.'

'I'm . . . thank you,' she managed to say before pointing

128

behind her. 'I . . . I have to see how Ingrid is doing.'

He nodded. 'Of course.'

Anni turned her back to him, trying not to run.

In the lounge, Ingrid had brought down a blanket, and filled it with her toys, including Runar's boat.

'We're on a journey,' she said, when Anni came in. 'We're travelling all around the world.'

'That's a good idea,' Anni said, sitting down next to her. 'Where are we going first?'

Ingrid thought about it. 'America,' she said. 'That's far away from here, isn't it?'

'Yes, that's on the other side of the ocean.' Anni picked up the boat. 'Good thing Runar made this for you, then.'

Ingrid nodded. 'Yes. He's my very best friend.'

Anni ruffled her hair. 'Yes, he is. You're lucky to have him.'

She sat down on the sofa, and picked up the basket where she kept clothes that needed mending. It was impossible to concentrate on anything.

Had he actually invited them to eat with him? And she had said thank you? Anni took a deep breath, trying to collect herself.

If it had been possible, she would have grabbed Ingrid and left the house. Instead, she had to sit on her sofa, with an old sock in her hand, reminding herself to beware of the enemy.

Chapter Ten

By dinnertime, it was still snowing, and Anni doubted there would be any cars coming by anytime soon.

Ingrid looked up from her dolly and teddy, who by now had arrived in China. 'I'm hungry, Mamma.'

'Me too. I have potatoes and more potatoes. Would you like that?' Anni said.

'Can we fry the potatoes?' Ingrid loved crispy potatoes, even those fried in cod liver oil.

'I'm sorry, sweet pea. I can't open the windows because of the wind. The whole house will be filled by smoke from the oil,' Anni said.

Ingrid wrinkled her nose. 'Can we have herring?'

'Yes, we can have herring.'

And more herring, Anni thought, trying not to reveal to Ingrid how tired she was of the salty fish. *When this war is over, I'll never eat fish again*, she swore to herself.

'You stay in here, while I go downstairs to find what we need,' Anni said.

Ingrid leant forward. 'But what about the bad man?'

Oh dear, Anni thought. 'Herr Kerber isn't a bad man. I've told you that. He's in his room and he won't bother us. I'll be gone for a few minutes. You wait here where it's warm. OK?'

'Yes, Mamma.' Ingrid didn't look convinced, but Anni knew she didn't like the cellar much.

She went out into the hallway to find the key, closing the door to the lounge behind her. There was nothing they could arrest her for hidden in the cellar now, but still. She had no intention of making it easy for Kerber.

The key was hidden in a crack in the door frame. Anni crouched down and fished it out. It wasn't visible to anyone, and the house had plenty of cracks.

Then she picked up her coat from the hallway before returning to the kitchen. The cellar door was always locked, she made sure of that. The habit was so ingrained, she never forgot.

Anni unlocked the door and put the key in her pocket.

'Damn,' she muttered. Better to keep the key in the key box from now on. A locked door would only make him more curious.

She turned the switch and the light bulb flickered on. The chill made her shudder.

The cellar was made up of two large rooms; the first one had shelves on every wall, filled with mostly empty glass jars. Anni sighed when she spotted a lonely tin of sardines in a corner. She had that saved for Christmas.

Ingrid loved the olive oil they used, a lot more than the cod liver oil.

The potato bin was closest to the staircase. Anni could see the levels were low, but she also knew there was no reason to panic. Not yet, anyway.

She took a pot from the top shelf, and put a few potatoes in it, enough for dinner and breakfast. From the bin next to the potatoes, she took a smaller turnip. *Not many left of those either*, she noticed.

Anni drew her breath. There was nothing to worry about. Guri had food in her cellar, more than enough for them and for possible refugees.

From a barrel in the corner, she picked out a herring. It smelt strongly of pickled fish, but she hardly noticed any more.

'What I would give for a piece of bacon,' she muttered.

The second room had its own light bulb, and when she turned it on, it cast a half light in the middle of the room. It was cold and damp in there, even more than in the food storage. The huge copper boiler almost filled a corner. Behind it was a large cupboard, with a door on one side.

Anni looked at it and sighed. Together with Guri and Martin, it had been used to hide refugees from time to time, but never in the winter. It would be far too cold.

Good thing it was empty when Kerber showed up, she thought.

She threw a wistful glance at the large bathtub on the other side. To get hot water in it, she would have to fire up under the copper boiler, and then use a hose to transfer the water into the bathtub. It took ages, but it was worth it.

'Damn thing,' she said out loud.

This was the time she could use a bath. Before Kerber's added firewood, she hadn't felt properly warm since before the war, summers included.

After turning off the light, she headed for the staircase. She was about to pick up the food she had left on one of the steps, when Ingrid started screaming her head off.

Anni forgot about the potatoes and ran up the stairs, and into the kitchen, calling for Ingrid.

It was eerily quiet in the house. Anni slammed the door from the kitchen.

'Ingrid?' she called again.

'Frau Odland? Please, I'm sorry.' Kerber stood in the lounge, turning towards her and for some reason holding his hands up.

'Where is she?' Anni held her fists up, ready to punch him if he tried something before she found Ingrid.

Kerber pointed to the closet under the stairs. Anni could see the door was ajar.

'The delivery arrived, and I think she got scared when I came into the lounge,' Kerber said. 'I thought you were here.'

Anni didn't hear a word he said. She hurried over to the cupboard and opened the door.

'Ingrid? You can come out now. There's nothing dangerous out here,' she said in Norwegian.

She could see her in the corner, holding her hands around her knees. 'Come out, sweet pea.'

Ingrid scooted towards her, and Anni took her hand. 'Good girl.'

She pulled her close and gave her a good, long mummy hug. 'Herr Kerber is sorry he scared you.'

'Bad men knocked on the door,' Ingrid whispered. 'I hid in the closet.'

'You did the right thing, but there's no bad men here now. You don't have to worry,' Anni assured her.

She looked up at Kerber, who stood watching them with a strange look on his face. *He looks ashamed*, Anni realised. She didn't know they could feel shame. She certainly hadn't seen it in any other soldier since they arrived.

'Excuse me,' he said, and left the lounge. She could hear him opening the front door and talking to someone.

Anni held Ingrid close until the little girl relaxed.

'I left the cellar door open, sweetie, and we need to close it. Want to come with me?'

Ingrid nodded. 'Yes,' she said in a small voice that broke Anni's heart.

What are we doing to her? she thought, getting up from the floor while holding Ingrid tight. She hardly weighed anything, and Anni knew potatoes wouldn't make much of a difference.

Ingrid held her hands around her neck when they headed for the kitchen.

'Mamma, look. What is he doing?' Ingrid's voice changed, sounding less timid.

Anni turned around.

Kerber was carrying a large box. 'Can I put this in the kitchen?' he asked.

'Yes, of course.' Anni regretted it immediately. 'I'm sorry, but the only thing we have today is potatoes and herring, and I don't want my daughter to be too disappointed.'

Kerber smiled and Anni's stomach did an annoying flip.

'I told you I'd get enough food for all of us,' he said.

Anni frowned and said the only word that fell into her head. 'Why?'

She stepped aside when he didn't answer at once, and instead put the box down on the counter. Then he looked at her. 'As a thank you. For letting me stay here.'

Letting you, Anni thought. *That's a lark*. She managed to hold her tongue and put Ingrid down on the floor. 'Sit by the table, sweet pea,' she said.

Kerber didn't say anything else; instead, he started to take things out of the box.

'It's not that much,' he said, putting a large loaf of bread on the counter next to him. 'There's a limit even to us, but since I was staying here all day, it was easier.'

The bread was followed by a rather large sausage, a bag of carrots, two onions and a smaller package of what she was pretty sure was butter.

Her stomach growled. He thankfully ignored her. 'I thought I'd make you both a proper meal,' he said.

She noticed that Ingrid was staring at the bread with an open mouth.

'You cook?' Anni sat down next to Ingrid and put her hand on her back to keep her calm.

'A casserole isn't actual cooking, is it? It's mostly chopping and mixing everything in a pot,' he said, looking around. 'Where do you keep your pots?'

'In the cupboard next to the cooker,' Anni said.

He found the largest pot she had and put it on the counter next to the food. "And you keep your knives . . . ?'

'Second drawer.' Anni relaxed. Watching a man cook was a new experience to her.

The first thing he did was cut a thick slice of the bread, butter it and hand it to Ingrid.

She looked at Anni for approval, and Anni smiled. 'You can eat it. Say thank you.'

Ingrid took the bread from him. 'Thank you,' she whispered.

He smiled, then turned away again, and started chopping onions.

Anni watched Ingrid study the bread from all angles.

'You'll like it, I promise,' she said.

Ingrid took a tentative bite, and her face lit up. She held the bread out to her. 'You taste, Mamma.'

'No, this is yours. I'm sure I'll get a piece too,' Anni said.

Ingrid took small bites, wanting to make it last longer.

Anni had to look away, blinking furiously not to show any tears. *This is what it should be like*, she thought. *Food that smells and tastes like food, unlimited bread for my skinny baby.*

'I didn't expect you to have an electric cooker,' Kerber said.

'We bought it before we moved in here,' Anni said. 'Lars, my husband, wanted me to have it easier than his mother. Although she refuses to use anything but her old wood stove, I'm afraid.'

She watched him put the pot on the stovetop and turn it on. The big dollop of butter he added almost stopped her breathing. She had to turn her head away.

'My mother was a firm believer that boys should know how to cook a few simple meals,' Kerber said, oblivious to her reaction.

'Sounds sensible,' Anni said. Lars couldn't cook water without burning it. Or at least he claimed so.

'She was that.' He looked at Ingrid. 'I'm sorry. I forgot to ask if you wanted a slice.'

Anni couldn't hide the smile. 'I was hoping for a taste.'

Oh, that sounded stupid, she thought, but he didn't seem to mind. He cut another slice of the bread, buttered it and handed it to her. 'I hope you enjoy it,' he said.

Anni stopped herself from putting the bread up to her nose, to get a deep sniff of the lovely smell.

'I'm sure I will,' she said and took a bite.

The bread was soft and sweet, and the crust as good as she remembered from before the war. The butter melted in her mouth. 'Delicious,' she said.

He beamed at her. 'Thank you,' he said, as if he had baked it himself.

Anni had to look away from his gaze, and focus on the bread. That something so simple as a piece of proper bread with butter could taste this good almost had her in tears.

'Mamma?' Ingrid put her hand on her arm.

Anni smiled at her. 'Don't worry, I'm fine. It's good bread, isn't it?'

'Much better than farty bread,' Ingrid said, giggling.

Kerber looked away from what he was doing. 'What did she say?'

Anni tried to explain it in German to him, and even if it took him a moment, he smiled at first, then his face seemed to fall.

'I didn't . . . I haven't tasted the bread here. I'm sorry,' he said.

Anni wondered if he meant it. She had her doubts. 'It is

how it is, there's nothing either of us can do about it. You probably wouldn't be able to buy it, anyway.'

'You mean, they wouldn't let me?' That seemed to surprise him.

'No, because you probably don't have a ration card, do you?' Anni smiled when he laughed.

'You're right. I don't have that, not here. In Germany I would, of course,' he said.

Anni eyed him. 'For civilians, you mean?'

He nodded. 'Yes. Most necessities are rationed, including food. Precisely like here.'

'Even with all the food your people ship out from the occupied countries?' Anni said. She wanted to see how he reacted. Something was off about him today.

'I'm afraid those supplies are mostly designated for the armed forces, and for the higher-ups,' he said. 'Very little reaches the general population.'

Anni wondered if he wanted her to express sympathy with Germans. The only sympathy she felt was towards her own people. Germans started the war by hailing Hitler, they kept it going, and if life was tough on them, it was no skin off her nose. She wasn't about to let him know how she felt, though.

'That's sad,' she said, trying to sound genuine.

He threw some finely cut carrots in the pot, then gave a piece to Ingrid. 'It is, but that's what they have done to us.'

Anni stared at him and asked the first thing that fell into her head. 'And your family, how are they managing?'

'I don't have any family left,' he said, not meeting her eyes.

Anni caught her breath. Even his little boy was gone? She couldn't even imagine the loss.

He still didn't look at her. 'My friends are gone; the school where I used to teach was hit by a bomb in 1943. So, there's no one,' he said with a certain calmness in his voice.

Anni couldn't tell what he was thinking. *There must be some way I can gain his trust*, she thought, trying to collect herself. So far, he had lived in her house for over a month, and she had nothing to show for it. Martin still hadn't come back to her about those names, and she hadn't found anything else.

'I'm so sorry. That must be lonely for you,' she said.

Kerber started slicing the sausage. He looked at her. 'I'd rather be alone the way things are now. I don't have to worry about anyone,' he said.

Anni frowned. 'You have no friends where you work?'

He smiled then, a sweet smile that made her so flustered she had to look away. When she looked up again, she caught him looking at her. She could sense he was hiding so much, and she wasn't sure if she wanted to know that much about him. It was easy for Martin to say she should be friendly, but he wasn't sitting there, looking at a man that made her feel something she hadn't felt in years. She forced herself to breathe.

'For us, there is no trust. It's every man for himself. All we can hope for is that we will survive these last days,' he said softly.

So he knows, Anni thought. *He knows that they're losing the war, and he's admitting it to me. Is he testing me?* She wasn't sure.

'I understand,' she said after a short pause.

He went back to his cutting again. 'I'm sure you do.'

Neither of them said anything after that. Anni watched him prepare the food. He had good hands, she noticed. Strong. He handled the knife as if he were a professional cook.

For a second, only for a second, she told herself later, she wondered what those hands would feel like on her skin.

And then she pulled herself back to reality, and started fussing over Ingrid to hide her confusion.

Chapter Eleven

Ingrid, twenty-three years old

London, 13th August 1961

Ingrid balanced the two cups, one in each hand, and tried to not spill half the tea before she reached her mum.

Esme barely noticed that she had gone. She sat staring into the wall as if it was the most interesting thing in the world. Around them, hospital life went on with no connection to either of them. Somewhere a radio was blaring. Some kind of wall had been put up in Berlin, and it was all anyone could talk about.

Ingrid hadn't paid much attention, but the radio started to grate on her. She tried to shut it out.

'Here, Mum. It's not very hot, I'm afraid. I got it from the WVS kiosk and that's on another floor.'

Esme gave her a quick look before taking the cup. 'Thank you, love.'

Her voice was listless and so different from what Ingrid

was used to, it scared her even more than her father's illness. From the very first time they met, Esme had been warm and loving, and always chatty. Now all that spark seemed to have been lost.

'Have the nurses told you anything while I was gone?'

Esme shook her head. 'Only to be patient and optimistic. Which is a bonkers thing to say to someone who's been sitting on her bum for bloody hours.'

They had sat there since early morning when Esme woke up to Lars's strained breathing, and yelled for help.

Ingrid had been sleeping in her room. Sometimes it was lovely to take a break from the small flat she shared with another girl. In all the ruckus with the ambulance and a sobbing Esme, she had completely forgotten to tell her job she wasn't coming in, and had used the opportunity to give them a call while she was getting tea.

'You haven't talked to anyone?' Ingrid had a hard knot in the middle of her stomach.

'Not for lack of trying, I can tell you that.' Esme took a sip of the tea and pulled a face of disgust. 'This should not be allowed in a hospital. It's practically poison. It's an insult to teas everywhere. It's an insult to every tea-producing country!'

'You haven't had anything to eat or drink since we got here, Mum,' Ingrid said. 'Here, I got us some crisps.'

Esme absentmindedly took the package from her, opened it and stuffed a handful of crisps in her mouth. 'Good,' she said.

'I can get you more. When the cafeteria opens, they'll have bacon butties for sure.' Ingrid struggled with opening her own bag of crisps, and Esme took it from her.

'You could never get the hang of this,' she said with a smile.

'You always helped me.' Ingrid returned the smile. 'Do you think Pappa will be fine?'

Esme blinked away a few tears. 'I hope so. He's had such a hard time of it since the war. He was torpedoed twice, you know, barely managed to avoid capture by the Germans one time. It happened in the North Sea, midwinter, so it was pitch dark. The sea was on fire, he told me once, and all he could hear was men screaming as they burnt.'

Ingrid didn't know the details from her father's war experiences, and this was the first time she'd learnt this much.

'How did he survive?'

'The first time, the ship he was on was in a convoy, heading for Canada when a U-boat caught them by surprise. He was on a cargo ship, and sometimes they lagged behind. Lars worked on the bridge then, first mate, and the torpedo hit them midships. They barely had time to jump overboard.'

Esme talked quietly and Ingrid thought it was better she talked than stare at the wall. 'One of the destroyers found the surviving men and picked them all up. The U-boat didn't return. Lars thought one of their own deep-water bombs must have hit them.'

She heaved a deep sigh, and finished the last of the crisps.

'The second time was in summer while they were off the coast of Iceland. You know how it is up north during that time, it's mostly daylight. You could see for miles, he said. But that day a storm darkened the sky. Without warning, a fleet of U-boats caught up with them. There were fifteen ships in the convoy and Lars remembered seeing four ships blown to smithereens before his ship was hit, this time in the stern. He was in the water for a long time. When they found him, he was barely alive and suffered a long bout with pneumonia. After that, he didn't have to go out again.'

Esme looked at Ingrid. 'I wanted you to know. It took him years to tell me this much. And he never wanted you to know how horrible it had been.'

'Why not?' Ingrid sighed. 'He could have told me. I wanted to know how it had been for him.'

'He always says you have your own war history, your own battle scars, and he wants to shield you.'

'That's so silly,' Ingrid said. 'I barely remember the war. Pappa knows that.'

Esme patted her knee. 'That's men for you. They need to be the great protector to feel useful. Especially the quiet types like your father.'

She fell silent again. Ingrid watched her. She looked haggard and tired.

'They're worried about his lungs. He's had pneumonia before, after the torpedoes. They think that might have weakened his lungs or something. I always nag him to stop smoking that rubbish pipe.' Esme dried away more tears. 'God, I hate this.'

Ingrid racked her brain to find something to distract her. 'How did you and Pappa meet? You never told me that.'

Esme looked bemused. 'I didn't?'

'No.' Ingrid smiled, relieved to see life back in her eyes. 'Tell me, please.'

'Oh, all right. I was out with my girlfriends one night, in a pub off Trafalgar Square. In comes this group of loud navy officers, clearly out for a good time. We saw right off that they weren't our lads. One of them spotted us and headed straight for our table. He was loud and brash, and wanted to buy us drinks.'

She sighed. 'I didn't like it, but one of my friends took a shine to him. She had a thing for tall, blond men, and she clung to him the rest of the evening.'

'What friend was this? She sounds like great fun.'

'I'll never tell. You know who it is, but she's not wild anymore.' Esme chuckled.

Ingrid pretended to be shocked. 'No! That wasn't Pappa, was it? Did you steal him from your friend?'

Esme gave her an exasperated look. 'I would never!'

'Then what happened?' Ingrid was enjoying herself.

'Lars sat down next to me and apologised for his friends' behaviour. His English wasn't great, and we had a good laugh about trying to find the right words. I liked him. He was handsome and kind, and he treated me far better than I was used to. And after that we were together whenever he had shore leave.'

Esme pressed her lips together and Ingrid could see that she was struggling. *One more question*, she thought. She had been wanting to ask Esme about this for a long time. Her father always said better to put the past to rest.

'When did Pappa tell you about me?' Ingrid held her breath.

Esme fumbled with the crisp bag and didn't look at her.

'I learnt about you when the letter came in 1945,' she said quietly. 'He showed me the picture your mum sent him.'

Esme looked at her. 'You were so adorable, and clearly

so happy. I've tried so hard to make you that happy again. I knew your mother had been wronged by Lars. Loving you was the only thing I could do for her.'

Ingrid knew the picture she mentioned. It was framed and hung on the wall in the flat. 'You know, I sometimes took down that picture to look at it. I tried so hard to remember when it was taken, but I never could. Once I even took it out of the frame, to see if there was something written on the back. There wasn't.'

'I'm sorry, Ingrid. When your grandmother's letter came, Lars translated for me, holding your picture all the time. Then he talked about the last time he had seen you, when you were a toddler. It broke my heart.' Esme dried her eyes.

Ingrid gave her a quick hug. 'I was so little then. I can barely remember how it was, and you know I'm happy now.'

'Yes, but you had lost so much of that happiness by the time you came to us.' Esme leant her head towards hers. 'I'm so sorry, love.'

Another question surfaced, but Ingrid didn't know how to say it. She closed her eyes for a second. 'You know I've tried to talk to Pappa about this, and he never gives me a proper answer. I know he's hiding things from me.'

Esme took a minute. 'I don't know much more. You know how he is.'

Ingrid knew all too well. 'Then tell me what you know. Not knowing what happened back then, what happened to my mother, is always with me. I can't let it go. It would be like letting go of myself.'

All the questions Ingrid had struggled with for years

146

bubbled up at once. Her throat restricted the moment she spoke. 'I don't know how or . . . or when they got divorced. Nobody ever told me.'

Esme didn't look at her at first. Her eyes were bright from holding back tears. 'I'm so sorry, Ingrid. I didn't know. At the time, I didn't know.'

'Mrs Odland?' A doctor appeared in front of them. 'Your husband has pneumonia, I'm afraid.'

He looked so serious; Ingrid knew in her heart what would happen. 'How . . . how bad is it?'

The doctor's face softened. 'We have him on antibiotics and fluids, and now we'll have to wait to see if it does the trick.'

Esme started crying and didn't manage to speak. Ingrid put her arm around her. 'When can we take him home?'

'Not for a while. We have to let the medication do its job. We have to be patient.'

Esme's sobs intensified. Ingrid took a deep breath. She couldn't fall apart now when her mum needed her. 'Can we see him, please?'

'You can go in and see him for a few minutes. He needs to rest, and he's barely conscious.'

Esme stood up and Ingrid followed her. The doctor held her back. 'Only one of you, please, Mrs Odland.'

Ingrid let go of Esme. 'You go, Mum. I'll be right here.' She sat down to wait.

Someone turned up the radio again. Ingrid frowned. Why on earth would they have a radio blaring in a hospital ward? Didn't patients need quiet?

It was the damn wall again. Her thoughts jumped to her father. He had always had a wall up around him. He loved her, she knew that, but he wasn't one for sharing his thoughts. Esme was the only one she could talk to.

What if Pappa dies? She thought. *What if he dies and I don't get any answers? What if he knows what happened to Mamma?*

She pressed her hands together, feeling a stab of guilt.

What am I on about? she thought. *What kind of person thinks about herself when her father might die at any moment?*

Ingrid searched for a handkerchief and couldn't find any. She had to use her sleeve instead. Then she pressed her hands against her eyes to stop the tears.

I can't cry now, she thought. *I have to be there for Mum. I have to take care of her. I'm all she has.*

That meant she couldn't ask her anything else for now. It would have to wait until Pappa felt better.

And he will. He has to, she thought. *And when he recovers, no more silence.* She would not let it go this time.

'Ingrid? You can come in now, love,' Esme called from the door.

Ingrid stood up at once. 'I thought the doctor said I couldn't.'

'To hell with the doctor. Come inside. Your father wants to talk to you.' Esme had cried again.

Ingrid quickly followed her inside.

She could hear his breathing at once. So strained and worrying.

'Pappa, I'm here,' she said, sitting down in a chair by the bed. She took his hand; it was cold, and she rubbed it gently between her hands to warm him up.

For a moment she thought she was too late, that he

would never talk to her again, and she cursed herself. *I should never have accepted his excuses.*

Then he opened his eyes and looked at her. His eyes softened.

'There you are.' He smiled and Ingrid had to blink away tears.

'Please don't scare us like this, Pappa. It's not fair,' she said.

'Don't trouble yourself with me, Ingrid,' he said.

She could hear his voice getting more strained and shook her head. 'Don't speak, Pappa. You need to rest.'

'No, you need to know this now,' he said.

There was an urgency in his voice that made Ingrid stop talking. She put one hand on his chest, finding comfort in feeling his breathing through her fingers.

He put his hands on hers. 'Listen to me, Ingrid. In my study, you'll find a file folder with your name on it. It's all the papers concerning the farm and the house. It's all in Norwegian, so Esme can't help you much, I'm afraid. Esme and I have written our wills, and everything should go smoothly.'

Ingrid sent Esme a horrified look, but her stepmother was sitting quietly, staring at her husband.

'Pappa, we can talk about this when you come home, when you're feeling better,' Ingrid said in a soothing voice.

'I know, but humour me. You'll also find a few other things in there. I should have talked to you about this a long time ago, but I couldn't make myself do it.'

A coughing fit interrupted him. Esme was there at once, supporting him while he coughed.

'Give me the glass of water, pet,' she said to Ingrid.

Ingrid handed her the glass, and watched Esme while she made him take a few sips.

He nodded. 'Thank you, love,' he said and leant his cheek on her hands for a second.

It made Ingrid smile. She never doubted the love they had for each other. It made her wonder how it had been between him and her mother. She had been a baby when he left, and had no memories of him until he came to pick her up. All she remembered were the stories her mother had told her about him. It had been more like fairy tales than anything else.

Lars turned to her. 'We'll talk more tomorrow,' he whispered.

Ingrid nodded, relieved to hear it. 'Yes, Pappa, I think so too.'

She stood up and bent over him, to kiss him on the cheek. He took her hand.

'Listen to me, my girl. No matter what anyone tells you about your mother, don't believe them. You have every reason to be proud of Anni and your grandmother. They risked their lives through the whole war,' he said, before having another coughing fit.

This time a nurse came barging in. She took one look at Lars and scowled at them.

She helped Lars lean forward before putting an oxygen mask over his mouth and nose. It seemed to take effect immediately. Lars closed his eyes and she gently laid him back on the pillow.

Ingrid had moved next to Esme. The nurse turned towards them.

'The doctor said one person for a few minutes,' she said.

'Go home now, and come back tomorrow.'

Esme protested. 'No, we want to stay. Please, we need to stay with him.'

The nurse looked at them, not unkindly. 'It's not allowed, I'm afraid. You can come back early in the morning.'

'But he needs us,' Esme said, sounding desperate. 'Ingrid, tell her.'

The nurse shook her head. 'I'm sorry, Mrs Odland. What he needs most is rest, and you're not doing him any good.'

Ingrid put her arm around Esme. 'Come along, Mum. We'll go home. You need a proper cup of tea, and some sleep. And so do I.'

Esme wasn't ready to leave yet. 'Will you call us if anything happens?'

The nurse nodded. 'Of course, Mrs Odland.'

All the way home, Ingrid wondered about the folder her father had told her about. Perhaps all the answers she needed to understand why her mother had left her were in there. The idea that he'd told her now made her angry. Why the hell had he waited so long?

All right, she thought. *There's no chance he will wriggle his way out of it this time. No chance at all.*

They had barely walked inside the house when the phone call came. And by the time they were back at the hospital it was too late. Lars was gone.

Ingrid held her stepmother close while the doctor explained what had happened, sharing her tears and feeling utterly lost.

The funeral had been exhausting. Ingrid looked at the mess in the kitchen and decided it could wait.

151

Lars had wanted the service to be held in the Norwegian Seamen's Church in Rotherhithe. The reverend had held the sermon in Norwegian and English, so it took a fair bit longer than expected.

Ingrid had been approached by a few of his friends from his time at sea. They all told her what a swell man he was, and how she should be proud of him.

She had smiled and thanked them, when all she wanted to do was scream. Why had he never told her whatever he knew about her mother? It was so hard trying to hide how . . . furious she was.

Esme had made sure that he was buried at the cemetery in Beckenham. She wanted him close, so she could visit often. Ingrid had let her take care of everything.

While she had tried to keep herself under control, Esme had run around the house, tending to the guests who came to the wake at their house. They were mostly from Esme's family.

'Ingrid? Where are you, love?' Esme called from the lounge after the last guest had left.

When she came in, Esme was sitting on the sofa, rubbing her feet. 'I'll never wear those shoes again,' she muttered.

'Leave the cleaning up to me, Mum. You should go to bed, get some rest. You've been on your feet all day,' Ingrid said.

Esme looked up at her. 'Yes, in a minute. Did you like the ceremony?'

'It was beautiful. You did a wonderful job. I don't know how you did it,' Ingrid said, sinking down onto the sofa next to her.

Esme looked around. 'I can't get used to him not being here.'

Ingrid put her arm around her shoulder. 'It's only been a week. It will take time.'

'You should move back to your flat,' Esme said suddenly.

'No, I think I should stay here and keep an eye on you.' Ingrid smiled at her. 'The flat is miserable anyway.'

'And your job?'

Ingrid shrugged. 'I'm on leave now, so I still have time to get everything sorted. I'd like to stay here. If you want me.'

Esme nudged her with her elbow. 'Silly girl. Of course I want you to stay. This is your home, you know that.'

They sat quietly for a moment. Ingrid leant her head on her shoulder, like she did when she was little.

With all that had happened since her father passed away, she hadn't thought about the file.

Maybe I should take a look tonight, she thought.

Esme seemed to sense what she was thinking. 'I'm going to bed. If I'm lucky, I'll sleep for a week.'

'I'll think I'll take a look at Pappa's file now,' Ingrid said.

Esme nodded. 'You should do that. I think you've avoided it long enough.'

She stood up from the sofa, kissed Ingrid on the top of her head and headed for the stairs.

Ingrid made herself a cup of tea and brought it into the study.

One wall was covered with bookshelves, the books more organised than at any library. He had encouraged her to read whatever books she wanted but made it clear that no dog ears were allowed, no breaking the spine of books and no scribbling inside. At some point or other, she had broken all the rules. He was never angry; she always felt safe.

Ingrid sniffled, then sat down by the desk where everything also was tidy and organised. He had told her often that on a ship, everything needed to be in its place or there would be chaos, and if there was chaos, nobody could do their jobs properly.

'Ship-shape and Bristol fashion,' she muttered, smiling at the expression. He would use it whenever he wanted her to tidy up her room.

The folder was an old accordion file organiser, scuffed and well used. It was tied together with string, and when Ingrid opened it, it folded out and revealed pockets with papers in all of them.

Ingrid sighed and started by taking a quick look through the contents. The first folders were all his papers concerning his time at sea; a small, blue book had entries of all his trips. Far more than she had realised.

She found the papers to the farm and the house and a letter from the county in Haugesund, dated a few weeks before he died. It was a declaration of expropriation of the farm from October next year. Ingrid frowned. They wanted to take over the farmland, and then tear down the farm because it was too close to the monument. There would be compensation, and she realised he had waited to tell her about this too. He had drafted a letter, accepting the offer, signed it and left her signature open.

Ingrid wasn't sure what to feel about the farm disappearing. Visiting Besta was always a treat, and she loved the place, as much as she loved her grandmother.

Finally, in the last folder, there was a small bundle of letters. Ingrid pulled it out and looked through it. She knew the letters were from Besta; she recognised her handwriting from birthday and Christmas cards.

She looked through them quickly. Most of the letters were about the farm and the weather, and enquiries about how Ingrid was doing. Some clearly also responded to her father asking her to move to London with them.

The last letter in the bundle was postmarked August 1945. Ingrid opened it. She noticed it didn't start with 'Dear Lars'.

Lars

Anni has disappeared. No one will tell me where she is. Martin has tried. He and Nina came by after he returned from Grini detention camp. Martin said he had submitted a letter to the authorities in Anni's defence, and it didn't make the least bit of difference. I've been down there to talk to them several times, and they can't be bothered. The interim police chief refuses to talk to me. This might change when there's a proper government in place, but I'm not holding my breath.

I'm not telling you everything here, because I'm not sure if they will read my letters. I don't want to give them a reason to, anyway. By now, I trust them about as much as the last government to be honest.

This whole, sorry mess falls on you, Lars. I know what you did to Anni, and I'm not sure I can ever forgive you. But this isn't about me and you, or even Anni. You must come home immediately and bring Ingrid back with you to London. They are bullying her at school every day, fighting, calling her terrible names, and I can't bear it. Our girl deserves better.

That awful school mistress came by after a boy attacked Ingrid and had the audacity to say Ingrid should be at a 'special school' because she was aggressive and uncontrollable, and that wasn't how little girls behaved. I almost spat in her face. When I later talked to the principal, he said he couldn't do anything, and that if the fighting continued, they might take Ingrid away from me. If that happens, they'll put her in some horrid orphanage where she'll be lost to both of us. So you see the urgency here.

Ingrid is your daughter, and she's unhappy. She shouldn't suffer for her parents' actions. I will tell you what I know about Anni when you come, and you'd better do your damnedest to make this right for Ingrid or you're not the man I raised you to be.

Your mother

Ingrid hadn't realised she had been holding her breath. *I had forgotten that fight,* she thought, suddenly remembering her dress had been torn and the rage she had felt.

Runar attacked me, and I defended myself. And they told Besta it was my *fault?*

Thank goodness Pappa came for me, she thought. Thinking about what would have happened had he not come made her shudder.

She looked at the letter again. There was so much she didn't understand. So much that made no sense. And it also told her that her father knew a lot more than he had ever told her.

And now it was all too late.

Ingrid folded the letter and put it back in the folder. Nobody told her anything. And she knew he hadn't told Esme either.

Poor Besta, she thought, fighting tears. She was sure Besta would have told her every little thing she knew once she was old enough. Besta always said that when she turned fifteen, she could spend summers at the farm, but that never happened.

I can't rely on anyone else to help me now, she thought. *I would have to return to Haugesund if I'm ever going to find Mamma.*

That's it, she thought. *I have to go back and talk to people. Somebody must know what happened to Mamma.*

Making the decision felt good. As soon as Esme was feeling better, she would go to Norway.

Chapter Twelve

Anni
Haugesund, December 1944

As soon as the storm ended, Anni and Ingrid headed for the farm to see how Guri was coping.

Ingrid carried her pail in one hand, holding Anni with the other. 'Do you think she'll like the casserole, Mamma?'

'I'm sure she will,' Anni said, smiling down at her.

She had the kindest heart, she thought. Hopefully that wouldn't be lost as she grew up.

'Look, Mamma. The goats are in the yard.' Ingrid looked up at her.

'Give me the pail, and you can run ahead,' Anni said.

Ingrid handed her the food and ran off. When she came to the gate, the goats discovered her and came running.

'Don't open the gate,' Anni called before Ingrid managed to lift the lock. 'The goats will run away.'

Ingrid leant into the gate and took a deep breath. 'We're here, Besta!'

Guri let the goats out of the house every day, to let them roam around. Anni knew she did it to air the house, although she told Ingrid it was to keep the goats happy.

She looked over the gate to the five white and brown goats, gathering closely by the fence. 'No running when I open the gate,' Anni warned them.

The nanny goat bleated back at her, and Ingrid giggled. 'She can't speak, Mamma.'

'Goats speak plenty,' Anni said, as the other goats joined in the bleating, making quite the ruckus.

Guri should have been alerted by the noise, Anni thought.

She lifted Ingrid over the fence. 'Chase them away, sweet pea, so they don't overrun me.'

Ingrid shushed them, and when that didn't work, she ran off. They followed her, and Anni could slip inside the yard, closing the gate behind her.

The goats could probably jump over the fence, yet they never did. Guri claimed the old nanny goat kept them in order.

She looked towards the barn. It seemed to have survived the storm unscathed. The still snow-clad roof was sagging in the middle, and she was pretty sure that it wouldn't survive another few winters.

I have to get someone to clear the snow off that roof, she thought.

When she got closer, she realised the front door was ajar. That was unusual, and Anni hastened her steps.

She pushed open the door to the house and peeked

inside. 'Guri? Why haven't you locked the door?'

This wasn't like Guri. Anni had a knot in her stomach and held her breath when she walked inside. *Had she been taken?* was her first thought. Had the Germans been inside the house? She threw a glance over her shoulder, but realised there would have been prints from their boots, and she was pretty sure they would have taken the goats, and not bothered with the gate.

The first thing she registered was the smell of burnt coffee.

Anni raced into the kitchen and pulled the coffee pot away from the stove. There was no way in hell Guri would have allowed the coffee to boil over like that. Anni put the pail on the counter.

'Guri?' She raised her voice, and startled Ingrid, who had been following her inside.

'Where's Besta?' Ingrid looked at her, clutching her hands to her chest.

'I don't know. We'll have to look for her. Can you run upstairs and see if she's there? Maybe she's taking a nap.'

And leaving the coffee like this? Not bloody likely.

Ingrid ran at once, while Anni searched downstairs. No sign of her. It was highly unlikely Guri was taking a nap in the middle of the day, but it would keep Ingrid busy.

If it wasn't for the coffee, Anni would have thought she had stepped out to the outhouse. Now she had a hard, ice-cold knot in her stomach.

She called for Ingrid. 'Did you find her, sweet pea?'

Ingrid came scrambling down the stairs. 'No! Where is she?'

'Maybe outside. I'll go to the barn, and you can look in the sheds.'

Ingrid ran off ahead, and Anni followed her. When she crossed the courtyard, she heard Ingrid calling for Guri at the top of her lungs.

One of the doors to the barn was ajar, and Anni's feeling of dread grew stronger by the minute. She walked with all her senses tingling.

If anything happened to Guri, if she had been careless and the Germans had got wind of what she was doing, her life would end. How could she tell Lars that his mother had been arrested by the Gestapo?

Inside the barn, Anni was met with the usual smell of goats and hay. The dust danced in what little light streamed through the narrow windows and cracks in the walls.

'Guri? Are you here?' She raised her voice. 'Guri!'

She listened for a moment, and then she heard a noise, as from an animal in agony. *That's not a goat*, she thought.

Anni followed the sound and came around the ladder leading up to the hayloft. Guri lay sprawled out on the wooden floor, her eyes closed and body completely still. She was covered with a blanket for some reason.

She looks dead, Anni thought. *Please don't let her be dead.*

'Do you know how long I've been on this bastard floor?' Guri's voice cut through the momentary panic.

'Bloody hell, I thought you were dead,' Anni said, and dropped down on her knees next to her. 'What happened?'

Guri opened her eyes and looked at her. 'I had to see if the barn had survived the storm, of course.'

Guri's hands were cold. 'You're freezing. How long have you been like this?'

'Only a couple of hours,' Guri said. 'Please don't fuss. It's nothing serious.'

'You fell. I'd say that's serious,' Anni said.

Guri grabbed her hand. 'Listen, we have a problem.'

'Yes, I can see that.' Anni didn't listen. 'Where are you hurt? Shall I call for the doctor? Did you break anything?'

'No, I didn't break anything. I hit my back pretty hard, and I think I sprained my ankle. Listen to me. I'm supposed to go out with Martin tonight. You have to do it.'

'Tonight? I can't do that. Not with Kerber in my house. It's too risky.' Anni shook her head. 'I thought Martin understood that.'

'Of course he does, but I can't get hold of him now, can I? And I can't go anywhere. It's too late to change the arrangements.' Guri looked up at the hayloft. 'Far too late.'

Anni followed her look and spotted a pale face staring back at her. Her mouth fell open in shock, before she turned to look at Guri again. 'What have you done?'

Guri patted her hand. 'What was I supposed to do? Send them away? Martin brought them three days ago, and then that bloody storm happened. But Martin said the boat is coming tonight for sure. If you help him, it will be fine. You know it's not possible for one person to do this job.'

Anni looked up again. 'How many are up there?'

'A married couple and their son from the hinterland. They operated a radio in the mountains and the Germans were getting too close,' Guri said.

'There's a child?' Anni could feel the bile in her throat.

'Yes, he's twelve, so he understands the seriousness. He's been good as gold, he has,' Guri said.

162

'Jesus, do they know how risky this is? Why not leave the boy with relatives or friends? The Germans aren't going to arrest him.'

'Who are you?'

Anni looked up again and spotted a boy who looked worried.

'Pappa went down to see how she was doing and gave her the blanket. He wanted to get help, but she said to leave her because someone was coming, and it took ages,' he said. 'Are you the one we were waiting for?'

A man showed up next to the boy before Anni could answer. Obviously his father. 'I'm sorry, Guri. We heard voices.'

Anni shook her head. 'You have to stay hidden, for God's sake.'

'I'm sorry. I heard your concern. We don't have any family we can leave Jonas with,' he said in a low voice. 'We can't leave him behind.'

'That's Jon,' Guri said. 'His wife, Kirsten, is in the back somewhere.'

Jon said something to the boy, and he disappeared. 'He's been through a lot. He'll be fine.'

'You stay out of sight until I come for you,' Anni said. 'There are patrols passing here sometimes.'

Jon nodded. 'We will. Thank you.'

He disappeared and Anni looked at Guri. A thought occurred to her. 'How did they manage up there during the storm?'

Guri smiled. 'They were in the house with me.'

Anni gaped. 'You're not right in the head. What if there had been a patrol?'

'In that storm? I don't think so. And if I hadn't, they would have frozen to death in here.'

Anni opened her mouth to say something, but Guri stopped her. 'Please, can we argue about that in the house? My back is killing me,' she said, trying to sit up. 'Damn,' she muttered.

'Watch your language. Ingrid is outside,' Anni said. She looked around for something that could help. 'Do you think you can climb on my back?'

'I'll try.' Guri looked at her. 'Are you sure you can manage?'

'You barely weigh more than Ingrid. Question is how I can get you up on my back.'

Guri waved her hand. 'Help me get hold of the ladder. I can use it for support.'

'Maybe we should try the wheelbarrow?' Anni said.

Guri scowled and Anni smiled at her. From upstairs, she could hear Jonas giggle, followed by his father shushing him.

With her support, Guri managed to pull herself up to semi-standing. She was sweating from the ordeal. 'Dear Lord, that hurts. Now what?'

'I guess that will have to do,' Anni said. She turned her back to Guri and bent down, the same way she would when Ingrid wanted a piggy-back ride.

Guri put her hands around her neck. 'I feel as dumb as goat shit,' she said.

'You should be. Climbing up there was stupid. Climbing down even dumber,' Anni said, slowly making her way out of the barn. 'But it's good you didn't have them help you into the house.'

'I told you, I'm not that dumb. And I knew you would be coming to check on me today, anyway. I didn't think you would come this late! Poor Jon and Kirsten were making a fuss earlier and wanted to go and get you!'

Anni took a better grip around Guri's knees. 'I'm happy you're still here.'

'So am I. The moment I slipped on the ladder and fell, I honestly thought my time had come,' Guri said. 'It's nothing serious, I've pulled a muscle, and perhaps gained a new bruise or two.'

Anni started walking, and Guri let out a stifled sound of pain. 'Shit,' she said, panting hard.

'Do you want me to stop?' Anni stopped anyway, to let Guri breathe a little.

'No, haul me into the house. I will be fine once I'm on my sofa.'

Ingrid was on her way to the barn when they came outside. She ran towards them. 'Besta?'

Anni was breathing hard. Guri was heavier than Ingrid. Not that she would dare to tell her that. 'Besta has hurt her back. She'll be fine.'

'Does it hurt, Besta?' Ingrid's eyes were brimming with tears.

'Not much, sweetie. Be a good girl and run along inside. Keep the doors open. I need to lie down.' Guri was talking through gritted teeth, and it made Anni even more worried.

She started moving again. The house seemed a long way away.

'I think your house is moving backwards,' she said, taking another little break.

'I wish it was closer.' Guri took a deep breath. 'I might

have hit my back harder than I thought.'

When they finally got into the house, and Anni managed to help her down onto the sofa, they were both exhausted.

Guri closed her eyes. 'I need to rest a few minutes,' she muttered.

'Not before I've had a look at your leg,' Anni said.

She pulled Guri's skirt up to the knee. The leg was swelling, and it didn't look encouraging.

'Can you wriggle your toes, please?' Anni could see Guri wasn't in the mood.

'Leave it be, Anni. I'm on my sofa, I'll be fine.'

'If it's a sprain, all we have to do is put your leg on a pillow, put something cold on it, and wait for the swelling to go down. But if it's broken, we have to call the doctor or go to the hospital.'

'No, I don't want to go to the bloody hospital. It's filled to the brim with Nazis. I'll say something to one of them and that will be it.' Guri lifted her hand and pointed at her. 'No hospital.'

'Then move your toes, or I'll drag you there myself.' Anni watched her foot. The toes wriggled and she looked at her. 'Does it hurt when you do that?'

'No. The calf hurts like holy . . .' She threw a quick glance Ingrid. 'It hurts.'

'I'll get you some cold flannel to keep on it. But you can't walk on that leg. I'll find you a stick or something,' Anni said, standing up.

She filled a small pot with ice-cold water and brought a flannel to put on the swelling. 'Don't move.'

Guri looked relieved the moment the cold flannel covered her leg. 'That's better,' she said.

'We'll keep it wet. Hopefully it will keep the swelling from getting worse,' Anni said.

Ingrid was standing by the end of the sofa, looking so concerned, Anni picked her up on her lap. 'Besta will be fine in a few days, I promise.'

'You promise?' Ingrid put her hand on her cheek and pulled her face towards her. 'Really promise?'

'I really, really promise.' Anni smiled at her. 'Do you know what I think will make Besta happy when she feels this poorly?'

Ingrid shook her head.

'I think if you and I stayed here for a few days to take proper care of her, she'd feel better much sooner. What do you say?'

'Can I put flannels on her leg?' Ingrid cheered up at once.

'You can do it later. Why don't you go and play with the goats while I look after Besta for a moment?'

Ingrid leant into Anni. 'What about our surprise?' she whispered.

'Oh, that. I put it on the kitchen counter. Why don't you bring it in here and show it to Besta before you go outside? Be careful when you take it down.'

Ingrid rushed off and came back, carrying the pail carefully.

Guri frowned. 'What's that?'

'We have brought you lovely casserole, Besta!' Ingrid held up her pail. 'It's *so* good.'

Guri took the pail from her and opened the lid. 'This smells wonderful.'

'There's sausage in it,' Ingrid said, brimming with joy

that her grandmother was impressed. 'We have some bread too. Good bread.'

'Thank you, little one. I'm going to enjoy this,' she said to Ingrid and hugged her. 'Now run along, sweetie, and play with the goats. After being cooped inside here during the storm, they're antsy and restless. When you get back inside, I'll feel a lot better,' Guri said.

'Are you sure, Besta?' Ingrid looked at Anni. 'Is that true?'

'Yes, absolutely it is. The flannel is magical,' Guri said.

That made the little girl feel better, and she skipped outside.

'Stay away from the barn,' Anni called after her.

'Yes, Mamma,' Ingrid called back.

Guri looked at Anni. 'How did you come by food like this?'

'Our lodger was snowed in too, and it turns out he can cook,' Anni said, trying to sound casual.

'He cooked for you?' Guri frowned. 'Why would he do that?'

Anni narrowed her eyes. 'He said Hagland closed down because of the snow, and he didn't want to stay stuck out there. And they had food delivered to him. I couldn't refuse when he offered to cook. It's like you said, most likely the food is taken from some of our own people.'

Guri nodded. 'I did say that, didn't I?'

'Yes, you did. Now tell me – will Martin come here?'

'No, it's too risky.' Guri looked at Anni. 'Martin will be waiting at the regular spot. You have to be there on time; it's going to be in the middle of the night.'

'Nothing new there,' Anni said.

'Martin said there'll be another boat waiting outside of Kvitsøy island. You have to row them out there.'

'We'll manage. We always do.' Anni smiled. 'I'll be glad to get out of the house, to be honest.'

'I'm sorry,' Guri said. 'I've climbed up that ladder a million times.'

Anni narrowed her eyes. 'Would you have told me if you hadn't? I strictly remember telling both you and Martin that these kinds of operations were far too risky now.'

'I couldn't say no.' Guri sighed. 'It's what we do, and we have managed so far, haven't we?'

'Yes, but that doesn't mean we're invincible. We can't be this careless,' Anni said.

Guri nodded, but Anni wasn't convinced. She would do whatever she wanted anyway.

'I'm sorry I've dragged you into this,' Guri said, looking regretful.

'Don't worry about it. I'll take care of everything. You make sure you and Ingrid are safe,' Anni said.

Guri nodded. 'We'll be fine. I'll stay on the sofa tonight. Ingrid and you can take my bed. Do you have the children tomorrow?'

'No, so that's a blessing. I can sleep in.' Anni got up. 'I'll fill a hot water bottle for your back, and bring you some aspirin.'

'Thank you.' Guri closed her eyes. 'I hate this so much.'

Anni scowled at her. 'You could have broken your neck.'

Guri muttered something. Anni was pretty sure it was swearing.

'I heard that,' she said, while preparing the kettle.

Guri kept the old woodstove burning with peat. It gave

off a sharp smell, but Anni didn't mind. The kitchen was always warm and cosy. 'I'll have the kettle boiling in no time,' she said.

While she found the aspirin and waited for the water to boil, she planned how to bring the family to the pier.

She brought the hot water bottle over to the sofa. 'Guri? This will help.'

Guri groaned, but managed to slip the hot water bottle under her lower back. 'I've only pulled a muscle, I'm sure of it.'

'Then you will feel better tomorrow. I hope Ingrid won't be a bother for you now,' Anni said.

'I've raised a boy, and she's a lot like him. We'll be fine.' Guri seemed more comfortable now. 'She'll be right here with me.'

'Good. I'll pop by the house and get our night things, and I also need to leave a note for Kerber,' Anni said.

Guri frowned. 'Why on earth would you do that? You don't answer to that . . . that person, do you?'

'No, but if I don't leave him a note, he might get suspicious, and might even come here. We can't risk that,' Anni said.

'No, I guess we can't,' Guri said.

'I can see your brain working. What is it?' Anni took the blanket at the end of the sofa and put it over Guri.

'Do you think it was a coincidence that he was with you during the storm?'

Anni shook her head. 'I don't think the Germans can control the weather.'

'No, I mean, it's odd that he decided to stay at the house at the exact moment these people showed up,' Guri said.

'If he did, then he'd be disappointed. He's back at Hagland today.'

Guri nodded. 'Be careful. That's all I say. Now go and get what you need for the night, and then we can eat. Can you turn the casserole into a soup? I think we should feed them before you leave.'

'Yes, I agree.' Anni looked at her. 'How have you been feeding your guests?'

'Martin brought some food, and I gave them milk and potatoes,' Guri said. 'The wife, she had some bread. I know they'll be fed when they arrive in Scotland, but it's a hell of a journey on an empty stomach. It's such bollocks that people have to hide like animals. I hate that.'

'You're not getting any arguments from me. How were you planning to get them past the neighbours?'

Guri shrugged. 'By using the pathway around the monument. It's longer, but safer. Martin will meet you halfway, help you cross the field and down to the pier. I checked the boat before the storm. You're not too worried, are you? You've done it lots. There shouldn't be a problem.'

Sure, unless they encountered a German patrol. They were rare, but that didn't mean they didn't show up at times. She wanted to say she had a bad feeling, but that happened every time. There was no choice anymore.

'I'll get them there,' she said instead.

After gathering a few necessary items and some of Ingrid's toys to keep her occupied, Anni and Ingrid returned to the farmhouse. Guri wasn't sleeping, but she smiled at them when they came in, and Anni sighed with relief.

'Why don't you stay inside here, Ingrid, and look after

Besta?' Anni said. 'I'm going to the kitchen to cook, and when I come back, we'll have some lovely soup.'

Ingrid flopped herself down on the floor. 'I'll play here, Mamma.'

'And be very quiet,' Anni said.

Anni knew she could trust her. Ingrid was never foolish, and she would sit by her grandmother for as long as it took.

To turn what was left of Kerber's casserole, meant for one person for two days, into a soup for six people wasn't difficult. Guri had potatoes and turnip, already cooked, and plenty of dried herbs from her garden.

Because of Kerber, she had been less involved with the resistance activities, and she felt guilty about it now. Guri shouldn't have had to deal with this on her own.

And she had every intention of telling her so. It didn't matter that that man was in her house; she could still find ways help Guri and Martin.

Chapter Thirteen

Behind Anni, Kirsten and Jonas held hands and braved the slippery ground. Jon came last. He kept looking over his shoulder, and she knew he was scared. Hell, she was scared. Anything else would be stupid.

When they arrived at Haraldshaugen, she stopped and waited, giving a sign to the family to be quiet. A faint whistle had her turn around and narrow her eyes.

'He's here,' she said to Jon before whistling back.

Less than a minute later, Martin showed up next to them. He was dressed much like her, in his thickest winter clothes.

He greeted them with a friendly smile, designed to keep them calm. Anni could see it worked.

Martin pulled Anni over. 'Did you come from your house? With the . . . him there?'

'No, of course not. I'm staying with Guri,' Anni said, frowning at him.

'Is that why you are here? She said she didn't want you involved.'

'Guri fell down the barn ladder,' Anni said. 'She hurt her ankle and her back.'

'I see. Let's move.' Martin wasn't one for small talk.

The coastline was too rough and riddled with cliffs and inlets to have any hope of detecting anyone or anything that might be dangerous. But Anni knew there were patrol boats, slowly sailing past the land, with sharp-eyed Kriegsmarine sailors watching every movement.

Martin seemed to know what she was thinking. 'I haven't seen any ground patrols or any of Kriegsmarine's boats,' he said. 'Hopefully the storm yesterday scared them to land.'

Anni hoped so too, following Martin around the monument, and heading closer to the water. She could hear the sea now, lapping at the water's edge.

The small path they were using to get down to the water led them by a narrow stretch of open land, clearly visible from the sea. Martin stopped.

Anni looked behind her at the family. They huddled together without saying a word. Jonas was holding both his parents' hands now, and she could see the fear on his face.

'We have to be quick across this field,' Anni whispered. 'Don't stop no matter what. And if I say so, drop down to the ground and stay absolutely still.'

She hoped they understood the consequences if they didn't.

Martin nodded at her, then ran across. She knew he'd be scouting the pier.

She waited for Martin's sign, and then waved at Jonas and Kirsten.

'Aim straight forward and Martin will send you to the boathouse. Stay there. We'll be right behind you.'

Kirsten stared at her, petrified. She was shaking.

Anni knew she would panic at the slightest noise. She smiled at her. 'Don't worry. Martin is the best.'

Jonas pulled his mother's arm. 'Come, Mamma. Let's go. Now.'

'I don't think I can do this. I'm sorry,' Kirsten said, tears streaming down her face.

Anni looked at Jon. 'You take her, and I'll be right behind you with Jonas. We can't risk standing here for too long.'

Jon nodded. 'Come along, dear. We have been through worse.'

He didn't give her time to answer but took her hand and held it tightly. 'We can do this. Together.'

Anni waited until the two of them were safely on the other side, before turning to Jonas. 'Are you ready?'

He grinned through the darkness. 'Yes!'

That's the spirit.' Anni took his hand and squeezed it. Then they ran. The grass was wet and slippery under her boots. She could hear Jonas panting next to her. A glimpse of his face revealed only determination.

On the other side, Martin waited alone. 'They're in the boathouse,' he whispered.

He looked at the boy as if he hadn't noticed him before. 'You're young,' he said.

'This is Jonas,' Anni said. 'He's the bravest refugee we've had so far.'

Jonas grew at least a foot.

'Well done.' Martin patted him on the back. 'Be careful down the steps. It's slippery.'

When they came down to the boathouse, Martin let Jonas go inside to his parents, then held Anni back.

'The fishing boat is out there. They responded to my light flash,' he said, unable to hide the relief in his voice.

Anni knew how he felt. There had been times when they had been waiting in the boathouse, and then had to take the refugees back to the farm. It wasn't a good situation for anyone.

She could see Martin had already made everything ready. Their old rowing boat was dipping in the water, tied to the wooden pier. She knew for a fact it hadn't been there before the storm. Martin had been here for a while.

'Let's get them out there before the bastards show up,' Anni said, grinning back.

The family was already outside, eager to go, when they turned around. Martin went into the boat first, holding it steady by grabbing on to the pier.

Anni guided them down into the boat. Kirsten had gathered herself, and now looked as determined as Jonas.

'Take Martin's hand, and he'll help you sit down,' she said.

It took a few minutes to get them all in the boat. Jon sat at the front, and Jonas and Kirsten next to each other in the aft.

Martin looked at his passengers. 'No talking from now on. We need to be as quiet as we possibly can.'

Anni could see they understood, as she knew they would. She had seen it so many times now. The moment people sat in the boat, they knew they would soon be safe. That wasn't true, there was still the long boat trip to Shetland, but still, people felt safer the moment they left land.

Martin and Anni took an oar each, and Anni used hers to push them away from the pier. The boat was big and heavy, but they were used to it and made good speed once they were clear of the pier.

For a while, all they could hear was the dipping of the oars, splashing through the water. The water was far from calm, and the wind even worse, but they knew what they were doing. Anni followed Martin's steady rhythm with the oars, and the boat cut through the waves.

It was freezing cold, and she could see Jonas sitting closer to his mother, her arm around him. Anni bent down quickly and handed them a blanket from the bottom of the boat. Without words, they huddled together under it.

Anni looked over her shoulder and caught a glimpse of the boathouse disappearing in the darkness.

Sometime later, Martin caught sight of the fishing boat, and gave a sigh of relief.

It wasn't any of the bigger boats that went to Shetland. This was smaller, and Anni knew they would sail out into the fishing grounds, mingle with the other boats out there and then transfer the refugees to one of the Shetland buses.

Martin gave her a grim smile when she nodded at him.

Minutes later, they glided along the boat side and waved up at the fishermen leaning on the railing. They pulled the oars inside the boat, and Anni held on to the ship's side, trying to keep the rowing boat steady. Two of the fishermen leant over and helped her.

Martin grabbed the rope one of the fishermen threw down and tied it around Jonas's waist. 'It's for safety,' he said to Jonas before lifting him up.

Jonas was quickly pulled up by the fishermen and put down on the deck. Kirsten followed without any fuss, and then finally Jon.

He hesitated. 'Thank you,' he said. 'We will be for ever grateful for this. Please send our love to Guri.'

'I will,' Anni said, smiling at him. 'Take care of yourself and your family. And hopefully you'll return home soon.'

He nodded. 'Yes, hopefully.'

Minutes later he was onboard with the others.

Anni waved at them as Martin pushed the rowing boat away, and they could put down the oars again.

No one on the boat called out, but she could see Jonas standing by the railing, lifting both his arms to them.

'I think you've made an impression,' Martin said, clearly amused.

'I doubt it.' Anni pulled at the oar, happy now that they could see the fishing boat drifting away, and after a while the *tuk-tuk* sound of the engine told them that their refugees' passage to a safe haven had started.

It wasn't over yet. There was so much that could go wrong still, and she really didn't want to think about it too much.

If the transfer to the bigger fishing boat went well, there would still be at least thirty hours of travel, depending on the weather. And then there was always the constant threat of U-boats or planes attacking them.

Anni tried not to think about it.

They rowed towards land again, and the sound of the fishing boat soon disappeared into the darkness. Anni looked at Martin.

'I hope they make it across,' she said.

'The Nazi bastards are terrified of the RAF,' he said, voice filled with contempt.

'Have you found out anything about the name list I found?' Anni looked at him.

Martin shook his head. 'We've sent a copy to Shetland, and I haven't heard anything back. It was strange, though, don't you think?'

'Yes, all the names were German.' Anni kept rowing, worried they would go off course. 'What do you think?'

Martin sighed again. 'Maybe they are important. Point is, we have no idea why.'

'They could be traitors, and he might be after them,' Anni said, hoping desperately she was wrong.

'Yes, but why isn't the Gestapo handling it? Do you think that's what he is?'

'He's not Gestapo,' Anni said firmly.

Martin turned his head. 'Perhaps not, but then again, how would we know?'

Anni didn't want to even consider Kerber to be Gestapo. It felt so . . . so wrong to think of him like that. But she couldn't tell Martin that.

'They're getting more scared by the day, Martin. They know they're losing,' Anni said, and told him what Kerber had said. 'They know it's a matter of weeks, maybe less.'

Martin frowned. 'Our biggest concern is what will happen when Germany is finally beaten. A lot of people on our side think that they'll never back down, and that means we might still have a long way to go. Can you get him to tell you about that?'

'I don't know,' Anni said. 'I can't simply ask him, you know that, right?'

Martin grinned at her. 'I know that. But whatever happens, we're not going down without a fight, Anni.'

He sounds so sure, Anni thought. *I wish I could be like that.*

They fell silent until they were back at the boathouse. Martin turned to her when they were safely by the monument.

'I don't want you to think I take this lightly,' he said, looking worried. 'We both know what will happen if they catch us, and I don't want to be caught this close to the end.'

Anni shook her head. 'Neither do I. We have to be more vigilant, that's all. I have a lot to lose. I won't risk that. The more desperate the Germans get, the more dangerous they will be. Keep that in mind, please.'

He nodded. 'I understand.'

'And, Martin, I don't want Guri to go out anymore. She's more fragile than she lets on, and I've neglected her since the German moved into my house.' Anni sighed. 'Next time, come to me and then we'll do it like tonight. You can hide people in her barn, but I will bring them out.'

Martin smiled. 'Thank you. I'll be in touch.'

Anni waited until he had disappeared. She followed the path around the huge monument and walked slowly towards the farm. Now the moon was shining, forming shadows among the pillars. It made the place look haunted and she liked that. She'd take ghosts over soldiers any day. The huge stones looked like arrows pointing at the sky. Anni wished she could have used those to defend what she loved.

A movement on the other side of the monument startled her. Anni froze in place.

It didn't look like a soldier; maybe it was one of the neighbours visiting their outhouse.

Anni sighed. The problem with curfews was that they didn't take into account that not everyone had indoor plumbing. She stood still, watching the shadows. Had they seen anything? She didn't think so, although the fear was a heavy lump in her stomach.

Recognising that the fear came from a desperate hope that no one had seen them, she crouched down and tried to walk around the fence.

It was most likely a stupid idea, and if it was the neighbour, there wasn't much she could do about that. But she also knew that if she didn't try to see who it was, she'd obsess over it later.

Quickly, she ran along the fence, hoping whoever it was didn't see her.

In her peripheral vision, she spotted another movement, heading in her direction. Anni threw herself to the ground, ignoring the wet snow and immediately regretting it.

What the hell am I doing?

She jumped up and brushed her clothes. *I'm not doing anything wrong*, she thought. At least not right now, and there was no reason why she shouldn't walk outside her own house.

Anni straightened her back and kept walking, following the edge of the monument.

He was standing so still, she almost walked into him.

'Frau Odland,' he said, stepping out of the shadows. '*Guten Abend*.'

Anni swallowed and it felt as if she was swallowing her tongue. She drew a sharp breath.

'Good evening, Herr Kerber.'

He looked back at her house. 'I couldn't help noticing you weren't home tonight.'

'I left a note,' she said.

'Yes, I found it,' he said, smiling slightly.

She had a flash vision of him entering her bedroom to see if she was there, perhaps sitting on her bed . . . Anni shook her head. *What am I doing?* she thought.

'How is your mother-in-law?'

'She's resting,' she said, keeping her voice as steady as possible. 'She had a fall.'

He nodded. 'I see. And are you on your way home to maybe pick up something?'

Anni shook her head, not wanting to go for a midnight stroll with him. 'No, I did that earlier, when I left you the note.'

He seemed puzzled. 'Then what are you doing outside?'

'I couldn't sleep. My mother-in-law keeps her goats in the house at night, and to be honest, I needed some fresh air.'

That made him chuckle. 'I can understand that. Goats have quite the pungent smell.'

'Yes, they do, and sometimes fresh air is the only thing that helps,' Anni said, relieved by his smile. 'I see you had the same idea.'

That seemed to amuse him. He looked up. 'The moon was so lovely tonight, and I enjoy the silence around here. It's a lovely place.'

'That it is,' Anni said, itching to turn around and sprint to the farm.

'There's a curfew, you know,' he said finally. 'Even out here.'

'Yes, I know,' Anni said.

She pushed her hands in the coat pockets. 'I'll go back now, before Ingrid wakes up and can't find me. Have a good night, Herr Kerber.'

'Good night, Frau Odland.'

Anni could feel his eyes in her back when she turned around.

After two steps, he called again. 'Frau Odland.'

His voice was soft. Anni turned to look at him.

'Be careful, Frau Odland.' He held her gaze, making sure she looked back. 'You never know who else is lurking in the darkness. Tonight, you were lucky.' Then he turned around and headed towards the house.

Anni stared after him for a second.

Suddenly she felt cold to the bone.

Guri was awake when she came back to the house. She looked better, and the lounge was warm and cosy. Anni sank down into one of the chairs.

'How did it go?' Guri looked worried.

'They're all safe onboard the fishing boat,' Anni said.

'You look exhausted,' Guri said.

'I am.' Anni rubbed her face. 'Did Ingrid settle in?'

Guri smiled and pulled the blanket to one side. Ingrid was sleeping close to her, thumb in her mouth.

'She refused to go upstairs, and it took me a minute to realise she was scared to be up there on her own. I told her I needed her to stay downstairs to look after me.' Guri touched the little girl's head. 'Bless her.'

'I'll take her with me. That doesn't look comfortable for you.' Anni smiled at her.

'She's never a bother, you know that,' Guri said, making sure Ingrid was covered by the blanket again.

'Have you seen how much she looks like Lars?' Anni leant forward on her knees.

'There's plenty of you in her too,' Guri said.

Anni could see she liked it, though. She stifled a yawn.

'You're tired; go to bed,' Guri said.

Anni nodded. 'In a minute. I need to settle my head first.'

'Something happened, didn't it?' Guri looked at her.

'Yes, but I'm not sure what to make of it,' Anni said.

Guri watched her while she told her about Kerber. When Anni stopped, Guri made a sharp intake of breath.

'Oh, my,' she said.

'Not helpful,' Anni said, trying to make light.

Guri shook her head. 'Do you think he was out before, when you were on your way to the boat?'

Anni tried to remember if anything had stood out. 'I don't think so. Martin came early, and he didn't notice anything.'

'I see. It's just that for him to happen to be there at the same time you were out sounds completely off.'

Anni knew she was right. 'I don't think he means me harm,' she said slowly.

Guri sent her a sharp look. 'You don't know that. He's likely trying to pull the wool over your eyes. I don't like it, Anni.'

'Neither do I, but what can we do?' Anni said, trying to see the ways they could be safer. It was almost impossible.

Guri nodded. 'You have to tell Martin. That man might have seen him. Even if they're not coming for you right now, they might chase after the rest of us.'

Anni put her hand on her arm. 'Like you,' she said.

Guri scoffed. 'Me? I'm an old woman. You have no idea how easy it is to fool people when you're my age. They think you're half-demented.'

'You're not demented. A little potty, maybe.' Anni stood up. 'I have to sleep.'

Guri nodded. 'We can talk more tomorrow.'

'Do you need anything before I go? I can heat up the water bottle again.'

'I'm fine, Anni. I've been to the outhouse while you were gone, and I've refilled the hot water bottle myself,' she said, looking pleased with herself.

'How did you manage that?' Anni wasn't sure if she should believe her.

'Very, very slowly, and with a lot of encouragement from Ingrid,' Guri said, grinning now.

Anni laughed. 'You're something else. I don't know what, but you are.'

She leant down and scooped up Ingrid. The little girl whimpered but didn't wake up. 'Good night, Guri.'

'Good night, Anni.'

Guri waited until they were at the stairs, then turned off the light.

Anni climbed upstairs and into Lars's old room. The bed was big enough for the both of them, and Ingrid loved to wake up in there.

She put Ingrid under the covers, then stripped down to her long johns and shirt.

Ingrid's warm body stuck to her and, oddly enough, made Anni feel safer. She put her arm around her and leant her chin on Ingrid's head.

Her mind filled up with images of how wrong their

operations could go if they were careless. They all knew the risks, what would happen if they were caught. Horror stories of what happened if you were in Gestapo custody was real.

But no one in their group had ever been caught. It had been her, Guri and Martin from the start, and then later Nina. Nobody outside of their circle knew they were involved. Only Martin knew that.

He organised the refugees and the drop-offs. Anni knew he used another name when he did that. She didn't know anyone or anything about that part.

It struck her that if any of Martin's contacts had been taken, she wouldn't know. It was for safety reasons, but it was an uncomfortable thought.

Anni closed her eyes and immediately her thoughts jumped to Kerber. He was different than any of the other Germans she had met during the last four years.

He was also the only one she had talked to as if he was an actual person, and not another possible monster in uniform.

Or perhaps I'm imagining him to be human, because I can't accept the thought we have a monster in the house. She thought about the 'German tarts'. *How easy it must be for them to be seduced by a man like that*, she thought. *And how dangerous.*

Anni looked at Ingrid again. *She doesn't think he's a monster*, she thought, remembering how he had seen Ingrid was scared when he was cooking for them, and then had handed her the fresh bread. And he had warned her, instead of arresting her.

But then again, it could all be an act.

Chapter Fourteen

The snow had settled over everything, making the world hushed and clean and white. The wind was cold, and Anni could see Ingrid's nose turning red.

'It will be a few more minutes before the bus comes,' she said. 'Why don't you make a snow angel?'

At least that would take her mind off the wait.

Ingrid threw herself backwards into a pile of snow and started moving her arms and legs.

'I'm making an angel, Mamma. Runar taught me,' she said.

Anni took her hands and pulled her up, then they stood for a moment to admire the Ingrid-shaped angel. 'It's lovely,' Anni said.

Ingrid grinned up at her. 'You do it, Mamma.'

Anni eyed the snow pile. There was plenty of room for a Mamma-shaped angel too.

She turned around and let herself fall backwards. There was more than enough snow to cushion the fall. Ingrid squealed with delight when Anni started to swipe her arms and legs to make the snow angel. She tried to avoid ruining the effect when she stood up, but it couldn't be helped.

'What do you think?' Anni brushed the snow off her clothes.

Ingrid took her time. *An art critic in the making*, Anni thought.

'I like them. Can we keep them?' Ingrid looked up at her, so sure that she could take care of everything.

Anni smiled. 'The sun will get them sooner or later. There's nothing we can do about that, sweet pea.'

While they were standing there, neither of them noticed the black car approaching until it stopped alongside them. Anni quickly pulled Ingrid closer to herself.

Kerber rolled down the window. 'If you are going to town, you are welcome to ride with me.'

Anni thought about it for a second, then nodded. 'Thank you, Herr Kerber,' she said.

Ingrid looked at Kerber with a huge smile. 'Hello,' she said.

'Hello, Ingrid,' he said, and smiled back at her.

Anni wasn't sure what to expect when she climbed into the car. The chauffeur didn't offer them a glance.

'We were waiting for the bus to take us into town,' Anni said, offering him a polite smile.

Kerber smiled back. 'It's much warmer in here than standing by the road.'

Ingrid had lost all fear of him after the meal he cooked for them. She sat quietly beside Anni, looking at Kerber with an adoring face.

'Do you have an errand to run?' Kerber pulled a face to make Ingrid laugh.

She giggled into Anni's arm.

'We are going to the photographer to have some photos taken,' Anni said. 'It's a gift for my mother-in-law. For Christmas.'

She felt foolish adding the Christmas part. He knew the holidays were coming. But he didn't need to know the pictures were for Lars.

'Of course.' He looked at Ingrid again. 'They change so much in such a short span of time, don't they? One minute you're holding this little chubby baby, and the next they're in school.'

Anni heard the soreness in his voice, remembering the family photo she had seen in his house. He must be thinking about his own boy. *Lars had to feel the same way,* she thought. It was a harrowing feeling.

'Yes, they grow like weeds,' she said in a light tone. 'Ingrid will be starting school next year.'

'I can see she is a bright girl,' he said. 'We need girls like her.'

She's not for your country, Anni thought. *No child of mine will have anything to do with any of you when this war is over.*

'Thank you. We'll see what she makes of herself,' she said, keeping her thoughts to herself.

The car rolled carefully across the road. Anni could see the snow piling up on the sides.

'Does it always snow this much here?' he asked.

'Not really. The snow usually comes late, and melts away in February. We have early springs here,' Anni said.

In the back of her head she noted the absurdity of making small talk with one of *them*.

But he's different, a small voice said. He had warned her when she was out with Martin. That had to mean something.

She met his eyes, and he smiled. His eyes were sad and tired, and he didn't seem at home in the car. Anni smiled back, then looked down.

He was still German, he was still a part of the Occupation force and he was still the enemy. No matter how she felt.

I don't feel anything, she corrected herself. *Not a thing. I'm a married woman. I would never even look at another man. No matter how long this war will last, I'll be faithful to Lars. So there.*

The air in the car seemed to grow heavier. She didn't trust herself to meet his eyes again.

Through the window, she could see that they didn't stop at the Hitler teeth control point. The sentries didn't even ask them to stop.

What was she thinking, being driven to town in a Nazi car? Suddenly she couldn't take it anymore. 'Please, can you let us off here?'

Kerber knocked on the window to the car, and the chauffeur stopped at once.

Anni opened the door and felt as if she hadn't had any fresh air for ages. She helped Ingrid out and forced herself to smile at him. '*Danke.*'

'*Bitte,*' he answered, then closed the car door.

Anni stood for a moment, while the car drove away. The chauffeur threw her a cold stare.

'Bastard,' Anni muttered.

She felt a small, cold hand in hers, and forgot her anger. She looked down at Ingrid. 'Now, why are we here again?'

'Mamma, you're silly. We need to take pictures for Besta,' Ingrid said, giggling.

Anni nodded. 'Yes, that's exactly what we are going to do. But it means you have to stand still for more than a blink of an eye. Can you do that?'

'Yes, I can,' Ingrid said with all the confidence of a six-year-old.

'Right then, let's go.'

The wind was biting as they crossed the streets leading down to the harbour. Anni could see people huddling down, or diving into shops for warmth.

The photographer's studio was a few houses from where they were standing. Ingrid hopped next to her.

'Still warm, sweet pea?' Anni smiled down at her.

'Yes, my toes are all toasty,' Ingrid said with a huge smile.

Inside the photographer's studio, it was a lot warmer and surprisingly empty. No other customers in sight.

'I'll be right there,' a cheerful voice called out from the backroom.

Anni sat down on her heels and helped Ingrid take off her coat and thick sweater.

'Good. Now, all we have to do is comb your hair and put a nice bow on, so you'll look good for Pappa.'

The photographer, a woman in her forties, came out from the backroom, beaming from ear to ear. 'If it isn't my favourite customer,' she said. She held out her hand to Ingrid. 'You're getting so big now, I might need to buy a bigger camera.'

'No, you don't. I'm small,' Ingrid assured her.

They followed Ragnhild inside the studio. Anni sat down on the chair, watching how she instructed Ingrid.

Ingrid smiled and twirled and showed off her new dress.

Ragnhild used the opportunity and clicked the camera several times, giving Ingrid instructions while doing so.

Anni knew the pictures would be perfect, and she would pick the best one to send to Lars.

She had no way of knowing if he would ever receive the picture. Martin would give the letter to one of the fishermen, and they would hand it off to the people on Shetland, who would then try to find out where Lars was. At least she hoped that's what they did.

'And what about your mamma?' Ragnhild waved her hand. 'You need to be in a few pictures too. The two of you together will be lovely.'

'Yes, of course.' She had almost forgotten that.

A quick look in the mirror revealed her hair was in a state, and she pulled her comb through it. Then straightened her blouse.

'I guess this will have to do,' she said to Ingrid.

Ragnhild told her to sit on a chair, with Ingrid next to her.

'Then your grandmother will always have a memory of how much you have grown, and how lovely your mamma is,' Ragnhild said.

Ingrid put her hand on Anni's knee. 'You have to smile, Mamma.'

Anni dutifully smiled. Suddenly an image of Kerber popped into her mind, and she could feel herself blush.

'Now that's lovely. You both look adorable.' Ragnhild

looked up from the camera. 'One with only Mamma?'

Anni shook her head. 'Absolutely not.'

Ragnhild nodded. 'Then that's it. You can pick them up in a few days. Do you want any of them framed?'

'Yes, two of them, please. One of the both of us, and then the one with only Ingrid needs to be on cardboard. It's to be sent to a . . . relative.'

Ragnhild smiled. 'I will make it the best cardboard in town,' she said.

'Thank you.' Anni looked at Ingrid, who was admiring her bow.

Anni looked towards the door before leaning closer to Ragnhild. 'How are the soldiers behaving when they come in here?'

Ragnhild whispered back. 'They seem to be more nervous lately, for one. The soldiers are talking a lot about their families and how they are struggling back home. They talk about the Soviet Union and how it will ruin the world. As if that's not what they themselves have tried to do. I think they're seeing the end of the line,' Ragnhild said with a smug smile.

'That's good, I hope. I'm not sure I can take another year of this.' Anni smiled at Ragnhild. 'It's the same for all of us, isn't it?'

Ragnhild nodded. 'I'm afraid so. Every day they come into my shop. They sit on a chair, with a mountain background, hat on their lap, and grin at me. They send their pictures to their families, wives, parents, maybe a sweetheart. They smile, pay me and thank me. And it's all so normal, you know?'

Anni nodded. 'As if they were regular people.'

'Exactly. Apart from the uniform and the shiny boots, of course,' Ragnhild said, rolling her eyes.

'Are you ever scared?' Anni looked at her.

Ragnhild nodded. 'All the time. I see everything that happens in the street from my window. Sometimes the view can be disturbing.'

Anni put her hand on her arm. 'I'm sorry, Ragnhild,' she said.

Ragnhild smirked. 'Me too. Every day I hope it will end, and nothing happens. Perhaps next year.'

'I can't even think that far ahead,' Anni said, shaking her head. 'I feel as if all we have been saying since 1940 is "next year". It's enough to drive me bonkers.'

Ingrid skipped over to them. 'I'm hungry,' she declared.

'And this from the little pea who didn't want breakfast,' Anni said. 'I have a surprise. We're meeting Nina at a café.'

'Really?' Ingrid lit up. 'Can I tell her about the pictures?'

'Yes, you can tell her,' Anni said.

They said thank you to Ragnhild and ventured off into Haraldsgaten. The main street was still busy.

'Can we buy oranges today?' Ingrid pointed at a grocery store.

Anni shook her head. 'I'm sorry, but I don't think they have anything like that today. There would have been a long queue outside if that was the case.'

Ingrid forgot the disappointment soon enough when they entered the little café where Nina waited.

She was sitting in the furthest corner, staring in the air. Ingrid ran over to her. 'Nina, we are here!'

Nina kissed her cheek. 'I'm so glad you finally came. I haven't eaten a stitch today.'

Ingrid took her hand. 'What's a stitch? Is it good?'

'Tasty. Like little girls,' Nina said, pretending to bite her.

'No! I'm not tasty!' Ingrid looked delighted at the thought.

Anni sank down on the chair. There were a few customers, but not many. Most were probably stuck in a queue somewhere.

'I've no idea what they have today,' Nina said. She looked at Anni. 'Do you remember the sandwiches we used to get here? The large ones with fish pudding, a big dollop of real mayo and covered in shrimps?'

Anni's stomach growled at the memory. 'Please stop.'

Inside the café it was warm and cosy. The café owner was a friend of Nina and came over herself to talk to them.

'You are lucky. I've saved you a treat. Enough for the three of you,' she said, and winked at Ingrid.

'I don't want to eat little girls,' Ingrid declared.

'God no, neither would I. They are far too sweet. Might give you a toothache,' the café owner said. 'Wait here.'

Nina sighed. 'I dream of proper food.'

Ingrid was sitting halfway on Nina's lap. 'We had casserole with sausages and potatoes and onions,' she said. 'The bad man made it.'

'The bad man?' Nina raised her eyebrows at Anni. 'Your German made soup?'

'For God's sake, don't say it like that. Everyone who hears you will think I'm a . . .' One look at Ingrid made her stop. 'You know. And it's absolutely not like that.'

Nina was shaking with suppressed laughter. 'You should see your face. Of course, I know it's not like that.'

'It was *so* good,' Ingrid said. 'And also he had lovely bread.'

Nina looked at her. 'You're going to make me cry. Did you save me some of this wonder food?'

Ingrid shook her head. 'No, we gave the rest to Besta.'

'Lucky Besta,' Nina said.

Anni smiled at her, feeling guilty now she hadn't brought any coffee or bread for her. 'I'll see what I can do,' she said.

Nina entertained Ingrid by singing to her. The little girl was fascinated and Anni relaxed.

They were on an outing, no different than any other mother and daughter, meeting a friend. Soon, hopefully, Ingrid's picture would find its way to Lars and he would know that they were thinking about him, hoping for him to come home soon, and all would be well.

And the man in her house would soon fade away amongst many of the other tedious war memories. Stored in the back of her head, together with memories of frying potatoes in cod liver oil, or standing in a queue for an orange.

Anni took a long breath and smiled at the café owner, who came over with a plate of open sandwiches.

'It's smoked razorbill, with almost proper mayonnaise and dill,' she said with a triumphant smile.

'Razorbill?' Nina scrutinised the sandwich. 'How I long for a good ham.'

The café owner looked around; none of the other guests seemed remotely interested in them. Then she leant closer. 'What you said,' she whispered.

Nina's eyes turned huge. 'Are you teasing me? It's real?'

'*Hysj.* Not so loud,' the café owner said. 'Yes, it is. Enjoy it while there is some left. And before you leave, have your ration cards ready. It's going to cost you some points.'

Anni and Nina exchanged looks.

'Do you think it's true?' Anni brought a sandwich over to her plate and looked at the thin slices of what could possibly be meat, but most likely was something else. 'I don't dare to taste, to be honest.'

'You'll only know if you dig in,' Nina said, taking a bite and closing her eyes. 'I haven't tasted anything like this in for ever.'

Anni looked at Ingrid, who stared at her sandwich with a small frown on her forehead.

'Taste it, sweet pea. I promise it's yummy.'

Ingrid took a bite and chewed carefully. 'It's good, Mamma.'

'You bet it is,' Nina said, happily munching her sandwich.

Anni could feel the tension disappear from her shoulders and her neck as she managed to stop thinking about Kerber.

'So,' Nina said after a while. 'How are you managing? With your you-know-what.'

Anni kept an eye on Ingrid, who picked pieces off her sandwich and put them to the teddy, then in her own mouth.

'It's . . . difficult,' she said slowly.

Nina also looked at Ingrid. 'Are the two of you safe?'

'Yes, I think we are. He's not like the ones you see in town. He's not a soldier for one. He's an administrator,' Anni said. 'Didn't Martin tell you?'

'You know how he's like.' Nina rolled her eyes. 'If I can get two syllables out of him, it's like the King's speech.'

They made sure to keep their voices down.

'Perhaps I should come and visit,' Nina said. 'Take a look at how things are.'

Anni smiled. 'As much as I would enjoy that, I'm not sure it's wise. For now, there's an equilibrium in the house, and I need that.' She looked at Ingrid again. 'Nothing else matters.'

'I understand,' Nina said, finishing the last bite. 'I don't like it either. Be careful, Anni.'

Anni sighed. 'I want this to be over.'

Nina smiled, a barely visible smile. 'I think we're all suffering from exhaustion now,' she said. 'I'm so tired of the marching in the streets, the shouting and singing, and the way they look at me when I pass them by. I never look anyone in the eye, I never say anything and I'm scared all the time.'

Nina put a hand on Ingrid's head. 'I think town is getting too noisy for me.'

'Perhaps I'm better off where I am,' Anni said.

She thought about it later, when they sat on the bus. Nina lived with her father in one of the small houses a few blocks over from the high street, and the majority of soldiers in the area were stationed in the town's schools and community buildings.

It was a constant reminder of how dangerous it all was.

But at least Martin and Nina have their flat to themselves, Anni thought, then immediately felt a pang of guilt.

When she came home, there was a brown paper package on the tabletop. Anni opened it and peered inside. Carrots and apples. And a note. *For Ingrid*, it said. Underneath the vegetables she found half a loaf of proper bread.

Anni lifted the bread to her nose and inhaled the smell. She put it away for later, as a surprise for Ingrid's tea.

He had also refilled the coffee tin, she discovered.

Perhaps I'm a traitor, she thought before taking an apple and biting into the fruit. *Perhaps it might just be worth it.*

Chapter Fifteen

It was the scrawniest Christmas tree she had ever seen. It looked as if it had been beaten up by all the other trees in the forest.

Anni sighed. The problem was that most trees had been chopped down for firewood, even spruce trees that could have become Christmas trees.

Ingrid looked at it as if it was the most precious thing she had ever seen. 'It's beautiful,' she whispered. She put her hands together and looked adoringly at the tree.

Anni smiled. *This will probably be the first tree she'll remember when she's older*, she thought. *I sometimes forget that the war is all she knows.*

'Can we decorate it now, Mamma?' Ingrid looked up at her, almost trembling with anticipation.

'Yes, we can. I think it needs all the decorations we have.

I'll hang up the glass baubles, and your job is to hang up the garlands we made with the children.'

'I like the red and green ones best,' Ingrid declared.

'They are pretty,' Anni said. Next to her was a large cardboard box, marked *Christmas*. She smiled when she opened it. Inside, all the decorations from her own childhood were neatly and safely packed, like her mother had taught her when she was little.

When she had married, she had imagined that the collection would grow with decorations brought home by Lars from all over the world. Instead, there were all the little things she had made with Ingrid.

All the more precious, she thought, picking up a little angel made from wool and papier mâché.

She unpacked the first bauble and held it up. It was glittery and shiny. Ingrid gasped. 'It's so pretty, Mamma,' she said, coming closer.

'Your grandmother was in America when she was young, and she brought it home, all across the Atlantic Ocean,' Anni said.

'Besta did?' Ingrid looked impressed.

Anni smiled. 'No, not Besta. Your other grandmother. My mamma.'

Ingrid stared at her. 'Where is she?'

'She went to heaven before you were born, sweet pea. She would have loved you,' Anni said, remembering so clearly her mother's face.

'She would? Was she nice like Besta?'

Anni nodded. 'Yes, she was. She always gave me the best hugs.'

'What was her name?' Ingrid leant on her knees and

Anni stroked her head.

'Ingrid.'

'That's my name!' Ingrid giggled.

'I named you after her. So you would be strong and kind like her.'

Ingrid looked thrilled. 'You did?'

Anni kissed her on the nose. 'Yes, I did. Now, go and finish the tree, or Besta will be disappointed when she comes to visit.'

Ingrid pointed at the bauble. 'Can I hang that up?'

'Yes, you can, but we need to hang it up high,' Anni said.

She picked Ingrid up on her hip, then the bauble with the other hand. 'Where do you think it should be?'

Ingrid looked at the tree, considering her options.

'Don't take too long; you're heavy like a tiny baby elephant, and I don't want to drop you,' Anni said.

Ingrid pointed. 'There, Mamma. Then we can see it from everywhere.'

Anni handed her the bauble. 'Ready, steady,' she said.

Ingrid had her tongue sticking out in concentration while she threaded the bauble onto the branch. Anni checked that it hung securely.

She kissed her on the cheek. 'You are very clever.'

Down on the floor again, Ingrid started draping garlands on the bottom branches, while Anni put up more of the baubles.

'When I was little, we had the loveliest cakes and sweets for Christmas,' Anni said.

'Like what?' Ingrid looked up at her.

'My mamma would make peppernuts with golden syrup,' she said. 'And I would be allowed to scrape the mixing bowl.'

'Can we make that?' Ingrid tried to get one of the paper baskets to fit on a branch.

'Maybe, if Guri still has some sugar left after making your pappa's birthday cake.'

Ingrid nodded several times. 'Besta always has.'

Anni smiled. 'I wouldn't be surprised.'

When all the decorations were up and the tree looked half decent, they celebrated with a cup of hot blackcurrant toddy.

Ingrid smacked her lips. 'Did your mamma make this for you when you were little?'

Anni thought back to when her mother would make hot cocoa, with proper chocolate and sugar, and top it with a generous amount of whipped cream. 'Sometimes she did, especially if I had a sore throat.'

'I don't have a sore throat,' Ingrid said.

'There you go, it's working already.' Anni wondered if she should talk to her about how it would be when the war was over.

Anni looked at her. Ingrid was sitting on the couch, skinny legs hanging, and enjoying her beverage. She didn't know anything different. The Germans had been in the country almost her whole life, and for her, that was normal life. It was a scary thought.

'Will Pappa come home for Christmas?'

Ingrid's question caught her by surprise. 'Why do you ask that?'

Ingrid looked down. 'Some children have their pappa at home,' she said.

'You know why, sweet pea. Your pappa is sailing all over the world, helping to end the war,' Anni said.

'But *when* will he come home again?' Ingrid wasn't about to give up that easily.

'Honestly? I don't know. I wish I did,' Anni said.

Ingrid frowned. 'Will Pappa come home when all the soldiers are dead?'

'Who told you that?' Anni didn't like the sound of that.

'I don't remember,' Ingrid muttered.

'Whoever said it is wrong. The soldiers will leave when the war is over, but not because they are dead. They will go home to their own country, to their own families. Do you understand?'

Ingrid looked relieved. 'And then Pappa will come home?'

'He will. And he'll be so happy to meet you.'

Ingrid frowned. 'How will he know it's me?'

'Your Pappa loved you even before you were born, and I know his heart must have broken when he realised he couldn't come home.'

Ingrid seemed happy with that explanation.

I hope I'm right, Anni thought. *I hope the war is over soon, I hope Lars comes back even sooner, and . . .*

Maybe, when the winter is over, we can go for a trip, out of town, she thought. *Guri too. We can bring her goats and live up in the mountains in a cabin or something, and not come down until he*, they, *all of them, have left.*

Later in the night, Anni was wide awake. Next to her, Ingrid was sleeping. She listened to her soft breathing, and wished she could sleep as deeply and soundly.

Finally, she gave up and got out of bed. Putting on the old dressing gown Lars had left behind, she walked downstairs to make herself a cup of tea. Perhaps that would work.

Anything was better than trying to fight thoughts she didn't want.

She didn't see Kerber at first and couldn't hold back a yelp when he suddenly turned towards her.

Anni pulled the dressing gown tighter. She couldn't go upstairs again now he'd seen her; it would look as if she was running.

'I'm sorry,' he said. 'Did I wake you?'

Anni shook her head. 'No, no, of course not. I couldn't sleep.'

He was standing in his office suit, hands behind his back. He looked tired.

'I'm about to make myself a cup of chamomile tea. My mother-in-law grows the flowers in her garden. Would you like a cup?' Anni said.

He smiled. '*Danke*. I would love that.'

She walked past him towards the kitchen. While she put the kettle on the hob, finding the tea and cups, he sat down by the table. He didn't say anything, but Anni was aware that he was watching her. It made her nervous. Her hands fumbled over a cup.

'I don't have anything to nibble on, I'm afraid,' she said when she put the cup in front of him. 'It's been a long time since we had any sweet biscuits to dunk in our coffee or tea.'

'I know.' He smiled at her. 'It's how it is these days, isn't it?'

'Yes, I suppose it is.' Anni turned her back to him to see to the water.

'Your Christmas tree is lovely,' he said.

Anni couldn't help laughing. 'It's awful, but we tried our best.'

She poured the tea in two mugs and set them on the table.

'The tree is lovely because of the decorations. I can see Ingrid has made some of them,' he said.

'Yes, we make them with the children when we're in the prayer house.' She decided to be more open with him. 'I know it's not much, but we have to give the children some feeling of normal life.'

'I'm sure they love it.' He shook his head. 'I can't remember the last time I had a real Christmas. By the time I was married and had a son, the Reich was in full control. All the old Christmas symbols are replaced by swastikas and pictures of the Führer. Somehow it failed to get me into the Christmas spirit,' he said quietly.

Anni didn't dare to interrupt him. Against her better judgement she wanted to know more about him. She tried to tell herself it was for Martin, but it wasn't true.

'I was born in 1914, a few months before the first war. My father realised what was coming and brought us to Switzerland. We stayed there until the war was over.' He looked at her with a lopsided smile. 'So many times in my life, I've wished that we had stayed there. My life would have been very different.'

Anni could picture it. 'At least he got you out. He would have been drafted into the war, wouldn't he? And you might have lost him.'

He smiled. 'Yes, that's true. But it was hard. Some people thought he had deserted Germany. They despised him for it. And my mother and me by association, of course.'

Anni looked at him. 'Did you feel the same way?'

Kerber frowned. 'When I was a boy, yes, I did. I grew up with boys who bragged about their fathers; they were war heroes. I wished he had been like them. Later, I understood he did the right thing. I should have done the same with my wife and son.'

'I'm sorry,' Anni said and she meant it. She couldn't help it. She could see he was in pain.

'Thank you, but there's no need to be sorry. We made our choices, and now we have to live with the consequences.'

He hesitated, and Anni stayed quiet. Perhaps he needed someone to talk to. She could understand that.

'My wife and son were staying on our farm outside Berlin. I thought they would be safe there. They were killed by Allied planes, aiming for the city.'

So he lost his whole family at once, Anni thought. Her own heart felt as if it was breaking too. For *him*.

'I read the papers,' she lied. It probably wasn't the same paper he read, but she didn't have to tell him that. 'They don't say much, but it's clear that conditions in Germany are hard for people.'

His mouth hardened. 'It is the price we pay for starting a war we could never win, I'm afraid. For listening to liars. Again. My father saw through it before the first war; I didn't see it until it was far too late.'

He caught her looking at him and smiled quickly. 'I'm sorry. I didn't mean to bring you down. Tell me something nice you remember from your Christmas celebrations. Please,' he added when she hesitated.

Anni decided it wouldn't do any harm to talk to him that way. 'We would have thick, sweet hot cocoa every Christmas. My mother always used real chocolate.' She laughed. 'Do you remember chocolate?'

He drew a long breath, then smiled. 'With whipped cream

and a hint of coffee? We used to go to an Austrian coffee shop in Berlin, to eat Sachertorte and drink hot chocolate in the winter. My mother loved Schwarzwald cake, with dark chocolate and sweet cherries.'

Anni could see something different in his eyes. A sadness over times lost. 'When did you lose your mother?'

He met her eyes. 'She passed away before the war broke out. She was a strong woman, determined to make the most of her life.'

'She sounds wonderful,' Anni said.

'Unfortunately, the . . . difficult times our country went through broke her heart. She got sick and, I believe, she decided not to fight it.'

He had such a gentle voice, not at all what Anni expected from a Nazi. He didn't speak as an officer.

'You have suffered many losses. Is that why you seem uncomfortable?' she said, studying his face.

Kerber smiled. 'How is it that you have seen through me in a few weeks, when everyone else I interact with has no idea?'

Anni shrugged. 'Because everyone you know are soldiers?'

He laughed then. 'Yes, that must be it. It's a role we play.'

'What is it you do at Hagland, at the fortress? I know it's a defence against the British, but you're not a builder or a guard, are you?' Anni hoped it wasn't too obvious that she was trying to extract useful information from him.

Kerber shook his head. 'I'm an office clerk. I fill in forms for supplies, I check to see all supplies have arrived, I make special requests for superior officers happen and I keep my head down.' He frowned. 'It's not at all where I had imagined my life at this point.'

'Nobody imagined what has happened, I suppose.' Anni wanted to ask him more about Hagland. Martin had said anything could be useful. 'So, what can you requisition with those forms?'

'When the motor pool needs equipment for their cars, or the cook wants to whip up something special, I can order it. It doesn't mean I'll get it, though. As lovely as your country is, it's not the centre of the world,' he said.

Anni sipped her tea. 'It is to us who live here.'

'Of course,' he said. 'I didn't mean to be disrespectful.'

She shrugged it off, regretting the remark already. *Information*, she thought. *That's all I want.* She decided to push on.

'If you don't mind, can I ask how you came to be here?'

'No, that's quite all right.' He smiled again, a smile that didn't reach his eyes. 'After they drafted me to work for the Wehrmacht, I was first sent to the Sudetenland and then to Russia. I was in a military convoy driving away from the fighting outside of Stalingrad. Running away is more correct, but I was lucky there was room for me.'

Anni remembered the illegal news telling how the Germans met their largest defeat at Stalingrad. It had been the best news since their defeat at Narvik. It had given everyone a genuine lift. *Kerber might have a different view*, she thought.

'How did you survive? Even here we learnt that it had been terrible,' she said, taking care how she formed her question.

'One of the good things about being an administrative clerk is that you are never actually at the front. You stay behind the lines with the Red Cross and the generals.' He rubbed his face, and Anni didn't dare to interrupt him.

'Everyone on that convoy knew we were running for our lives. Nobody spoke a word. There would be a day, perhaps hours, and then we would be overrun by the Russians, hell bent on revenge.'

He rubbed his elbow, seemingly unaware that he was doing so.

'We thought we were safe, and then the bombing started. I've no idea where it came from. It was complete chaos. The car in front of us was hit, it toppled over, and I dragged an officer to safety. The driver of our car managed to get us away from there. It turned out the officer was well connected. He arranged for me to pick my own commission. Norway sounded like a perfect place to sit out the rest of this wretched war.' He smiled when she frowned at her. 'This part of the Reich is a lot more peaceful than other places.'

It grated her. It was such a flippant comment. Whatever he thought, Norway wasn't 'part' of his damn Reich, nor was it peaceful for the people who lived through their Occupation.

'Didn't you want to return to Germany?' she said instead.

He shook his head. 'No, I had no family left, and I've always wanted to visit Norway.' Again, he smiled at her. 'Although I haven't seen much of the country since I arrived.'

'It's not the time to be a tourist, I guess,' Anni said.

'That's true.' He laughed again.

Anni knew there might not be another opportunity to gain his confidence. If she managed that, perhaps she could ask him about the list. 'If you could be a tourist, what would you like to see?'

'The mountains, the fjords, the aurora borealis and the

north. I read your Knut Hamsun when I was young, and the way he describes everything is mesmerising.' He picked up on her frown. 'What?'

'Hamsun is a personal friend of your Führer, I believe.' Anni couldn't help herself.

'Ah, I see.' He hesitated. 'Is that why you don't have any of his books here?'

So, he'd gone through the bookshelves, even if he didn't speak Norwegian. *Good thing I had removed the books he likes, then*, she thought. 'I was never too fond of his books, even before the war,' she said, trying to keep her voice neutral.

'May I ask you why?'

'I prefer Sigrid Undset,' she said, and looked at him.

Everyone knew that Sigrid Undset hated the Nazis. They wanted her so badly, she'd had to escape to Sweden.

'The Nobel Laureate,' he said, surprising her. 'I enjoy her novels too.'

He smiled and she tried not to smile back. It wouldn't do.

Anni nodded, trying to stay serious. 'Yes, they are quite good.'

The silence in the room wasn't uncomfortable. She felt safe, and that disturbed her. She suddenly felt that if she stayed, she would overstep. Or say something she would regret later. She realised that she had enjoyed talking to him, despite the gulf between them. And it had to stop. She couldn't risk making him think she was too comfortable with him. He might get ideas, and she had to nip that in the bud.

Anni stood up. 'I have to see to Ingrid. Good night, Herr Kerber.'

'Good night, Frau Odland,' he said, standing up too.

She was still at the bottom of the stairs when he spoke again. 'Frau Odland? Thank you.'

Anni could barely meet his eyes. 'For what?'

'For listening. I don't think I've spoken like that with anyone for longer than I can remember,' he said.

That wasn't what she'd expected. She had no idea what to say, so all she did was nod, and then walk up the stairs.

Inside her room, she sat down on her bed. Her hands gripped the bedframe, holding on as if she was afraid of falling.

I've been on my own for too long, she thought, breathing hard. *I barely remember being close to a man, and I miss it. I miss Lars*, she corrected herself.

She tried to remember the last time she had been with Lars, and for a horrible moment her mind went blank. *The night before he left*, she thought. *Yes, of course.* Ingrid was in her own room and sleeping. Or so they had thought. Until Ingrid screamed her head off, and they had to stop. It had been a struggle, with lots of laughing and groaning.

Ingrid had ended up sleeping between them, and that had been fine too. They had held hands across the little girl. He had promised to come home again soon.

Anni smiled at the memory. *Yes, I did have that, and this man downstairs, he can't take that away. He can't change that.*

I won't let him, she thought. *I won't.*

Chapter Sixteen

Ingrid, twenty-four years old

Haugesund, June 1962

Travelling from London to this little coastal town had taken two days. First, they had taken an aeroplane to Copenhagen, then changed planes to continue to Stavanger and finally a choppy boat trip across a fjord to Haugesund. *Good thing we stayed over in Stavanger*, Ingrid thought.

'I thought it would be like England, and raining all the time,' Esme said, looking pleased with the summery day.

'So did I. But we have lovely summers in England, Mum,' Ingrid said.

It had taken some time to find someone to run the shop, because Esme insisted on coming. Ingrid was glad of the company. Now that she had arrived, it felt a lot more scary than she had imagined.

She had decided to sell their house, and since the authorities wanted the farm and the land, it had seemed the best thing to do. The sale of the house could have been handled by a local lawyer. But she wanted to see if there was anything in the farm or the house that could give her information about Mamma. And she needed to see it for herself. Maybe she would remember something.

A big, white building came up on the right side, and Ingrid pulled the string above their head to signal the driver to stop. 'This is it, Mum. See, there's Gard, the school.'

It took a few minutes before they found themselves on the narrow pavement with their suitcases. Esme looked at the building. 'You remember this?'

Ingrid frowned. 'I beat up Runar right here where we are standing. Other children cheered him on, but I beat him. I didn't remember who it was until I read Besta's letter.'

Esme nodded. 'She was quite the warrior. I loved how she dressed down the teacher. I can't believe they blamed you.'

'I was seven and Runar was a year older. And bigger. I remember how furious I was. I didn't care what happened to me.'

Esme looked concerned, and Ingrid smiled at her. 'It was a long time ago.'

Ingrid looked across the road and pointed at a smaller, white building on the other side. 'There's the prayer house. I went there with my mother. She looked after the smaller children when their mothers had to work.'

'Wouldn't they be at school?' Esme said, looking at the white building behind them.

'It was taken over by the Nazis at some point,' Ingrid said.

'That must have been difficult,' Esme said, still looking at the school. 'Why aren't there any children here now?'

'Summer holidays start in June here,' Ingrid said, picking up her suitcase. Then stopping to think. 'I remember starting school in August.'

'I'm surprised you remember anything. You were only in school for a couple of weeks, I think,' Esme said.

'It felt longer,' Ingrid said.

'It took Lars some time to come and pick you up,' Esme said. 'Then you both stayed for a few days with your grandmother. Lars hadn't seen his mother or you since 1940. They had a lot to talk about. She wasn't too happy about me; I can tell you that.'

Ingrid thought about the letter from Besta. 'I wish he had told you what they talked about. It would have helped.'

Esme nodded. 'So do I, but Lars only said it concerned the farm.'

'There was so much he never told me.' Ingrid tried not to be angry about it, but the feeling clung to her. She had told Esme about everything she had found in the folder.

'I'm sorry, pet. I should have tried harder,' Esme said.

'Please don't apologise, Mum. This isn't on you at all,' Ingrid said. 'Let's see if we can find the house. And hopefully we'll find answers.'

Esme looked around. 'Where do we go?'

Ingrid took a sharp breath. 'If we follow this road, I think we'll come to the farm sooner.'

Esme took her arm. 'Don't you want to see the house you lived in with your mother first?'

Ingrid smiled. 'Yes, I do.'

As they started walking, Esme kept the conversation light, and mostly one-sided, commenting on everything they

215

saw. Ingrid had a hard time paying attention.

Something tugged at her memory. She pointed at a large field to the left of the dirt road. 'I think there was a fairground over there. We could hear the music in the summer. Mamma used to dance with me when we heard it. A few times she would take me to ride the carousel.' She turned to Esme, with a huge smile on her face. 'I just remembered that!'

'That's good, isn't it?' Esme smiled at her enthusiasm.

'Yes, but what if that's all I'll ever remember?' Ingrid said. Her face fell at the thought. 'A silly fairground and nothing more.'

'Are you worried, pet?'

Ingrid sighed. 'I'm not sure if I'm worried. It's strange being back here.'

'You were this skinny little girl, with cotton-white hair, and so confused,' Esme said. 'You kept asking about your mamma. And of course, your dad had no idea how to talk to you.'

Ingrid laughed. 'I remember you giving me a hug and telling me everything was going to be fine.'

'Fat lot of good that did you since you didn't speak a word of English,' Esme said, making her laugh.

'I still remember that hug,' Ingrid said. 'You smelt good and you made me feel welcome. I didn't have to know the words to understand you.'

The road was lined with bushes. She smiled at Esme. 'We used to pick raspberries here. I can still remember the taste. They were delicious.'

Suddenly she stopped. 'Mum, look, there it is.'

A small wooden house, painted white, like most houses

in these parts, stood by the side of the road. The paint on the sides flaked, and she could see the windows needed repairs.

'I didn't realise it was this close to the sea,' Esme said, looking past the house.

'I could hear it from my bedroom every night.' Ingrid stopped in front of the house. 'I thought it would be bigger.'

'You were little,' Esme said, studying the house. 'It's always sad to see an empty house, I think. Houses need people.'

It had been empty for a while now, no new tenants since her father passed away.

She looked at her. 'I don't want to go inside now. I'm not sure I can face it.'

Esme nodded. 'In your own time, pet. There's no need to rush.'

Ingrid put down the suitcase again. She looked at her stepmother. 'What am I doing here, Mum? Mamma is probably dead, since she never came back for me. I should be able to put this all behind me.'

'Sometimes you have to look back to be able to go forward,' Esme said.

'Maybe you're right. Once the farm is handed over to the county, the house is sold and we're back home in London, I'll feel better.'

Esme took her hand. 'Let's go and see this farm of yours, shall we? The caretaker said that was the best place to stay for us, and not in this house, remember?'

Ingrid looked at her old house and then took Esme's hand. 'Yes, let's see the farm.'

'That's something else,' Esme said, stopping to look at the big monument. 'What is it?'

'I'm not sure. Something about a king, I think. Vikings, maybe?'

'Sounds interesting,' Esme said.

'Mamma would take us here, and we played hide and seek among the pillars.'

Esme was fascinated, she could see that.

'We can explore it later,' Ingrid said, quickly losing interest. She wanted to know about her own history, not some old stones, or whatever they were.

When they finally stood in front of Besta's farm, Ingrid couldn't speak. She tried not to, but she was staring through a veil of tears.

'It's lovely,' Esme said softly.

Ingrid blinked several times. Not much had changed. The tenant farmer had clearly been taking care of the buildings as well as the land, even if he hadn't lived there himself.

The farmhouse was covered in pink roses, and the garden looked well cared for too. 'I used to play with Besta's goats in the yard,' Ingrid said, laughing at the memory.

'The barn looks bad,' Esme said.

The roof was sagging and several of the boards had rotted away.

'Shouldn't the tenant take care of all the buildings?'

'I don't see anyone,' Esme said, looking around. 'I thought he was supposed to meet us.'

'Let's go inside,' Ingrid said and headed for the front door. It was, after all, still her farm.

'How will we get inside if there's nobody here?' Esme looked at her.

'There's an extra key here, somewhere. I remember Besta

used to hide it in case she lost her own key.' Ingrid let her hand run on top of the door and smiled in triumph when her fingers caught hold of a key. 'Yes!'

Esme shook her head. 'I can't believe you remembered that.'

'I saw her put it up here all the time.' Ingrid put the key in the keyhole and wriggled it around. 'And voilà.'

Esme wrinkled her nose. 'It needs a proper airing out. Let's get all the windows open and let the summer air in.'

'The lounge is in here,' Ingrid said, opening a door.

Everything looked much the same, only tidier and cleaner than she had expected. Ingrid didn't know what to feel, seeing it all again.

'Where's the dust?' She turned to look at Esme. 'This house hasn't been lived in for three years, not since the last tenants moved out.'

Esme looked around with a puzzled look on her face. 'Then either you have very clean ghosts, or the caretaker has kept the house in order.' She picked up a pillow and slapped it, revealing a small dust cloud. 'As well as a man can do.'

Esme put down the pillow and threw up her arms. 'Now, where do we sleep, and is there anywhere we can get some food?'

Ingrid pulled a face. 'I think there used to be a corner shop not far from here. I hope it's still there.'

While she was talking, she went into the kitchen, and opened the cupboards. 'I don't think you have to worry, Mum,' she said over her shoulder.

'Oh, my,' Esme said, clearly relieved when she joined her.

The cupboard was filled with food: dry goods and cans, neatly organised, and from what Ingrid could see, dust free and new. 'He must be some caretaker,' she said.

Esme came over to inspect the food. 'This is lovely. Is there any tea?'

'No, but I brought a package to tide us over for a while,' Ingrid said.

'We'll be peachy, then.' Esme beamed at her.

Ingrid handed her a package. 'I think this is sugar. What else do we need?'

'Milk would be lovely,' Esme said, clearly enjoying herself now.

'If there's a corner shop, it might be closed, you know,' Ingrid said, pulling out cans and handing them to Esme for inspection.

'Since we're in the countryside, perhaps we can find a cow?' Esme said.

Esme had grown up in the middle of London. Ingrid doubted she had ever seen a cow.

'Excuse me? I know that look, young lady. I can milk a cow. I'm a real-life milk maiden, my girl,' Esme declared.

'How are you a milk maiden?' Ingrid pulled a few other cans closer to her. She didn't have any problem reading the labels. 'None of these are milk powder or canned milk.'

'I walked out with a milkman once,' Esme said.

Ingrid laughed so hard, she didn't see the man entering the lounge. He stared at her with shock in his eyes. Ingrid stopped laughing.

'Hello,' Esme said, taking a step closer to Ingrid as if she was trying to protect her.

The man didn't take his eyes off Ingrid. 'I would have

recognised you anywhere,' he said in Norwegian.

Ingrid drew a sharp breath. She could feel her mind racing through memories, trying to fit one to this man. He was tall and had those broad shoulders only a working man would have. His brown hair was pushed back without any concern to how it looked, but it was his eyes that caught her attention the most.

And then she remembered how much she hated him.

'What are you doing here?'

Esme looked at her. 'Do you know this man?'

Ingrid cleared her throat. 'Mum, this is Runar.'

Esme raised her eyebrows at her. '*That* Runar?'

Ingrid nodded, unable to speak for a moment.

He was my best friend and then he wasn't, she thought, watching Esme greet Runar with a suspicious look on her face.

He looked confused by this small woman being so short with him. 'Hello,' he said.

'What are you doing here?' Ingrid said again.

Runar looked startled. 'I'm the tenant farmer. The caretaker,' he added.

'You? Since when?' Ingrid didn't realise her voice was shaking, until Esme took her arm.

Runar frowned. 'For the last three years. I've only been tending to the land. You know, planting crops and whatnot. There hasn't been any livestock to take care of, after you . . . after Mrs Odland passed.'

'I can't remember seeing your name on the lease,' Ingrid said.

'It's there. My mother divorced my father and remarried. I have my stepfather's name,' Runar said.

'So you lied about who you are?' Ingrid looked down at Esme. 'He lied,' she said in English.

'About what?' Esme turned to Runar. 'What did you lie about?'

Runar seemed to struggle to find the words. He turned to Esme when he answered. 'My stepfather adopted me when I was eleven. That's not lying,' he said in English.

Ingrid narrowed her eyes. 'Yes, it is.'

Looking at him only brought back bad memories.

'I have to . . . go upstairs,' she said, and headed for the stairs.

Behind her, she could hear Esme gasping.

She didn't stop until she was in Besta's room. It didn't look anything like she remembered. She thought the bed was the same, but she couldn't be sure.

Ingrid sank down on the bed, trying to remember the last time she had slept in this room.

It had to be one of the times when Mamma wasn't there. She wondered why. Where did she go?

It was a new question.

'Ingrid? Darling? Are you all right?' Esme came into the room, looking worried.

'I'm fine, Mum,' Ingrid said.

'I sent him on his merry way and told him to come back tomorrow when you're feeling better.' She sat down next to Ingrid and took her hand. 'Tell me. You're never like this.'

'Remember the fight I told you about?'

Esme nodded. 'Yes, of course.'

'It's all I could think about when I saw him. I was so angry at him. How do I know he's not thinking the same thing now?' Ingrid said.

'I understand, love, but that was years ago. I'm sure he wouldn't be a tenant here if he still felt the same. He was a little boy. Perhaps you shouldn't be so hard on him,' Esme said.

'Yes, I know, but everyone kept yelling at me that I was a German bastard, and no one ever explained why.'

'Now you have a chance to find out. He's older than you, and he has lived here longer. Perhaps he can answer some of your questions.'

Ingrid shook her head. 'I can't. Not yet. He was my best friend, he loved Mamma and he always took care of me. And when he turned on me like that, he broke my heart. Suddenly I didn't have anyone in the whole world.'

Esme looked as if she was about to cry, and Ingrid put her arm around her shoulders. 'If you cry, then I cry, and it's going to be a mess.'

'Yes, well, there's nothing wrong with a good cry.' Esme leant her head on her shoulder for a minute. 'But it isn't true, you know. You're still hurting.'

Ingrid pulled a face. 'I was hoping it would help to come here, but now I'm not so sure.'

Esme patted her knee. 'You need to find out what happened to your mother, Ingrid. And I do think Runar is a good place to start.'

Ingrid nodded. 'I know. I'll talk to him tomorrow.'

'Good girl. Now, let's find something to eat,' Esme said.

Ingrid smiled at her. 'Have I told you how happy I am that you're here with me?'

'A few times. Now, get yourself cleaned up and come downstairs. Did you know they have no gas in this country? Only electricity? I don't understand how they manage.'

Ingrid tried to avoid thinking about Runar when she followed Esme. She didn't want to see him again.

Ingrid woke early, unable to sleep again. They had polished off a lot of the food before going to bed. And with the long journey, it had taken the last of her strength.

She slipped out of bed and quickly got dressed. They had shared Besta's bed, reminding her of how she had done that with Mamma when she was little.

Esme didn't even react when she tiptoed across the creaky floor, heading downstairs.

She opened the kitchen window and let the summer air in. It was so early, she could see dew on the grass outside. Somewhere birds were singing.

It was so peaceful and quiet.

She closed her eyes, letting the smell of Besta's roses and briny sea air fill her with memories.

Like the goat milk Besta made her drink every day.

'Yuck, disgusting,' she muttered.

It was too early to wake up Esme, so she decided to go and look for that corner shop. Esme would love fresh milk for her morning tea.

She grabbed a sweater from the hallway and went outside.

It was such a beautiful morning.

Besta's roses had grown wild, but they were still there, filling the air with a sweet fragrance.

Ingrid looked around. How strange everything was. Everything seemed smaller and more forlorn than she remembered.

Memories seeped into her mind. She turned around

and her eyes fell on the barn.

The roof sagged in the middle now, and there were tiles missing. It probably should have been torn down years ago.

But there was something else tugging at her.

She walked over and pulled one of the doors open. There was an intense smell of dry hay inside, and she smiled, looking up at the hayloft.

'I've tried to keep it like it was,' a low voice said behind her.

Ingrid almost jumped out of her skin. 'What the hell are you doing?'

Runar stood in the door, daylight behind him. 'I'm sorry. I was coming from the shop and saw you going in here.'

'You could have made some noise instead of sneaking up on me like that,' she said with an unsteady voice.

'I'm sorry,' he said. It wasn't an apology for the here and now. He looked solemn. The silence hung heavily between them.

'I thought you were my friend,' Ingrid finally said, acknowledging that she understood. 'I trusted you.'

'I've regretted fighting with you ever since it happened. That's why you left, isn't it? Why Mrs Odland sent you to your father?' Runar said.

'Yes, but it wasn't merely about the fight. It was because the whole school shunned me,' Ingrid said.

Runar stepped closer. Ingrid could see his face in the shadowy light. She could also see the little boy she remembered, somewhere there in this grown man's features. She knew she had already forgiven him. They had both been children, trying to navigate an adults' world neither of them fully understood.

'I'm truly sorry, Ingrid. You shouldn't have been treated like that,' he said.

'Why did you and the others hate me so much? I never understood that, Runar,' Ingrid said, sensing something had changed between them.

'It was because of the German who lived in your house. There were rumours about him and your mum,' Runar said. 'You didn't know?'

Ingrid frowned. She had memories of a man smiling at her, giving her cake and a Christmas present.

'No, I didn't. I liked him,' Ingrid said. 'He was nice.'

'Maybe, but he was also the enemy. It was common knowledge that he lived in your house, with your mother . . . it made people gossip. And then she was arrested, the gossip got even nastier.'

Ingrid stared at him. 'Arrested? Mamma was never arrested. I would have remembered that.'

'People talked about how Mrs Odland had been arrested,' Runar said, frowning slightly. 'You really didn't know any of this?'

'I had no idea.' Ingrid shook her head. 'Why didn't the German try to stop his people from arresting her?'

Runar looked surprised. 'He had been taken away earlier.'

Ingrid tried to make sense of what he said. 'Why would the Germans arrest one of their own?'

'No, no, you've got it all wrong. This all happened after the war,' Runar said. 'The Milorg did the arresting when the war ended. They arrested all the NS people, the Germans and anyone else that was suspected of collaborating with the enemy.'

Ingrid rubbed her temple. 'What is Milorg?'

'Milorg was our military organisation, run from London, and created to fight the Nazis here,' Runar said. 'Most of the men received their training from England and Scotland. They did all sorts of things: sabotage, raids, espionage. And when the war was over, they took care of things until the King and government returned home. They're our heroes, Ingrid.'

Ingrid sighed. 'OK. Tell me what happened when the war ended. Maybe I'll understand more then.'

'The Germans gave up, even though everyone thought they would fight back. The Wehrmacht soldiers around here were gone by the autumn of 1945, but the last of the German soldiers in Norway weren't returned to Germany until the summer of 1946. They prioritised prisoners of war and misplaced persons,' Runar said. 'And your mamma was still here when the war ended. The only ones who could have arrested her, were the Milorg.'

Ingrid stared at him. 'Why would they do that? It makes no sense.

'I don't know what happened,' Runar said.

'Why not? You said people were talking about Mamma. Someone must have said something.' Ingrid pressed on, feeling like she was finally getting somewhere.

Runar shook his head. 'My mother and I left Haugesund right after my father left us, before Christmas in 1946. I grew up in Oslo.'

'Then why did you come back here?' Ingrid found it odd that they had both moved away.

Runar looked at her and smiled. 'I hoped you would come back,' he said simply.

Ingrid could feel herself blushing and she didn't like it. 'That's the most preposterous thing I've ever heard.'

He shrugged. 'Maybe, but it's still true. I never stopped thinking about you.'

Ingrid folded her arms across her chest, not sure how she was supposed to react to that. He meant the guilt for fighting with her, of course. Although for a second, she had imagined something else. *I am so bonkers*, she thought.

Finally, she looked up. 'You're an idiot,' she said, before walking out of the barn.

She couldn't slam the door behind her. It would most likely bring down the barn on his head.

What was he on about? she thought. *How idiotic was that?*

Behind her she heard Runar closing the barn door.

'It's still true,' he said again.

'Idiot,' Ingrid replied.

She was still muttering to herself when she came back into the house.

Chapter Seventeen

After that, Runar stayed away. Ingrid was glad. He was annoying.

Perhaps I won't forgive him after all, she thought. *I don't have time for him anyway. Besides, I have other things to worry about, haven't I? I didn't come all this way to find Runar. I'm here to find Mamma.*

They had taken the bus into town and were walking down towards the harbour from the bus station. The summer weather had disappeared and been replaced by a grey sky and drizzle.

Esme had found an umbrella in the house and was enjoying the sights.

'It's a nice town,' she said. 'Although why so many buildings are painted white, I don't understand.'

'That building isn't white,' Ingrid said, pointing at a

grey building right below a large, red brick church. 'Nor is the church.'

'No, but most of the houses built with wood are,' Esme said.

'Maybe white paint is extra cheap,' Ingrid said to make her laugh.

'Or maybe it's a rule of sorts.' Esme looked at her. 'Do you think there's any place we can get at proper cup of tea? Before we start this search of yours?'

'I have no idea,' Ingrid said. 'Perhaps somewhere in the main street. I'm sure we'll find a place.'

Esme took her arm, including her under her umbrella. 'Do you remember anything of this?'

Ingrid looked around. 'I'm not sure. I recognise the church, yes, but I don't think we ever went inside,' she said.

They turned towards the harbour. Ingrid kept looking at buildings and people passing them, hoping to see something familiar. Something that made her feel as if she had once belonged to this place.

'Let's go and find some tea. I'm parched,' she said, slightly disappointed she didn't recognise anything.

They found a bakery after a few minutes. Inside, a delicious scent of coffee and vanilla made Ingrid realise how hungry she was. The glass counter was filled with all sorts of cakes and pastries and caught Esme's attention.

'No Victoria sponge,' she said, looking a tad disappointed.

'That's foreign countries for you,' Ingrid said, taking a step back when Esme swatted at her.

'Don't be cheeky,' she said. 'I can adapt just fine, thank you very much.'

The woman behind the counter wore a pristine uniform, complete with a laced headband. She came over at once and said something to Esme.

'I'm sorry, dear. I don't speak a lick of Norwegian,' Esme said, smiling broadly at the woman.

She looked confused. 'Oh,' she stuttered.

Ingrid jumped in. 'I speak Norwegian. Not fluently, but I can order two cups of tea, and a chocolate cake for me.' She turned to Esme. 'Mum, what do you want?'

Esme frowned. 'I don't like too much cream on a cake,' she said, scanning the selection. 'That one. The one that looks like it's made with sweet crust pastry. What's that?'

She pointed on a thin cake, decorated with braided pattern.

'*Fyrstekake?*' the woman said.

Ingrid translated. 'She says it's called prince's cake. And there's some kind of almond filling in it. Looks good.'

Esme nodded. 'Yes, let's have a piece of that.'

They headed for a table in a corner and sat down.

Ingrid looked around. Most tables were filled by women. Some older, most younger with children. They were chatting and laughing, like they would do in any café in London.

These women could be girls I went to school with, Ingrid thought. *I could have been one of them. If Pappa hadn't left, if the war hadn't happened, if Mamma had stayed, this would have been my life.*

It was too painful to think about, and she had no intention of bursting into tears in the middle of eating cake. She pulled herself together and turned her attention to Esme.

'This looks lovely, dear,' Esme said to the waitress when she brought them their order.

The tea was Yellow Lipton teabags, cold milk in a pitcher on the side, and a small bowl of sugar lumps.

'*Tusen takk*,' Ingrid said.

The waitress hesitated. 'I don't mean to be rude, but can I ask where you learnt Norwegian? Your accent sounds like it's from here, you see,' she added quickly.

Ingrid smiled. 'I learnt by talking to my parents. I was born here in Haugesund.'

'Really?' The waitress beamed. 'But where did you grow up then?'

'In London with my father and stepmother,' Ingrid said.

'Are you back to visit family?'

Ingrid searched for the right words. 'Yes, in a manner of speaking,' she said. 'My father passed away last year, and I'm trying to find out what happened to my mother, Anni Odland. She disappeared in 1945.'

Ingrid couldn't make herself say she was arrested. It somehow sounded as if her mother had been a criminal, and she refused to even think of that as a possibility.

The waitress's face went blank for a split second; her smile disappeared. 'I . . . I don't know anything, I'm afraid,' she said in a hurry.

'Of course,' Ingrid said. 'I never knew what happened to her, and I don't know anyone here.'

She was sure the woman knew something. The look on her face was clearly shock.

The woman took a quick look around, then leant closer.

'I . . . the police station is the best place to start,' she said, then hurried away from them.

'You mentioned your mother.' Esme looked up from her cake. 'What did she say?'

'She told me to try the police station,' Ingrid said, watching the waitress. She didn't look back at them.

Esme looked at her. 'You already knew that. If your mamma was arrested, they would have information about that, of course.'

Ingrid had told her what Runar had said. 'Yes, I know that.'

Esme smiled. 'What? You have a funny look on your face.'

'No, it's nothing. I'm being silly.' Ingrid smiled. 'How is your cake?'

Esme nodded. 'Not bad, actually. It's very buttery and not too sweet, and the crust is delicious. Tuck into yours, so we can go to the police and see what they can do to help you.'

Ingrid watched her stepmother pour tea, tutting at the teabag and the cold milk, and then handing her a cup.

The tea was fine, and the chocolate cake a wonderful distraction. Rich with cream and a touch of coffee. Ingrid couldn't eat all of it, so handed half the cake to Esme. 'It's too rich.'

'I'm going to need new clothes if this keeps up,' Esme said.

She still ate the cake. Ingrid smiled at her.

'I'm so glad you decided to come with me,' she said.

Esme looked alarmed. 'You didn't think I was going to let you go dallying around on your own, did you? Your father would never forgive me.'

Ingrid laughed. 'I don't need a chaperone, Mum, but

still, I'm happy I don't have to do this alone.'

'Good. Now, let's go. We need to get some proper fresh food, so keep your eyes out for a butcher. And then perhaps we can get some rolls or bread from here?'

Ingrid nodded. She was eager to start searching for her mother. That was what they were here for. To find information about her.

'What if I go to the police now, and then we can meet back here afterwards? Will you be fine with that?' she asked.

Esme patted her hand. 'I'll rest my feet, if you don't mind. Perhaps I'll have more cake, and then look for a butcher.'

Ingrid leant over and hugged her. 'Thank you, Mum.'

The police station was a small, grey house, tucked back from the main street. A huge tree sat on a small plot of grass at the front, looking lush and green.

It looked cosy, she thought. Friendly, and yet someone in there had arrested Mamma for no good reason.

Ingrid took a deep breath. 'Whatever they tell me, it's good,' she muttered.

She walked inside and a man in uniform looked up from the counter. He smiled. 'Hello. Can I help you?'

He was too young to have been at the police station in 1945, but she supposed she would've been very lucky to meet someone with first-hand experience immediately.

'I'd like to talk to someone in charge,' she said, smiling back at him. 'Someone senior?'

The man frowned. 'Like my boss, you mean?'

'Maybe. I'm not sure,' Ingrid admitted. 'I need someone

who can give me information about the end of the war.'

She wasn't explaining herself very well. She could see he was confused.

'Are you a journalist or something?'

'No, not at all. I'm looking for my mother. She was arrested in 1945.'

He shook his head. 'I'm sorry, but I think all the Nazi records were sent to Oslo, or Bergen.'

Ingrid closed her eyes for a second. 'Is there anyone I can talk to? It's only been seventeen years. Perhaps someone who worked here at the time?'

'Wait here,' he said, then hesitated. 'What's your name?'

'Ingrid Odland,' she said.

He nodded, then disappeared through a door in the back that she presumed led into an office.

Ingrid looked around while she waited. The walls were the same grey as on the outside. *Perhaps a sale on grey paint too*, she thought.

There were posters on the wall, and the windows looked as if they hadn't been washed in a while. Ingrid could feel her hands sweating. *This is a terrible idea*, she thought. *Why am I here? Mamma is probably dead, anyway.*

She was debating with herself whether or not to leave when the policeman came back.

'Police Secretary Hansen will talk to you,' he said. 'You can go right in.'

Ingrid nodded. 'Thank you.'

She passed him and walked quickly over the floor. There was no turning back now.

The secretary stood up when she entered the office. 'Good morning. This is regarding a case in 1945?'

He's a lot older than the constable, old enough to have been at the station when Mamma was here, she thought. Ingrid sat down in the chair he pointed at. 'Yes, it is. I'm hoping you can help me.'

'I need a bit more to go on, I'm afraid,' he said with a friendly smile.

'I'm trying to find out what happened to my mother, Anni Odland. She was arrested after the war, probably in May 1945.'

That seemed to surprise him. 'Are you sure?'

'No, but that's what I've been told,' Ingrid said.

'We're a small police station, and all the records from the Nazi Occupation aren't kept here anymore. I'm afraid I can't help you there,' he said.

'No, that's the thing. Like I said, Mamma was arrested *after* the war. By Norwegians, either by the Milorg, the Home Front or the local police,' Ingrid said, remembering what Runar had said.

That startled him. 'Why?'

'That's what I'm hoping you could tell me,' Ingrid said, trying to be patient.

He scratched his neck. 'When were you born?'

Ingrid frowned. 'Why does that matter?'

'It will clarify something for me,' he said.

'I was born in 1938, in this town. My father's name is Lars Odland, who sailed abroad during the war. My mother, my grandmother, Guri Odland, and I lived at Gard for the entire war. I don't remember much, but I remember my mother suddenly gone, and nobody would tell me what happened,' Ingrid said.

'Gard?' He looked confused.

'Yes,' Ingrid said. 'We lived close to Haraldshaugen, the monument. My grandmother had a farm out there.'

He suddenly stood up from the chair. 'Wait here for a minute. I'll see what I can find.'

Ingrid felt hopeful again. All she needed was some kind of clue as to where Mamma had gone. She could be alive somewhere.

The little office felt more claustrophobic the longer she had to wait. And she regretted not having Esme with her. Esme wouldn't have let her panic.

Finally, the police secretary came back with a thick ledger in his hands. He dropped it on the desk and sat down.

'This is our day ledger. It's all we have here from the liberation and the rest of 1945. That means that even if I find your mother in here it would simply be a registration, and her actual file would have been sent somewhere else,' he said, and started to flip the pages.

Ingrid's throat felt dry as sand. She couldn't do anything but nod and wait for what he came up with.

'Right, here we have something,' he said. 'Anni Odland was arrested 10th May, released two days later, and then arrested again in June. She wasn't here long, though. She was sent somewhere else.' He was reading the words as if they made sense to Ingrid, then folded his hands on top of the page. 'I'm afraid that's all we have.'

'But that makes no sense. If she was arrested for a crime, wouldn't there have been a trial? They do have them here in Norway, don't they? Even in 1945?' Ingrid could hear her voice getting shrill and stopped herself.

He had a strange look in his eyes when he talked again.

'Do you know why your mother was arrested?'

'I don't know anything. All I know is that she went away in the summer, and in August my father came home to bring me with him to London,' Ingrid said, exasperated at how dim he was.

'And your father told you nothing about your mother? Because I find it unlikely that he didn't know what this meant,' he said, and nodded to the ledger.

'If he did, he died before he told me,' Ingrid said. 'As did my grandmother, who passed away when I was fourteen. So you see, I don't have anyone who can clear this up for me.' The icy lump in her stomach made it hard to speak.

His facial expression changed. 'I understand.'

'That's more than I do. Please tell me what you know,' Ingrid said.

'Then I'm sorry to have to be the one to tell you this. Your mother was arrested because she was . . . involved with a Nazi.'

Ingrid was lost for words. 'It's not true,' she finally said.

'I'm only telling you what it says here. He lived in her house for about six months,' the police secretary said. 'He was arrested with all the other Germans the moment the war ended, of course.'

Ingrid remembered the gossip Runar told her about. But she didn't even know how long the German lived with them. But surely her mother wouldn't get involved with a Nazi?

Nothing of what he was saying made any sense to her. 'She was arrested because this man lived in our house? How . . . was that a crime?' she finally said.

The police secretary cleared his throat. 'Many women

were arrested all over the country for fraternising with the enemy, as in having sexual relationships. Some claimed it was romantic, of course. Love, if you will, but that would be impossible. No decent Norwegian woman would love one of those people. So the German *sluts* had to face the consequences of their actions after the war.'

He said it so matter-of-factly and with such contempt, Ingrid felt sick.

'How do you even know if my mother was involved with him like that?' She said.

He pointed at the ledger. 'It says here that she was arrested in accordance with the Provisionary Police Procedure of 1943, paragraph 6. It was used to protect those women.'

Ingrid leant forward, trying to get a glimpse of the page. 'Protect them from what?'

He cleared his throat again. 'Women like that, they were in danger from retaliations from the public. Some women had their heads shaved, or they were beaten up. You obviously don't know how it was after the war. There were a lot of angry people.'

Ingrid got herself under control. 'Tell me where my mother is, please.'

'I wouldn't know. The only thing I can find is that she was sent to Bergen in June 1945.' He looked up from the ledger. 'That's all we have.'

Ingrid knitted her fingers together. 'Then where do I start looking for her?'

He closed the ledger and looked at her. 'All our files were sent off to Oslo. You might want to contact the Department of Justice or the State Archives. Someone there might be able to help you.'

Ingrid stood up. 'Even if she did . . . even if she did what you say, how was that a crime? Why would women be arrested for something like that?'

'The war was a difficult time for all of us. Your mother's choice to be with a German, it wasn't something people forgave easily,' he said.

'Why would anyone need to forgive her?' Ingrid was baffled.

'These women, they were regarded as traitors and collaborators, and in people's opinion they betrayed their country,' he said, his voice changing markedly. 'You must understand there were strong feelings about that kind of behaviour.'

'Wait. You said the police procedure was from 1943. Does that mean it was a Nazi procedure?'

His face turned dark. 'Of course not. The exile government in London made the laws. They rightly predicted that this *thing*, with these girls, would become a problem. So, they updated the procedures, and they were implemented immediately after the peace.'

Ingrid stood up to leave, then changed her mind. 'My father told me I have every reason to be proud of my mother. She worked with the resistance movement, he said.'

'Your father spent the war outside of Norway, didn't he?' The police secretary looked uninterested now.

'Yes, he was in the merchant navy. He was torpedoed twice,' Ingrid said.

'Well, he would have said that to you, wouldn't he? To console you when you were a child?'

There was a smugness to his voice, and Ingrid wasn't having it.

'My mother didn't do this. Your ledger is wrong. Someone made a terrible mistake,' Ingrid said, the anger boiling up inside.

He stood up too. 'You're her daughter, so I understand your feelings. But in this case, you're wrong.'

Ingrid narrowed her eyes. 'Is that in your ledger too?'

He turned the ledger around, opened it again and pointed at an entry. 'See for yourself. They wouldn't have done this unless she was guilty.'

He gave her a sympathetic look. 'I'm sorry, but the truth is, she did what she did, and she had to live with the consequences.'

Ingrid refused to believe it, but she saw no point in arguing with him. He had given her all the information he had.

The next morning, Runar came back to the farm. Ingrid was sitting outside again, drinking tea when he appeared. Esme was asleep upstairs.

Ingrid had been awake most of the night, trying to make sense of what she had learnt. It changed everything. She had no idea how to deal with it.

'You know, you'd be a brilliant milkman,' she said, when he came inside the yard.

Runar looked puzzled. 'Sorry?'

'It's so early even the birds are rubbing their eyes,' she said.

Runar sat down next to her. 'I did drive for a brewery at one point.'

Ingrid looked at him. 'I thought most boys here would head for sea the moment they were old enough. Did you do that?'

Runar shook his head. 'I prefer to keep my feet firmly on the ground.'

'You don't like the sea?' Ingrid said.

'I like the sea, but I never wanted to be a sailor,' he said.

'Your father was a sailor!' Ingrid laughed a little. 'I just remembered that. Isn't that odd?'

He nodded. 'As was yours, I think. Didn't he sail through the war?'

'Yes, he did. He barely survived a couple of torpedo attacks. But not without injury. His lungs suffered, and he never quite recovered,' Ingrid said. 'Did that happen to your father?'

'He was torpedoed, too, yes. Listening to him brag, he won the Battle of the Atlantic all by himself.' Runar didn't look at her. 'He drank, and claimed it was because of the war. My mother told me he had always been a drunk, and he was mean. That's why my mother and I left for Oslo. To get away from him.'

Ingrid put her hand on his arm. 'I'm sorry. That must have been painful for you both. Is he the reason you came back here?'

'No, not really. My father didn't stay here. He found a ship and disappeared. As far as I know, he never came back. I couldn't bear the thought of running into him in some harbour somewhere.' He smiled at her. 'And that's the extent of my sad story.'

Ingrid couldn't help but smile back. 'Your mother did the right thing by taking you away. She must be brave.'

'Yes, she is.'

They fell silent. Ingrid discovered she didn't mind sitting like that, enjoying the morning with him. She threw a glance at him. He had grown into a handsome man, but she could clearly see the freckled boy who had saved his snacks for her. She had loved him then and mourned the loss of his friendship.

Runar noticed her watching him. 'What are you doing outside so early? Are you a milkman in London?'

She laughed. 'I run a sweet shop with Mum. Her dad started it, and then she took over, and now she's training me to take over one day.'

'Do you enjoy it?' Runar smiled.

'Yes, I do. It's always busy, there's always laughter and fun, and of course, children love coming to us,' she said.

'Is this what you want to do?'

'You mean for the rest of my life?' Ingrid nodded. 'Yes, I hope so.'

Runar pulled a tuft of grass from the ground. 'And is there a Mr Sweet Shop?'

Ingrid burst into laughter. 'A Mr Sweet Shop?'

He shrugged his shoulders. 'It's a reasonable question. You're young and beautiful, and there are surely men who also like sweets.'

'At the moment, there's no one I fancy,' she admitted.

'Good,' he said.

Ingrid had no intention of letting him get away with it. 'What about you? Is there a handyman slash driver woman?'

He looked at her, and Ingrid wasn't sure she read his eyes right.

'There's nobody I like for more than a short while,' he said, smiling again.

It did something to her, something she didn't expect.

Oh no, she thought, turning away from him, trying to collect her feelings. *This is silly*, she thought. Had he carried a torch for her since they were children? That was absurd.

After a short while, she turned back to him. 'Do you have the key to my old house?'

'Yes, of course I have,' he said.

'I'd like to see it. I haven't been in there since I was seven, and I'd like to see if I can remember more.'

'Would you like me to come with you?'

Ingrid could see he wanted to, and to be honest, she wasn't too keen on going in there alone.

'Yes, I would.' She stood up from the grass and brushed the leaves off her trousers.

'Do you need to tell your mum?' Runar nodded towards the house.

Ingrid shook her head. 'No, she's sleeping. It's been an exhausting few days for her.'

'Then let's go,' Runar said.

They followed the narrow path past the huge monument. 'I remember that,' Ingrid said.

'It would be hard to forget,' Runar said, putting his hands in his pockets. 'We used to play there. Your mother took us sometimes.'

Ingrid pulled a face. 'I don't remember that. Sorry.'

They stood outside the house a few minutes later. It looked sad, and in need of a new coat of paint.

'I was happy here,' she said. 'Mamma made me happy.'

'I remember once your mother and grandmother celebrated your dad's birthday, and I came over for dinner,' Runar said. 'Only that was at the farm. You showed me the goats.'

'You made me a boat! I loved it.' Ingrid turned to him. 'I'm sorry, I don't know what happened to it.'

'That's OK.' Runar found a set of keys from his pocket. 'The house has good bones. I make sure all is in good repair. You'll find a seller in no time.'

Ingrid sighed. 'The county wants to appropriate the rest of the farm, and I think it would be silly to keep this house.'

'So you're sure you're not going to come back here?' Runar opened the door and let her inside ahead of him.

'My life is in London now,' Ingrid said. 'I was part of Mum's family from the moment I arrived, and I wouldn't know what to do with myself alone here.' She sighed. 'When Besta told me I would be going to London, I didn't want to. I was so sure Mamma would come back for me.'

'And that if you weren't here, she wouldn't find you,' Runar said softly.

Ingrid nodded, but the words choked when she tried to say something.

'Let's go inside,' Runar said.

Ingrid looked around the narrow hallway they entered. She knew there wouldn't be any furniture. About ten years earlier, her father had emptied the house so that any new tenants could put their own furniture in there.

'The lounge is on the right,' Runar said.

Ingrid laughed a little. 'I know.'

In the lounge, she pointed at the door under the stairs. 'I would hide in there. From the bad men.'

Runar smiled. 'I remember that. We hid in there together sometimes. You were hiding from the Nazis.'

'I don't remember much from the war,' Ingrid said. 'Is it strange that I would hide like that?'

He shrugged. 'I don't think so. I used to hide under my bed, although that was to hide from my father, not the Nazis.'

Ingrid looked inside the closet. It seemed so small and dark now, but she had a flash of herself sitting cross-legged and listening to voices from outside. Mamma talking to someone. Could it have been the German who lived in the house? She had no idea.

'Did you meet the man who lived here, Runar?'

Runar had come in after her. 'I don't think so. If I did, I can't recall it.'

She walked through the first floor, entering room after room. They were all empty, and the echo from her steps sounded too loud.

In the kitchen she stopped for a moment, but it was nothing more than a kitchen with appliances and some sad curtains in the window. The only other door opened to a cold basement.

'I can't even remember Mamma in here,' she said when they were back in the hallway. 'It seems strange that I don't.'

Runar was leaning his shoulder to the door frame. 'Perhaps not. A lot happened to you between then and now. You were very young.'

'I guess.' Ingrid looked at the staircase. 'I'll pop up and take a look at the bedrooms. Will you wait here?'

'I'll be here,' he said.

Ingrid headed up the stairs and opened a door to what looked like a box room. 'No, not here,' she muttered.

The second door led to the master bedroom. The only things in there were dust bunnies and dead flies on the windowsills.

'There's nothing,' she said to herself. 'There's nothing of her here.'

She hugged herself, realising that despite her better judgement, she had nursed a hope to find Mamma here, that she would be waiting for her to return. *I will always find you*, Mamma had said.

Perhaps she can't, Ingrid thought. *Perhaps I have to find her.*

Filled with a new determination, she went downstairs again. Runar smiled up at her, then frowned. 'Have you been crying?'

'That's not such a surprise, is it?' She smiled when he turned even more serious. 'I'm fine, Runar.'

'Did you find anything?'

'No, nothing but dust. Nothing to tell me anything about Mamma.'

'OK, then. I'll walk with you back to the farm,' he said.

Outside, the sun was warmer. From the top of the steps, Ingrid could see the ocean. 'It's so beautiful here.'

'Yes, you likely won't see anything like this in London,' Runar said with a wide grin.

'No, but you're never far from the ocean when you live on an island,' Ingrid said.

They started the walk back to the farm. Ingrid took a deep breath. 'I went to the police station yesterday,' she said. 'I talked to the police secretary.'

Runar stopped. 'Was he helpful?'

'In a manner of speaking. He confirmed the arrests, but he said it was because she was involved with the German who stayed here,' Ingrid said, watching him.

Runar sighed. 'I'm sorry, Ingrid. I didn't know that. I would have warned you if I did.'

Ingrid believed him. 'It's hardly your fault.'

'Did they treat you badly?' Runar took a step closer to her.

'No, he wasn't mean at all, but it was clear that he didn't like why I was there. I think he knew more than he was willing to share.' Ingrid shook her head. 'I couldn't persuade him. Not until I was ready to leave.'

Runar looked at her. 'Did he tell you what happened to her? Where she is?'

'No, not where she is now. He showed me what their ledger said. Mamma had been sent to an internment camp in Bergen in June of 1945.'

Runar looked shock. 'Internment camp? What on earth does that mean?'

'It sounded as if they had sent her to some concentration camp, but they wouldn't have done that, would they?'

Runar shook his head vigorously. 'There weren't any concentration camps in Norway after the war. I can promise you that. That's outrageous. Didn't he give you anything else to go on? Nothing at all?'

Ingrid shrugged. 'He told me to contact the Department of Justice and the State Archives. Whatever file they have on her would most likely be there.'

'Wouldn't the police in Bergen know something?' Runar seemed to be thinking hard.

Ingrid felt so much better after telling him. He understood. She wasn't sure if Esme would.

'You should contact them before you leave here,' Runar said. 'And if there were any internment camps here, they must have written about them in the newspapers.'

'You think so?' Ingrid felt the smallest of hopes flicker.

'Yes, I do. You should talk to the newspapers here too, no, wait,' he said.

'No or yes?' Ingrid had to smile.

'If you contact the newspapers, they might want to make a story on you. Is that something you would consider?'

Ingrid shook her head. 'No, not at all. At least not for now.'

'Then the best place is to see if the library has newspaper clippings that mentions things like that,' he said. 'They're really helpful over there.'

Ingrid smiled at him. 'Do you know the librarians?'

'I go there at least once a week,' Runar said.

'You read a lot?' Ingrid sighed inwardly. What a silly thing to ask, she thought.

Runar seemed unfazed. 'Yes, I do. I didn't go to middle school, but that doesn't mean I can't learn more.'

'I agree. Good for you,' Ingrid said, grinning at him.

He laughed. 'Are you making fun of me?'

'A little, but I'm not judging you,' she said. 'I always have a book under the counter in the shop for when there's no customers around.'

'Do you like the job?' They walked around the edge of the monument, getting closer to the sea.

'I love it,' Ingrid said. 'It's a lovely place and one day I'll take over from mum.'

'Tell me about it,' Runar said, leading the way down to a wooden pier with an old, rickety boathouse.

Ingrid took a deep breath. 'Oh, this is gorgeous.'

The view from the pier seemed to stretch for miles. 'To

the left is Shetland, to the right is Iceland, and straight ahead is America,' she said slowly.

Runar laughed. 'I guess that's right.'

'Mamma told me.' Ingrid looked around. 'I remember this place now. We would come down here for picnics.'

'See?' Runar touched her shoulder. 'You have good memories.'

Ingrid nodded. 'I guess I have. In time, I hope I can remember them all.'

They stood in silence for a few moments, enjoying each other's company. Ingrid had almost forgotten about Esme.

'I'm sorry, Runar, I have to return to the farm. Mum will worry if she doesn't find me.'

He looked disappointed but nodded. 'Of course.'

'Would you like to stay for breakfast? We would love the company,' she said, suddenly feeling shy about it.

Runar smiled. 'I was hoping you'd say that.'

Chapter Eighteen

Anni

Haugesund, Christmas 1944

The only sounds came from the crackling in the fireplace. Anni had put her feet up on the sofa and was enjoying the warm lounge.

She pretended to read, but her thoughts went to Herr Kerber no matter what she did. He had been sitting on the floor with Ingrid and was helping her draw trees with the crayons he had brought her. Ingrid had been giggling, and he had laughed too.

Suddenly she hadn't seen the serious and tired man; instead, she got a glimpse of the man he had been before everything happened to him.

'I shouldn't have done that,' she muttered to herself, and looked at the book again.

She managed half a page before thinking about Kerber again. Somehow, she couldn't stop herself anymore.

Kerber had told her he would have to go to Bergen to spend New Year's with his superiors. He had looked at her and said he'd rather stay here, with her. She hadn't been able to say anything.

He would return tonight. Anni took a deep breath. She wasn't looking forward to it, and it had nothing to do with the restlessness she felt. Not at all.

Anni walked over to the window and looked out. More snow. She wondered how the roads were. Slippery, most likely. *Maybe he wouldn't come*, she thought. Maybe that would be for the best.

At least the house was warm. All the extra firewood Kerber had brought kept them cosy and comfortable.

Kerber had been lovely during Christmas. Thanks to him, they'd had proper food. Ingrid had loved her sweets and her presents, and there had been laughter and smiles.

It had felt like the first proper Christmas in years.

She drew a sharp breath. And oh, how disturbing it had all been.

Especially the almost kiss.

It had happened the night before he left. Ingrid was sound asleep on her bed, and she had gone downstairs to thank him. He had smiled softly, and she felt as if she was melting. Her lounge had felt so small, all of a sudden, and she had been so aware of him standing there, looking at her. He seemed relaxed, happy, even, and Anni had forgotten to be on her guard.

Kerber had thanked her, then he touched her cheek, and Anni couldn't move. But then he leant closer, and she knew he wanted to kiss her; *she* had wanted him to kiss her so badly she could almost taste him. And at the last second, she came to her senses. She stepped back and ran upstairs, not looking back at him.

He must think I'm an idiot, she thought.

I never thought for a second that I would almost kiss a man because of the food he brought, Anni scolded herself, trying to fool even herself about the rising attraction she felt for the man. *I'm worse than the German sluts hanging on some soldier's arm with no shame.*

She found it hard to accept she had been so close to him and, in a moment of weakness, had almost broken her vows.

'I'm Lars's wife,' she muttered. *And soon, maybe even this year, the war will be over, and Kerber will be gone for good. And . . . and Lars will come home, and life will be as if the war never happened.*

Anni stared at the Christmas tree. She knew she should take down all the decorations, and use the tree for firewood, but she didn't have the heart to do it yet.

She wrapped the knitted rug around herself and felt warm and contented. Soon, she fell asleep on the sofa.

When someone hammered on the door, she almost fell on the floor. Confused, she hesitated to answer it. Could it be soldiers? Perhaps Kerber had decided to show his true self and had sent them to arrest her.

She realised Ingrid would wake up if she didn't put a stop to it. She pulled the rug tighter around her shoulders and hurried out of the lounge.

When she came out in the hallway, she closed the door behind her, and put on her coat. She knew it would be freezing out there.

She opened the door and the cold wind woke her up.

There wasn't anyone on the doorstep. There were no signs of the dreaded soldiers.

What the hell is going on? she thought.

Anni looked around again and caught sight of Martin in the shadows.

'What are you doing here?' she said, walking over to him. 'What if Kerber had been in the house?'

Martin shook his head. 'I know he's not, Anni. He's gone to Bergen. They said so at Hagland.'

Anni shook her head too. 'You have to be quick, Martin. He's coming back tonight, and he could be here any moment.'

Martin looked concerned. 'This couldn't wait,' he said.

'What's the emergency?' Anni sighed. 'It's Guri, isn't it? She did something foolish. Is she OK? Should I go to the farm?'

'No, no, nothing is wrong with Guri. This is something else,' he said, looking more and more uncomfortable. 'I have a letter for you. I thought you would want it as soon as possible.' Martin didn't meet her eyes. Something was off.

Anni felt a sharp pain in her stomach. 'It's Lars, isn't it? Is he dead? Did a torpedo sink his ship?'

'No, as far as I know, he's fine, but I'm sorry.' Martin looked took a deep breath. 'I'm so sorry.'

'Stop saying that.' Anni touched his arm. 'What's going on? Is Lars sick, is that it?'

Martin handed her a thin envelope. 'Read the letter, Anni. Please.'

Anni looked at the envelope, scared to open it. It had been such a long time since they had last heard from Lars. She didn't want to read it. Judging from Martin's face, it was bad news. If Lars wasn't sick or dead, then what?

'Did you read it?' Anni's mind was racing with horrible scenarios.

'No.' Martin looked horrified at the thought. 'I would never do that.'

'But you know what it's about? Because why else would you apologise to me?'

Martin nodded. 'You're right. I do know.'

Anni opened the letter. She could see from the date that it was written over a year ago. 'Damn,' she said. 'This isn't a response to my letter. He hasn't received the photos of Ingrid.'

'I don't know how this letter found its way to Shetland. You know how it is,' Martin said.

Anni nodded, not looking up from the letter. Lars's handwriting was so familiar, it made her want to cry. *Guri will be delighted when she sees this. We've waited so long to hear from Lars*, she thought but then she started reading properly.

> *Dear Anni,*
> *I hope this letter finds you well.*

The rest of the letter made no sense.

She had to read it several times to understand what it said. Her heart crumbled. That's what it felt like. As if somehow her whole body crumbled to pieces, like a light bulb that broke when it hit the floor, and yet she was still standing.

The icy wind didn't even faze her anymore. She felt numb.

Martin took a step forward and grabbed her arm when she started shaking. 'I'm sorry, Anni.'

He kept saying it as if it somehow would make it better.

Anni tried to breathe. It was all too much. 'It must be a mistake,' she whispered. 'A terrible, awful mistake.'

'No, it's not.' Martin had that look of sympathy on his face, reserved for a grieving widow.

'How do you know that? You said you haven't read the letter,' Anni said. She could hear her voice breaking, and pressed her lips together.

'The letter was handed to me by someone who knows him. He told me what Lars has done. I have no reason to doubt him.'

'No,' Anni said. 'No. Lars wouldn't do . . . this to us.'

I can't even say this out loud, she thought. *I can't tell him that right now, I'd rather have news that Lars died. That's how horrible this is.*

'How is it even possible?' she said, pulling herself together. 'I don't understand.'

'I don't know either. Apparently, the London-government changed the Marriage Act's paragraphs about divorce, making it easier for people outside of Norway to divorce their spouse and marry again.'

'The government legalised bigamy?' Anni could feel the rage building up. 'What kind of bullshit is that?' She was shaking the letter in his face. 'What am I going to do now?'

Martin looked crestfallen. 'Anni, I can only tell you what I was told. It's all to do with the war. The law used to say that if a couple has been separated for three years, one of them could apply for a divorce. The other spouse would then have to be informed and would have their say, then the courts would decide. During the war if someone wanted a divorce, they could apply to the exile governments Department of Justice in London, and they didn't have to inform or ask the spouse back home.'

'How can the exile government do that? Why wasn't I told? Lars says he married this . . . this woman in 1943! All this time I've been waiting for him. I've been faithful to him. All this time, I have been divorced without even knowing about it. And what about Ingrid? What on earth am I supposed to tell her?'

'You'll get no argument from me. This is despicable. I can't understand what would make the government do something like this,' Martin said. 'Or how Lars could do it.'

'To hell with them all, then. This will not stand when the war is over. It cannot stand.' Anni shook her head.

Martin looked worried. 'I'm sorry.'

'Please stop saying you're sorry, Martin. It's not helping at all.' Anni pulled herself together. Whatever Lars had done, it wasn't on Martin. 'Thank you for bringing it to me. I never expected to hear anything from him until . . . until all this was over. Now I probably never will.'

She was choking on the words, and swallowed hard. 'What if I had dragged Ingrid with me to town to meet her father when this wretched war is over, and he arrived with his shiny new wife on his arm? How can I possibly explain something like this to her?' She shook her head. 'And how in holy hell am I going to tell this to Guri?'

'Maybe it's better for you both to know,' Martin said gently.

Anni frowned. 'I'm not so sure about that,' she said, and suddenly realised she was freezing. 'You should leave. I don't want Kerber to find us frozen to death outside my door.'

He hid a smile. 'Yes, of course. We'll talk soon.'

He turned to leave, but Anni stopped him. 'Martin,

please don't tell any of this to Guri. I will tell her myself. Or to anyone else for that matter, not even Nina.'

Martin nodded. 'Of course not. You can trust me.'

He turned around again and disappeared into the shadows.

Anni ran inside the house and closed the door behind her. Her fingers felt frozen to the bone. She huddled in front of the fireplace and looked at the letter again. Perhaps the best thing would be to burn it. Pretend it never existed.

Maybe that would make it feel as if it had been a nightmare. Something she could wake up from and know wasn't real.

She held the paper in her hands, then read it again and almost gagged. But she couldn't make herself burn it. It would still be Lars's words and actions. She could never ignore that.

I wonder what Guri will make of this, she thought. *Will she disown him? Or me?* She didn't believe the last one. Guri loved Ingrid too much to cut them out of her life. Especially not after Lars's betrayal.

She threw a glance at the wedding photo on the shelf and couldn't help wondering if it was her fault. *If I had taken Ingrid and Guri to Shetland, then we would have been fine*, she thought.

Anni looked at the letter again.

No, she thought. *This is not my fault. I haven't been a bad wife; I've done everything I possibly can to keep his child and his mother safe. I've been faithful to him. I've made sure Ingrid loves him, despite not remembering him. And this damn war isn't my damn fault.*

But still. It felt as if it was her fault.

258

She sat quietly for a moment, attempting to sort her thoughts and feelings.

'Oh, God,' Anni muttered. The truth was, she felt ashamed because her first reaction hadn't been anger. It had been shock first, then a moment of relief, before finally anger.

'I'm as bad as Lars is,' she said.

Anni stood up from the floor to avoid the temptation of shoving the letter into the fire. Instead, she shoved it deep into a drawer.

She curled up on the sofa with the rug around her. She knew she wouldn't be able to sleep, and she couldn't lie next to Ingrid while tossing and turning. She was furious.

How dare he? How dare he get married to someone else, then write a damn letter to tell me? And how could it even be legal?

She was sure the British authorities didn't take bigamy lightly, even if the Norwegian exile government decided it was legitimate.

'Bastard,' she muttered. 'Coward! Telling me something like this in a letter. He didn't even have the guts to tell me to my face. And now he has left the whole sorry mess to me – it will be me who has to tell Guri and Ingrid.'

She felt sick.

Anni swore under her breath, then burst into tears. She cried until she felt exhausted and stupid, then threw off the rug and went into the kitchen, splashing cold water on her face.

The window was blacked out, so she couldn't see anything. Not that it mattered, since there would be no lights to see anyway.

'Frau Odland?' His voice was so soft, and yet it startled her.

She grabbed a tea towel before turning, brushing it over her face.

Kerber looked concerned. 'I didn't expect you to be up,' he said.

'Umm, I couldn't sleep,' Anni said, forcing herself to smile. 'You're late coming back. I didn't hear the car.'

He nodded. 'There are all sorts of things happening at the moment. A lot of troop movements, soldiers heading home to Germany, a lot to keep on top of.'

'Really? That must be taxing.' Anni was sure that Martin would find that interesting, but tonight she couldn't care one hoot about what anyone else wanted.

Her mind raced. She didn't want him to disappear into his room. 'Would you like some coffee?'

Kerber took a step closer. 'Are you all right? You look as if you have cried.'

Anni put away the towel, trying to compose herself. She didn't feel foolish; she had every reason to cry. Didn't mean she wanted him to know about it.

'I've had some upsetting news,' she finally said, and forced herself to smile at him. 'I'll be fine in the morning.'

Kerber came closer. 'Are you sure?'

Feeling exposed, Anni huddled herself. 'I'm used to bad news, Herr Kerber. There has been nothing but bad news for five years. I'll manage.'

He gently put his hand on her shoulder. 'But how often do you cry from them?'

Anni trembled and it wasn't because she was cold. *It would be so easy to seek comfort from him*, she thought. So easy. He was here, looking at her with such compassion, such warmth, she almost started crying again.

All this time I've held back, was her next thought. *All this time, I've been faithful to Lars when I didn't have to be. The dutiful wife who would never even look at another man.* But the letter had changed everything. Lars had changed everything. *I'm not married any more.*

She leant into him, and Kerber pulled her close.

The kiss was everything she had imagined and then some, and for the moment, she forgot every thought about Lars's betrayal.

Later, much later, Anni felt the warmth of Kerber's body against hers, and all she could think of was why she had resisted so long. *All that time wasted*, she thought.

She looked at him. His hair was ruffled and that guarded look she had noticed the first day was gone. 'It's odd to call you Hugo,' she said.

'Anni,' he whispered, and stroked her face with his fingers. 'You have no idea.'

Anni smiled. 'I guess I surprised you,' she said.

'In the best way. You seemed so upset. I hope I didn't take advantage of you,' he said.

Anni burst out laughing. 'I think I'm the one who took advantage of you.'

'I don't mind.' He let his finger run along her face. 'You've been in my thoughts since the first day we met. I knew you didn't want me in your house, but I had no choice. I was afraid you would think I was a monster.'

'I didn't.' Anni smiled. 'But I was terrified, I'll admit to that.'

He shifted his position on the narrow bed. 'I'm sorry about that. I never meant to scare you.'

'I didn't know you then,' she said. 'All I saw was another enemy. You didn't have the uniform, but you were still coming into my house, taking what you wanted.'

His face darkened. 'Yes, I understood that. I hated that.'

'I think you can safely think that I don't anymore,' Anni said.

After a few minutes, he spoke so softly she could hardly hear him. 'Would you like to tell me what happened to make you so upset? Something must have happened today.'

Anni shook her head. 'No, I'd rather not. It's too soon to tell anyone. I decided to act on my . . . impulses, that's all.'

'You certainly did,' he said, smiling at her.

'It was probably inevitable, I think.' Anni had so many questions for him, but she wasn't sure how to ask. Or even if she wanted to ask. Maybe all she could do was to enjoy the moment and forget about the war and the letter.

She closed her eyes. *I'm in bed with a man, an attractive man, and now I don't have to feel guilty or be ashamed about how I feel about him.*

Hugo tilted her face up. 'I'm happy you acted on your impulse. And you need to know, anything you tell me stays between us. Do you understand?'

Anni blinked away tears. 'Thank you,' she whispered.

He kissed the top of her head, and it made her smile.

There were things she wouldn't tell him. No matter how lovely he was, she couldn't put the others in danger.

For now, all she wanted to do was enjoy him.

Finally, the enemy was good for something.

Chapter Nineteen

Anni

Haugesund, March 1945

When March arrived, the weather finally turned. The last of the snow melted and left slush and ice. But there was a warmth in the wind and the days slowly became longer, spring was coming. The black car had come to pick up Hugo a few minutes earlier, and Anni sat by the kitchen table enjoying her coffee. The weeks since Lars's letter arrived had given her time to calm down, although thinking about it left the bitter taste of bile in her mouth. She couldn't do anything about Lars until the war ended, but Guri didn't know yet, and neither did Ingrid.

Ingrid was sitting under the table, singing to her doll, blissfully ignorant there would be no happy ending for her parents whenever the war was over, no big reunion with her pappa.

There was not going to be a right time for this, and she

still had time. Guri would learn soon enough what Lars had done when the war ended. Ingrid didn't need to know either. Maybe she would try to explain it to her when she was older. That should give her enough time to come up with a good story.

'Not bloody likely,' she muttered and rubbed her eyes.

Since the beginning of the war, when she realised Lars wouldn't come home any time soon, she had pictured herself waiting for the ship that would bring Lars back, standing there with all the other families hoping to see their wayward son, father or husband. Ingrid would have been in her finest dress, bow in her hair, waving a flag, and Guri would be all spruced up. Probably with a hat and dress.

Anni knew she would have been wearing a new dress, hair done properly for the first time since the war started, and they would wave and call his name when he ran down the gangplank.

It would have been awkward at first. After living apart for so long, this was to be expected. He would have to get used to the chubby toddler he had kissed goodbye being a scrawny little girl.

But eventually they'd find their way back to each other again, and life would be normal. Perhaps they would have had more children. Lars might've been away at sea for long periods, but they would be safe with the knowledge that he would always come back.

Anni snorted.

All the while he had been happy with someone else. More than cheating on her with another woman, he had married her. The idea that she had been divorced for years still made her sick. The fact that her own government had decided this despicable *thing* to help sad, lonely sailors marry their girlfriends made her even more sick. What were they thinking?

She knew the old saying that sailors had a girl in every port, but that's no excuse to cheat on your wife, marry some trollop and not even try to let your wife know you're divorcing her. *Coward*, she thought. *I will never forgive him this.*

Until the war was over, nobody would know how many other wives and children would experience this. It could be so many.

'Imagine standing there on the harbour, and he'd come waltzing down with *her*, that trollop, on his arm?' she muttered to herself.

It was exhausting trying to make sense of what had happened. In one night, she had lost a husband and her life, and gained a lover.

With the end of the war getting closer every day, the last thing she had imagined was sleeping with an enemy. It wasn't what she had thought peace would be like.

But Anni was happy. She refused to consider how other people would view what she had with Hugo. She didn't want to call it a relationship. There were too many obstacles for them to have any kind of future. For now, she settled for being happy.

She was so immersed in her thoughts, she didn't notice Guri bursting through the door until she heard it slam behind her.

Ingrid crawled out from under the table. 'Besta!'

One look at her mother-in-law's ashen face was enough to tell her something was wrong. The last time she had seen her this distressed was when the Germans arrived in 1940.

'Ingrid, why don't you go upstairs and get dressed? Besta will still be here when you come down again,' she said, keeping her voice calm and reassuring.

Ingrid hugged Guri before running out.

Anni looked at Guri. 'What happened?'

Guri sank down on Ingrid's chair. 'It's Martin,' she said in a low whisper, and leant forward, hiding her face in her hands. 'I can't breathe.'

Anni sat down in front of her. 'Take a deep breath and count to five,' she said.

Guri did what she said, then looked at Anni with an exasperated expression in her eyes. 'How is this helpful?'

'It's supposed to help you focus on something else,' Anni said. 'It certainly works with children.'

'Not with grandmothers. Now I'm nauseous and terrified.' Guri pressed a hand against her stomach.

'How about a glass of water?' Anni didn't know how to deal with Guri falling apart. She was always in such control of herself, so calm in any storm. To see her like this was unsettling.

Guri nodded. 'Yes. Thank you.'

Anni filled a glass with water and put it on the table in front of Guri. 'What's this about Martin?'

Guri folded her hands around the glass. 'They've arrested him,' she said in the same strained voice.

Anni stared at her. 'Arrested? No, it can't be.'

'Yes.' Guri almost choked on the water, drinking too fast.

'How do you know? Who told you?'

Guri seemed to breathe easier now. 'I was in town, and everyone was talking about it.'

'What about Nina? Is she safe?'

Guri nodded. 'For now, yes. But I'm worried about you. If they know about Martin, then it's you and me next. You know that.'

Anni stared at her. 'Why would they do that? Martin would never snitch on any of us.'

'He might snitch on me because I'm expendable,' Guri said, looking at her with clear eyes now.

'What the hell does that mean?' Anni could hear her voice shaking.

'It means that if, or rather when, Martin is tortured by the Gestapo, he'll give them my name as a last resort. Not you, not Nina, not anyone else. I'm the oldest, and the Germans won't treat me as harshly. Anyway, that's the idea. We talked about it at length, Martin and I, before we started this malarky.'

Anni turned around for a second to collect herself. Then she looked back at her. 'You're insane. Why haven't you told me this before?'

'You wouldn't have approved.' Guri knitted her hands in her lap. 'The most important thing for us has always been to keep Ingrid safe. You know that. For Martin that's Nina.'

'I can't believe what I'm hearing.' Anni folded her arms across her chest. 'You've gone completely off the rafters now.'

Guri finally smiled. 'Listen, they might not come. Martin is a clever man. He knows what he's doing, and he won't break easily. You know that too.'

Anni nodded. 'Yes, I do, but we can't be sure, can we?'

Guri shuddered. 'I suppose not.'

From upstairs came the sounds of Ingrid running around. *She wasn't exactly light-footed*, Anni thought. 'You have to leave the farm, Guri. At least until we know what's going on.'

'I can't stay away indefinitely. There are my goats to look after and my garden.' Guri sent her a defiant look.

Anni didn't budge. 'You know the Occupation can't last much longer. Maybe a few weeks, a few months at the most.'

At least that's what Hugo had said.

Guri shook her head. 'They'll think I'm guilty. They will go after you if I run. We can't risk it.'

Anni thought about it. 'Then we'll have to pretend nothing happened. Perhaps you, as the advanced old lady that you claim to be, can pretend to be soft in the head if they come for you.'

'Soft in my head?' Guri raised her eyebrows. 'How old do you think I am?'

Anni couldn't help smiling. 'I know how old you are. I didn't say you're soft, I said you should pretend to be. You can do that, right?'

Guri ignored the question. 'Do you have any of the bastard's coffee left?'

'Yes, of course. It's mixed with the sugarbeet substitute you gave me,' Anni said, and went to the stove to fetch a cup for her.

'Sugarbeets are hard to come by. I hope you don't waste it on that man,' Guri said.

Anni wondered how she would have reacted had she known she was spending every night with Hugo. 'I'm sure he only drinks proper coffee at Hagland,' she said, keeping her voice calm.

Guri snorted. 'Bastards,' she muttered when Anni put the cup in front of her. It didn't stop her from enjoying the coffee, though.

'Then we agree? Do nothing and hope they pass us by?' Anni said.

Guri nodded. 'I don't see what else we can do.'

Anni wondered if she could ask Hugo for help but dismissed the thought immediately. She might sleep with him and enjoy it, but that didn't mean she trusted him entirely. Not with other people's lives at risk.

'I agree. Do you want us to stay with you for a few days? Until this blows over or the war ends, whichever comes first,' Anni said.

'God, no. If the bastards come for me, I don't want you anywhere near them.' Guri shuddered at the thought.

'You could stay here. We can put the goats in one of the sheds or in the cellar, and with Herr Kerber in the house, I don't think they'll come looking for you here,' Anni said.

'Or perhaps that's what that man wants us to think.' Guri shook her head several times. 'No, absolutely not. If they come for me, I'll handle it.'

Anni didn't argue with her anymore. It was no use, and it wasn't as if she was wrong.

'Right. Then we wait.'

Guri took another sip of the coffee. 'I hate waiting.'

As long as nothing bad happens, I'm happy to wait, Anni thought.

Any more conversation was interrupted by Ingrid rambling into the kitchen.

She climbed up on Guri's lap and leant against her. 'Besta, I missed you.'

'You saw me two days ago,' Guri said, clearly pleased with the statement.

Anni watched them. Ingrid chatted, thrilled to have Besta in the house. Guri seemed to forget her worries, and relaxed when Ingrid told her about what had happen the last two days. There were a lot of details.

'Runar says the war will be over soon. Do you think so, Besta?'

'I hope so,' Guri said.

'And then Pappa will come home?' Ingrid held her hands on her grandmother's.

Guri kissed Ingrid on the top of her head. 'I'm sure he will. I'm sure he misses you and your mamma so much.'

Not bloody likely, Anni thought. She sipped her coffee, and her mind wandered to Hugo again. It was hard to believe she had been in his bed only a few hours earlier.

Anni spent the rest of the day trying to calm Guri. She'd jump every time they heard a sound from outside the house. Anni kept having images of the three of them taken away by soldiers.

There was a Gestapo house in Haugesund, and if half the rumours about what was going on in there were true, Martin was in serious trouble, and so were they.

She put a hand on her heart, trying to calm herself down. *Perhaps we should go somewhere, perhaps to Shetland or up in the mountains*, she thought. *The three of us and Nina, including the goats. Guri would never leave without them.*

'You take one like that, and then the other across,' Guri said, showing Ingrid how to hold the knitting needles.

The little girl had her tongue in the corner of her mouth

and was totally focused on what she was doing. 'Besta, like this?'

Guri gently guided her fingers. 'Exactly like that. Look how clever you are.'

Anni leant back in the chair. It could have been a perfect day apart from everything. She longed to see Hugo, and she also feared it. She worried about Guri, but mostly she worried about what would happen to Ingrid if they were both arrested.

It was time to make provisions for Ingrid. Someone to take care of her if the absolute worst happened. She had taken it for granted that they would be fine for far too long.

She realised that Guri was watching and smiled at her. 'Can I bring you anything?'

'No, I think I've had enough coffee.' Guri smiled. 'I might be awake for a week now.'

'It's almost like before,' Anni said, with a sigh.

Guri patted her knee. 'It soon will be. We only have to stay strong until it's over.'

Anni sighed again. 'When? This year, this summer, another Christmas?'

'Nobody knows when, Anni. But we do know that they are on the run in France and Germany, and that the Russians are chasing Nazis in Finnmark, and we have hope now, more than in a long time.' Guri was serious now. 'Don't lose that.'

Anni thought about Hugo. What would happen to him when the war ended? She hadn't given that a thought before either. It was a whole new dilemma.

The resistance was preparing for peace, she knew that. Martin and she had helped bring in heavy crates with guns, grenades, ammunition, handheld radios and who knew what else from fishing boats, handing them over to men she didn't know, for when the war ended.

She remembered when Martin had first suggested that they should start their small resistance group and it had seemed like the most foolish idea. How on earth could they believe that they could fight back against the Germans?

But as the Occupation forces took over the country, and it became more and more difficult to live, to pretend they weren't there, their little group did good things. She had lost count of how many people they have helped over to Shetland. They had done well. They kept a low profile. But still.

Anni didn't like the odds.

There were thousands of German soldiers all over the country. Hundreds of thousands. At least four to five thousand just in Haugesund, and they had access to plenty more powerful weapons than any resistance groups would have. No tanks would fit in a fishing boat.

She looked at Ingrid, still busy with her first knitting project.

'You look scared.' Guri watched her. 'I don't want you to worry about me.'

'Of course I worry,' Anni said. 'I'm only hoping it will be over before they get to us.'

Ingrid piped up. 'Can I sleep at Besta's tonight?'

Guri shook her head before Anni had a chance to say something.

'Not today, little one,' she said. 'Next week, maybe.'

Ingrid wanted to protest, but Anni stopped her. 'Besta decides, sweet pea.'

She wouldn't have minded Guri taking Ingrid for the night, but considering the farm might suddenly swarm with soldiers, the decision was easy.

Guri stood up. 'It's time to go home,' she said.

Anni followed her out. 'Are you sure you wouldn't rather stay here? I'd feel a lot better if you did.'

She looked at her mother-in-law with a sudden feeling of dread.

Guri smiled sweetly. 'I have to look after the animals.'

Anni put her hand on her arm. 'No, please, Guri. I have a bad feeling. Get on your bike and leave now. Stay with some of your friends in the hinterland. I'll get a message to you when it's safe.'

Guri sighed. 'How will you explain that I'm gone?'

Anni frowned. 'Everyone knows you're gone from time to time. There's nothing unusual in that.'

'I want to stay at home, Anni.' Guri had a determined expression on her face.

Anni couldn't let it go. 'Please, Guri.'

'I'm not going to hide,' Guri said.

'Could you stop being so damn stubborn?' Anni's voice rose, and Ingrid slid down from the sofa.

'It's fine, sweet pea,' Anni said. 'Go in the kitchen, please.'

Ingrid looked worried but did what she was told.

Anni folded her arms across her chest. 'I mean it, Guri. That's the smart thing to do. Please be smart.'

'You're serious?' Guri said.

'I don't even think you should go home. I have a packed rucksack in the closet with everything you'll need,' Anni said.

'You have?' Guri looked surprised.

'Of course I have. I'll take out the stuff for Ingrid, and you take the rest.' Anni turned around to get what she needed.

Guri followed. 'I can't believe you're so ready to run.'

'You mean you're not?' Anni opened the door to the closet and found the rucksack. 'Here, hold this, while I get some food for you. And don't worry, I'll raid your house tomorrow when I go to see to the goats.'

'I guess I don't have any choice, then,' Guri said with a faint smile.

Anni nodded. 'You don't. Ingrid and I, we need you to be safe and to come home again.'

While Guri put on her overcoat, Anni went into the kitchen, where Ingrid was sitting on a chair, looking miserable.

'No need to look so sad, sweet pea,' Anni said, kissing her on the top of her head. 'Go and say good night to Besta.'

Ingrid jumped down and ran into the lounge. 'Besta!'

Anni put the rucksack on the counter and took out everything Guri wouldn't need. Then she switched Ingrid's clothes and toys for food, including most of the coffee.

When she came out, Ingrid was hugging her grandmother and whispering to her.

'Here.' Anni handed Guri the rucksack and then pulled Ingrid gently towards her. 'You be safe now.'

Guri nodded. 'You too.'

Anni lifted up Ingrid. 'Besta will come back soon. She's going on one of her trips.'

Ingrid held out her teddy bear. 'You can have it, Besta.'

Guri smiled. 'For me? I'm too old for teddy bears, little one.'

Ingrid shook her head. 'No, he'll keep you safe, Besta.'

'You'd better take it, Guri. I think she means it,' Anni said.

Guri relented. 'I will keep him safe.'

Ingrid kissed the bear and handed it over to Guri. 'Bye, Besta.'

Anni leant over and hugged Guri. Ingrid did the same.

'Oh, my,' Guri said, smiling at them both. 'I will see you soon.'

Anni waited until Guri disappeared in the dark. Then she closed the door and looked at Ingrid. 'Why don't you show me your knitting?'

Ingrid looked dejected. 'Why did Besta have to leave now?'

Little ears, Anni thought. 'She went to see a friend who is sick,' she said.

Ingrid seemed to accept that. She picked up the little knitting project and tried to do what Guri had shown her. Anni kept an eye on her. She could see her brain working.

'Are the bad soldiers coming?' Ingrid didn't look up.

'No, they're not. You don't have to worry about that,' Anni said, keeping her voice soft.

'Promise?'

'I promise, sweet pea. Nothing will happen. Not to Besta and not to us.' Anni held out her hand. 'Let me see how you're doing.'

Ingrid climbed into her lap and leant her head against her shoulder. 'It's not a scarf,' she said.

'No, you need more wool for that. What do you want it to be?'

Anni held it up and gave it a little wave. Ingrid giggled.

'It's nothing,' she said.

'That's perfect. I've needed a nothing for a long time,' Anni said.

Ingrid giggled again. 'But what can you do with a nothing?'

Anni pretended to think. 'Hmm. Let me see. I can put it in my hair, or on the Christmas tree next year. Or I can use it as an earring. There are so many things you can use a nothing for.'

Ingrid had forgotten what she was afraid of, and Anni could relax.

But she kept looking at the clock. Would Hugo come early? She hoped not. She wanted Ingrid tucked safely in bed before he came home.

Came back, she corrected herself. This wasn't his home.

She hugged Ingrid closer, suddenly realising she felt unsafe without Guri nearby.

She knew she had to do her best to keep them all safe. *Starting with checking up on Nina*, she thought. The poor girl had to be terrified for Martin.

Chapter Twenty

Next morning, Anni hauled Ingrid to town and headed for the barter store.

Nina was standing in a corner, folding baby clothes. She didn't look up until Anni stood in front of her.

Her eyes were huge and she looked as if she hadn't slept in days. 'Hi, Anni,' she said.

'Oh, sweetie,' Anni said. 'I'm so sorry.'

Nina tried to smile, but it was clear she was struggling to hold back tears.

'Can we go outside? I need to talk to you,' Anni said.

It didn't seem like anyone was interested in them, and Nina followed her outside.

'Guri told me what happened. Do you know where Martin is?'

'All I know is that they have taken him to Bergen.' Nina's

voice broke. 'He was arrested with a friend from work; they were both in the harbour at the time. I'm so scared, Anni.'

Anni put her arms around her and let her cry on her shoulder. 'You're so brave.'

Nina sniffled a few times. 'Not even close,' she finally said, forcing a smile.

'Yes, you are, and Martin is so proud of you.' Anni looked around. The street was busy, but nobody seemed to pay them any attention. She couldn't see any soldiers. 'Are you safe? Are you sure you should be here in the store?'

'I'm staying with a friend and her family. They're good Norwegians, so I'm safe. Pappa didn't want me to stay in our flat in case something like this happened.'

Anni held her arm. 'Guri has left for the hinterland. Perhaps you should too.'

'No, we planned for this, Pappa and me. I know what I'm supposed to do,' Nina said.

When Anni tried to interrupt her, Nina shook her head. 'No, you don't have to worry about me. Pappa made up a ruse to fool the Gestapo. His friend was in on it too. They had agreed that if they were ever arrested, they would confess to buying smuggled goods from a man from outside of town. A man they only knew by first name.'

'And you think that will work?' Anni was doubtful. 'Listen, the Germans aren't stupid.'

Nina nodded, eager now. 'I know that, and so does Pappa. He said that they would repeat this story over and over again, and that sooner or later, the Gestapo would believe them. And I think it has worked. Otherwise they would have come for all of us by now.'

Anni considered it. 'I hope you're right. I really, really do.'

'I don't take any chances, that's for sure. After today, I'll stay away from the barter shop too.' She looked at Anni. 'What about you? Are you staying at home with Ingrid?'

'Yes, I am. I think that I'm safe with my lodger in the house. He would have had me arrested a long time ago if he had any suspicions,' Anni said.

That wasn't strictly true. After the warning he had given her when she had come back from sending Jonas and his parents away, she knew he was aware that something was going on. Although neither of them had said it out loud.

'Are you sure?' Nina put a hand on her arm.

'As sure as I can be, I suppose,' Anni said.

Nina bit her lip. 'What about the farm now that Guri isn't there?'

'We'll check on the goats every day. You know how they are. Left on their own, they would probably eat at the house,' she said.

'Yes, that's goats for you.' Nina folded her arms. 'Please tell me if there's anything I can do. Or if you want me to come and look after Ingrid. Anything.'

Anni smiled. 'Thank you, Nina. We'll be fine. I would have asked you to stay with us, but with that man in the house, I'm not sure it would be wise.'

Nina shuddered. 'God no, I couldn't stay that near any of them. I'd be afraid to be attacked in my sleep.' She grinned. 'Or that I would attack him.'

'I know how you feel,' Anni said, sounding a lot lighter than she felt. 'Anyway, Guri knows how to take care of herself.'

'She'll never let them get her,' Nina said.

Anni nodded. 'I hope so. I don't know what to do with myself without Guri.'

Ingrid was jumping from foot to foot. 'My boots are lovely, Nina,' she said.

'I can see that. They sure look good,' Nina said.

'Thank you.' Ingrid looked like a little angel, showing off her lovely boots.

'You're welcome.' Nina looked at Anni again. 'I'll come by if I find out something.'

'So will I. Thank you.' Anni gave her a quick hug. 'Be careful.'

Nina nodded. 'I will.'

Anni took Ingrid's hand. 'We'll see you soon, then.'

Nina turned back as she walked into the shop. She did a little wave, and Ingrid waved back.

Afterwards she looked up at Anni. 'I like Nina,' she said.

'Yes, we all do. Nina is a lovely girl.'

Anni felt better on the bus ride home. She had needed to see with her own eyes that Nina was safe.

Anni curled up against Hugo, enjoying his warmth and his breath on her face. She looked at him. He was on his back, with his eyes closed and a smile on his lips. He sensed that she was watching him and opened his eyes, his smile widening. 'Are you looking at me?'

'Yes, I am.' Anni leant on her elbow. 'Why did you move in with us?'

She wanted to know why he had picked her house.

'It was part of the orders I received when I arrived here,' Hugo said. 'They think someone in the area is helping the resistance.'

'The resistance?' Anni's heart sank. Exactly what they had thought from the start. He was there to spy on them. Her thoughts raced, and she fought back a moment of panic. 'Honestly, that's hardly likely.'

Hugo didn't seem to notice. 'They know fishing boats are used for smuggling all sorts of things,' he said calmly. 'Both in and out of the country. Black market goods, resistance people, guns. All things that are illegal.'

Anni frowned. 'Sure, but why would they think it happens here? I mean, we're so close to the soldiers at Hagland and Gard, and the town is a couple of kilometres from here. It would be far too risky, surely.'

Hugo held a hand on her arm, stroking her skin with his fingertips. 'It's going on all over the country, you know that as well as I do. With a coastline like yours, it's impossible for the Kriegsmarine to control everything.'

She couldn't tell him anything real, she knew that. 'I haven't seen anything to worry about. There's no one like that around here. I mean, there's bound to be smugglers, but they are people who would risk anything for profit.'

Hugo nodded. 'I'm sure. It doesn't matter if someone is caught with a package of British cigarettes, or a boatful of people or weapons. The punishment is equally severe in either case.'

'That's not very cheerful, now, is it?' she said, trying to keep a lighter tone.

'No, it's not. You need to understand something, Anni.' Hugo put his face close to hers. 'The authorities, *my* authorities, are finally realising that the war is lost. Not all of them are accepting the facts, but a lot of us are. In a matter of months, maybe even weeks, the Third Reich will collapse, and that scares them. All that power they have accumulated will disappear. And when people like that get scared, they also get extremely dangerous.'

'What will they do?' Anni said, knowing he told the truth.

'I don't know yet. Right now, at Hagland and everywhere else, there's all sorts of rumours and speculations, but the fact is that the Allied forces have breached the borders of Germany. Every day the Russians are coming closer to Berlin and they have a lot to avenge. And do you know where Herr Hitler is?' He whispered the name as if he was scared to say it out loud.

Anni frowned. 'Right now, you mean? In Berlin, I'm guessing.'

'He is hiding in an underground bunker, right below the Reichstag building. Like the coward he is,' he said, with a bitterness that surprised her. 'He's surrounded by his inner circle and his SS guards and waiting for something to happen to save his thousand-year Reich. It won't happen, though.'

Anni realised he knew more than she could hope for. 'Do you think the Russians can get to him there?'

'I don't know, but I hope so. I think the more loyal and fanatic of our leaders will do his bidding until the last moment. That might come sooner if the Russians grab him.'

'Do you have any idea what will happen here? To us?' Anni bit her lip. 'There are so many soldiers in Norway.'

He stroked his fingers over her chin. 'No, *mein Liebling*, I don't know, but I'm doing my best to find out.'

'They must be disappointed with me, then, the people who sent you to me,' Anni said in a voice she could hear was a bit too thin.

'What do you mean?' Hugo smiled at her.

'I mean, I haven't done anything worth reporting,' Anni said. 'I live a quiet life. All I want is to get my little girl safely through this war.'

'And that's what I want too,' he said. 'They sent me to watch this area, not only you. I haven't told them anything,' he said, kissing the top of her head. 'Unfortunately, there might be others doing the same that I don't know about.'

Anni turned to look at him. 'You don't know? Aren't you one of them?'

Hugo didn't smile any more. 'I'm not military, Anni. If the *Sicherheitspolizei* or the Gestapo have an operation out here, as a civilian I more than likely wouldn't be told.'

Anni had to think about that. 'Oh,' she said. That was a surprise.

'Remember when I first moved in here? And you went to your mother-in-law for the night?' He asked the question with some hesitation.

Anni couldn't hide her surprise. 'Did you know there was a patrol when you met me at the monument?'

'I knew they were in the area but I wasn't informed in advance,' he said.

Anni's thoughts went to Guri, who could be anywhere, and here *she* was, in the arms of one of the men now holding Martin. She had to ask him, to test him.

'What do you know about the people they arrest here?' she asked. 'What happens to them?'

Hugo looked at her. 'Most likely they are sent to Bergen for further interrogation. After that, most are sent to the detention camp at Grini, and then shipped off to Germany. I think you know what happens next.'

'They end up in concentration camps,' Anni said, her voice lagging in her throat.

'Yes, and when they get there, anything can happen to them.' Hugo heaved a deep sigh. 'I'm sorry. Do you know anyone who has been arrested?'

Anni thought about Nina worrying about Martin, and Guri running away from everything she loved. She had to take the risk. 'If I do, can you find out what happened to them? Or will that put you in danger too?'

Hugo smiled. 'You don't have to worry about me. I can find out. What's their name?'

Anni hesitated. Martin was already arrested. There wasn't any risk to her or Guri unless he turned her in. 'Can I trust you?'

She knew that was a rhetorical question. He could lie or laugh it away. Instead, he nodded.

'Yes, you can trust me. I would never do anything to harm you.'

Anni chose to believe him. 'My husband's friend Martin Foss was arrested, and his family is worried about him. Could you find out what happened to him?'

Hugo nodded. 'I will see what I can do.'

'Thank you,' Anni said.

They were both silent for a moment. Anni was suddenly lost for words. This was a new step in the relationship, something she hadn't expected to encounter.

Hugo picked up on her reservations. 'I'm not going to put you or Ingrid in any danger, Anni. I would never do that, but I want to help.'

'Help, how?' Anni couldn't quite believe him.

'I will find out what I can about your friend, but you

must understand, I can't get him out. I hold no power with the Gestapo,' he said.

'Can you find out if his family can visit him? Unless he's already been sent to Germany, of course,' Anni said.

Hugo stroked her face. 'I will do my best.'

'Why will you, though? I mean, you could get in trouble, couldn't you?'

'It's highly unlikely. They have no reason to think that I'm not on their side. I say and do all the correct things, acting the part of a proper Nazi, and follower of the great Reich. I stay under their radar because I do my job, and act friendly, and then I come back here to you, and I can breathe. I don't know how I would have managed these months without you,' he whispered. 'I feel safe with you.'

Anni almost cried. 'I feel safe with you too.'

'I promise you, I won't get in trouble,' he said.

She wanted to believe him, she needed to, but she held back.

He seemed to pick up on her hesitation. 'I want you to trust me,' he said. 'Ask me anything.'

Anni thought about the list but wasn't sure. 'Tell me why you're travelling so much.'

He smiled. 'I will, but you should know that if you tell anyone, you'll put us all in danger.'

'I can keep a secret,' she said.

'There are people who don't want the war to end, and there are people who want it to be over. I work for them. I can't give you any names, but one of the reasons I travel is to talk to those people. To make sure we have enough people on our side to end this war as quickly and as peacefully as possible.'

The list, Anni thought. They were the people he talked to. 'And these people, can you trust them?'

'That's what I'm trying to find out. You can see how risky this is.'

Anni took a deep breath. 'I saw the list under your bed,' she said slowly. 'Are they the people you talk to?'

Hugo looked surprised but nodded. 'Yes, they are some of them. Have you showed the list to anyone?'

She shook her head, afraid to get Martin in more trouble.

'No, I didn't understand what it meant, so I left it where I found it.'

'Good. I don't want you to be in danger.'

'Be careful, Hugo. It's a dangerous game you're playing. How can you be sure any of these people won't betray you?' she said.

'I doubt it. We're not talking to the fanatics.' Hugo kissed her gently. 'Promise me that you'll stay out of any dangerous situations. I don't want you to take any risks at this point.'

Anni wanted to tell him what she had suspected for a while now, but she didn't know how to. It was all too overwhelming. And right now, the more pressing thing was to get a message to the resistance about the list. Perhaps knowing about people like that would help secure a safer peace.

She considered telling him, but decided against it. It was dangerous enough asking him about Martin. If he was arrested, or lying to her, she could put members of the resistance in real danger. For now, she would do what she had to do, and hope he was honest.

Chapter Twenty-One

Ingrid, thirty-two years old

London, 1970

Ingrid could hear the girls squealing outside, followed by Runar's voice, talking to them in Norwegian. He loved picking them up from school and insisted on doing it every day. They would take a detour to the park, and if the weather was good, stop for an ice lolly on the way.

These last eight years had been the best years of her life. Ingrid smiled at the memories. They had married in London with Esme and the rest of the family. Esme gave her away, and it had been a wonderful party afterwards.

Runar's mother had come from Oslo, together with Runar's stepfather. Her wall in the office was covered in photographs, reminding her of the memories they had made together.

There was this little voice telling her that she had no family. There was a deep longing inside her that never quite went away.

The entrance door slammed open, and she could hear that they had both had a lovely day, or at least a lovely trip to the park.

She loved the sound of their voices. The girls singing in silly Norwegian now, and Runar laughing and joining in.

How did I get so lucky? she thought, smiling to herself.

Ingrid looked down at the ledgers again. She and Runar was the de facto owners of the sweet shop now, and doing the books was part of her job. Esme still worked at the shop, but fewer hours. She was preparing herself for retirement, apparently. Even talking about moving to Benidorm for the winters.

On her desk was the photograph of her mother and herself, taken in 1944. Ingrid kept it there as a reminder never to give up the search. All the letters she had sent out for the last eight years had come back with no answers.

The information about her mother had to be out there, but for some reason she couldn't get access to it. Nobody would tell her anything. It was exhausting and infuriating, and she had worked so hard to not let it take over her life.

She had her own file now, filled with newspaper clippings, rejection letters from police stations and archives, quite a few from the Department of Justice. They all claimed it was classified information, and refused to confirm that there even existed a file on Anni Odland.

The last two years Ingrid had focused on the State Archive of Norway. She started by writing to them once a month, then once a week. If anything existed that could tell her about her mother, it would be there. She was sure of it.

A light knock on the door made her look up. Runar was leaning against the door frame, one hand behind his back.

He had a funny look on his face, and Ingrid frowned.

'Are the girls OK?'

'Peachy. They're changing out of their school uniforms, then I'll give them a snack to hold them over for dinner.'

'Thank you,' she said, smiling at him. 'You are so sweet.'

'Indeed I am, and I have something that might make you find me even sweeter,' he said, before coming over to the desk.

He leant over and kissed her lightly.

'That's it? That's your big surprise?' Ingrid realised he was still holding his hand behind his back. 'Did you buy me flowers?'

'No, this is better. Or at least I hope it is.' He handed her an envelope. 'It's from the archive, Ingrid. And I don't think it's their usual response.'

Ingrid looked at the envelope. He was right. Every other correspondence from them had been a short formal letter, sent in the usual white business envelope. The answer always the same: *We don't know anything about Anni Odland.*

'I'm guessing that writing every week had them thinking you'd never stop,' Runar said.

'They thought right. I was planning to write every day.' Ingrid held the brown envelope in her hands. She couldn't bring herself to open it. It wasn't heavy, but there was something in it, more than a rejection letter.

'Last time I told them I would be contacting newspapers if they didn't send whatever they had to me,' she said.

'There you go,' Runar said. 'Threats work.'

Ingrid looked up at him, aware she had tears in her eyes. 'I'm scared. What if Mamma is dead?'

Runa smiled, the same smile she had loved for so many

years. 'That may be so, but you won't let that stop you. You still need to know what happened.'

Ingrid looked at him. 'I don't deserve you,' she said, smiling at him.

'Yes, you do.' Runar kissed her again. 'You're not a coward, Ingrid. Open the envelope.'

The girls came running down the stairs, and Runar rolled his eyes to make her smile. 'I'll be in the kitchen when you're ready.'

He left her, and Ingrid turned her attention to the envelope. She took a deep breath and opened it carefully.

Inside she found a short formal letter on top, and a few pages after that.

Ingrid read the letter first, making sure she understood everything.

'*We have found a file on your mother, Anni Odland, and have decided to release the papers to you. We have no further information*,' Ingrid read aloud, snorting at the last words.

She put it aside and read the rest of the papers.

There wasn't much, but what there was crushed her hopes.

Ingrid pushed away the papers and put her head in her arms on the desk. It was over. She'd never find her mamma.

A short time later, Runar found her sobbing over the desk. He came over at once and put his hand on her back. 'Ingrid, what did they say?'

'She went with him to Germany.' Ingrid looked up at him, drying her eyes on her sleeve. She put her hands on the papers. 'Mamma married the German who lived in our house, and then she signed away her Norwegian citizenship. I can't believe the archive people fought me for so long. They could have told me this the first time I wrote to them and saved me years of pain. It's bullshit, Runar.'

Runar frowned. 'There was nothing else?'

'There's nothing after 1946. Nothing at all. It's as if Mamma disappeared into thin air.'

Runar frowned. 'I'm not sure anyone would know what became of her. Germany was completely ruined.'

Ingrid shook her head. 'It doesn't matter. She left me behind to go to Germany of all places. Whatever happened is on her.'

'They could have told you that the first time you contacted them. Why drag it out all this time? That's strange, don't you think?' Runar sat down next to her.

Ingrid shrugged, overwhelmed with the whole thing. 'I don't know. I don't understand this at all.'

'Listen, I know this is a shock. Something like this, it's awful, but you don't know if that's the whole truth,' Runar insisted.

Ingrid handed him two pieces of papers. 'I think it is. She signed this, Runar. And when she did, when she decided she didn't want to be Norwegian anymore, she also signed away me.' She didn't want to start crying again. 'I'll go and sit with the girls.'

Runar nodded. 'Can I read it?'

'Sure. Afterwards stuff it back in the envelope and in a drawer. It makes me sick to look at it,' she said.

Leaving the office, her feet felt as if they weighed a ton. The hope of being reunited with Mamma had disappeared in a few seconds.

The police secretary in Haugesund had been right all the time. *He probably knew this, and didn't tell me*, she thought. No wonder he had looked as if he despised them both.

Ingrid took a deep breath. She had to face the facts. Her mamma had married a German. She had done what they arrested her for. The realisation that she had left her behind so easily . . .

The girls were sitting by the table, eating toast. They both turned towards her and their little faces lit up.

'Mummy! We saw a puppy in the park. Can we have a puppy, please?' Guri, the five-year-old, held her hands together. 'Pleeease?'

'Yes, Mummy, can we have a puppy?' Joanna, her first baby, already almost seven, had the same hopeful look on her face.

They were talking over each other, trying to compete for her attention, like they always did.

Ingrid almost burst into tears again. 'No, puppies are too much work, and I have enough with taking care of you two.'

'But we'll take care of it.' Again, with the synchronised words.

'Perhaps when you're older,' she said.

They looked disappointed, but soon started telling her about their day.

Ingrid sat down between them and pulled Guri on her lap. 'You smell so good,' she said.

'Like the sweet shop?' Guri giggled.

'Yes, you're like a raspberry fudge, or maybe a vanilla marshmallow,' Ingrid said.

'No, she smells like poo,' Joanna declared.

Guri narrowed her eyes. 'You look like poo.'

'No name-calling, girls. Eat your toast,' Ingrid said, trying to hide a smile.

Mamma is losing out on all this, she thought, kissing Guri on the head. *She wasn't there for our wedding, she wasn't there when the girls were born, she won't see them grow up, see how wonderful they are. Nothing. We have already lost twenty-five years, a quarter of a century.*

All these years, I've nursed a hope that wasn't real. It never occurred to me that she would simply turn her back on me. I never even thought it possible that she had been a 'German slut', she thought. *It's too hard to even think about.*

'Mummy, why are you crying?' Joanna slipped down her chair and came over to her. 'Are you sad?'

The little one looked at her with huge eyes. 'Mummy?'

Ingrid pulled a face to make them think she was silly. 'I'm sorry. I think I worked on the numbers too much. I'm a little tired.'

They seemed to accept that. Ingrid smiled. 'Who wants more toast?'

'Me, me,' they sang in tune.

Ingrid busied herself with toast and jam. *Don't scare the girls*, she told herself.

The smell of the bread reminded her of the first time she had tasted proper bread. It had been that German who had brought it, and he had buttered it. It had been the best thing in the world.

'Mummy is smiling,' Guri whispered.

Ingrid sat down between them. 'Yes, I am. I remember

the first time I tasted proper bread. I was six years old, and it was wonderful.'

'Why didn't you have proper bread?' Joanna looked concerned again.

'There wasn't any lovely bread like this during the war. The bakers had poor flour, and it was a struggle for them to bake even one type of bread. Can you guess what it was called?'

Ingrid smiled when they both shook their heads. 'You're going to like this. Everyone called it farty bread.'

The girls fell into giggles.

'And do you know who told me that?'

They shook their heads. 'Who did, Mummy? Who did?'

'That would be me,' Runar said from the door. 'It was a terrible bread, all sticky and almost black, and everyone who ate it farted.'

The word had them in stitches again.

Runar looked at her over their heads. 'I think I found something,' he said, lowering his voice.

Ingrid bit her lower lip, then nodded. 'Tell me.'

'Come back to the study.'

The girls, Ingrid thought. They hadn't been told about the search for their lost grandmother. They didn't even know about her.

In the study, the envelope was still on the table. Ingrid folded her arms around her. 'I don't want to see it,' she said.

Runar lifted his hand. 'I'll put it away. If that's what you want. Did you read all of it?'

Ingrid shook her head. 'I stopped after the document where she signed me off.'

Runar held up a piece of paper. 'This is a letter from a man who said he worked with your mother and grandmother during the war, Ingrid. A testimony, if you want. And there's more.'

'But it doesn't matter, Runar. She left with him.' Ingrid started getting hot. 'What's the point?'

He acted as if he didn't hear her. 'These letters are from people who knew her, they sent them to the police to speak on her behalf. There's a Martin Foss who says she worked with him in the resistance, and there's also a letter from his daughter, Nina Foss. She confirms what her father told them.'

'Yes, but it made no difference to them,' Ingrid said.

'No, but it might to you. Don't you think we should find Martin and Nina? Anni mattered to them, Ingrid. She really did,' Runar said. 'Working together, taking risks like that, that creates bonds. They were family to her.'

Ingrid shook her head. 'I don't know. I . . . right now I'm so sick of it all.'

'You told me you wanted to know more about what Guri and Anni did during the war. These people can give you answers to that,' he said.

I don't know if I want to find her anymore, she thought. *Not after what I read.*

'Perhaps it's time to let it go,' she said, avoiding looking at him.

Runar gasped. 'You must be joking. You've finally found the best trace since you started this, and you want to give up now? That's not like you.'

Ingrid finally looked at him. She could see the love in his eyes, and she couldn't stop the tears flowing again.

'She chose a Nazi over me. How could she do that? I

would never leave my girls behind. Especially not for a . . . a fling with some man.'

Runar came over and took her hands, holding them to his chest.

'I don't think she left you because of a fling,' Runar said.

'How can you believe that?' Ingrid looked at him.

'Because I remember the two of you together,' Runar said softly. 'You had that incredible bond that you have with our girls. You have that from her, from your mother. It's a bond that nothing can sever, no matter how hard anyone would try. There has to be another explanation, Ingrid. Something other than what those few papers tell you.'

Ingrid shook her head. 'I don't know, Runar.'

'Sleep on it. This has been a huge shock for you. Do you want me to bring Esme here?'

'No. I'll go upstairs and see if I can take a nap.' Ingrid could see how worried he was. She put her hand on his chest. 'I'm fine, I promise.'

'You're a force of nature,' he said.

Ingrid leant into him, feeling his strength and taking solace from it.

'You are the sweetest, and I love you,' she said, and kissed him.

Behind them the girls were giggling and whispering together.

As long as I have Runar and my girls, I'll be fine. I don't need Mamma, Ingrid thought. *Not anymore.*

Chapter Twenty-Two

Anni

Haugesund, March 1945

On the way to the farm, Ingrid discovered a small cluster of horse foot flowers. Their tiny, yellow flower petals in between patches of almost melted snow brightened up the path.

'Look, Mamma! Can I pick them?' Ingrid was already bending down.

'Are you sure? They look so pretty where they are,' Anni said. Ingrid frowned and pondered for a second. This was a dilemma, obviously.

Anni laughed. 'Why don't you pick a few, and leave the rest?'

Ingrid carefully picked four flowers, making sure not to pull the roots. 'Can we put them in a vase at the farm, for when Besta comes back?'

'Yes, we can do that.' Anni refused to think Guri would stay away for much longer.

'Look, Mamma. There's Nina!' Ingrid looked up at her. 'Can I give her the flowers?'

'Yes, if you want to.'

Nina was coming out of the house, carrying a small bag in her hand. She stopped when she discovered them.

Ingrid skipped towards her, waving the flowers in her hand. 'These are for you.'

'Oh, thank you, Ingrid. These are the first ones I've seen.' Nina took the flowers and smiled at Anni. 'They're so pretty.'

'Yes, they are. Why are you here, Nina?' Anni hadn't expected her to be at the farm.

'I needed to see you,' Nina said.

Anni could see she was distraught. 'What's going on?'

Nina bit her lower lip. 'I . . . well, you know if Pappa was here, this wouldn't be a problem, and now that Guri isn't here either . . .'

Anni looked over her shoulder. Ingrid was skipping on the pathway again.

'Please don't tell me there's someone in the barn now.'

Nina pulled a face. 'I'm sorry, Anni, but it couldn't be helped.'

'Why on earth would you do this? It's too dangerous the way things are now.' Anni struggled to keep her voice down, so as not to frighten Ingrid.

'I couldn't say no,' Nina said, following her to the barn. 'It's an emergency, and they didn't know Guri wasn't here. There's a boat coming for him tonight. They told me that when they brought him.'

'The Germans could be looking for Guri, for God's sake.'

'He's only here for a few hours,' Nina muttered.

'For all we know, they might have this place under

surveillance, you silly girl,' Anni said, getting more exasperated by the second. 'What if the boat doesn't come?'

'Yes, I know it's stupid, but they had nowhere else to send him. And this man in there? He's something else. That was a hell of a surprise,' Nina said.

'Why? And what's in the bag?' Anni asked.

'He's wounded in his leg and his arm, so I was bringing supplies to see if I could help.'

Anni held out her hand, and Nina gave her the bag. Inside were rolls of bandages, aspirin and a small bottle of iodine.

'Does he need a doctor?' Anni didn't like that at all.

Nina shrugged. 'Actually, they didn't say. He was already here by the time I arrived, and they had to leave in a hurry. You know how it is.'

'Yes, I do.' The refugees would be brought to them either by sea in someone's rowing boat, or someone would bring them in a cart or even by bicycle. Even Guri didn't always know the people who brought them to the farm.

Nina seemed to have put the initial shock behind her. 'This one is a real surprise,' she said, grinning.

Anni didn't even try to hide how cross she was. 'Aren't they all,' she said.

'Not like this one, I can promise you that,' Nina said, smiling at her private joke. 'Oh, and he only speaks English.'

'That's hardly a surprise. They're mostly British.' Anni wondered what was actually going on. 'Do you know how he got here? How he ended up in Norway, I mean?'

'I haven't spoken to him, he was so out of it when they brought him and only moaned a few words in a language I've never heard,' Nina said. 'Besides, you speak better English than me, don't you?'

'I'll try.' Anni pushed open the heavy door, but paused and turned to Nina. 'Watch Ingrid, please.'

Nina looked disappointed but didn't argue.

Crossing the yard to the barn seemed longer than usual. Anni had to admit to herself that she wasn't prepared for doing this without Guri and Martin. They were always so efficient and confident, not like her at all. She knitted her hands to stop them from trembling.

But he was a refugee, and she was the only one who could help him. Nina was too young, and Martin would never forgive her if something happened to his daughter. The responsibility was all hers.

Anni took a deep breath and pushed open the barn door.

Inside she was met by the usual dusty, stuffy air, smelling strongly of dried hay and goats. She climbed up the ladder to the hayloft. 'Hello?' she called softly. 'Don't worry. I'm a friend.'

The only sounds she heard were the creaking of the wood in the ladder when she put weight on it, and the rustling of the hay when she stepped off the last step. Anni imagined she could sense someone holding their breath. Someone who was terrified, or ready to pounce on her. Either way, he didn't know who she was.

She cleared her throat. 'Please don't be scared. I'm the daughter-in-law of the woman who owns the farm. I'm a friend,' she said in English, hoping there wasn't a gang of Nazi soldiers hiding in the hay.

There was some rustling in the hay, but still no response.

Anni tried again. 'My friend told me you were hurt. I can help.'

She pulled aside some of the hay and peeked inside Lars's

secret boyhood room. The daylight streamed through cracks in the wall, enough that she could see a man lying under a blanket, facing the wall in the corner.

The man turned his head and Anni couldn't hide her surprise. He had short, black hair, eyes darker than any she had ever seen, and the colour of his skin would make him stick out like a sore thumb in town.

'Oh dear,' she muttered.

He stared at her. 'You speak English,' he said.

'Yes, I do. Are you in pain?'

He tried to sit up and flinched. 'I've been worse. Thank you.'

Maybe not British, Anni thought. *But not quite American either*. She had rescued both.

She put down the bag Nina had given her, and started taking out the contents.

'How on earth did you end up here?' she said, smiling at him.

It was a valid question, and it would hopefully take his mind off what was to come.

'I'm a fighter pilot with the Royal Canadian Air Force, and I crashed my plane,' he said, smiling now, clearly enjoying how shocked she was. 'Technically the Nazis shot me down, but I crashed it when it hit the ground,' he added.

'You look like you probably shouldn't be here,' she said, raising her eyebrows.

'I wasn't supposed to be here, but I also wasn't supposed to crash, of course,' he added with a lopsided grin.

'Honestly, this is probably the last place someone like you should be,' Anni said.

'There's no hiding me,' he said, laughing when she gasped.

'I've been in this country for two weeks now, and everyone I've met has been wonderful, but they all started out with the same shocked expression on their face you had.'

'I'm glad people have been looking after you. Hopefully, this will be your last stretch,' Anni said.

'That young woman who came in her earlier, she's not your mother-in-law, is she?' He looked bemused at the thought.

'She's six years younger than me, so no. Even if she had a son, he would not be of marriageable age,' Anni said.

It made him smile, but he looked poorly.

She sat down on the mattress next to him. 'I'm Anni.'

'My name is Harbans Singh, but you can call me Hari. Everybody does,' he said.

This close, Anni could see he looked worried. 'You look fairly young for a pilot, Hari,' she said.

'I'm old enough to fly.' He tried to sit up again but grimaced with pain. 'And to get shot down.'

'Tell me about your wounds, please.'

'I banged my arm pretty badly when the plane hit the ground, and there's a cut on my leg.' He sighed. 'I think it's infected. And my head hurts like holy hell. Sorry, ma'am.'

'I have some aspirin for your head and general pain, and some iodine and bandages for your wounds. Can I take a look at your arm first?'

'Are you a nurse?' He looked nervous but tried to take off his flight jacket.

It was badly ripped on one side and had clearly been through a rough time.

'No, but I look after young children,' Anni said, smiling when he laughed. 'I'm used to blood and scrapes.'

She held out her hands and helped him sit up. The effort had him sweating at the brow. 'How come you speak English?' he said, panting with the effort.

'I studied English and German in school. I thought it would be useful. The English hasn't been much so far,' she said. 'The German has been, unfortunately.'

'I bet.' He watched her while she pulled away the shirt sleeve and exposed a rough bandage.

'Did a doctor take a look at you?' Anni could see blood had seeped through the bandage.

'Someone did, but I'm not sure if he was a doctor. My plane crashed in a forest, and I passed out. Then I woke up in a bed, much like this one, with a man bandaging my arm. It hurt like hell. He kept talking to me and at first, I thought he was speaking Nazi.'

'He didn't look like a Nazi, did he?' Anni couldn't help smiling at him.

'Not at all. He looked like a farmer or fisherman,' Hari said.

'Most of us do,' Anni said, while digging through Nina's bag in search of a pair of scissors, nodding her approval when she found one. 'Here we go. Keep still, please.'

'Where am I?' Hari frowned when she lifted his arm.

'You are on the west coast of Norway, a few kilometres from Haugesund,' Anni said.

'And where's that?' Hari looked away when she touched the bandage.

'The town is almost right in the middle between Bergen and Stavanger,' she said, waving her hand.

'I'm not even sure how I got to this place, to be honest. I think I was much further north, and I definitely didn't crash

303

on the coast. It was higher up. They only moved me when it was dark.'

Anni took away the bandage and examined the wound. It was a large, nasty-looking gash, going from the shoulder all the way across the elbow. 'You're right,' she said. 'It looks inflamed.'

She took a flannel and opened the bottle of iodine. 'This will sting a lot.'

He squeezed his eyes shut and reminded her of Ingrid whenever she had to do this to her. Anni cleaned the wound as best she could and applied a fresh bandage.

'I usually give my kids a crayon or a glossy picture when they've been brave, but I didn't bring any with me,' she said, smiling at him.

'Thank you, ma'am, but I don't need a shiny picture,' he said with a bright smile. 'I'm a pilot in the Royal Canadian Air Force. That's pretty shiny.'

'You'll probably get a medal when you get to Shetland,' Anni said to cheer him up. 'How old are you, Hari?'

He took the two aspirin she handed him and swallowed them quickly. 'I'm twenty-five, ma'am.' Hari lifted his arm and frowned. 'If my arm is busted bad, they're going to ground me.'

'I don't think there's any damaged tendons or bones,' Anni said. 'Make sure to keep the wound clean, and when you're in Shetland, have a proper doctor look at it.'

'Thank you. It feels better now,' he said.

'Good. All right, then. Let's have a look at your leg,' Anni said.

He pulled away the blanket. Someone had cut his trouser leg up to the middle of his thigh. Mostly what she could see was faint bruises and some swelling. When she touched the skin, he flinched again.

'Can you walk on it?'

'I can, but not very well, I'm afraid. I've probably strained something,' he said, pulling a face.

Anni tried not to show how concerned that made her. He had to make it. There was no way she could hide him for long, even if the war was over soon.

'Do you remember how you got hurt?' She pulled the blanket over his legs again.

He shook his head. 'Not at all, I'm afraid. My plane was totally crushed. My bomber didn't make it. It doesn't seem fair, does it? Why did I survive and not him?'

It clearly weighed heavily on his mind. Anni guessed he hadn't been able to talk about it with anyone since the crash.

She took his arm and looked him in the eyes. 'Hari, listen. We don't know why some people live and some don't. It's a question nobody can answer.'

'And I'm supposed to live with that?' He looked down when he said it.

'What else can you do? Who are you going to ask?' Anni patted his hand. 'It's war, Hari. And if there's any answer at all, that's the one. Terrible things happen in war and it makes little or no sense.'

He looked up and smiled at her. 'Thank you. My *beeji* would call it a miracle that I survived.'

'Your *beeji*?' Anni asked.

'Sorry. My grandmother. She's strong in her faith, and great with wise words,' he said. 'She lives in Vancouver with the rest of the family. She'd like you, that's for sure.'

'Do you have a big family?'

'Yes, but not everyone is living in Canada. We still have family in India,' he said.

'We'll do our best to get you back to them,' Anni said, putting everything back in the bag again.

'Can I ask you something?' He looked pensive.

Anni nodded. 'Anything.'

'My bomber. What would the Nazis do with his body? Do you know?'

Anni smiled. 'He would have received a full military funeral by the Germans. All honours. Honestly, they do that with everyone in a uniform. And after the war, I'm sure his family will be notified of what happened to him.'

Hari smiled from ear to ear at that. 'That's a relief. I was afraid they would burn him or something.'

'Not at all. They honour everything military,' Anni assured him.

'Thank you, that puts my mind at ease. When I get back home, I'll write to his family and tell them. It will hopefully be of some comfort to them.'

'I'm sure it will be. I have to go back now. You need to rest; it's a bit of a trek to the sea. I'll come back for you in a few hours when it's darker, OK?' she said.

He hesitated, and Anni smiled at him in what she hoped was a soothing manner. 'You're safe here,' she said.

'As safe as I can be,' he said.

'Yes, I'm afraid so.'

Chapter Twenty-Three

By the time it was dark enough to leave the barn, Anni had a gnawing feeling in her guts. Every time she went out with Guri and Martin, she worried it would be the last time. And this time she was alone.

She pulled her woollen socks on, then dressed in Lars's old sweater and boots. She knew she had to pull herself together. Hari's life depended on it, and there was also the risk to Nina and herself, and to Ingrid.

'I can do this,' she muttered.

Ingrid was fast asleep in Guri's bed when Anni checked on her.

Downstairs, Nina was sitting on the sofa, wrapped in one of Guri's blankets. She looked like a little girl, afraid of the dark.

'I should come with you,' she said. 'Pappa says there has

to be two people in case something goes wrong.'

'No, Martin would have my head if anything happened to you, and besides, I need you to look after Ingrid,' Anni said. 'I'll be back in a couple of hours.'

'Fine, but if you're away for longer than that, I'm coming after you.' Nina had a defiant look on her face.

Anni narrowed her eyes. 'Absolutely not,' she said in her sternest voice. 'If I'm caught, there's nobody else to take care of Ingrid. I need you to stay here with my child, no matter what happens. Promise me.'

Nina nodded. 'I promise, Anni. I won't leave her alone for a second.'

'Good. Right now, you and I are all we have.' Anni took the walking cane Nina had found and smiled. 'Thank you. This will do the trick.'

'Do you need help to get him down from the hayloft?' Nina said. 'Or maybe that was silly. I did say I wouldn't leave the house.'

Anni pulled a face. 'Smarty pants. But yes, that might be a good idea. I'd rather not have him falling down and breaking something else.'

Nina was on her feet before Anni had finished the sentence.

To their surprise, there was no need for the two of them. Hari had already managed to get himself down the ladder and was sitting on the floor by the time they came inside.

He looked exhausted, and grinned when he saw them. 'Took me ages to get down here,' he said.

Anni scowled at him. 'That was a foolish thing to do, Hari. You could have fallen, and if you had been more injured, we would all have been in a hell of a dangerous situation.'

He got a sheepish look on his face. 'I do apologise.'

Nina pulled at Anni's arm. 'He did save us a lot of time.'

'I guess so.' Anni was still frowning. 'Go back to the house.'

Nina didn't argue, and walked over to the door. She looked outside, then turned her head. 'All quiet.'

Anni rolled her eyes at her. 'Go back into the house, you silly goose.'

Hari looked serious when she turned her attention to him. 'I'm so sorry,' he said again.

'No need,' Anni said. 'We brought you a cane. It's a fair bit to walk, I'm afraid, and we need to hurry.'

Hari took the cane and managed to stand up. 'This will do,' he said.

Anni patted her shoulder. 'Lean on me, that's safer. I don't want to risk you falling.'

Hari nodded. 'Got you. What if we meet someone?'

'If we do, then I'm afraid we'll be done for,' Anni said.

'You're not one for pep talks, are you?'

Anni frowned. 'I don't know that word, I'm afraid.'

'It's what you do when you want to energise people,' Hari said.

'This is not that kind of situation, I'm afraid. We either make it, or we don't.' Anni hoped that would make him realise how serious she was.

'See, pep talk,' Hari said in a shaky voice.

Anni walked as fast as she could, and Hari did his best to keep up.

They walked the long path around the monument.

Anni didn't want to take any chances. The sky was lighter than she liked, not surprising for April, but it made her nervous.

Not much I can do about that, she thought.

When they came up to the monument, Hari stopped. He was breathing hard, and Anni let him take a minute.

She looked around, trying to see through the shadows for movement, or anything that might be out of order.

Hari gave her a light nudge, making it clear that he was ready to walk again. Anni smiled at him, and they forged ahead.

Coming around to the other side of the monument, they stopped where they had to cross the field.

'We usually run across here,' Anni said. 'But we'll have to be as quick about it as we can. Will you manage?'

Hari nodded, a determined look on his face. 'Let's do this.'

They stepped out on the field, out in the open, and started moving.

Anni could see Hari was in pain. He was barely putting any weight on the wounded leg. She put her arm around his waist and hoped he would manage.

They were almost across when she heard a noise behind her.

Anni froze on the spot. Hari looked at her. 'What?'

She shook her head, then shot a quick look behind her. She was sure she heard someone calling her name.

Oh my God, she thought. *Hugo?* Her heart sank. Was this moment he would show his real self? The idea that he would be the one to destroy her world was unbearable.

Maybe they could outrun him.

She smiled at Hari, in an encouraging way, she hoped. 'We need to reach the boulders. Can you manage?'

Hari nodded, and they started walking again. 'Do you have a gun hidden over there?'

'No, not really,' Anni said, bracing herself when she heard Hugo calling her name again. 'I'm sorry, Hari. We have to stop.'

She let Hari catch his breath again as they waited for the inevitable. And there he was. Her German.

When Hugo caught up with them, he was panting. 'Anni, listen to me. There are soldiers on their way here.'

Anni frowned. 'They're not with you?'

He looked horrified. 'No, of course not. We have no time for explanations. You have to return to the farm.'

Anni threw a quick glance at Hari, who was staring at her with terror written all over his face. She had forgotten they were talking in German. Anni still held her arm around Hari, and she could feel him shaking. 'Hugo is a friend,' she said in English.

Hugo looked at Hari for the first time. 'Oh my God,' he said.

'We can't stay here.' Anni pulled Hari forward. 'How far away are they?'

'Maybe half an hour. I took a car and went straight here as soon as I heard.' He noticed that Hari had trouble walking, and went over to the other side, trying to do the same thing Anni was doing.

Hari shook his head. 'No, no.'

'It's fine, Hari. He's here to help. We have to get you in the boat and get the hell out of here.'

'How can you be sure?' Hari didn't look confident.

'Trust me. Hugo says there are soldiers on their way. We have no time to waste.' Anni nodded at Hugo, and changed to German again. 'We need to get him to the boathouse.'

She had no choice but to trust him. It would be impossible to hide Hari in the barn again. He wouldn't be safe, and he needed medical care.

To her surprise Hugo didn't argue. He took a firmer grip around Hari's waist, and they more or less carried him between them.

When they finally stood on the pier, they were all exhausted.

'No time to rest,' Anni said.

She went in the wobbly boat first, then helped Hari in.

'Sit in the back, Hari. Whatever you do, don't stand up until I tell you to,' she said.

Hari grabbed hold of the gunwale and nodded.

Anni looked up at Hugo. 'Do you need help too?'

Hugo hesitated. 'Perhaps I should go back, and try to deflect the soldiers.'

'Can you row?' Anni was more interested in getting away than anything else.

'I'm not sure,' Hugo admitted. 'Are you sure I should go with you?'

'I need you to help me row,' she said, holding out her hand. 'We'll get out of here quicker if there's two of us.'

He nodded. 'Of course.'

Once they were all in the boat, she pushed off and sat down to take the oars, instructing Hugo what to do. Thankfully, he picked up on it quickly.

As the boat moved away from the shore, she tried to see if there was anyone there. By now, the sky had darkened, and she was hoping that meant the soldiers wouldn't notice them.

Hugo realised what she was doing. 'I promise you, when they're there, we'll know. There's nothing quiet about that lot.'

Anni caught a glimpse of Hari's face. He had his eyes focused on Hugo. He had to be scared out of his mind. *Poor boy*, she thought, forgetting that he was actually a year older than she was.

Anni suddenly remembered something else. 'Will the soldiers go to the farm, do you think? Ingrid is there.'

'Alone?' Hugo looked concerned.

'No, of course not, but the babysitter is only nineteen years old. She'll be no match for a battalion of soldiers.'

Hugo shook his head. 'It will be a small group of soldiers, and I'm sure they'll be heading for the beach. They are looking for smugglers.'

Anni looked at him. 'What about patrol boats?'

'I doubt it. They're more concerned with the stretch between Hagland and Bergen.'

'But you can't be sure of that, can you?' Anni said, pulling at the oar.

'No, I can't.' Hugo followed her rhythm. 'So, the faster we get to where you're taking us, the better.'

Anni focused on the rowing. Whatever questions she had would have to wait.

They kept rowing, trying to keep as quiet as possible. Anni could feel her arms straining with every pull of the oar. Hugo didn't seem to have the same problem.

He noticed she was watching him. 'How much further?'

Anni shook her head. 'Any moment, actually. Keep on

the lookout for a bigger boat than ours.'

Hugo narrowed his eyes. 'How are you supposed to see a boat out here? It's pitch black.'

Anni smiled. 'That's where experience comes in. Be quiet for a moment.'

They fell silent and Anni closed her eyes. Somewhere out there was a boat with an engine. They would probably have turned it off, she thought, but still.

'That way,' she said, and nodded towards south. 'It's close.'

She managed to turn the boat around, and they started rowing.

'How would you know that?' Hugo was panting next to her.

'I heard coughing,' Anni said. 'Let's hope it's my people and not yours.'

They rowed for a few more minutes, and then Anni lifted her oar, giving Hugo the signal to do the same. The boat had momentum and kept going forward.

'We're here,' she said. 'Hari? Be ready.'

She looked at Hugo. 'And you, please don't say a word. You might get us all shot.'

He nodded, a grim expression on his face.

Hari sat up when their boat scraped alongside the bigger boat. It sounded so loud, Anni cringed.

She looked up at two pale-faced fishermen. 'We weren't sure you would find us,' one of them said.

'Funny, neither did we,' Anni said.

The fishermen grinned at her. 'How many of you are we talking with us?'

'Only one. A pilot from Canada, eager to return home.

He's injured. He'll need proper doctoring when he's in friendly waters,' Anni said.

'Bring him onboard. We'll take good care of him.'

Anni helped Hari stand up in the boat. The fishermen dropped down a rope and she tied it around his chest.

'Hold on to this, Hari. They've done this before, these boys. You're in good hands,' she said. 'Have a safe trip home.'

Hari had a serious look in his eyes. '*Sat sri akal*, Anni. I will never forget you, or any of the others who have risked so much to save me. Thank you. And if you're ever in Canada, come visit.'

He put his hands together and made a little bow.

'I will. Go now.' Anni smiled at him.

She signalled for the fishermen to pull him up. She held on gently to his legs, while balancing in the boat. Hugo kept the boat still.

Finally, Hari was safe inside the fishing boat, and she could breathe a little easier.

She pushed them away from the side of the boat and sat down next to Hugo.

They sat quietly next to each other until they could hear the engine of the fishing boat vanishing into the night.

Anni turned to Hugo. 'I need to ask you a question. Please, tell me the truth.'

He was holding both oars and nodded. 'I will.'

'How did you know about tonight? That they would be out looking for us?'

Hugo pulled a face. 'I know because one of my officer friends told me. He's in charge of surveillance plans on this coast,' he said. 'He's on the list, Anni.'

Anni turned towards the fishing boat, suddenly scared that perhaps one of the Kriegsmarine patrol boats was coming. 'Are they out there now?'

'No, don't worry. If they haven't come by now, it means they're searching further north,' he said.

'And your friend is on your list?' Anni asked.

'He can be trusted, yes.' Hugo looked at her. 'You don't have to worry.'

Anni nodded. 'I won't, then.' She took the oar from him and used it to turn the boat around, heading back to shore.

Hugo put his arm around her and kissed her cheek. 'I found out about your friend.'

'Martin? Is he safe?' Anni stopped rowing.

Hugo nodded and looked pleased with himself. 'He's held at Grini prison camp in Oslo. He was on the list to be sent to Sachsenhausen concentration camp in Germany, but I managed to keep him in Norway. He will stay at Grini until all this is over. I'm sorry that I wasn't able to get him back home,' he said.

Anni gaped at him. 'No, no, thank you. Anything is better than Germany right now. You know that. Do you think his family can visit, or at least send him letters?'

Hugo nodded. 'I would think so, yes.'

'That's good. They'll be pleased.' Anni put down the oar again and they started rowing towards the shore. With Hari safe on the boat and Martin still in Norway, she couldn't ask for anything more, given the situation. 'I have to pop by the farm and check on Ingrid. Then we can go home.'

Home, she thought. *What a strange thing to say to him.*

* * *

Nina was sleeping on the sofa when Anni came into the house. Making sure Ingrid was safe and sound asleep in Guri's bed, she woke Nina and told her what Hugo had told her about Martin. Nina cried and hugged her.

'We'll talk tomorrow when I come to pick up Ingrid,' Anni said. 'I have to go home right now.'

'Why? Aren't you staying with us?' Nina looked worried.

'No, I need to talk to Kerber. He might have more information for us,' Anni said quickly, hoping Nina didn't realise what she was hiding about Hugo.

'Can you thank the German from me?' Nina said, then shook her head. 'There's something I never thought I'd say. Be safe, OK?'

Anni smiled. 'I will. Sleep tight.'

When she came outside, Hugo was standing by the gate, looking at the barn with a frown on his face.

'Hi,' she said. 'What are you looking at?'

'I think your barn needs repairs. The roof is sagging,' he said, smiling at her.

Anni shrugged. 'No point. Lack of materials and no available carpenters to do the work.'

'Because they're all at Hagland,' he said, slipping his arm around her shoulder. 'I'm sorry.'

'No need.' Anni yawned. 'Now I'm sorry.'

He laughed and pulled her closer. 'I'm glad I could help tonight.'

'So am I, even if you scared me half to death.' Anni leant against him when they started walking back to the house. 'I'm absolutely knackered,' she said, and yawned again.

Hugo laughed. 'By tomorrow it will probably feel as if my arms have fallen off.'

'Not used to manual work, are you? And I thought your people are all about the physical force,' Anni teased.

'No, people like me do paperwork,' he said quietly. 'It's nothing like what you have done.'

'I never feel as if I do enough,' Anni said.

Hugo looked surprised. 'Anni, I think you are the bravest person I have ever met.'

Anni laughed. 'You're exaggerating.'

It was hard to believe that a short while ago, they had been in so much danger. It seemed all so absurd, so surreal.

'Not at all. Thanks to you, a young man was saved,' Hugo said. 'My people would have killed him on sight. I can promise you that.'

Anni looked at him. 'How can you live with people like that?'

He stopped and nodded slightly towards a Wehrmacht officer and two soldiers coming towards them. Anni drew a sharp breath. 'Don't let on that you understand German,' he said quietly.

He waved at the soldiers and called out a greeting. All Anni could think about was Nina and Ingrid. What if the soldiers went to the farm? She looked over her shoulder, ready to run.

'Don't, Anni.' He squeezed her hand. 'Trust me.'

Anni stayed quiet while he walked over to the officer in charge. She couldn't hear what they said. The two soldiers stared at her, measuring her, she thought. Anni looked down, scared they would see the panic in her eyes.

After what seemed like an eternity, Hugo came back to her. He took her hand and squeezed it gently.

The officer tipped his hat to them and barked an order

at the two soldiers. They turned around and left. Anni looked at Hugo. 'What did he say?'

'They're returning to Gard,' he said, nodding towards the monument. 'They were patrolling the beach and found nothing.'

Anni frowned. 'What about the farm?'

'It's safe. They were never in that area. I gave them no reason to think they should be.' He put his arm around her again. 'Do you want to go back?'

Anni thought about it. 'No, I don't want to scare them now. Let's go.'

When they arrived at the house, she didn't want to bring him up to the bedroom she had shared with Lars.

Instead, she took his hand and led him to his bedroom, to the narrow bed that had become the safest place in the world to her.

Chapter Twenty-Four

April came with almost summery weather. The wildflowers on the fields surrounding the monument made everything seem cheerful and hopeful.

They could sense now that the end of the war was close. Shamefully, Anni admitted to herself that she had mixed feelings. She wanted the fighting and suffering to be over. More than anything she wanted the Occupation to end. But she didn't want Hugo to leave. She was happy, as crazy as it was. It was a feeling she had almost forgotten. He made her happy, and she knew she did the same for him. Couldn't that be enough for now?

Ingrid had picked a colourful bouquet of spring flowers and smiled up at her.

'Can we put some in Herr Kerber's room?' she asked when they entered the house.

'Of course you can. He would like that, I'm sure.'

Anni smiled at the sight of Hugo's coat on one of the hangers. It was nice to have a man in the house.

He had proven himself useful. Nina would never forget what he had done for Martin; nor would Anni. Nina had already written to Martin several times and he had been allowed to answer. Now she was planning a trip to Oslo for a visit.

Anni reminded herself to be careful. This relationship . . . or affair, or whatever she wanted to call it, wouldn't last long. When the war ended, Hugo would return to Germany. And she would be left to pick up the pieces after Lars's bombshell.

Not tonight, she thought. *I don't want to think about any of that. Not now.* Hugo had been in Oslo for a week, and she couldn't wait to see him again.

She knew she was selfish; she knew she should have stayed away from him. The attitude towards the girls who went with Germans had become increasingly hostile. She could see it in the way people looked at them when she was in town. And she was one of them, even if it was in secret.

I have no regrets, she thought when she came into the lounge and found him sitting on her sofa, reading a book.

Ingrid waved her flowers at him. 'For your room,' she said.

Anni translated and he smiled at the little girl. 'Thank you, Ingrid,' he said. 'They are beautiful. Like you.'

That made Ingrid giggle and look at her mother for translation.

'He says they're pretty, and so are you. Go and put the flowers in a glass of water. We'll start dinner soon,' Anni said, smiling at her.

Ingrid scrambled into the kitchen, and they could hear her sing to herself.

She stood still, watching him watch her. He smiled, and she felt as if her heart expanded.

'How was your day?' he asked and stood up from the sofa.

'Fine.' Anni held out her hand. 'Not too close. I don't want Ingrid to be confused.'

He looked tired. 'She's in the kitchen.'

Before she could protest, he leant forward and kissed her. 'I've missed you,' he said.

'I missed you too.' Anni held her hand on his cheek for a second. 'How was your trip?'

'Exhausting. They were celebrating Hitler's birthday as if nothing was going on. As if Germany isn't in ruins and the Soviets aren't bombing Berlin to rubble. It was surreal,' he said.

'Everyone must know the war is coming to an end,' Anni said.

Hugo looked sad. 'When the Reich falls, it won't be easy. So many people still cling to the lies, to Hitler. The good thing is that more and more people want to surrender. That's something, I guess.'

Anni hugged him. 'We'll be strong and brave, and we'll believe everything will work out in the end.'

Hugo ran his finger along her cheek. 'You really believe that?'

'Yes, I do. I believe there will be a future after this, a place where my little girl can be free and happy.' Anni smiled. 'Otherwise, what has it all been for?'

'I hope you're right.' Hugo straightened his back. 'In the

meantime, I think we should have a plan for us.'

'Such as?' Anni was distracted by him standing so close to her.

'Will you marry me, Anni?' he said, looking so serious.

Anni's breath caught in her chest. She hadn't told him about Lars's betrayal. She never thought she would have to. 'Oh.'

'I know you're still married, but I was hoping you would consider it anyway,' he said.

'And come with you to Germany?' she said, trying to make sense of it.

He nodded, eager now. 'Not until I know you and Ingrid will be comfortable,' he said. 'The only thing I have left in Germany is my family's farm. After all this, I'd like to see if I can make a living off the land. I love you, Anni. I don't want to lose you.'

Anni was at a loss for words. She found it difficult to imagine her life without him, but this was impossible. 'I . . . I don't know what to say,' she said. 'It's not something I can decide for myself. There's Ingrid and Guri, and . . . then Lars will come home.'

Somehow, she couldn't make herself tell him about Lars's marriage in England. What if he thought she had only gone to bed with him because her no-good husband cheated on her? She was too ashamed to admit it to him.

'I know it won't be easy, but we can make it happen if you love me too.' Hugo's smile lit up his face. 'I will do my best to give you and Ingrid the life you deserve.'

Anni looked behind her to see if Ingrid was there before leaning closer. 'All I can think about right now is you,' she said, and kissed him.

* * *

They spent hours dreaming up their new life. Hugo told her about the farm, and he made it sound so idyllic. By now they all knew Germany was destroyed, but she didn't care. It was a sweet fantasy.

She lived in bliss, until May, when Hugo came back from Hagland, looking like a ghost.

Anni was in the kitchen, and Ingrid had been given the important role of running to Guri's farm to feed the goats.

'Anni,' he said, standing in the door. 'I have to leave. Today.'

She frowned. 'Now? Why? I thought you could stay here until the end.'

He came closer to her and took her hands. 'Listen, this is not official knowledge, so be careful whom you tell it to. Two days ago, Hitler killed himself in the bunker in Berlin.'

Anni swallowed. 'He's dead? Are you sure?'

'Yes, he appointed Grossadmiral Dönitz as the new leader. When our soldiers learn of this, there's no way to predict how they will react.'

'I see. But why does that mean you have to leave? Can't you stay here?'

He shook his head. 'I've been ordered to Oslo, to help prepare the transition that will come. The people who want this to end peacefully, who want to make sure there's no fighting, are under great pressure by those who want to fight until death.'

'You mean like Reichskommissar Terboven and his allies?' Anni put her hands on her stomach. 'I didn't realise.'

He held her close now. 'I will come back for you. Don't give up on me.'

Anni smiled. 'I won't. I never will.'

She kissed him, and they made love for the last time. Anni knew she couldn't tell him about the baby, not now. It would only make him more worried.

I'll tell him when I see him again. A lovely surprise for him, and for me, she thought.

Later, after Hugo had left, Ingrid came running home, yelling that Besta was at the farm. *One less thing to worry about*, Anni thought, relieved her mother-in-law was safe.

Chapter Twenty-Five

Anni

7th May, 1945. Liberation comes to Norway

It felt as if everyone was holding their breath, waiting for the worst, hoping for the best. Anni stood outside the house and looked towards the school. The swastika still fluttered from the flagpole.

She didn't have a radio, but everyone knew that in a matter of hours the war would officially be over. *After five long years*, she thought, not sure if she could even believe it.

People were already celebrating. She could hear shouting and music coming from the fairground. Ingrid was standing next to her, and she could see that she was worried. 'It will be fine, sweet pea,' she said, hoping she would be right.

She didn't know how the situation was in town, but she didn't want to go in there, not with Ingrid, not when there was still a chance the Germans might fight back. There were plenty of soldiers and officers who talked about defending Norway from the 'Allied invasion'.

Anni pulled a face. *Defending*, she thought. *What world are they living in, I wonder. We don't need any more defending, thank you very much.*

But the reality was that about four hundred thousand German soldiers were still in Norway, scared and angry. Although many men from the Home Front and Milorg were in the country by now, they wouldn't be enough if the Germans fought back.

Anni sighed. Her fear would make absolutely no difference in the end. She had no idea where Hugo was, or if they would be able to find each other on 'the other side'. She put her hands on her stomach. It was too early for her to show, but she knew. This would change everything. She didn't know how yet, but she couldn't have the baby and hope nobody would notice.

And for now, she was still the only one who knew Lars had divorced her.

Suddenly the swastika disappeared from the school, followed by the Norwegian flag being hoisted up in its place. Anni stared at it, not noticing tears streaming down her face. How on earth had they managed to hide the flag for so long? She put her hand over her mouth, not sure if she was laughing or crying.

'Mamma?' Ingrid took her hand and shook it lightly. 'Mamma, what is it? Why are you crying?'

Anni smiled down at her. 'Do you see the flag, sweet pea?'

Ingrid looked at the school. 'What is it?'

'Can't you see? It's the Norwegian flag. That means that peace has finally come. The war is over.' She dried her tears before lifting Ingrid up and giving her a big kiss. 'We're free, Ingrid. It's over.'

Ingrid threw her arms around her. 'Can we have cake now?'

'Yes, as much as we can possibly find.' Anni gave her another kiss and put her down. 'Come, let's run to Besta. Maybe she doesn't know yet.'

They ran down the path, Ingrid squealing with laughter.

Anni kept having to dry her face. It felt so impossibly wonderful, as if the shadow of the last five years had suddenly disappeared.

When they arrived at the farm, the front door was wide open and they could hear voices from within.

Ingrid pulled loose from her hand and ran inside. 'Besta! We're here!'

Guri sat in the lounge, tears streaming down her face, when they came inside. She was pressing a handkerchief to her face.

Ingrid ran to her and threw her arms around her. 'Don't be sad, Besta. Peace has come, and now Pappa will come too.'

From the radio bellowing in the corner came the reassuring voice of King Haakon, talking from London. Even his soft Danish voice had taken on a twinge of excitement.

Anni didn't realise she was crying again too, until her nose started dripping. She found a handkerchief in her pocket and blew her nose. 'We weren't sure if you knew. How did you get a radio?'

Guri looked up at her, not hearing the question. 'It's over, Anni,' she said, awe in her voice. 'It's finally over.'

'Have they surrendered?' Anni couldn't grasp the meaning of the King's words.

'Not officially yet, but they're saying that Terboven has been stripped of his powers, and that general, what's his name, has taken over the command of the forces in Norway.'

'General Böhme,' Anni said, remembering that Hugo had said the general was a loyal Nazi, but that Admiral Dönitz wasn't, and he had been appointed by Hitler himself. 'I'm not sure he's like Terboven,' she said.

'I'm waiting for them to tell us that that bastard Quisling has been strung up somewhere,' Guri said.

She spat the words out, and for once Anni didn't stop her from swearing.

Ingrid sat curled up in Guri's lap. She frowned. 'Why is that man talking funny on that box?'

'That's our king, sweet pea. He speaks Danish, and that's a radio,' Anni said. 'I forgot you've never seen one of these.'

She sank down on the floor and stared at the radio cabinet. 'How on earth did you manage to get this thing in here by yourself, Guri? It's monstrous.'

Guri shrugged. 'I've always had it in the house. I hid it with the goats.'

Anni burst out laughing. Somehow that seemed the most hilarious thing she had ever heard.

Guri clapped her hands. 'We can't sit here as if we're forgotten wallflowers. Let's go.'

'Where, Besta?' Ingrid looked up at her.

'To town, of course. I'm sure everyone and their uncle is there to join in.'

Anni hesitated. 'Are you sure it will be safe?'

'Yes. There is no way I'll be sitting here like an old woman muttering to myself with all that is going on. It's historical, isn't it?' Guri pushed herself up from the chair. 'I'm going to feed the goats, put on a proper frock, and then I'm off to town.'

Ingrid looked at Anni. 'Can we, Mamma? Can we please go?'

'Yes, Besta is right. We don't want to miss this.' Anni stood up too. 'And we have to look our best, don't we?'

Ingrid nodded. 'Can I wear my dress?'

'Yes, you can. Not sure I even have one,' Anni said to Guri. 'I can't remember the last time I wore a dress.'

'Then come as you are. Nobody is going to care.'

Anni didn't have a dress. She had refashioned most of her pre-war dresses and skirts into clothes for Ingrid.

She put on some clean trousers, a blouse that was too big, and an even looser light jacket over that. Looking in the mirror, she felt safe with her secret.

Ingrid had already managed to pull on the dress Guri had bartered for her. She smiled at her, and Anni realised how much she had grown since before Christmas. 'Is one of your front teeth loose?'

Ingrid looked cross-eyed along her nose and stuck out her tongue. 'Yes, it is, Mamma,' she said, horrified and excited at the same time.

'Don't worry. When it falls out, the tooth fairy will give you two *øre* for it,' Anni said.

Ingrid's eyes grew wide. 'She will? Why?'

'I don't know, sweet pea. It's what she does,' Anni said.

Ingrid pondered that for a minute. 'She sounds nice.'

'I'm sure she is.' Anni tied up her hair and looked at her. 'Now, how do I look?'

'You look pretty today, Mamma,' she said, giggling.

'And so do you,' Anni said. 'Let's go and find the Peace, shall we?'

They walked down the road, past the prayer house, and stopped at the bus stop. There was no sign of Guri.

'Will the bus come, Mamma?'

'I hope so. I think we should wait and see what comes along,' Anni said.

They sat down on the grass. It was a lovely day. To distract Ingrid, she pulled grass straws and tried to teach her how to make noise. Ingrid couldn't get the hang of it, but she did have fun.

There wasn't a lot of traffic. At some point a Wehrmacht lorry filled with German soldiers passed them, coming from town. Her whole body stiffened, anticipating the worst.

'Look, Mamma. Look at the flags. They are different!' Ingrid looked up at her with a big smile.

Anni noticed it too. On the lorry they had put Norwegian flags, flying in the wind. The driver, obviously a Norwegian, waved at them, shouting something she didn't catch, grinning from ear to ear.

'Why is he shouting congratulations?' Ingrid was confounded.

Anni waved back at the man. 'Because the country is ours again. You can wave back.'

Ingrid waved and when the lorry passed them, Anni spotted several Norwegian men in the back, next to a group of German soldiers. The Norwegians were fully equipped with weapons. They waved back to Ingrid, smiling at her.

Anni watched the German soldiers. They looked defeated, tired, hanging their heads down.

She felt a stab of hatred, so sharp she almost threw up, then controlled herself. They were defeated. It was over. They could all finally look forward again.

Anni put a hand on her stomach. *Who am I to hate them?* she thought.

She turned to Ingrid, who was still waving. 'Maybe we should go back and get the bike. I'm not sure the bus will come today.'

Ingrid didn't listen. She pointed at another lorry coming towards them. It was filled with people, shouting and laughing.

When the driver caught eye of them, he stopped, and leant over. 'Are you going into town?'

Anni smiled. 'Yes, but I don't think there's a bus.'

'Not today, Mrs. Hop up in the back. We're giving everyone a lift.'

Anni walked around to the back and eager hands lifted Ingrid up, then a young man pulled her up too. Someone handed Ingrid a flag to wave, and when they started to sing the national anthem, Anni joined in. Ingrid was having great fun, especially when someone gave her a piece of candy.

A military lorry passed them, and Anni could see there was armed guards on this too. But the men sitting there were civilians. Behind her, the young people howled at them, yelling dirty words. Anni threw a glance at Ingrid, who was sitting with her mouth open.

Anni wasn't sure how to deal with it. She figured Ingrid

didn't understand most of it, anyway, since most of the insults were said in German.

She looked at the lorry again. The people wore suits and hats and looked like they had come right from the office. *They all looked like Hugo*, an unbidden thought said. But she couldn't think of him now, not today.

A young man flopped down next to her.

'I'm sorry about that. People are going overboard today,' he said.

'If not today, then when?' Anni said.

'Yeah, that's what I say too,' he said, beaming at her. 'I'm hoping we'll be able to raid the liquor cabinet in the Wehrmacht offices in town. I've heard that they have barrels of the good stuff in there. I think we deserve a proper drink.'

Anni nodded to the next lorry that passed them. 'Where are they taking them?'

The man dismissed the lorry with a short wave. 'To Hagland. They've made the fortress into a camp for the Germans. I hope they shoot the bastards,' he said, unable to hide his anger. 'If it were up to me, I'd give weapons to the Russian prisoners, let them handle it.'

I hope not, Anni thought. 'Were those people soldiers too?'

He shrugged. 'I don't know. I think maybe officers. There are rumours that some of them ditch their uniforms to try and hide. But they won't get away with it. I've heard that the resistance has collected name lists from the start. The London-government has them too. They'll be caught.'

Anni wondered if Hugo was in a place like Hagland somewhere. She hadn't heard from him since he left for Oslo. Watching the lorries made her scared for him. Where was he? And more importantly, how was he?

'Are they . . . are they shooting Germans?' she asked.

The young man frowned. 'No, not anyone from our side. Have you had an opportunity to listen to the radio? My old man hid ours in the old hunting cabin up in the mountain. We brought it down two days ago.'

'What did you hear?'

He spotted Ingrid. 'Don't look scared, little one. It's all right now. I promise.'

Ingrid beamed at him but didn't say anything.

He turned to Anni again. 'They're saying that the official surrender will be midnight tonight. But we all know it's over, so I'm not worried they will fight back. They would have done so by now. But I heard from someone that Terboven is cowering at the Crown Prince's Estate outside Oslo with Police Minister Jonas Lie and a few of the other bastards. I've no idea where Quisling is. I hope they all go the same way as their horrible boss.'

Anni found it difficult to process. 'Are you sure we're all safe?'

He nodded. 'Absolutely. There's Milorg and Home Front boys everywhere, all over the country. We have nothing to worry about anymore.'

When they arrived in town, Norwegian flags were everywhere. More than she had ever seen at any 17th May celebrations before the war.

'The Hitler teeth are gone,' she said, when the car drove down the hill.

'Yes, we did that yesterday. It was quite a job.' The boy grinned at her again. 'My arms are still smarting.'

Anni couldn't help laughing. 'Well done.'

334

The lorry had to stop before they got close to the main street. There were too many people milling about.

Anni jumped down and he lifted Ingrid down to her. 'Thank you for the lift,' she said.

'Have a lovely peace,' he said, grinning from ear to ear, as the lorry drove off after finding a gap in the crowd.

Ingrid skipped next to her. 'Where's Besta?'

'Besta is around here somewhere,' Anni said, watching the crowds filling Haraldsgaten. 'Or she will be soon. We'll head over to the post office to wait for her. Don't let go of my hand, Ingrid.'

'I can't see her.' Ingrid tried to strain her neck.

'Don't worry. We'll find her.'

Probably dancing in the middle of the street, Anni thought.

She held on tightly to Ingrid's hand while they tried to make their way through the crowds.

People were running and singing, completely oblivious to anything else than pure joy. *There will be a lot of babies over Christmas*, she thought.

Anni couldn't help smiling. She felt the way they did, of course she did, but there was also the worry for Hugo. She was sure now he was probably arrested in Oslo with the rest of them, but how was she going to find out? She had no idea.

'Anni! Anni!'

Nina came running towards them, then threw herself around Anni's neck, sobbing and laughing. 'I'm so happy to see you!'

She let go of Anni, then hugged Ingrid, then Anni again. Finally, she settled down. 'I had a telephone call from Oslo.

Pappa will be released. He's coming home, Anni. Any day now. And it's all thanks to you.'

Nina burst into tears again, but now Anni knew that she was happy.

'That's the best news, Nina. Even better than all this ruckus,' she said and kissed her on the forehead.

Nina sniffled a few times, then looked around. 'Isn't it wonderful?'

'More than wonderful. I've been so worried about Martin,' Anni said.

'And Lars will be coming home soon too, I'm sure,' Nina said, not noticing Anni flinching.

She didn't have to answer. Someone started shouting close by, and then there was more shouting.

Anni took a firmer grip on Ingrid's hand. 'What's going on?'

Nina stood on her toes. 'I think they're attacking a girl,' she said, looking shocked.

Anni decided to see what was going on. 'Stay close,' she said to Ingrid.

As they got closer, Anni could see a group of young men, screaming at a woman. She suddenly heard what they were yelling.

'Where's your lover now, German slut? Did he leave you with a Nazi bastard in your belly?' One of the men, barely out of his teens, was clearly the aggressor. The other men gathered around the woman, screaming obscenities.

'Let's cut her hair!' one of them yelled. The others cheered.

Nina grabbed Anni's arm. 'Come, let's go.'

'No, we have to help her,' Anni said.

Nina shook her head. 'She deserves it,' she said in a voice dripping with contempt. 'Running with a German like that? They all knew there would be a price to pay.'

'How do you know that it's true?' Anni couldn't move.

'Mamma?' Ingrid pulled at her hand. 'I'm scared.'

Anni picked her up and put her on her hip, holding her close. 'Don't worry. We're perfectly safe.'

She followed Nina past the men, and almost stopped. If it hadn't been for Ingrid hiding her face against her neck, she would have.

She noticed another man a few steps away. A policeman, watching what was going on with a small smile. Anni couldn't believe he didn't stop it.

'Are you going let them do this to the poor girl?' she said, her voice shaking with anger.

'She should be ashamed of herself; she's a Nazi slut,' he said, looking at her.

There was that word again. She hugged Ingrid tighter. 'Do you treat quislings, the people who made big money on the Nazis, this way, or is that reserved for women you don't know are guilty of anything? I think the shame is yours.'

She didn't wait for him to respond, turned around and walked over to where Nina was standing.

'Why did you do that?' Nina said. 'What if they had turned on you?'

'Bunch of bullies, going after the weakest,' Anni muttered. 'If that's peace, they can all go to hell.'

Nina put a hand over her mouth. Anni wasn't sure if she was shocked or laughing.

'Martin would never have allowed it,' she added.

Nina looked upset. 'I know. You're right.'

After a few steps, Anni turned. The woman was bundled up against the wall, crying, trying to hide her face. Anni handed Ingrid to Nina. 'Wait here.'

Nina grabbed her arm. 'No, Anni. The policeman will take care of it. Look.'

Without looking in her direction, the policeman took action. 'Run along, boys,' he said. 'You've had your fun.'

The men ran off, laughing when they did so. The policeman looked at the crying woman, then threw a glance at Anni before he too walked away.

'Stay here,' she said again.

Anni hurried over to the woman, only to discover she was frightfully young, barely older than Nina. Her face was swollen and blotchy, and she was sobbing so hard, she could barely breathe.

'How can I help?' Anni said, touching her shoulder gently. 'Is there anywhere I can take you?'

The woman looked up at her. 'My mother's shop is over there,' she managed to say.

She took Anni's hand and got on her feet. 'I look a right mess,' she muttered. 'At least they didn't cut my hair.'

'Are you going to be OK?' Anni didn't want to let her go in the state she was in.

The woman smiled sadly at her. 'Thank you. They were wrong, you know. I've never gone with a soldier. My mum would have my hide if I'd as much as looked at one.'

She thanked her again, before hurrying across the street and disappearing into a shop.

Anni ran over to the others, hoping Ingrid hadn't been too scared.

Ingrid had been crying. Anni sat down in front of her. 'It's OK now. The policeman chased them away. You don't have to be scared.'

'Jesus,' Nina said, when Anni stood up and lifted Ingrid on her hip again. Ingrid held her arms tight around her neck.

'You are not right in the head; I swear to God I thought those guys were going after you next.' Nina shook her head. 'What if they had attacked you?'

'Bullies like that are easy to deal with. Show them no fear, and they crumble,' Anni said, a lot more confidently than she felt.

Anni hugged Ingrid and kissed her on the cheek. The knowledge that this could happen to her had unsettled her.

She had to talk to Guri about the baby before it was too late.

Chapter Twenty-Six

Anni had left Ingrid with Guri to go to the milk shop. Guri had insisted they would have cheese. Anni doubted it. *It would take more than three days until things were back to normal*, she thought and opened the door. Women's voices floated outside, talking and laughing, and it made Anni smile too. It had been too long since the atmosphere had been this relaxed.

The shop had wall to wall shelves, still filled with empty cans with faded labels, much as it had looked the last five years. All the ordinances from the Occupation forces had been taken down, she noticed. *Ripped down*, she thought. Whoever did that, had done it in anger. There were pieces of paper stuck to the nails.

Good for you, she thought.

The shopkeeper looked up, noticed her and nodded

curtly. Not his usual greeting, although Anni didn't think much about it. Not until she noticed that everybody had gone silent.

She smiled at the women in there, most of whom she'd known for years. No one smiled back.

Not today. Today they glared at her.

Anni felt uncomfortable but didn't want to show it. She took a step forward, and the other women all moved out of the way.

She smiled at the shopkeeper. 'My mother-in-law heard you have cheese today,' she said.

His eyes shifted to the women behind her. 'We're all out, Mrs Odland.'

Anni looked behind him. 'Are you sure? Because I can see you have more.'

'I don't want to get in trouble, Mrs Odland, but those are for my regular customers,' he said.

'I'm one of you regular customers. This is my regular store,' she said, keeping her voice calm while mostly wanting to scream at him.

'We don't want your kind here, and I'm sending in a complaint to the authorities about you,' one of the women shrieked behind her.

Anni turned around and looked at her. 'What did you say? What's *my* kind?'

The woman narrowed her eyes. 'You were with a German. Behaving no better than a common tart. We all knew it. Him staying at your house and all.'

A couple of the other women nodded, but most looked away.

Anni stood her ground. 'How dare you accuse me of

something like that?' she said, keeping her voice levelled and calm.

'Someone saw you with him,' the same woman said. 'You kissed him.'

She almost asked how anyone could have seen that, but that would absolutely get her in trouble.

Anni stepped away from the counter, standing closer to the woman. She didn't know her, and it enraged her that a stranger would talk to her like that. Even if she was right . . .

'That is a filthy lie,' she said, narrowing her eyes. 'Don't you dare make up stories about me.'

'He lived in your house, didn't he?' The woman wasn't about to give up that easily.

'Do you think I could have refused a Nazi when he decided to billet in my house? Or are you so thick you pretend to not know what would have happened to me if I had tried to say no?'

The woman looked around for help. 'You looked far too friendly,' she said.

'So, if one of them had decided to move into your house, you would have told him you didn't want any Nazi soldiers in your house?'

'I wouldn't promenade with someone like him in the middle of the night,' the woman said, more unsure now.

Damn, Anni thought. The walk from the monument after they had helped Hari. That was what this was all about. But she hadn't kissed Hugo then, not outside the house.

'Some of you left your children with me while that man was in my house. It didn't bother you then.' Anni looked around at the other women. 'Would you have said "To hell with you," if he had come to your house?'

None of them said a word, and the shopkeeper looked worried.

'The war is over, and they'll be sent back to bloody Germany. Or they'll be shot. They don't deserve any better. And neither do sluts like you!' The woman tried to stare her down. 'Carrying on like that, a married woman with a child!'

Anni couldn't stop herself. She slapped her across the face, and the other women gasped.

'I've done nothing wrong.' Anni looked around, challenging them to say something. 'You're all as bad as she is if you think I have.'

Anni didn't wait for an answer. She sent an icy look at the shopkeeper. 'Keep your damn cheese. I hope you all choke on it.'

After that, she turned around and left the shop.

She felt pretty good when she stood outside. Too bad about the cheese, though. Behind her she heard the women talking again. Somebody laughed.

'Oh, God,' she muttered. 'I should have kept my mouth shut.'

On the way to the farm, she knew she was running out of time. She needed to talk to Guri now.

Anni stopped at her house to find Lars's letter. She couldn't tell Guri the truth without also telling her how it had happened. She had no intention of letting Guri think she had cheated on Lars.

Anni waited until Ingrid had fallen asleep in Guri's bed. She had asked if they could stay over, and Guri had been more than happy to comply.

When they sat down in Guri's lounge, her mother-in-law turned to her.

'You've been like a skittish cat ever since you returned from the shop, and without the cheese, mind you,' Guri said.

'This is worse than cheese,' Anni said, trying to collect her thoughts. She hadn't told Guri the details about what happened.

Guri frowned. 'How much worse?'

Anni could hear her voice shaking slightly. 'I am so sorry about this, Guri.'

Guri leant forward. Her face was lined with worry.

Anni took a deep breath. 'I hate doing this to you.'

'Get to it, Anni. You're scaring me.'

Anni jumped right into it. 'I'm pregnant.'

She waited for a response from Guri and could see her face crumble. 'I'm so sorry to load this on you, but I need your help.'

Guri gaped at her. 'It's that German, isn't it? Did he force you? He must have. I knew there was something wrong.'

'No, it wasn't like that. He never forced me to do anything, Guri. It was my choice,' Anni said.

'But you swore to me that you were faithful to Lars. How will he react when he learns that you're having another man's child? And an enemy at that,' Guri said with bitterness in her voice.

Now comes the worst part, Anni thought.

'Lars won't care.' She took out the letter and handed it to her.

Guri took it and opened the envelope. 'What's this?'

'Martin gave me this in January. I'm sorry I've kept it

from you all these months, but I couldn't show it to you. We had enough to worry about.' Anni knew she was rambling, but Guri's silence was unnerving. She pressed a hand against her mouth, forcing herself not to cry. *If I start, I can't stop*, she thought.

Guri read everything, then put the letter down on the table. She looked as if she had aged in the few minutes it had taken her to read it. 'Oh my God,' she said quietly.

Anni tried to say something, but Guri stopped her.

'You did right by not telling me. I would have been on the next boat to Shetland to give him a piece of my mind,' she said. 'This is worse than anything I could ever have imagined.'

She looked up at Anni. 'This is why you involved yourself with the German, isn't it? Were you trying to get back at Lars?'

Anni shook her head. 'No, it wasn't like that. The attraction between us had been there for a while. But I would never have acted on it if it hadn't been for this. Going with Hugo wasn't cheating. I wasn't married anymore.'

'And what Lars has done is legal? How is that possible?'

Anni could see that Guri was trying so hard to keep her emotions in check. 'Martin said that the London-government had changed a paragraph in the law that would allow Norwegians outside of Norway to get divorced and marry someone else. They saw no need to inform the wives about this. No need at all.' Anni pressed her hands together. 'I could see so clearly how I would stand down at the harbour, waiting for him to walk off the boat, with his new wife, and tell me I wasn't a married woman anymore. So, yes, I was furious and heartbroken.'

'And that's why you decided to sleep with this man.' Guri didn't ask this time.

'I . . . it felt as if it gave me the permission, the freedom to act on something I had wanted for some time, yes.' Anni took a deep breath. 'But I wish it hadn't happened. I wish I could have gone back to a life with Lars, for us to raise Ingrid together. I would have been happy with that. I think it would have been a good life. But Lars took that from me, Guri.'

Guri knitted her hands and was visibly shaking with anger. 'I can't think of Lars right now. I'll deal with him later.'

Anni didn't say anything. She felt exhausted, drained of all energy. It was a relief telling it to someone she trusted, but the situation was still a mess.

Guri thought so too. 'How could you let this happen? There are methods, I think, and . . . and someone like him would surely know how to procure things?'

Anni swallowed hard. 'I honestly didn't think it was possible for me to become pregnant. My monthlies have been so irregular the last few years, and the doctor said it was to be expected with the food we have and the whole situation.'

'Why are you telling me?' Guri had tears in her eyes. 'Why now?'

Anni looked away. 'Because a woman in the store accused me of being with Hugo. I can't hide the pregnancy much longer, and I need to protect Ingrid.'

Guri did something she hadn't expected. She leant over and put both her hands over hers.

'I'm sorry,' she said, looking more serious than Anni had

ever seen her. 'I feel so betrayed, and I can't even imagine what you felt when you learnt this.'

Anni took a deep breath. 'I made my bed, and I don't regret it. Unfortunately, I didn't think of the consequences.'

Guri folded her hands. 'Tell me what you need from me.'

'I have to leave as soon as possible, and I can't return until after the baby is born,' Anni said, with a lump in her throat choking her.

Guri was silent for a moment. 'And then what?' she said, her voice so gentle Anni almost burst into tears.

'I'll give the baby up for . . . for adoption, and then come home for Ingrid,' Anni said, trying her best to keep her voice steady.

Guri watched her. 'Can you? Can you give up a child that easily?'

Anni tried to smile. 'I don't have any choice. Ingrid needs me more than ever now, and I've seen how they talk about the women who had relations with Germans. Ingrid doesn't deserve to hear that. Nor does the baby.'

'That's an impossible choice,' Guri said.

'Yes, I know.' Anni bit her lip, forcing back tears. 'I don't know what to do.'

Guri held on to her hand. 'Maybe we can find another way,' she said.

'None that I can see. I've been thinking about nothing else for weeks,' Anni said.

'You can go away and have the baby, and I can bring Ingrid to you when you're settled,' Guri said with a steady voice. 'That way you can keep them both.'

Anni could hardly believe it. 'You would do that?'

'Yes, I would. Lars has a new wife in London. It curdles my blood to think about it. But it also means that it's unlikely he'll come home.' Guri waved her hands. 'I haven't heard anything from him yet, but I sent a letter to the Seamen's Church and asked them to help me find him.'

Anni drew a sharp breath. 'What if he takes Ingrid with him when I'm not here?'

Guri shook her head. 'No, I would never let him. She belongs with you, Anni. I know that much. The bond you two have, it's special. Lars is not a bad man, but I don't know anything about this wife of his. What kind of woman marries a man who is already married? She must be horrible.'

Anni couldn't help but smile. 'We don't know that.'

'Of course not. But it's only a matter of months, right? When are you due?'

'Early January, I think,' Anni said, putting a hand on her stomach as she spoke.

'The baby will be born then, and you'll have Ingrid with you again before her next birthday.' Guri smiled. 'That's not long at all.'

More than enough time to get everything in order, Anni thought. *More than enough time to create a home for all three of us.*

Guri frowned. 'What about him, the father?'

'Hugo went to Oslo a week before the Peace. Most likely, he's already been sent back to Germany, and I'll never see him again,' Anni said, feeling a stab in her heart when she said it.

'I have an old schoolfriend in Tromsø. She'll take you in,' Guri said.

Anni shook her head. 'The north is too bombed out. The last thing they need is a pregnant woman.'

Guri sighed. 'I suppose you're right.'

'I'll go to Oslo,' Anni said, nodding. 'That's far enough away from here, and nobody will know me. I'll tell people I'm a widow. It will be easier in a big city.'

'Good. I have a friend in Oslo too; she'll look after you,' Guri said. 'I'll send her a letter tomorrow.'

'Thank you, Guri.' Anni fought back tears of relief. 'I want you to know that I might decide not to keep the baby.'

'When you have the baby, you can decide what to do,' Guri said in a soft voice. 'It's your child, as much as Ingrid is. It's not a package or a baby goat.'

Anni swallowed hard. 'I'll leave as soon as I can. That will give me enough time to prepare Ingrid.'

'I'll help you. You know this is going to be hard for her,' Guri said.

'I've failed her so badly. I couldn't protect her from the war or from what Lars has done, and I can't protect her from what I've done,' Anni said, crying softly now.

'You know she's safe with me. I'll protect her. I promise,' Guri said, and hugged her.

Anni couldn't get another word out. She felt exhausted and guilty, and it was all too much.

Chapter Twenty-Seven

They came two days later, early in the morning. Anni was about to put on the kettle for coffee when she heard knocking on the door.

She took the tea towel with her, drying her hands while she walked through the lounge. When she opened the door, a policeman was standing on the steps, looking at her with cold eyes.

'Mrs Odland?'

Anni looked over his shoulder. She could see three more men, one in army uniform, the two others in casual clothes. The black armbands told her they were from the Milorg.

She wasn't sure why they were there. Maybe it had something to do with Martin.

She smiled at them. 'Yes, that's me. Do you have news about Martin Foss?'

'We're here to take you to the police station. You're under arrest for fraternising with the enemy,' he said, ignoring her question.

Anni didn't notice that the tea towel dropped to the floor. 'Excuse me?'

He pulled out a piece of paper. 'Says so right here.'

Anni took a step backwards. 'No. I haven't done anything. You have no right to arrest me.'

The policeman smirked. 'We have every right. We represent the government of the free Norway, Mrs Odland. People like you will face justice now.'

Anni couldn't make sense of what he was saying. 'No,' she said again.

One of the Milorg men took a step forward. 'There's no point arguing. You'll have your say at the station. You can come with us peacefully, or we will carry you.'

Anni became aware of Ingrid pressing against her. 'I can't leave my child alone.'

He looked at Ingrid with an expressionless face. 'That's not our problem. The children of Germans are not our problem.'

Anni faced him, so furious she could have hit him. 'My daughter was born in 1938,' she said, her voice colder than his eyes. 'Her father is Lars Odland, an officer in the Norwegian merchant marine, who has sailed for this country since long before 1940. So don't you dare talk about her like that.'

He looked taken aback. 'Fine. Is there anyone who can take her? Otherwise, we have to bring her with us.'

Anni looked down at Ingrid's pale face, putting her hand on her head. 'No, I don't want her at the police station.

Her grandmother lives on a farm a few minutes' walk from here. She'll take her.'

'Good,' he said. 'Can the girl go there by herself?'

Anni looked down at Ingrid again, who was shaking. She was terrified. Anni had to think on her feet. It was clear that the men had no intention of leaving without her.

'Her name is Ingrid Odland, and she's old enough to go alone,' Anni said, trying to control her anger.

'I don't want to, Mamma,' Ingrid said, tears running down her cheeks. 'Please, don't make me.'

Anni crouched down and held her arms gently. 'Listen to me, sweet pea. I want you to run to Besta and stay with her until I'm back. Can you do that?'

'Are you coming back soon?' Ingrid sniffled.

'Yes, very soon. This is a misunderstanding, and when it's sorted, I'm coming home.'

Ingrid looked at her. 'Do you promise?'

'Yes, sweet pea, I promise. I will always come back to you.'

She kissed her on the forehead and gave her a gentle push out the door. 'Run as fast as you can and don't look back until you're at the farm. Stay with Besta.'

Ingrid looked at the policeman and the three other men. Anni held her breath.

She would never forget her little girl walking towards the men and stopping in front of them.

'My Pappa is coming home soon, and he'll beat all of you,' she said, lifting her finger and waving it at them. 'He will!'

Then she started running towards the pathway, her blonde hair flying behind her.

Anni hid a smile. *That's my girl*, she thought. She waited until she couldn't see her anymore, before turning to the policeman.

She grabbed a coat, making sure her belly would be hidden. She knew what they meant by fraternising and didn't want them to see proof of her so-called crime.

Anni kept her head high during the drive and made sure to have an indifferent expression on her face. She had hidden her activities from the damn Nazis all through the war; she could manage a few hours more.

An hour later, she was sitting in a room reeking of bad coffee and men's sweat. Outside there was chaos and a lot of angry people shouting.

They had marched her up to the front door with people shouting obscenities at her. It was terrifying. *This was madness*, she thought, ducking her head when someone tried to attack her. She couldn't believe the anger and hatred in their faces. They looked ready to string her up in the tree in front of the building.

When they entered the police station, Anni recognised some of the other people gathered in the reception room: a few Nazi party members, a shopkeeper who had business with the Germans, even a few former policemen, and some women. Presumably ones who were there for the same reason she was.

The policeman shoved her in the room and shut the door. He never looked at her or said another word.

Anni kept her hands in her lap, sitting upright and quiet, making sure her coat covered all of her. She focused on staying calm, remembering what Martin had said in case the Nazis arrested them. *Show them no fear, stay in control*, he said.

These were not Nazis, they were her own countrymen, but the fear she felt was real. She took a deep breath and closed her eyes for a moment.

Finally, another policeman came inside, and closed the door behind him. He was carrying a clipboard.

Anni recognised him at once from the incident on Liberation Day. He was the policeman who had stood by, the one she had told to be ashamed. Was this what it was? Revenge?

But how did he know who she was? She hadn't told him her name. *Stay calm*, Anni told herself. As soon as this ridiculous accusation was cleared up, she could return to Ingrid.

'I hope our people weren't too brutal, Mrs Odland,' he said, showing no signs of recognising her.

Anni had read in the paper that half the police force had been arrested, mostly for having membership in the NS – the Norwegian Nazi party. She wondered what he thought of that.

He sat down and looked at her, apparently waiting for her to speak.

Not on your life, she thought.

'Right, then,' he said, clearing his throat. 'I see here that a German civilian lived with you in your house from November 1944 until the war ended in May 1945. Is that correct?'

'No, he didn't live with me,' Anni said.

'He was in your house, yes?' He looked at her now. 'Answering will make this quicker.'

Anni frowned. 'Herr Kerber was billeted to my house. I had no choice in the matter.'

'Right,' he said. 'Yes, I can see it says that here.'

He rustled the papers again, before looking at her. *He had cold eyes*, Anni thought.

'How long after he moved into your house did you start having sexual relations with him?'

The question threw her. Anni stared at him. 'Excuse me?'

'You heard me. Answer the question,' he said.

'There was no relationship,' Anni said, sounding shrill to her own ears.

'My information says otherwise. You had a sexual relationship with this German. What do you have to say to that?'

Anni frowned. 'That your information is wrong.'

He put away his pen. 'I don't think so.'

Anni did her best to stay indifferent. She didn't look down on her belly, she didn't hold her hands too tightly, she didn't flinch. Instead, she stared him straight in the eyes. It was time to stop this nonsense.

'Does your information tell you that I worked with my mother-in-law and Martin Foss for the resistance? Helping refugees leave the country safely, and bringing in weapons and supplies for the Home Front? We started up in 1940 and the last person I helped got out safely in April this year.'

No need to mention Hugo's help, she thought.

The policeman didn't blink. 'Martin Foss was arrested in January and subsequently sent to Grini prisoner camp where he was put on the list to be sent on to Germany. He never mentioned you or your grandmother.'

Anni sighed. 'How do you know he never mentioned us?'

'There's nothing in the records to imply that,' the man said.

Something clicked in place in Anni's head. 'Are you talking about records from the Gestapo interrogating him?'

'Yes, and as far as we can see, he never mentioned anyone, except a friend who he smuggled cigarettes with.'

'Of course he didn't. If he had mentioned me or Guri, we would both have been sent to Grini as well.'

He seemed unfazed. 'Perhaps. Or it could simply be that your German lover made sure that you would never end up there.'

Anni was getting angry and she knew that it wouldn't do her any good. She didn't respond.

He looked down on his clipboard again. From what Anni could see, there wasn't anything on it.

'Tell me, did you tell your lover about Martin Foss? Is that why the Gestapo arrested him?'

'This is absurd,' Anni said. 'I would never have done anything like that to Martin. He's a close friend.'

'Then how did Gestapo find him and not you?'

Anni tried to find the right word to convince this man that she was innocent of whatever he was accusing her of.

'I wouldn't know,' she finally said.

'Could it have been pillow talk? Something you told this . . .' He looked down at his clipboard. '. . . Kerber? Did you share secrets with him for food?'

Anni was horrified. 'Are you mad? Nothing like that happened.'

'You had a German in your house. You're young and pretty in a way those people seem to like. I'm sure he could have charmed secrets from you for a pound of coffee or some sugar.' He looked at her with prying eyes while talking. 'You wouldn't be the first German slut to do that.'

Anni felt sick. She hadn't thought to get rid of the sugar or coffee from Hugo. She had no reason to. Now this man was using that against her.

'Whatever extra food is in my house belonged to him. He used my kitchen as he pleased and when he left my house, he left the food behind.' She stared back at him. 'Are you arresting everyone who had soldiers billeted in their houses, or just me? Because that happened all over the country. As you well know.'

'Yes, I do. I also know that while there might not have been immoral relations between every woman and the soldiers living in their houses, some women did cross that line,' he said.

Anni felt sick to her stomach. 'Why is the government arresting women who might have slept with a German? What about the quislings? The politicians who embraced the Nazis, the people who reported neighbours, friends or family, the sadists who tortured and even executed other Norwegians? The people who profited from the Germans? Who worked with the Gestapo? Or the police? What will happen to them?'

Anni knew she should have kept her mouth shut. Making them angry would only make matters worse. She realised that now.

He narrowed his eyes. 'It is not your concern, but they will be brought to justice. We're cleaning house, Mrs Odland. This country needs a fresh start. We can't have traitors among us.'

'I couldn't agree more, but it has nothing to do with

me,' she said. 'I would like to return to my daughter now. How can it be a crime to have an enemy soldier billeted at my house, when the Nazis would have considered it a crime if I tried to refuse? That makes no sense.'

He looked down at his clipboard, before lifting his head. 'Perhaps you're right. At least for now. It will take great effort from all of us to cleanse our country from the stench of the Occupation. Be assured that there will be new laws and procedures coming soon,' he said.

Anni held her breath. Did that mean he would let her go? She knew that Guri and Ingrid would worry about her, more so if she had to stay overnight.

He waved his hand. 'You can go.'

Anni wanted to ask if she was safe from their nonsense, but she was too scared. Instead, she stood up from the chair and walked towards the door.

'Why did you interfere with the girl on the street?' he said.

And there it was, she thought. Anni looked back at him.

'I had to,' she said. 'I didn't want my daughter to think that's how our people behave towards each other. I told her how happy everyone would be when the war was over. I also taught her that she could trust policemen. I didn't want her to think I lied to her.'

He didn't respond to that, only waved her away again.

Anni hurried outside before he changed his mind, half expecting him to stop her.

In the reception room she spotted a woman in a corner, crying in her hands. She was clearly pregnant.

That could be me right now, she thought.

Anni didn't stop. She hurried through the doors, kept

her head down and walked through the crowd still standing there.

Nobody talked to her or shouted at her this time. Anni headed for the street leading up to the bus stop. As soon as she was out of sight from the police station, she started running.

She ran until she couldn't breathe any more, knowing she had to get herself home as fast as possible. She didn't trust that policeman for a second.

Chapter Twenty-Eight

Ingrid, forty-two years old

London, 1980

Esme had her feet up on the sofa and a duvet around her shoulders. 'I hate being poorly,' she declared, sneezing into her handkerchief.

Ingrid put a cup of tea and a plate of biscuits on the table. 'A cold is hardly the end of the world.'

'It's undignified, is what it is. I'm too old for the sniffles.' She leant back and smiled at her. 'I'm whining, aren't I?'

Ingrid nodded. 'Little bit. Now drink your tea and if you're still whining after that, I'll get you some Lemsip.'

Esme pulled a disgusted face. 'God, no. Tea will do, thank you very much.'

The door slammed and two animated voices filled the house. 'What do you mean you "borrowed" my earrings? Stop lying!' Joanna's voice turned shrill.

'You keep yelling like that, only dogs can hear you!' Guri retorted.

Two heavy thuds followed. Esme looked at Ingrid, and grinned. 'Now, that takes me back.'

Ingrid rolled her eyes. 'I'd better go and see.'

In the kitchen, the girls were facing each other like two boxers in a ring.

'Keep it down. Nanna is feeling poorly and needs to rest,' she said.

The girls forgot the fight and looked abashed.

'Is Nanna OK?' Guri said.

'She has a cold. So, no arguments, no dropping schoolbags on the floor and no screaming at each other,' Ingrid said. 'Is that understood?'

They both nodded. Joanna frowned. 'We can see her, right? She's not hospital sick or anything like that?'

'No, she's not, you can see her after your tea. Where's your father?'

Ingrid looked around as if Runar would materialise from thin air.

'Outside. He's super excited about something, but wouldn't tell us why,' Joanna said.

Guri piped in, 'Even though we begged him, he wouldn't.'

'I'd better go outside then,' Ingrid said, hiding her smile over the girls' snubbed expressions.

She walked outside and found Runar hauling grocery bags from the back of the car.

'What's the excitement, love?' she asked, smiling at him.

'To see you, of course,' he said, planting a quick kiss on her lips.

Ingrid laughed. 'As nice as that was, there has to be something else. Tell me.'

Runar took out a folded paper from his pocket. 'I went by the Seamen's Church earlier today and found this. There's a woman holding a lecture about her father. Look.'

Ingrid unfolded the paper and read it. 'Martin Foss,' Ingrid said slowly. 'I remember. He was in Mamma's file.'

'See, his daughter will be at Norway House on Trafalgar Square in a few days. I think we should go,' Runar said, handing her a full grocery bag.

Ingrid wasn't having it. 'I'm finished with that, Runar. You know that. I have no need to find my mother anymore.'

Runar took the last two bags. He smiled at her. 'You know what? You can say that as often as you like, but it doesn't make it true.'

Ingrid scowled at him. 'Don't start.'

'Fine. But I'm going, and you can tag along if you want to.'

'I won't.' Ingrid was adamant about it.

'Fine,' Runar said again, looking annoyingly pleased with himself.

Ingrid didn't tell Runar that she remembered Martin and Nina from before, from when she was little. She was furious. Thinking he was so clever. *Damn*, she thought.

Ingrid was still mad when they jumped off the bus at Trafalgar Square. Not only had Runar decided to go, but so had the girls and Esme, who was suddenly feeling a lot better.

She still thought it was a bad idea, stirring up old wounds for nothing.

'You're all bullies,' she muttered.

'Oh, stop it,' Esme said cheerfully. 'You're here now, so stop whinging.'

Norway House was the tall building opposite Canada House at the end of the square. Ingrid had never been inside before. It looked dark and foreboding to her.

Joanna looked at Runar. 'This woman is Norwegian, right?'

'Yes, she is, but she's lived in Canada for years,' he said.

'Why do we have to come to a boring lecture?' Guri didn't look too thrilled.

'This woman knew your mamma when she was a little girl. What she will talk about is part of your history too,' Runar said.

Ingrid smiled at them. 'Don't look so worried, you two.'

A sign led them to a large room with a podium. The chairs were mostly filled already. The majority of the audience consisted of older people.

They found seats in the back and Ingrid sat down closest to the door. There was something unsettling about the situation and she felt uncomfortable.

Esme picked up on it and took her hand. She didn't say anything and Ingrid breathed easier. Esme always helped.

When Martin Foss's daughter came out onto the podium, introduced by a man Ingrid hadn't even noticed was there, her mind flooded with memories of Nina. And then Nina started talking about her father's experiences during the war. Ingrid held her breath.

'My father always said that he would never have survived the war without two amazing women. Guri and Anni Odland saved so many people, including him,' Nina said. 'And neither received the recognition they rightly deserved for their sacrifices.'

There was so much Ingrid had never heard before. It brought back all the hurt from not being told anything by her father and grandmother.

Towards the end of the lecture, she didn't notice she was crying before Esme put her arm around her shoulder.

'I'll wait outside,' she whispered, and stood up abruptly, before Esme had time to protest. The girls stood up too, but she shook her head. On the way out, she heard Runar's voice behind her, but she didn't turn around.

Ingrid didn't stop until she stood outside. The traffic noises on Trafalgar Square were oddly soothing. She pressed a hand to her stomach, forcing herself to breathe.

This is stupid. So far, far beyond stupid. I have to pull myself together and go back in. I'm scaring the girls, she thought, trying to gain control over herself. She turned around, when Nina Foss appeared in the door.

'Ingrid?' Nina smiled; the same bright smile Ingrid remembered. 'It really is you. I was so hoping you'd come.'

Ingrid found herself enveloped in a hug. She started crying again but managed to control herself. *This won't do*, she thought, and pulled away. 'Please, don't.'

Nina had the warmest eyes, she looked so concerned. 'Please, come inside again. We need to talk.'

Ingrid shook her head. 'I'm sorry, but I have to get my girls home.'

It sounded so pathetic, but it was all she could think of. She was fighting her feelings so hard; she could barely breathe.

'Please, Ingrid. I'm returning to Canada tomorrow,' Nina said with desperation in her voice.

Ingrid shook her head emphatically. 'I'm sorry, but I can't.'

Runar came outside with his arm around Joanna and Esme holding Guri's hand. Both girls looked worried.

'Ingrid, please.' Nina tried again. 'I promised Anni that I would stay in touch with you, and I failed.'

The mentioning of her mother's name felt like a sharp knife to the stomach.

'I'm not interested.' Ingrid couldn't hide the bitterness in her voice. 'She left me for a stranger, someone she must have barely known, and worse, a Nazi.'

Nina gasped. 'What? That's not what happened at all.'

But Ingrid didn't want to hear any more. 'I'm sorry, but no.'

She turned away from Nina and put a smile on her face for her family. 'Let's go home.'

Runar tried to say something, but she interrupted him. 'The bus is coming.'

Nina tried one last time. 'I know what happened to Anni. It's not at all what you think. She never wanted to leave you behind, Ingrid. They gave her no choice.'

Ingrid clenched her fists so hard the nails cut into her palms. *Why doesn't she understand?* she thought. *I've wasted enough time as it is on this nonsense.*

Runar looked around. 'Esme, why don't you take the girls to that café while we talk to Nina?'

'Don't.' Ingrid could feel her hands shaking and pressed them together. 'We're leaving.'

Runar nodded to Esme. 'It's OK.'

'Come along, girls. We'll be right next door,' Esme said in strained voice.

The girls followed Esme without protesting, and Ingrid felt so guilty, she almost cried again.

Runar touched her arm, and she turned to him, suddenly furious.

'I can't believe you did that,' she said, glaring at him.

'It's up to you, love,' Runar said. 'But she's here now. If we leave, you will always wonder what she could have told you.'

Ingrid closed her eyes for a moment. Runar was right. She would regret it.

'To hell with it. Let's get this over,' she said.

'Good girl.' Runar took her hand and turned to go back inside. Nina waited at the door and looked on the brink of tears. 'Thank you,' she said.

Ingrid held on to Runar's hand, dreading the whole situation.

Nina brought them into what looked like a dining room for staff.

'There are still people in the building, so I asked if we could sit somewhere private,' Nina said, smiling apologetically.

Ingrid hesitated. Suddenly so much depended on what Nina could tell her. *I'm scared*, she thought.

'It's fine, Nina,' Runar said.

They found a table by the window. Nina sank down on a chair and fished out a package of cigarettes from her purse. 'I hope this is OK. I'm nervous,' she said.

'So am I,' Ingrid said, forcing a smile.

Nina lit a cigarette and looked at her. 'I've been so afraid I'd never see you again. You look exactly the same.'

'Hardly. Last you saw me I was, what, six or seven?' Ingrid said.

'Six, I think. But your eyes and your smile? I'd recognise you anywhere.'

'You used to chase Besta's goats with me,' Ingrid said.

Nina laughed. 'Little monsters.' She looked at Runar. 'I don't remember you.'

'He's Runar Borgen. My husband,' Ingrid said. 'He was in Mamma's crèche.'

'How romantic.' Nina laughed. 'Then you remember Anni and Guri too.'

Runar shook her hand. 'I do. Nice to meet you.'

'Thank you.' Nina put her hand on Ingrid's arm. 'I've waited so long for this day to come. I promised Anni to keep in touch with you, and I failed her. Every letter I sent to London came unopened in return. I wrote to Guri, but she said not to worry. She assured me you were happy and safe and that she didn't want you to be confused with our letters. She and Lars would tell you about us when you got older.'

Ingrid sighed. *Guri was keeping things from me too*, she thought. *What else do I not know?*

'Why did you leave Norway?' Runar asked.

Ingrid knew what he was doing and loved him for it. Always the one who took care of everything and everyone. Nina's eyes twinkled. 'I fell in love with a Canadian soldier who came to Haugesund looking for his brother after the war ended. Pappa didn't want to stay either, so we both followed John to Toronto.'

'Is this the first time you've come back in Europe?' Runar said.

Nina nodded. 'John will be taking early retirement next

367

year, and this year our daughter and her family moved here. We want to be closer to them.'

She reached out and put her hand on Ingrid's arm. 'Your girls are so lovely. What are their names?'

Ingrid smiled. 'Joanna and Guri, but they can be a handful.'

'Guri would have loved that,' Nina said, her eyes softening.

'Besta came to visit once a year until she passed away when I was fourteen, my father followed a few years later,' Ingrid said, the words almost stuck in her throat. 'They never told me about any letters. They never told me anything.'

'That must be sad for you, that Joanna and Guri have missed out on everything,' Nina said quietly. 'I'm so sorry.'

Ingrid swallowed hard. 'Esme, my stepmum, is a wonderful grandmother to them. So was Runar's mum.'

'Good. That's good,' Nina said.

'But you're right. I think about what they missed.' Ingrid swallowed a lump in her throat. 'I'm sorry, but you said you know what happened to her.'

'I'll tell you what I know. But I'm surprised you don't know anything,' Nina said.

'I know she married the German and left me behind,' Ingrid said, keeping her voice steady. 'I have a copy of her file from the State Archive in Norway.'

'That's how you found out?' Nina looked shocked. 'I thought Guri would tell you. Or your father.'

'They both waited too long.' Ingrid frowned. 'I found out Mamma was arrested by the police after the war, and that they thought she was a German . . .' She couldn't bring herself to say it aloud.

368

'A German slut,' Nina said quietly. 'That's not the whole story.'

'How is that not the whole story? She married him, didn't she?' Ingrid didn't take her eyes off Nina.

Nina nodded. 'I was fourteen when the war started and, in the beginning, I had no idea what Pappa was doing. When I caught on, I wanted to help. I wanted to fight the Nazis. After a lot of begging and nagging from my side, Pappa let me distribute illegal newspapers. Later, I ran errands for them, I babysat you when they took refugees out to the fishing boats, and when Pappa was arrested and sent to Grini prison camp, I took over from him.'

'Pappa always told me I had every reason to be proud of Besta and Mamma,' Ingrid said.

'You do. They were in on it from the start. Pappa recruited them. What they did was extremely dangerous; people were shot for less. Anni didn't stop, not even when Kerber was billeted to your house. At first Anni was sure he was there to spy on their group. Pappa was so worried.'

Ingrid found it hard to process everything. 'She must have been so scared.'

Nina pulled a face. 'At first, yes. We all were, but Kerber wasn't a bad person. He saved my father after all. Honestly, I didn't ask too many questions about him.'

'How did he save your father?' Runar said.

'Pappa was supposed to be sent to Germany to one of those horrendous camps. But at the last minute, his name was taken off the list and he spent the last few weeks of the war at Grini,' Nina said. 'Anni asked Kerber to help, and he managed to arrange for Pappa to stay.'

Ingrid listened, feeling slightly better. 'She did that?'

'Yes, and he did it for her.' Nina smiled. 'Thank God for that. I might have lost Pappa otherwise.'

Ingrid took a deep breath. 'Do you know why Mamma was arrested twice? Why she never came back for me? That was never explained in the papers I received.'

'After the peace, they arrested lots of women for fraternising, even some who had barely exchanged a word with a soldier,' Nina said, looking down at the table. 'A lot of people had scores to settle. Kerber had stayed at your house, brought food and firewood; that was enough to make people jealous.'

'I know that much,' Ingrid said. 'You are the only one left who can tell me more about what happened.'

'In May she was only questioned, she was back home the same day. But when she was arrested again in June, they didn't let her go.' Nina took a deep puff of her cigarette. 'We didn't find her again until the year after.'

Ingrid found it hard to believe. 'I don't understand. If Mamma was a member of the resistance, surely they wouldn't do something like that to her?'

Nina looked uncomfortable. 'This will be difficult for you to hear.'

'I'm not seven anymore, Nina,' Ingrid said quietly. 'I have been protected for too long.'

'OK.' Nina put the lighter down. 'What do you remember about Kerber?'

'I remember the food he brought.'

'Yes, Anni shared with us too.' Nina sighed. 'He wasn't a fanatic Nazi. She couldn't have been with him if he was. He didn't want to be there any more than we wanted him to be.'

'Do you think someone told the police about them?'
Ingrid had a hard lump in her stomach, like a sharp cramp.
'How would anyone know?'

'I honestly don't know. The fact is that after the war,
Anni's name ended up on a list of women who had sexual
relations with Germans,' Nina said. She fidgeted with the
cigarette pack when she talked. 'When they came to arrest
her the second time, she knew she had waited too long.'

She spotted Ingrid's confusion. 'I mean, she was all set to
leave anyway. She knew time was running out. I guess Guri
never told you that either.'

Ingrid's stomach cramped. 'What do you mean?'

Nina sighed. 'Your mother was pregnant. She had decided
to go away to have the baby, give it up for adoption, and
then come home to you.'

'Pregnant?' Ingrid felt dizzy and clenched her fists so
hard her nails dug into her palms.

'Ingrid?' Runar's voice was gentle. 'You're white as a
sheet.'

'Poor Mamma,' she whispered, without lifting her head.
'That's why Besta and Pappa never told me the truth. They
didn't want me to think that she was a German slut, like
they all said.'

The children at school, she remembered them screaming
at her, filled with hate and rage. The teachers who treated
her with such contempt. And it was all Mamma's fault.
They had all been right, and she'd had to pay the price for
her mother's sins.

Runar put his arm around her. 'She was no such thing.
She was the nicest, loveliest women I ever knew.'

Ingrid burst into tears. She cried against his shirt. 'I

should have let it be,' she finally said. 'I didn't need to know this. It's too much.'

Runar lifted her chin and looked at her. 'You deserve the truth about what happened. You can't stop now. Let Nina finish the story.'

Nina lit a cigarette and sounded so sad when she spoke again.

'Pappa never believed what they said about her, Ingrid. Neither of us did. He told me she decided to treat Kerber as a guest, to spy on him,' Nina said. 'Whatever information she gathered, she shared with Pappa.'

'And for that she was punished, is that what you're telling me?' Ingrid could hardly believe it.

'Yes, I'm afraid so, and in the process, so were you,' Nina said.

'You said it took you and your father a year to find her. Why?' Runar said.

'Guri was so upset when Anni was arrested again. She went to the police station every day. They wouldn't tell her anything, until one of them blurted out that Anni had been sent to a place for "that kind of woman".'

'What kind of place?' Ingrid couldn't help but interrupt her.

'Internment camps,' Nina said with a disgusted look on her face. 'It happened all over the country. It was horrible.'

Ingrid swallowed. 'I don't understand why Mamma risked everything for Kerber. Why would she do that?'

Nina wouldn't meet Ingrid's eyes. 'Guri told me that a letter from Lars had come through in January 1945, a little over two months after the German moved in. In the letter, he wrote that he had been granted a divorce and had married someone else in 1943.' Nina shook her head. 'Can you imagine how she felt when she received that?'

'Jesus,' Runar muttered. 'The exile government came up with that monstrosity in 1943.'

'Yes, it happened to a lot of women whose husbands were out of the country for the whole war. I don't know how many. All the while, their families were waiting back home,' Nina said sarcastically.

'I know he did that,' Ingrid said. The lump in her throat made her struggle to speak. 'My stepmother told me years ago,' she said, when Nina looked confused.

'She told you?' Nina gasped.

'Pappa had told her he'd divorced my mother before the war. It wasn't until Besta asked him to take me to London that he told her the truth.'

'Bloody hell!' Nina exclaimed. 'You've had to carry the burden for all of them, haven't you?'

Ingrid waved her hand, wanting to know more about her mother. 'I've seen the letters your father wrote to the police. Why didn't they help?'

'Like I said, Anni was pregnant and Kerber lived in her house. That was proof enough in the eyes of the new government,' Nina said. 'You have to understand what it was like back then. It was like a witch hunt. People were so nasty, you wouldn't believe the things that were said about these women and their children.'

Ingrid shook her head, finding it hard to understand what Nina was telling her. 'You said you didn't find Mamma until 1946?'

'Pappa refused to give up,' Nina said with a smile. 'Anni managed to smuggle out letters for us with the help from one of the guards who knew Pappa. That's how we found out she had been sent to a national internment camp for *German women*, on one of the islands in the Oslo fjord. Pappa's time at Grini was a great place to make friends.'

'When was this?' Ingrid felt as if her world was breaking apart.

'We met Anni in May 1946 when the internment camp was closed down by the authorities. Oskar was almost four months and so cute and chubby,' Nina said with a sad smile.

'Oskar? Wait a minute.' Ingrid couldn't help interrupting her. 'I have a brother?'

Nina smiled. 'Yes, you do.'

A brother. Ingrid fell back in her chair. She had a brother; the girls had an uncle. 'I always wanted a sibling,' she said.

'I hope you get to meet him one day,' Nina said, looking pleased for the first time since they came.

Ingrid frowned. 'You said she wanted to give him away. What made her change her mind? Did she choose Kerber over me?'

'If it had only been Kerber, she would never have left you. But you need to understand how badly the children of German soldiers and Norwegian women were treated after the war. Anni told me Oskar wouldn't have anyone if she left him, and she couldn't bring him home. He would be alone in a place where people would hate him for his father. You had Guri and Lars to love you. But it almost broke her. I'm convinced she'll never have recovered.'

'Poor Mamma,' Ingrid said again, thinking about her girls. She couldn't imagine having to leave one of them behind. 'How awful it must have been for her.'

'I didn't understand how hard that must have been for her

until I became a mother myself. The pain of having to choose between my children? I can't even imagine,' Nina said softly.

'Why haven't Ingrid or you heard from Anni in all this time?' Runar asked.

'I don't know,' Nina said. 'Anni told me she would come back to Norway as soon as it would be possible. And when the postal services resumed between Germany and Norway, we all waited for letters from her. She had all our addresses, even yours here in London,' she said to Ingrid. 'Pappa tried everywhere, hoping someone could help. Finally, someone in the Justice Department told him that after Anni left Norway in 1946, they had no records of her whereabouts.'

'But that can't be right,' Runar said. 'There have to be records of them somewhere. She's Norwegian and so is Oskar.'

Nina shook her head profoundly. 'No, you see, that's the thing. The Norwegian government amended the Norwegian Nationality Act in 1945, making it so that any woman who married a German would lose her Norwegian citizenship because they married a man from an enemy country. Anni became a German and so did Oskar. That meant the two of them weren't the Norwegian authorities' problem anymore.'

'Another law was changed?' Runar said. 'Why would they do that?'

'I don't know. All I know is that the amendment was designed for women like her. Pappa always thought of it as a punishment. Mind you, it was only for the women. The few Norwegian men who married German women didn't get punished and they kept their citizenship,' Nina said, shaking her head.

'So, she had an affair with a German and got pregnant, then she married him and was stripped of her nationality as a punishment? How is that a crime?' Ingrid was angry and confused.

'It wasn't,' Runar said. 'We need to find out more about this.'

'Yes,' Ingrid said, feeling a new sense of determination. For the first time she was angry at someone else other than her mother. 'I want to find Oskar, and I want to know where my mother is buried.'

'Do you think Anni is dead?' Nina looked surprised.

'Yes,' Ingrid said firmly. 'Yes, I do. She would have found me otherwise. She promised. Nothing would have stopped her from coming back to me.'

'You could be wrong,' Nina said softly. 'There could be so many reasons Anni never got in touch with any of us.'

Ingrid put her hand to her chest. 'I would have felt it if she's alive.'

'I think you need to contact the German authorities. You're her daughter, so they will be more helpful to you,' Nina said. 'You can visit the West German Embassy here in London, can't you? Have them look into it for you.'

Ingrid nodded. 'You're right.' She leant forward and put her arms on the table. 'Tell me everything you know. The more I know, the more details I can give them.'

While Nina jotted down what she remembered, Ingrid's mind wandered. *What if Mamma is alive?* But she couldn't make herself believe that, dreading another disappointment. Somehow, now that she hadn't been abandoned out of selfishness, it was too much to hope for seeing her again.

* * *

It took another month before they heard from Germany. Esme brought the envelope inside the sweet shop and handed it to Ingrid. 'It says *Bundesarchiv* on the address. What's that?'

'Their national archives, I think. I remember that from when we were at the embassy,' Ingrid said.

'Let's hope it's good news, pet,' Esme said.

Ingrid looked at the envelope. 'I'm not sure I want to open it, Mum. What if she's dead?'

Esme folded her arms across her chest. 'Whatever else will you do with it? Hang it on the wall? Besides, what about your brother? You've always wanted someone to argue with, haven't you?'

Ingrid had to laugh. 'Oh, bugger, you're right. Let's do this before I lose my nerve.'

She ripped open the envelope with a dramatic flair that had Esme chuckle.

Ingrid struggled to understand what the letter said. It almost broke her heart, all over again. When she finally looked up at Esme, she felt so defeated. 'They found her,' she said, fighting back tears.

Esme took a step forward and put her arm around Ingrid's shoulders. 'I'm so sorry.'

'She's not dead, but she might as well be,' Ingrid said, not recognising her own voice. 'God, I hate this. It never bloody ends!'

Esme looked at her. 'I don't understand.'

'Mamma is in East Germany. Behind the bloody Iron Curtain.' Ingrid put a hand on Esme's arm. 'All this time, all the time and energy and money we have spent, and it's all for nothing. She might as well be living on Mars.'

'Are you bonkers?' Esme shook her head. 'In my view, alive is better than dead any day. Your mother is alive. East Germany is a hurdle, but it's not hopeless.'

'How so? I can't imagine us trying to break her out of there. We'd end up spending the rest of our lives in some gulag somewhere,' Ingrid said.

'Sooner or later the GDR will fall, mark my words. Dictatorships always do in the end. Always,' Esme said calmly.

Ingrid leant her head against hers. 'You are the most optimistic person I know.'

'I had to be, didn't I? You and your father had all the gloom of the Nordics about you, someone had to keep the faith.' Esme smiled at her. 'Now, take this and tell Runar and Nina what you've found. They'll be elated, I can promise you that.'

Ingrid sighed. 'Why is it that every time we find new information, it feels as if she slips further away from me?'

Esme looked at her. 'As long as she's alive, you can find her. Don't lose hope.'

Ingrid smiled. 'I won't, I promise,' she said.

Esme reached out and picked up a jar with soft liquorice.

'Take your treat and go and do what I told you,' she said, smiling at her.

Ingrid took a handful of sweets, tucked the letter into her pocket and went upstairs to find Runar and call Nina. Her head was spinning. *Where there's life, there's hope*, she thought. *Mum might be right. Walls fall down every day. Why not the Berlin Wall too?*

Chapter Twenty-Nine

Anni

Oslo, January 1946

Anni looked out of the window and saw rows of yellow multi-storey brick buildings spread out over large grounds. Everything covered in snow. She had never seen a hospital like this. It seemed too . . . big. Especially after all those months on the island.

In the background she could hear crying babies. She closed her eyes and took a deep breath. 'Don't think about the baby,' she whispered to herself.

But how could she not? He was so alone and it was all her fault.

Everyone knew the father of her baby was a German and, while most of the staff clearly didn't approve, a few of them were kind and gentle and obviously felt sorry for her.

One of the nurses in the delivery room had showed him to her right after he was born.

'A beautiful boy,' she said, and held the bundle towards her.

Anni knew she shouldn't look at him, but she had to. Whatever else he was, he was innocent.

The nurse saw her soften and put him in her arms. 'Until we get you cleaned up and back on the ward,' she whispered.

Anni didn't hear her. All she could see was this angry, little face, waving his fists about. She touched one of his hands with her finger, and he grabbed on. He tried to open his eyes and the urge to cry stuck in her throat. Like most newborns, his eyes were blue, but she could see they had Hugo's shape. *His eyes will turn brown soon*, she thought.

Apparently, it's my destiny to have children who look like their fathers. Attempting to make jokes didn't make her feel better.

His weight on her chest felt so right. He belonged with her, but she couldn't keep him. She couldn't choose him over Ingrid. It wouldn't be fair. *No matter what I do, I'll be failing one of them*, she thought. The baby had fallen asleep, still holding her finger. Anni couldn't get enough of him. 'You are so beautiful,' she whispered.

When the nurse came to take him, she reluctantly let him go. 'Where are you taking him?'

'He'll be in the nursery. While you're on the ward, they'll bring him to you for his meals,' she said.

Anni shook her head. 'No, I'm putting him up for adoption.'

The nurse looked at her with sympathy. 'I'm so sorry. But I'm sure they'll find a good home for him. Lots of people want baby boys,' she said.

'I hope so,' Anni said.

When they brought her back to the ward, she was put with other new mothers. They put a screen around her bed, for her privacy, they said.

Anni felt sore all over, and so tired. Not only from the birth, although that had taken almost twenty-four hours, but from everything. From being shuffled around from camp to camp, from having her body and mind prodded by strangers, from being denied having any contact with the people she loved, and from worrying about Ingrid.

She closed her eyes and fell asleep.

For a whole day, she pretended the baby wasn't real. She took the pills they gave her to stop the milk, and hoped he would fade into her memories.

When she was in her bed, hidden by the screen, she could hear the other mothers chatting about their husbands, their homes and families. Every day during visiting hours siblings and family would fill the halls with laughter and talking and all-round happiness.

Anni would slink away and find a place in a stairwell until visiting hours were over. The memories of when Ingrid was born were in such stark contrast. Lars had been pacing outside for hours, Guri telling him to sit down about every ten minutes. Later she had told Anni in detail how he had been completely useless. But she always told the story with a proud smile.

Lars had made a lovely new crib, Guri had knitted enough outfits to last Ingrid for a lifetime, of which she grew out of in a matter of months.

But this baby had nothing. Nobody greeted him into the

world with kisses and hugs, or lovingly crocheted hats or onesies.

Anni couldn't bear it.

On the second day, she went to the nursery, but stopped outside the door, unable to muster the courage to go inside.

A nurse opened the door from the inside. She discovered Anni and looked at her with a frown on her face. 'What do you want?'

'I . . . I . . . nothing,' Anni said, turning around, then changed her mind. 'I wanted to see my baby.'

'You're leaving him behind, aren't you?' The nurse's face didn't reveal what she was thinking.

'Yes, he'll be adopted,' Anni said, feeling more and more uncomfortable.

The nurse nodded. 'Clever girl. Probably the most sensible thing for you. I mean, you're young, you can have other children with better blood.'

She said it so casually that Anni didn't react at first.

'Excuse me?' she said after a second.

'You know what I mean. Children who will have a good Norwegian father, not some degenerate Nazi. Everyone knows their children are no good. It's bad blood, isn't it?' the nurse went on. 'Best you forget all about him.'

She gave Anni a curt nod, then closed the door. Anni couldn't move. Is that what they thought? All of them? She shoved her hands deep into the pockets of the hospital gown. She was shaking but didn't know if it was rage or shock.

Anni woke up crying. She knew they would come for her in a few days, to take her back to the island, and after that she would never see the baby again. When she had arrived at the camp, she was supposed to stay for sixty days, but then she was foolish and asked the director if she could send letters to her family. Arguing with the man hadn't been wise. It was the same for all the women in the camp. They could keep them indefinitely if they wanted to.

Anni dried her tears. She had to see the baby one more time. Carefully she got out of bed and slipped out into the corridor. It was cold, but she didn't notice.

The light was on in the nursery. Anni took a deep breath and opened the door.

It smelt of soap, disinfectant and something sweet that could only come from the babies.

She shut the door behind her and stood with her back pressed up against it for a moment.

I shouldn't be doing this, she thought. *I should have asked to see him, and they would probably have let me. Maybe not that nurse, but others, the nicer ones.*

But she didn't want to wait. She had to see him now.

There were babies in five of the cribs in there. Anni carefully checked the name tags, but he wasn't among them.

Her heart almost stopped. *They couldn't have found an adoptive family this quickly. Surely not. He's only two days old.*

Perhaps they have taken him for a feed, or to change his nappy, something they probably don't do in the nursery for fear of waking the other babies, she thought.

Anni looked around and found a door in the back of the room. The door was ajar. When she came closer, she could hear a woman singing softly. Anni looked inside.

A young nurse was sitting in a chair, bottle feeding a

baby. She looked startled when Anni came inside. 'Who are you?'

For a second Anni didn't know what to say. 'My baby,' she said, unable to hide how scared she was. 'Where is he?'

The nurse seemed too surprised to speak.

Anni took a step closer. 'I'm Anni Odland. My boy isn't in the nursery. Is that him?'

The nurse stopped her by stretching out her hand. 'No, this one is a girl. Did you say Odland?'

Anni nodded. 'He was born two days ago. Why isn't he in the nursery?'

The baby let go of the bottle, and the nurse lifted her to her shoulder.

'Have they taken him away?' Anni pressed her hands together.

'No, he's still here,' the nurse said, gently tapping the baby on her back.

Anni frowned. 'Then why isn't he out there with the other babies?'

The nurse looked uncomfortable. 'I'm not allowed to let anyone in here,' she said, avoiding her look.

'All I want is to see him, to know how he's doing.' Anni couldn't imagine why her boy should be separated from the others. 'Is he sick? Is that it?'

The baby on the nurse's shoulder burped and the nurse smiled. 'Hang on a second, I'll put her back in her crib. Then I'll take you to him but promise me you won't tell anyone.'

Anni waited with growing impatience while the nurse put away the baby, made sure she was comfortable and finally turned to her. 'Come with me, Mrs Odland.'

She opened a door, leading into the bathroom. There was a crib there, with a sleeping baby. Anni recognised him immediately. 'Why is he in the bathroom?'

The nurse sighed. 'I'm not allowed to say.'

'But he's not sick?' Anni touched his cheek gently. 'He doesn't have a fever.'

'No, it's not like that. He's in here because he's German. They want to keep him away from the others,' the nurse said with an embarrassed look on her face.

Anni looked up from her son. 'He's not German. He's my son, and I'm Norwegian. That's nonsense.'

'But his father is German, isn't he? That's what I was told,' the nurse said.

Anni looked at the baby. 'He doesn't have a father.'

'We were told that you came here from the camp at Hovedøya. They say that the women there have syphilis and all sorts of horrid diseases. I think they put him in here in case . . . in case he has something,' the nurse said, her words tumbling over each other.

'Bollocks,' Anni said. 'I've been tested repeatedly for everything they could think of, and if anyone had bothered to check my medical records, they would have realised that. I've never had a venereal disease in my life. I'm not a whore. Neither are any of the other women on the island.'

The nurse looked worried. 'All I know is what they told me.'

'I don't understand. They must know there's nothing wrong with him,' Anni said.

'I understand you're upset, but I can't help you.' The nurse looked more nervous. 'Perhaps you should leave.'

Anni looked at her son. He seemed perfectly at peace,

completely ignorant of what the world might think about him. 'What else are they saying about him?'

'You must understand, I don't agree with any of this. I don't believe children are born bad,' the nurse said.

'Of course they're not.' Anni understood now. 'They think he's born Nazi? There's no such thing. He's an innocent baby. He shouldn't have to pay for his parents' sin.'

The nurse looked at her. 'Then you should take him with you.'

Anni shook her head. 'I can't. I have to get back to my daughter. She's innocent too.'

'You don't understand,' the nurse said quickly. 'Nobody wants to adopt a German child, Mrs Odland. Your son will be sent to an orphanage for . . . for children who don't fit in. I read in the newspaper that children from the Lebensborn homes have been sent there already.'

'Why would they do that?' Anni could feel the warmth from the baby through her hand. She knew about the Lebensborn homes, where Norwegian women had gone to have their babies during the war, but she hadn't realised there had been children still there when the war ended.

'Because they're saying that children like your son have low intelligence, that their mothers have low intelligence, because that's the only way any woman would have been with Germans in the first place.' The nurse was so serious, Anni got scared.

'Who says such horrid things?'

The nurse looked at the baby and her face softened. 'Everybody. It's in the newspapers. The psychiatric doctors here at the hospital, the government – everyone. They call children like him "fifth columnists", saying that they will become Hitler's army in twenty years' time and then the war will start all over again.'

'What utter rubbish,' Anni muttered. 'It's not his fault what I did.'

'Believe me, I agree. But people fear and hate the German children. I'm sorry, but it's true. If you don't believe me, pick up any newspaper and see for yourself.'

Anni looked at her son. He wrinkled his nose in his sleep, and she knew that whatever happened, she couldn't leave him behind. He needed her. He needed her to be his mother.

More than anything she wanted to take him at once, leave the hospital and disappear, but she couldn't do that. She had no place to go, no money, nothing. The authorities would find her and likely take the baby away. She would never see him again.

'I'll keep you safe,' she whispered against his head. He smelt faintly of milk and soap. 'I'm so sorry.'

She caught the eye of the nurse, who gave her a kindly smile.

'You should tell them as soon as possible. Tell them that you're keeping him,' she said.

Anni nodded and dried the tears off her cheeks. 'I'll tell them tomorrow.'

She didn't want to pick him up since he was sleeping so peacefully, but she stayed with him even after the nurse had gone to check on the others.

'Hello, Oskar,' she whispered. 'I'm your mamma.'

Chapter Thirty

Anni

Oslo, May 1946

Anni threw one last look around the tiny room that had been her home for the last eight months. What little she owned was crammed in an old rucksack, with Oskar's things making the bulk of it. The baby was on the bed, wrapped in a knitted blanket.

'We're off to our new life soon, Oskar,' she said.

A visit to the camp from the Minister of Social Affairs a month earlier had changed everything. The minister was a survivor of Sachsenhausen concentration camp in Germany. He was horrified when he arrived at the island. To him, the barbed wire fences, the searchlights and the armed guards were no different than Nazi camps. He closed down the camp with immediate effect.

It had taken a month to find placements for everyone that didn't have anywhere to go. Anni had been placed in a maternity home in Oslo. *Hopefully it will be better than this*, she thought.

The last thing she packed was a small package of letters from Guri, Nina and Martin.

'Martin wanted to find your father, but I said no. I hope I did the right thing,' she said to Oskar, who was busy chewing his hand.

She put the rucksack on and lifted Oskar up from the bed. Outside, she joined the other women waiting to be led down to the pier. Anni looked back at the huts, wondering how she had survived with her sanity intact. But it was over now, she had Oskar and soon she would have Ingrid. *I have to believe that*, she thought.

Walking through the forest, the women chatted and laughed, but as they got closer to the pier they fell silent. While they had been there, they were not allowed letters or newspapers, and none of them knew what to expect from the outside world.

There was no sign of the ferry when they came out of the forest and one of the old guards came over to Anni.

'I'm going to miss this little one,' he said and gently knocked the tip of Oskar's nose with his finger.

Anni put a hand on his arm. 'We'll miss you too, Gunnar.'

'I'm glad I could help.' He smiled at her. 'Your friends are waiting for you; I called Martin to tell him today you're free.'

Anni swallowed a hard lump in her throat. Gunnar had offered to send letters for her, having noticed Martin's name on an envelope. They had been prisoners at Grini together and he'd helped her the best he could. It was all thanks to him she knew Ingrid was in London with Lars.

'Thank you for all your kindness,' she said and hugged

him. 'Please tell your wife Oskar loves his blanket.'

'I will, Anni. You take good care of both of you now,' he said. 'I'm staying until the next ferry; we're the last of the last.' He nodded at two other guards.

The ferry had begun docking. 'Time to go,' he said and followed her down the slope.

From the pier, she could see over to the mainland and Akershus Fortress. Most of the buildings lining the pier were assorted warehouses. She barely remembered what it looked like, the arrival had been a fog of fear and exhaustion. Anni found a place on one of the wooden seats and smiled at Oskar. 'We're on our way to our new life now, little one. It won't be grand, but we'll do our best.'

Oskar jabbed his fist in her ear. 'Ouch,' she said, and was rewarded by a big, sloppy kiss.

She smiled at him. 'Don't do that. Look at the birds instead. See the big ones? Those are seagulls.'

He couldn't care less.

He looked more like her now, but he had Hugo's eyes and dark hair. As always, her thoughts went to Ingrid. How did she look now? She could have grown so much in a year. In her letter Guri had said Ingrid was happy in London with Lars and his new wife, but how would she know? *Now that I'm out, I need to ask Guri for pictures*, she thought.

As soon as they left the boat, Oskar let out a wail and she laughed. 'I know how you feel,' she said, turning to discover Nina a few feet away, jumping up and down, waving her arms. 'Anni!'

Next to her, Martin, as solemn looking as ever, waved too.

The sheer relief of seeing them had her in tears. She took

a deep breath, so as not to scare the baby. 'Look, Oskar, there's Nina and Martin. Can you wave?'

He was chewing on his fist, and Anni laughed. She waved back at Nina, not noticing tears streaming down her cheeks.

She smiled at Martin when he came towards her. Nina was faster and hugged her, careful not to squash the baby. 'Can I hold him?'

'Of course.' Anni handed Oskar over and he didn't seem to mind. He smiled and babbled at Nina, who fussed over him.

'You are too adorable,' she cooed.

Martin shook his head. 'Girls and babies, it's a lethal combination.'

'It certainly is,' Anni said, trying to find a handkerchief in her pocket.

'Anni, it's so good to see you,' Martin said, and gave her a warm hug. 'How are you?'

'Better now with you two here,' Anny said. 'I had hoped Guri was with you. Is she all right?'

'She's in London, visiting Ingrid,' Martin said. 'We didn't know you'd be released so soon, otherwise she would have been here, you know that.'

It stung, thinking of Ingrid with Lars and the woman who was now Ingrid's stepmother. She closed her eyes for a second, fighting the guilt that threatened to overwhelm her yet again. 'Yes, I know,' she said, barely making a sound. 'I'm sorry.'

'No, Anni. I'm sorry,' Martin said. 'If only I had been at home. I would never have allowed them to take you.'

Anni finally found the handkerchief in her pocket and wiped her eyes. 'No, Martin. This is all on me,' she said, trying to sound light-hearted. 'I have many regrets, but Oskar isn't one. I'm grateful for him.'

Martin almost smiled. 'I did ask you to get friendly with the man, didn't I?'

Anni laughed. 'I don't think you meant that friendly.'

That made him smile. 'No, but still. The punishment you have been subjected to is a disgrace and will for ever be a stain on our country.'

Nina looked over her shoulder. 'Hurry up. John can't wait for ever.'

Anni took Martin's arm. 'Who's John?'

'Nina took a fancy to one of the Canadian soldiers who came to Haugesund right after the liberation. He's her fiancé now.' Martin had a grim look on his face. 'We're emigrating to Canada when the necessary paperwork is in order.'

'I'm sorry you're leaving, though that sounds like a wonderful fresh start,' Anni said, her heart aching at losing them again.

'Yes, well,' he said, pulling a face. 'You risked your life for five years, and they treat you like a traitor for having a baby. It makes no sense to me.'

'I made my bed; I can't blame anyone for that,' Anni said.

'Perhaps not, but what you did isn't a crime. Not by the Treason Act or any criminal laws in this country. You haven't broken any laws at all, yet you have been jailed for almost a year. This is pure hate and resentment, sanctioned by the authorities. I can't stand it.' Martin sighed. 'Did you know that they call it the Bigamy law now? And that the government ended it last year? There was quite the outcry.'

Anni shook her head. 'It doesn't matter anymore. I did

what I did. But it's over now, I want to look forward to creating a new life for Oskar and Ingrid.'

'There's one more thing you need to consider,' Martin said. 'I know you didn't want me to, but I located Kerber. He's in one of the army camps where they keep the Germans waiting to be returned home. He's still here, Anni.'

She was so surprised she didn't know what to say.

'I went to see him, to thank him for saving my life, and he asked about you.' Martin looked worried. 'I told him what they had done to you and promised to give you a letter from him.'

'Did you . . . did you tell him about Oskar?' Anni said.

'No, but I asked him about his intentions should he meet you again.'

'Intentions?' Anni didn't know if she should laugh or scold him. 'Why?'

'He said if it was up to him, he would never leave you again.' Martin watched her. 'He seemed sincere, Anni.'

'You shouldn't have,' Anni said, trying to ignore the pain.

Martin frowned. 'I'm sorry if I overstepped.'

'I have a place at a maternity home here in Oslo,' she said, more to herself than to Martin.

'The camp is about an hour away,' he said softly.

I'll likely never have this chance again, Anni thought. *Hugo will leave and be gone, and I will regret it.* She looked at Oskar trying to grab Nina's nose. But to only see him once, and then never again? How could she?

She looked at Martin. 'I'm not sure it's a good idea.'

He handed her the letter from Hugo. 'Read this before you decide. I'll be over there with Nina and Oskar. Take all the time you need.'

Anni took the letter, her hand was shaking. For a second, she considered ripping it up and throwing the pieces away. But she couldn't make herself do it. Instead, she opened it in a hurry, before she lost her nerve.

The letter was short but as she read, she could hear his voice in her head.

Mein Liebling,

Your friend Martin has told me what you and Ingrid are going through because of me. I never imagined it would be this bad for you. I don't know when they will send us home, but I'm not allowed to leave the camp. Please, see if you can find it in your heart to come and see me, even for one last time. I love you.

Hugo

Anni realised she was sobbing. She folded the letter together, and knew Martin was right. She had to see Hugo again even if only to say a last goodbye.

Nina and Martin waited for her by a car, next to a tall, broad-shouldered man who was trying to make Oskar laugh. It looked so idyllic, Anni had to smile.

'Anni, this is John. He's teaching me how to better my English,' Nina said, giggling.

'Lovely to meet you, ma'am,' he said, and shook her hand. 'That's a lovely little guy you've got there.'

'Thank you,' Anni said, taking an immediate liking to him. His accent reminded her of Hari.

Martin smiled. 'We'll be happy to drive you to the camp, Anni.'

'Thank you, but I'd rather take the train,' Anni said. 'I need some time to think.'

When they arrived at the station, Anni took both of Nina's hands. 'Promise me that you'll keep in touch with Guri. Tell her that I will come back for Ingrid when I'm settled.'

Nina was sobbing. 'You have my word.'

'The conditions in Germany are pretty grim now. If you decide to stay with him,' Martin said. 'You need to know that too.'

'I'll let you know what I decide to do,' she said, convinced she would be at the maternity home later. She didn't say it, but it was important to her not to be a burden to anyone, not even them.

Nina tried again. 'Come with us to Canada, Anni. We'll help you.'

Anni shook her head. 'I can't live that far from Ingrid. Please don't tell her about Oskar. I have to be the one to do that.'

Nina was crying, and John had his arm around her. Martin handed Anni a suitcase from the car. 'There's food and things for you and Oskar, mostly clothes and nappies. We even put in a tin of coffee, courtesy of the Canadian here.'

John grinned. 'And some of Canada's finest chocolate.'

'That's more than I could ever hope for,' Anni said.

Before they left, Martin handed her another envelope. 'It's not much, but we all chipped in, Guri too. John's address in Montreal is in there, as well as Lars's in London,'

Martin said, his voice trembling slightly.

Anni couldn't refuse. 'Thank you, Martin.'

After a new round of hugs, Anni picked up the suitcase and with Oskar on her hip boarded the train.

She put the suitcase on the top shelf and sat down with Oskar on her lap. He quickly fell asleep against her chest.

Anni held him closely while she quietly cried for the daughter and life she was leaving behind.

By the time the train stopped at her station, she was done with crying. There was nothing to be done about the past, and she had the rest of her life to live. To do that, she needed to accept her fate and look forward.

One day, not long from now, I'll have my girl in my arms again, she thought. *All I want is to see my children grow up together.*

The camp wasn't too far from the station. She walked along a single-track gravel road, with deep tracks from heavy vehicles. Spring was in full bloom. She spotted wildflowers in the ditches and farmers ploughing their fields. One of them lifted his hand and waved at her. Anni waved back.

'Look, Oskar. See the cows?' She showed him the reddish-brown cows on the field, who paid no attention to them.

The landscape out here, far away from the fjord and the sea, was different from what she was used to. Instead of boulders and heather, there were rows of huge, leafy trees, and a lot more greenery than she was accustomed to from home.

'It's lovely,' she whispered to Oskar.

When they finally arrived at the camp, it wasn't as foreboding as she had imagined. No high towers or barbed wire for one. *If this is how they guard Nazis, how dangerous did they think we were?* she wondered.

As they came closer, she saw children playing and their laughter calmed her down. It sounded so normal.

'It's better than where we were,' she said to Oskar.

At the gate, she was surprised to see that the guards were German soldiers. She told them her name and asked for Hugo. They told her to wait.

She put down the suitcase and sat down on it, trying to keep Oskar entertained. He was having none of it. He needed a change of clothes and food.

Anni wondered how they would react if she attempted to feed him right there, in front of their gate.

Instead, she found a piece of bread in her pocket and let him suck on that. It stopped the screaming, but she knew it wouldn't last long.

'Be patient, Oskar,' she said, kissing the top of his head.

She kept an eye on the gate and discovered Hugo running out of one of the barracks, calling her name.

Anni stood up from the suitcase. She had no idea how she looked, it had been an emotional and exhausting day, but soon realised Hugo didn't care.

Watching him run towards them, she suddenly felt so weak. As if all her strength had been holding her up for this moment, and now that he was there, her body almost failed her.

Hugo stopped in front of her. 'I almost lost hope of seeing you again.'

'I was lost,' Anni said, trying to stay calm.

Oskar stopped crying and stared wide-eyed at the new stranger. He decided to whack him with his soggy bread piece, then give him a beaming smile. Hugo's face softened. 'He looks like you,' he said quietly. 'He's beautiful.'

Good boy, Oskar, Anni thought. 'Oskar, be nice to your pappa.'

'Why didn't you tell me before I left, Anni? You shouldn't have gone through all this alone.'

Anni shook her head. 'I didn't want you to worry about me.'

Hugo took a step closer and enveloped them both in an embrace. Anni cried; so did Hugo.

'Nobody would tell me anything until Martin came. I'm so sorry. I never should have left you,' he whispered.

Anni tried to answer, but Oskar had finally had enough. He let out a wail and threw the bread to the ground.

'I'm sorry. He's hungry and he needs clean clothes,' Anni said.

'Follow me.' Hugo grinned at the furious baby. 'He's perfect, Anni. Absolutely perfect.'

Hugo took the rucksack and the suitcase from her. He smiled and suddenly she could see she had done the right thing. Not by Ingrid, that would never heal, but she was right where she and Oskar belonged.

Now that the war was over, things would surely improve, even for women like her. Perhaps they could stay in Norway and be reunited with Ingrid. *I can hope again*, she thought.

Chapter Thirty-One

Ingrid, fifty-one years old

London, 1989

Ingrid handed Runar the salad bowl. 'Did you bring that wine you promised?'

He grinned. 'It's only Thursday. I thought that was for the weekend.'

'Don't you get Norwegian on me. I've made your favourite dinner,' Ingrid said, pointing at the fried fish in the pan.

Runar smiled. 'You're my favourite.'

'Ah, you do know how to flatter,' Ingrid said, laughing at him.

The phone suddenly ringing startled her, making Runar laugh again. 'It's probably one of the girls. You are getting jumpy in your old age.'

Ingrid scowled at him. 'Just answer it, will you?'

She found the wine glasses in the cupboard and turned around to see Runar's shocked face.

'What is it? What's wrong?'

Runar handed her the phone without saying a word and turned on the TV.

Joanna was on the other end. 'Mum, you have to watch the news. We're on our way, but I couldn't wait to tell you.'

Ingrid looked at the TV screen, and without noticing, she dropped the handset.

The screen was filled with people screaming from the top of the Berlin Wall. The announcer had the biggest smile she'd ever seen when he told them that the wall was finally coming down.

'*Twenty-eight years ago, the world watched on in horror as the Berlin Wall went up. Today it is falling,*' he said. '*Look at the joy on everyone's faces!*'

Ingrid had to grab the counter. 'Oh my God,' she whispered.

Runar was with her in two steps. 'Come on, love. Sit down. I don't want you to faint on me and hurt your head or something.'

She didn't hear him, unable to tear her eyes away from the screen. She grabbed his arm and looked up at him. 'We can find her now, Runar. We can finally find Mamma,' she whispered in a hoarse voice.

Runar held her close while she cried.

Ingrid shoved her hands in her pockets. *Who knew Berlin would be this freezing?* she thought.

Runar was holding his arm around her shoulders, lending her his support. 'Are you OK?' He rubbed her arm.

My rock, she thought. *I could never had done this without him.* She gave him a quick kiss. 'Yes, I'm nervous and scared. It has taken so long to find Mamma, and now that we're meeting her, I feel like I need more time. Isn't that silly?'

Nina had found Anni, or rather, her connections in Germany had. Over the last few years, Nina had spent a lot of time helping the Norwegian war children find their German fathers and families, and she had told them there was a man in Germany who could help.

'I know, but we're finally here now, and everything will turn out fine.' Runar hugged her close.

'It's been so long,' Ingrid said. 'Maybe too long.'

'Not after all you have done to get here,' Runar said.

While they had waited for news, and hopefully an address, Ingrid had tried to write letters to her mother, but had ended up throwing them all away. She had no idea what to say to her.

All those years between them, all that missing time. Almost forty-five years. It was a lifetime. Her mother could have passed away, and the thought of standing by a grave scared her so much, she had nightmares.

Then Nina called. They had located Anni, alive and well, in a suburb on the outskirts of East Berlin, and she wanted to meet them.

Runar had bought plane tickets for the three of them, since she wanted Esme with her too. And to her delight, Nina and John wanted to come as well. This was not an undertaking she wanted to face on her own.

Nina, John and Esme were waiting in a coffee shop nearby, but she wanted Runar with her at their first meeting.

On top of the wall, covered in years of graffiti, people were hacking away at the concrete, not only to bring the wall down, but also for a memento of what had been such a dark symbol of the Cold War. Or maybe they wanted to sell pieces of rock for souvenirs.

'Look at them go,' Runar said in an attempt to distract her. 'We need to get a piece of that wall too.'

Ingrid wasn't paying attention. She had a horrible feeling this would be the worst mistake of her life. 'Maybe we should go.'

He pulled her closer. 'There's no shame in being scared. I'm sure she's as scared as you are, if not more. Imagine the guilt she must have carried all these years.'

'I know that, and I understand the choices she had to make. But I remember the pain from being abandoned. One day Mamma was there, the next day it was as if she had never existed. I don't know what she'll expect from me.' Ingrid looked at him. 'And I don't feel that I owe her anything.'

'I agree, you don't. But you owe it to yourself to talk to her. You need to ask her how she has lived all these years, and if she thought about you, if she missed you. All the things you're wondering about, love.'

Now they were here, standing by the famous Checkpoint Charlie, waiting for her mother to emerge at any moment. It was like waiting for a memory to materialise.

How would she look? Ingrid tried to remember the last time she had seen her, but she had been seven years old and crying so hard she could still feel the stinging in her chest. At that time, she had believed that Mamma would come back soon.

'I will come back soon, sweet pea,' she had said and kissed her on the forehead. 'I will always find you.'

So many lies, Ingrid thought, and realised she was crying. She wiped the tears away with a swift movement.

She was clutching the photograph of the two of them they had taken that last Christmas. If she didn't recognise her, she would show it to whomever she thought could be her mother.

'Ingrid. Look. I think that's her.' Runar lifted a hand and waved.

Ingrid resisted the urge to stop him before her mother discovered him. She could see three people standing close together, huddling as if they were cold too, looking in all directions.

'I think they're waiting for you,' Runar said. 'Do you recognise her?'

Ingrid couldn't speak a word. She could barely breathe.

Runar let go of her hand and Ingrid walked towards her mother. She hadn't noticed her yet, so Ingrid had time to observe her. First, she thought the man could be her brother, but soon realised he was too old. It had to be Kerber. *The one who took her away from me*, she thought, then turned to her mother again.

She was tall, but not as tall as she remembered. Her hair was covered by a woollen hat and her coat had seen better days. Next to her stood a young girl, about twelve or thirteen years old. She was holding her hand and looked both nervous and excited.

Ingrid pressed her hand against her mouth, forcing back a sob. *She's here*, she thought. *My mamma is finally here.*

Hilda tugged at Anni's hand. 'Where is she, Oma? I thought she would be here.'

Anni smiled at her. 'I haven't seen Ingrid since she was younger than you. It might take some time for me to recognise her.'

Hilda was looking smart in her new winter coat, bought with the money the West German authorities had given them. They had also bought proper food to bring home to the flat. *West German authorities, they did their best, bless them*, Anni thought.

'Don't worry,' Hugo whispered in her ear. 'She's coming. I know it.'

'No, you don't,' she said, glancing at him.

'Of course I do. I remember so clearly the two of you together. She has never forgotten you, your *kleine* Ingrid,' he said, touching her cheek.

Anni nodded. 'I hope you're right. So many years lost.'

She still found it hard to understand how a regime like the GDR could fall apart in a matter of hours. Nobody seemed to know what happened. They had been told that the West and East Germanys' authorities were talking, but not much more than that. The world was opening up at last. It seemed impossible that the wall would close again.

Seeing that hated wall fall down, after all those years living in a prison, it was almost impossible to believe. She looked at Hugo again. His smile reassured her. '*Keine Angst, mein Liebling.*'

'Oma, that man is waving at us.' Hilda pulled at her hand. 'Do you know him?'

Anni turned to look at the man. He waved, but her eyes fell on the woman walking slowly towards her. 'Oh my God,' she whispered.

She put her hand in front of her mouth, trying to stop

the sobs. Without noticing she let go of Hilda's hand and walked to meet her.

Ingrid was so tall, and her hair had greyed a little, but she knew her immediately.

'Sweet pea,' Anni muttered, feeling so weak, she was afraid she would fall to the ground.

'Mamma?'

Anni couldn't hold back a whimper. She blinked furiously, and the next thing she knew, Ingrid was hugging her.

'It's me, Mamma,' Ingrid said, holding her tight. 'I wasn't sure if you would recognise me.'

Anni sniffled, then let go of the grip. She put her hands on Ingrid's face. 'I would know you anywhere. You look the same. Older, yes, but you are still my beautiful little girl.'

That had them crying again, and Anni knew they must be scaring Hilda. She pulled herself together.

'I want you to meet someone,' she said, holding out her free hand to Hilda and Hugo.

Ingrid blew her nose in a handkerchief and smiled. 'I have someone I want you to meet too.'

Hugo brought Hilda to them, and the girl smiled shyly at Ingrid. Hugo smiled. 'I'm so pleased to see you again, Ingrid. Anni worried for you, all these years.'

Anni held her breath, suddenly anxious Ingrid would reject him, or worse, blame him for her actions.

Ingrid looked at him, then smiled. 'I remember you. You were always so nice to me. I'm glad she had you.'

Hugo smiled. 'Thank you.'

Anni put her arm around her granddaughter. 'Hilda, this is your *Tante* Ingrid.'

Hilda held out her hand, and curtsied. 'Hello, Aunt

Ingrid. I am very pleased to meet you,' she said carefully in English.

'Hello, Hilda. I'm pleased to meet you too,' Ingrid said, bending down and giving the girl a warm hug.

Anni used the moment to gain control over herself. There was so much she needed to tell Ingrid, so much to make up for. She hardly knew where to begin. She barely noticed Hugo gently putting his hand on her shoulder for reassurance.

'Hilda speaks fairly good Norwegian too,' she said as the waving man who had been hovering a few steps behind them stepped forward.

Anni frowned. There was something vaguely familiar about him. He smiled at her, and she suddenly remembered. 'Runar? Is that you?'

'Yes, it's me, Mrs Odland,' he said, laughing now.

'That hasn't been my name for a very long time, Runar. Please, call me Anni,' she said, giving him a hug.

Ingrid took his hand. 'We've been married for twenty-six years, and you have two grown granddaughters, Mamma.'

Anni had to blink again. 'You have two daughters?'

'Yes, Joanna and Guri.' Ingrid's voice was shaking and Anni could see she was as overwhelmed as she was.

Runar smiled at Hilda. 'Since I'm your *Onkel* Runar, what if you and your grandfather show me what's going on here while we let Ingrid and Anni catch up?'

He waved at the wall. Hilda seemed to be taking an instant liking to him. 'They are wanting to break down all the wall,' she said.

'They are? Did you get a piece for yourself?' Runar said.

She put her hand in her pocket, taking out a few pebbles.

'I brought them for *Tante* Ingrid, but you can have one too.'

Runar took one and looked at it. 'That is the best piece of wall I've ever seen.'

Hilda giggled. 'Opa, you must come too. Uncle Runar, this is my *Opa*. He is very nice.'

Hugo shook his hand, then looked at Anni to make sure she was all right.

'I'll be fine. Go with Hilda, please,' she said.

Anni watched them walk towards the wall, then swallowed hard, choking down the rush of emotions threatening to overwhelm her. *Not now*, she thought. *I can do that later.*

Anni took Ingrid's hands. 'I know you must have so many questions for me, but before we start . . .' She took a deep breath. 'I'm so sorry I left you behind, Ingrid. What I did to you has been my greatest regret, my greatest loss. I always meant to come back for you. Please forgive me, if you can.'

Ingrid squeezed her hand. 'I forgave you a long time ago, Mamma. I never stopped looking for you, hoping to see you, to find you. And now we can't waste any more time.'

Anni was so relieved, she struggled to keep her composure. She laughed shakily. 'I'm doing my best not to cry again. I feel I've done nothing but cry for years.'

'It's exhausting. Let's stop,' Ingrid said.

Anni touched her cheek. 'Have you had a good life, sweet pea?'

'Yes, Mamma. I haven't lacked for anything but you. I've missed you every day. That never went away.'

It was so hard to listen to, so hard to accept that her baby had grown up without her. Anni tried to speak, but she felt as if she had lost her voice.

Ingrid frowned. 'Nina told me I had a brother. Isn't he here with you?'

Anni forced herself to talk. The pain from losing her little boy was still raw in her heart.

'Oskar and his wife were caught distributing illegal papers in 1978. We don't have all the details of what happened to them. Hilda was a baby back then. She has been so excited to meet you. I've told her everything I remember about you and about home,' she said, not daring to stop, in case she would burst into tears again.

'I'm so sorry that you lost Oskar, Mamma. I would have loved to meet him, to have a brother.' Ingrid held her close again.

'I think perhaps it was the price I had to pay for what I did,' Anni said quietly. 'But whatever happened in my life, it has brought me here, to see you again. I'm so grateful for that, sweet pea.'

Ingrid laughed. 'Nobody has called me that since you.'

Anni didn't want to let her go. 'How long are you staying in Berlin?'

'We have hotel rooms for a week, not too far from here. Runar is the great organiser in the family. We didn't bring the girls, since we thought it might be too many and too much at once. But we brought Nina and her husband, John; they're so excited to see you again.'

'I remember John,' Anni said, smiling at the memory. 'He was very sweet and lovely.'

'Yes, he's a darling. Nina has worked so hard to find you since we discovered you were in East Berlin,' Ingrid said. 'I also asked my stepmum, Esme, to come. I hope that's OK.'

'Of course it is.' Anni blinked away tears again. 'What about Guri and Martin?'

'I'm sorry, but Besta passed away when I was fourteen, and Martin died in Canada almost fifteen years ago,' Ingrid said. 'Pappa too.'

Anni looked at her. 'Thank you for telling me.'

There would be time to mourn them later, she thought. *For now, I am allowed to enjoy my daughter again.*

Ingrid smiled at her. 'Let's join the others. They're all warm and cosy in a coffee house close by. I don't know about you, but I'm freezing,' Ingrid said, waving at Runar to come back.

Anni was finally walking with her daughter, and they were laughing and talking, as if they had never been apart. She could hardly believe it was real.

Hilda ran up next to her and took her other hand. 'Where are we going, Oma?'

'We are meeting other family members who are so eager to see you. Are you OK with all this?' Anni asked.

Hilda nodded, beaming at her. 'Yes, we're not alone anymore, Oma. I love that.'

'So do I, sweetie. So do I,' Anni said.

Author's Notes

Norway's wartime Bigamy law

After the liberation in 1945, many wives and children waited day after day at the quay or the train station. They were looking for a long-awaited husband and father who was supposed to come home from the war. Some of these women received completely unexpected and shocking news: they were informed that their husbands were alive but had established new families, with the blessing of the exile government.

The Bigamy Law allowed Norwegian men who had found new partners abroad during the war to get a divorce from their unsuspecting spouses and remarry. Many of their new foreign wives were not aware that their husbands were already married and possibly had children.

Norway was the only country during the Second World War to pass such a law.

The shame hung heavily over the victims of the Bigamy Law. At that time, even a woman who had waited faithfully through the hard years of war for her husband – raising, clothing, and feeding his children on strict rations – was expected to bow her head, endure the gossip, and stay silent about her misfortune.

In addition to the despair over their husband's betrayal, many abandoned wives faced terrible financial worries following this change in their circumstances.

While our story focusses on Anni, who is the wife of a sailor, it was not primarily seafarers who took advantage of the law, as many have assumed, but often Norwegians in administrative positions in the UK, USA and Sweden. The Bigamy Law stipulated as a condition for divorce through the Norwegian Ministry of Justice in London that it was not possible for the applicant to contact their spouse. There is evidence that the ministry took this detail lightly, for it was usually possible for Norwegians abroad to reach their families through so-called Red Cross telegrams.

The Norwegian authorities in London did nothing to inform spouses in Norway that they were divorced so they could take steps to protect their interests.

This book is for the women and children who lived with the consequences of the Bigamy law and were considered insignificant by the authorities of the time.

Anan Singh and Natalie Normann, August 2024.

Acknowledgements

So many lovely people have helped us with this book, and we want to thank them all.

Our agent extraordinaire, Lina Langlee of The North Agency, who never gave up. We're very impressed.

Our editor at Allison & Busby, Lesley Crooks, whose editorial feedback we love.

Huge thanks to our Norwegian historian, Kristian Magnus Vikse, who as a young boy delivered illegal newspapers during the war. He's also an author and former chief editor of *Haugesunds Avis*.

To our Norwegian author friend, Salmund Kyvik, who has written eighteen books set during World War Two and pretty much knows everything.

Several authors read the book and without their encouragement the book would have been harder to finish.

Christina Courtenay, Jan Baynham, Luisa A. Jones,

Pernille Hughes, Fiona Leitch and Andie Newton. Thank you all for taking the time to read and give your honest feedback. It helped, even if we didn't always appreciate it at the moment. Every one of these wonderful authors are worth a trip to Amazon or your nearest bookshop.

And to you, dear reader, we say thank you for reading Anni and Ingrid's story. We hope you enjoyed it.

ANNA NORMANN is the pseudonym of authors ANAN SINGH and NATALIE NORMANN. Anan was born in India and had his first short story published at fourteen. Natalie grew up on the west coast of Norway and has always been fascinated with the country's period of occupation. She is a bestselling historical romance writer in her native language and more recently published two contemporary Norwegian-set romances in English. *The Silent Resistance* is their first collaboration in English.

natalienormannauthor.com
Instagram @natalienormann | X @ natalienormann1